AT THE END OF THE
RIVER STYX

MICHELLE KULWICKI

PAGE STREET YA

PAGE STREET YA

First published in 2024 by
Page Street Publishing Co.
27 Congress Street, Suite 1511
Salem, MA 01970
www.pagestreetpublishing.com

Distributed by Macmillan, sales in Canada by The Canadian Manda Group.

28   27   26   25   24   1   2   3   4   5

ISBN-13: 979-8-89003-960-6
Special Edition ISBN-13: 979-8-89003-216-4
Library of Congress Control Number: 2023945411

Book design by Laura Benton for Page Street Publishing Co.

Printed and bound in China

ⵥⵥⵥⵥⵥⵥⵥⵥⵥ

To Atreyu and Cymorene.
To Alana, to my Prince, to Ronan,
and Gansey, and Adam, and Blue.
To Zachary and Ged, Nighteyes, and
Pip. To all the characters I love and
all the worlds I'll never forget.

ⵥⵥⵥⵥⵥⵥⵥⵥⵥ

PROLOGUE

The Asopos River, Greece
499 Years Ago

Zan ran, hand clenched around the two copper obols he'd stolen from the house where his mother lay dying. They were meant to be placed on his mother's eyes to pay the Ferryman's fee.

Zan would bribe him for her life instead.

The heat of his palms warmed the copper, and with every beat of his heart, the two obols pressed harder against his lifeline, growing heavier and heavier. The trees thickened, cluttered branches scratching lines down his arms with taloned claws, but he forced himself forward until he burst free of them all, coming to the bank of the Asopos, which flowed along the edge of the village. Gasping for breath, he tried to shake the echo of his mother's labored, fluid-filled gasps from his ears. The sound of her dying refused to fade.

Choking back a sob, Zan fell to his knees.

The water had risen high enough in the last week to soak the entire bank and begin flooding the plain. Thick mud bubbled around his legs as Zan forced himself to lay back, stretching out and wriggling his body against the ground. There was no moon above, only a dim spatter of stars that barely shone against an inky black sky. Zan's pulse thrashed in his ears, but he tried to stay calm, eyes following the lines of the constellations he knew.

They are where we came from, his mother used to whisper to him, long after his younger siblings had gone to sleep. *The stars hold our stories. Never forget your roots, Alexander. Never forget the old gods.*

"Ferryman," Zan whispered.

The sacrificial ritual was simple—one he'd found scrawled along the page edges of a book his mother kept hidden underneath a loose floorboard. *Obols. Water. Will. Death.*

"Ferryman," Zan called again, voice scratchy and thick with fear. He worked his arms, carving out larger and larger swaths of mud around his body. The river water leaked in over the bank, pooling around his legs, creeping over his throat. The cold dribbled into his ears, and he cringed away from the water, but he sucked in another breath—waiting for the clay to drag him down and paralyze his body.

Bitter cold bit at his arms as the river filled the gaps between his fingers, sloshed over his legs, brushed against his jaw, then his cheeks. Zan's fingers tightened around the coins, metal biting into his flesh as the water closed over his nose.

He could hear his heartbeat. *Thump. Thump. Thumpthump. Thumpthump. Thumpthumpthumpthump—*

The river grew heavy above him, roiling to life with sudden power. Zan's fingers scrabbled at the mud as his lungs heaved, but the heavy clay of the riverbank had done its job and held him steady. The current raged above him, and Zan struggled, opened his mouth in a miserable quest for air—

How long does it take to drown? he thought desperately.

Mud clung to his eyelashes, making it impossible for him to blink. Clay kicked up by the water caked Zan's arms, his legs, his throat. His eyes burned, crusted, and forced open, but all he could see were flickering edges of light barely bright enough to seep through the heavy silt.

There were no gods above him, no one to listen to his plea. There was nothing but the weight of the river settling heavy on his chest, nothing but the devastating fear of failure.

Death was supposed to be painful, then over—not this. Not awareness, not desperation, not the frantic jackrabbiting of his heart in his chest as he struggled to move, not the horrible burning of lungs so desperate for air. His teeth bit into his lower lip, sharp enough that he could taste coppery blood, and the water darkened as black crept in. Thick, oily, darker than anything Zan had ever seen, it looped coils around his wrists, tugged at his ankles, circled his neck, and pulled him even deeper into the mud.

Zan wrenched his head up and frantically tried to kick away, but his limbs wouldn't move. A bubble escaped his nose and pushed against the black. His head hurt. There was a pressure in his chest, then a burst of searing heat as his body finally gave in, as he inhaled bitter river water and felt his lungs crumple in his chest. *Please*, Zan tried to scream, vision going spotty and white. *Please, help me, save her, please, please.*

The black pulled harder, and the mud gave way. Zan fell, muscles cramping, stomach rising in his throat—

He popped through the bottom of the river. His whole body was a writhing mass of pain as he retched out water and dirt, and gasped in cool, damp air. It felt like an eternity before his breath stopped stuttering, and when he finally opened his eyes, all he could hear was the faint trickling sound of water and the metallic *clang, clang* of two obols clattering to his feet. Zan blinked and tilted his head toward the faint spattering of stars that coated a murky sky. He tried to ground himself, to find the constellations, but a deep gray fog rolled in—eating away at his senses until he was so dizzy he had to look back down.

The black still clung to his wrists. It dripped from his fingers, pooling to the ground, then clumped together, little pieces of liquid darkness becoming bigger, growing hooves, wings, carapace, antlers, and the piercing shine of a scythe.

Obols. Water. Will. Death. An eternity of servitude, exchanged for one life.

Zan brushed wet curls from his eyes and watched the creature fatten until it was larger than he was—an amalgamation of every animal he'd ever seen. Shuddering, Zan curled his arms around his body, willing himself to stop shaking.

"Alexander," the creature hissed from a beetle's chitinous mandible.

Zan coughed, dislodging a jagged pebble from the back of his molars. He rolled it around on his tongue for a moment before carefully spitting it out. "Ferryman," he whispered.

The Ferryman's mouth curved into a venomous smile, revealing fangs dripping black. "She will live," he said. "I accept your sacrifice."

Two obols sat on the tip of his tongue.

The Ferryman swallowed.

CHAPTER ONE

Portland, Oregon | Present Day

N *ame and location of death . . .*

Bastian shuddered as the disembodied voice of the nightmare he'd been having for months echoed through his head. Gray hallway. Gray walls. Gray fog. An endless stretch of mirror-black water that he walked across, so still the only movement was the steady beat of his footsteps, echoed vibrations that disappeared into a distance he could never reach.

And the steady, bored-sounding voice of another boy: *Name and location of death . . .*

A city bus tore past him, splashing muddy water up on the sidewalk, narrowly missing his shoes. Bastian scrubbed a hand through his hair, then drew to a stop in front of a weathered wooden door.

The bookstore was an unassuming hole-in-the-wall exactly one block north of the *other* bookstore that drew tourists and locals alike. It was sandwiched between a reasonably priced doughnut shop and a slate-gray building plastered in posters that advertised things like College Night, Girlz Girlz Girlz, and Shrimp Specials.

Bastian liked it that way. It was more hidden.

"Bash Barnes, that is literally a strip club!"

He sighed and looked over his shoulder. His best friend, Riley Kim, stood frozen, her face lit by the pink-and-purple strobe lights of the club.

Bastian's eyes flicked back up to the gray building. Mirage, the neon sign above the black door flashed. There were no windows. "Do they have shrimp specials at strip clubs?" he pondered, eyeing one of the posters.

She pulled her messenger bag to the front of her body and clenched her fingers tightly around the strap—as though the tight grip of a four-foot-eleven Korean girl was going to protect the contents from a motivated mugger. "Apparently," she answered, face twisting in disgust. "This is *so* trashy."

"You coming or not?" Bastian called. He squatted and unzipped the front pocket of his backpack, digging around.

No key.

Grunting in irritation, he unzipped the next pocket and shoved his hands in. Lots of paper. A squashed notebook with French scribbled across the front. A handful of dirt-crusted change.

Still no key.

"It smells like garbage," Riley said primly, stepping up behind him.

"It smells like doughnuts."

"And garbage."

"Noted," Bastian muttered. He unzipped the top pocket of his backpack and forced his hand between two textbooks. It had to be here. When he'd signed the contract last week, the impeccably dressed, fancy-lawyer son of the old man who'd owned the place had handed over the key. Bastian had definitely, *definitely* stuck it in his backpack, because he vividly remembered the squinty-eyed look of disbelief Fancy-Lawyer shot him as he fumbled with the zippers. "College kid?" Fancy-Lawyer had asked hesitantly. Which Bastian definitely was not, but he also wasn't going to cop to still being a senior in high school. An eighteen-year-old senior in high school, so an adult, but still. High school.

Instead, Bastian had tried to stammer out something vaguely intelligible about being a recent grad (lie) and this being a renovation project he'd share with his father (also a lie), and Fancy-Lawyer had shrugged and said, "Better you than me," before he walked out of the building.

So he had it. Somewhere underneath the bulk of homework he had no intention of doing, somewhere . . . somewhere . . .

Bastian's fingers closed around the teeth of the key, and he sighed in relief. He pulled it out, stood up, and stepped up to the dusty window of Cavendish Books & Collectibles. Other than a single golden letter D that had stood the test of time, the letters stenciled on the glass were flaky and stained brown.

Riley stepped around him and rubbed at it. Bits of paint blistered under her fingers. "Seriously, Bash?" She paused, peering at him owlishly. "You look awful."

He winced. "Thanks."

He *did* look awful. He looked like he hadn't slept for the past year, which was depressingly accurate because ever since the accident, every time he closed his eyes he had that stupid, awful nightmare.

Name and location of death . . .

A haunting voice, frigid air, the splashing of water under his feet, and sometimes, the worst times . . . black, oily tendrils that looped around his ankles and tried to tug him down.

7

Sleeping wasn't exactly restful.

Bastian sucked in a deep breath and stepped over to the door as the clouds above them broke and started to drizzle.

"How much did you pay for this place?" Riley asked, wriggling out of her school blazer and pulling it through the strap of her messenger bag. She held it over her long, gleaming black hair.

A lot more than he wanted to admit to. Shrugging in response, Bastian forced the key into the lock.

It stuck, refusing to settle in a bolt that was probably rusted out from the constant misting rain of the city, but Bastian gave it a wriggle, pushing hard until he heard the click of the lock engaging. The door still didn't budge. He threw his entire body weight against it. It slowly screeched open, frame dragging over a wooden floor that had buckled with age and humidity.

"How the heck did you even get in here to see it?" Riley muttered, following him inside.

"I managed," Bastian grunted, forcing the door closed behind them. "It's not really that bad."

The door made a pitiful moan as it edged across the floor.

"That is the stupidest thing I've ever heard."

He didn't answer. He only had eyes for the store. The sky had darkened, but there was still enough light coming in through the big front window to illuminate the place. Hundreds of bookcases. Thousands of books.

They sprawled across counters, on top of bookcases, surrounding chairs. Piles fanned across the warped floor and tumbled from shelves that had snapped in half from far too much weight left for far too long.

Bastian ran a finger along the edge of the case closest to the door. It came away caked in dust and grime. His stomach swooped with now-familiar nauseous excitement he'd been feeling since the moment he'd walked away with the key last week. This place was perfect. This place was *his*.

Purchasing it was also completely irresponsible, ridiculous, and (in the words of one of his favorite books from childhood), a terrible, horrible, no good, very bad idea.

"They seriously didn't take anything?" Riley asked from behind him, gawking at a huge pile of books precariously perched on a dusty stool.

"Told you. As is."

"You think you'll find a million dollars in here?"

His eyebrows rose.

"Or a dead body. Probably more likely. God, I wonder if there are rats. Do you think there are rats?"

"Riley."

A dusty Persian rug was draped over a countertop in the front corner. A decrepit-looking cash register and a huge pile of books sat on top of it—as if in one moment, someone had been in the middle of making a purchase, and in the next, everything had gone dead.

Riley stepped over to it and pulled the top book from a pile filled with crime thrillers. Her mouth curled in judgment. "Gross."

"Popular, though," Bastian murmured. There was a light switch by the front door, and he tried flipping it, but only a single fluorescent strip light crackled on. The rest were burned out.

"This place looks like it's a hundred years old," she said, setting the book down. A pile of dust poofed out from around it.

"Nah. It shut down five years ago. Old guy owned it, there was some family battle over his property when he died, no one touched the place, fancy-lawyer son put it up for sale a couple weeks ago. Enter me."

"Enter you," she said. "Sole proprietor. Expert on books, business, and marketing. How lucky they are to have you."

"Hey, I paid cash in full, they're happy."

Her lips pursed as she turned another circle. "So you bought a run-down bookstore because hey, why not, and now you're . . . what?" She crossed her arms. "Living here? I don't get it. You're graduating in six months!" She shook her head, nose scrunching up in the way it always did when she got one of her great Riley-Ideas that she was going to force on everyone. "Flip it. Sell it again. My brother's a contractor, I'll get him to help. You'll make back what you paid and more."

And here was the terrible, horrible, no good, very bad part. He didn't want to graduate, and he didn't want to just live here. He wanted to fix it. Renovate. Open to the public. Sell books. *Breathe* books.

Because he didn't know what else to live for.

"I'm not flipping it."

Riley shot him a very unimpressed-looking glare. "Why sink so much money into the place if you have no intention of fixing it?"

"I didn't say I had no intention of fixing it," Bastian mumbled. "I said I wasn't *flipping* it."

She crossed her arms. "Joon does great work. He can fix *anything*. I bet someone would totally snatch this place up if you let him reno."

"You sound like a Property Brother," Bastian muttered. "The dumbass one."

"Dorian is going to kill you."

Bastian rolled his eyes. "Dorian doesn't need to know every little detail of my life."

"He's your *brother*," she stressed, flicking back her hair with one hand. "Your *twin* brother. I'm not keeping secrets. Don't force us to choose sides in your weird little guilt war. Everything's already messed up enough."

Bastian forced a hand in his back pocket and came up with a pack of cinnamon gum. He offered a piece to her, she shook her head, and he took one for himself.

"Whatever," she sighed, peering distrustfully around a bookcase. "What's the plan here? I'm definitely not cleaning."

He'd been banking on her sifting through some of the mess with him, but before he could tell her that, his phone buzzed in his pocket. He pulled it out.

Dorian [3:19 PM]: 10 minutes, please don't be late

Chewing his lower lip, Bastian studied the message for a moment before swiping it clear without answering. He tucked his phone back in his pocket. When he looked up, Riley had disappeared down one of the aisles.

"Riley?"

There was a scuffling sound. "There's sheet music!" she yelled.

Bastian frowned. "Point?"

"There's a lot of it!"

He couldn't help the sudden upwelling of relief that surged through his chest. He didn't expect this to last once she found out what he was actually planning on doing, but there was still a part of him that wanted to run her down and hug her for not immediately stalking out of the place. "Not interesting," he called back. "Look for my million dollars!"

She didn't answer. Bastian picked his way through piles of books to a back alcove draped with a moldy-looking piece of velvet. He poked at it, but no rats scurried out.

Riley could be a pain in the ass, but she was also logical.

He wasn't. He hadn't considered rats.

Finally satisfied that nothing was living in the thick piece of fabric, he pushed it all the way to one side and stepped through into a tiny back office.

There was an empty desk and a clock above it that had one hand frozen on the seven and another frozen between eleven and twelve. The walls were painted dark orange and lined with olive-green filing cabinets—the sort of colors that looked good on a disco floor, fifty years ago.

He walked over and yanked a drawer loose to find folders upon folders stuffed inside. He pulled one out.

Hundreds of receipts spilled on the swollen wood floor.

Cavendish Books & Collectibles they read.

Sale: 6.75

Sale: 1.25

Sale: 3.25

Bastian nudged them until he'd pushed all the curled bits of paper into the corner of the room, next to a frumpy plaid sofa. A fat spider scurried out. He cursed and jumped out of the way. It froze on the floor, almost blending into the dusty gray carpet.

His ears were starting to ring. Riley was right: This entire thing was stupid. He'd blown the majority of the life insurance money on this, and it wasn't going to solve anything. The smell of gasoline was right at the edge of his consciousness every time he closed his eyes. Sometimes he could still hear screaming. Dorian was going to be furious, and Riley would eventually side with him because everyone sided with Dorian. He was the reasonable twin. The twin who did his homework in the hospital after the accident, and showed up to school the next week, and smiled at everyone like nothing had ever happened, and aced every test, and spent only a tiny portion of his share of the money on a car so he had reasonable transportation around the city, and saved the rest for college. He didn't make bad decisions. Dorian was *responsible*.

The rushing in his ears reached its peak, and Bastian kicked the sofa as hard as he could.

It hit the back wall with a bang, and an enormous dust cloud erupted from the cushions.

"Stop hitting things," Riley yelled.

Bastian squeezed his eyes closed, took a deep breath, and forced everything back down again. Emotion. Gasoline. Screams. His phone buzzed again.

Dorian [3:32 PM]: Where are you?

Not at couples therapy with you, Bastian thought grimly. He tucked his phone back in his pocket and didn't answer.

"Hey, Bash!" Riley called.

His eyes flicked open. "Yeah?"

"Uh . . . you've got a hole in the back window. Like, covered in plywood but . . . definitely a hole."

"I'm aware."

"Uh . . . you've also got a cat?"

This was punctuated by a feral hiss, the sound of Riley giving an inhuman yelp, and moments later, a blur of orange fur whizzing by Bastian's feet.

He cursed, jumping out of the way, only to get completely tangled up in the filthy velvet curtains where he promptly inhaled a mouthful of dust and started hacking all over the place.

"Lovely," Riley said primly, stepping into view and wiping her hands on her khaki uniform skirt. "Hole in the window. And cat. Who I presume came in through the hole in the window. Great real estate, Bash, absolutely prime use of funds."

"Shut it," he coughed.

She cocked an eye at him while he untangled himself from the drapes. The orange fur blur had solidified into a grimy cat daintily cleaning one torn-up ear with a dust-covered paw.

Bastian scowled at it.

The cat promptly dropped his paw, dipped his head, and started licking his ass.

"Well," Riley said. "I can see you'll get along fabulously."

"Come on," Bastian said, pushing past her and back into the belly of the store. "Help me move books."

She followed, and Bastian tried to force himself through the positives about the situation. The store was his. There was a tiny apartment upstairs. A shower. A kitchenette. A single window with a single air-conditioning unit that he'd hauled up the stairs yesterday and beat into submission. He could hear the hum of it running now. And underneath the smell of age, and grime, and dust?

The smell of paper.

Of books.

He'd coax it back to life. Dorian wouldn't understand, but their mom would have.

"You think your brother would actually help?" he murmured.

Riley paused, one hand reaching toward a dust-covered shelf.

"If I decided to renovate? You could ask him?" Bastian pushed.

Her eyes narrowed suspiciously. "You're calling him," she finally said. "I'm not your go-between."

"Riley," Bastian pleaded, but she darted close and snatched his cell phone from his pocket before he could stop her.

"He doesn't bite," she said, typing in the number. "Grow a pair, buddy."

Sighing, he took his phone back, then wound his way through the maze of bookshelves, bookcases, and book piles until coming to the very back wall of the store. Gummy-looking beige wainscoting ran the entire perimeter of the wall. Underneath was retro wood paneling. Above that was exposed brick. It was truly hideous. Bastian tucked a finger underneath the loop of twine he wore around his left wrist and tugged until the string rubbed hard against his skin. "Here," he said.

"Here what?"

He pointed to the bookshelves in front of them. "We'll empty those, then stack them up around this spot."

"You're so weird," Riley moaned, but she walked over to the next bookcase and started emptying it.

Grunting, Bastian started pulling books off the shelves and then piling them at his feet. The dust wound up around him, motes hovering in stray beams of light from the window. Once he had one barren bookcase, he grabbed ahold of the sides and started pushing. It moved with an awful scratching sound against the floor, leaving a patch of gleaming, untouched wood in its wake. He could get a cleaning company in here. Get rid of the dust, inspect the place for mold, get all the utilities working again, not just electric. He was already pulling Wi-Fi from the doughnut place next door, but running water would be a plus.

This could work. This had been a horrible idea, but it was *his* horrible idea and that made all the difference.

He forced the bookcase up against the wood paneling. Stepping back, he studied it, jaw working around the piece of gum that had already gone stale. Should only take a couple more bookcases to form a perimeter, then he'd have an alcove away from the window.

A section of the store.

He could hang a sign above it, Fantasy, Mystery, Romance, anything. This was a place that was his and only his—not Dorian's, not their shared, perfectly pristine townhouse purchased by their perfectly pristine aunt who wanted them to have a perfectly pristine life after the accident. He didn't know if this would help stop the creeping, oily nightmare that wouldn't allow him a single night's rest, but it was a a step.

Closing his eyes, Bastian took a deep breath in, letting the smell of books overwhelm the memory of gasoline.

CHAPTER TWO

Styx

Zan spun himself around on the orange plush-covered barstool, feet kicking the burnished gold pole that ran along the bottom of the bar.

He was bored. He was *always* bored.

The entire room was frozen in motion, the echoed memory of a dead woman who'd eventually passed of carbon monoxide poisoning—a boring way to go, but it had netted her twelve hours on Styx as her body fought to stay alive on Earth. He'd followed her through an extravagant church wedding, the birth of her first son, and for some reason, this weird little bar, before the barrier had thinned and the Ferryman ate her soul.

Then, the memory had been alive. The busboys had been dancing. A woman with chunky pearl earrings and three buttons popped open on her silk blouse had leaned over her martini and winked.

Now, the room was so silent it made his ears feel like they were popping. Now, that same woman had one hand frozen in the act of tucking a stray bit of hair heavily doused in Aqua Net behind her ear, the other forever reaching for the delicate stem of her cocktail glass. Zan gave her stool a push, watching her spin just enough that her fingers knocked against the glass and caused it to tip.

It shattered against the bar top, vodka dripping down the heavily lacquered wood paneling.

Leaning over the counter, Zan swiped a bottle of crème de menthe, then pushed himself off the stool and wandered the length of the bar.

The carpets were orange shag, and the walls were lined with sparkling chevron backsplash in brown, teal, and gold. It was a hideous combination.

He looked down at his shoes—white with blue stripes, the triangle logo of some company everybody seemed to like affixed broadly to the front of the tongue. He'd stolen them off a rack in a crappy run-down mall. The drunk frat boy reliving the memory with him had laughed, but they were comfortable.

Zan took a long swallow of crème de menthe, wincing as the sugary sweetness coated the back of his tongue.

He passed one of the booths—orange lacquer wood exposed on the bottom; the rest covered in sticky orange vinyl. Two women dressed in matching pantsuits and a man in a purple paisley shirt sat there, drinking bright-pink, fruity-looking somethings out of piña colada glasses. One of the women had dark-green eyes, the color of his mother's. Zan didn't ever like to look at her. He turned toward the man instead, caught midlaugh, head thrown back, throat completely exposed. Zan watched the lump of his Adam's apple for a long moment, waiting, *wishing* for the man to swallow, but it never moved.

Tugging the cork out of his bottle, Zan topped off the three glasses on the table, smiling as the cream swirled and discolored the pink liquid.

Sometimes, when he got really morbid, he'd come here and skip the sugar, just go straight for the house red wine. He'd drink enough to make himself sick, remembering the entire time how his mother despised drunkenness. He'd wander around the frozen bar, smashing glasses, throwing chairs, thinking with petulant glee that she'd be so upset if only she could see him now.

He'd always end up in the bathroom, squeezed between the toilet and the wall, stomach sloshing and roiling in a way that made him think of horrible rivers and horrible deals. He'd think of mistakes. He'd think of how he'd give anything to hear her yell at him; then he'd think of how he had nothing left to barter.

ᘓᘓᘓᘓᘓᘓᘓᘓᘓᘓᘓ

His mother had always prayed to the old gods, believing they watched. She'd fashioned votaries of clay—tiny horses, graceful swans, dancing children. Every year she'd enlist Zan to place them in the windows, not only warding off evil, but pledging her thanks for their grace. *The gods require sacrifice,* she told him. *You must always be open. Willing.* It was old magic that Zan's father had hated when he'd been alive and that his siblings were too young to understand.

But *she* believed.

And as she lay dying from a disease the medics couldn't cure, as his siblings cried, too young to take care of themselves, Zan realized they wouldn't survive without her.

The choice to appeal to her gods was easy: *Obols, Water, Will, Death.*

After the deal, he'd been given a single room as his living space—a tiny octagonal office lit by glowing lamps and surrounded by battered, eclectic bookshelves. The rushing sound of the dead river filled the small space, hard to ignore, impossible to escape.

There were rules on Styx. Not every soul wandered the river, only those stuck in limbo. Zan's job was easy.

Step 1: Record the name and location of death.

Step 2: Guide them to the Ferryman.

Step 3: Hand them over; let the Ferryman eat their souls.

Step 4: Begin again.

The world may move on without him, but if he served for five hundred years, then he could leave Styx. He could earn another chance at life.

The Ferryman liked to taunt him that Zan's sacrifice had come at the perfect time. The woman before had begged for death only four years into her term, leaving Styx awash with souls who couldn't cross the barrier.

"She screamed when I tore into her heart," the Ferryman hissed, legs coalescing to form the smoky body of a viper, one skeletal hand pointing toward a smudge of oily black on the floor-board near the large office desk.

Zan tried to scrub it off during his first week, but it wouldn't budge.

The Ferryman liked to brag about how long it took a servant's eyes to grow dark, how long it took them to break. Lack of water can kill a person in three days. Loneliness is just as deadly.

The Ferryman liked to brag that no one ever lasted their full term. That the souls of his servants tasted even better than the souls of the dead.

Zan didn't listen because he had his own rule on Styx.

Don't give up.

CHAPTER THREE

Portland, Oregon

The pointed tip of the paper airplane smacked into the back of his neck. Bastian caught it before it fell to the floor, crumpling it into a sad little ball as the bell began to ring. He forced himself to sit up from his desk where he'd been hunched over, half asleep, as his classmates filed out of the classroom in a flurry of conversation.

"That was a good one," moaned Mathais from behind him, "and you squished it!"

Bastian didn't turn around, just dropped the ball to the ground. Mathais sighed, squeezing into Bastian's peripheral vision and sitting at the desk next to him.

"Wake up," Mathais said, thumping Bastian on the back of his head. "You slept through Calc. What's wrong with you?"

Groaning, Bastian burrowed his head back in his arms and ignored him. He'd managed to get most of his stuff hauled up to the apartment above the bookstore, but between the constant scuttling of roaches across the buckling floorboards, the booming bass that leaked in through the window from the club next door, and the fact that every time he closed his eyes, he was being haunted by the disembodied voice of a boy he couldn't see, sleep was in short supply.

Mathais thumped him again.

Bastian was vaguely nauseous.

"We have exactly two minutes to make it to French," Mathais said. He leaned over and grabbed Bastian's backpack. "Come. Onward. To the beautiful French countryside, to the smell of lavender, and the romance of a country packed with people who still smoke cigarettes."

"Onward to sleeping through conjugation."

"*Oui, tu comprends!*"

Bastian rolled his eyes, but he squeezed out from behind the desk and took his backpack from Mathais. "Did Dorian put you up to this? I don't need babysitting. I can make it to class on my own."

"As evidenced by you skipping seventh hour three times last week." Mathais grinned. "Your track record sucks. Riley got to follow you yesterday. I get you today." He pulled on his own backpack and tried to tug his uniform straight. It didn't do much. No matter how much adjusting Mathais did, his school sweater bunched around his torso in wrinkled, creased clumps, the cuffs of his sleeves sagged around his wrists from constantly pushing them all the way up to his forearms, and his pants had long lost their perfectly pressed seam—and while Mathais's family more than had the means to hire a laundering service, he refused to do it on principle. He was a football player.

Football players were not supposed to look perfectly pressed.

Bastian looked down at his own sweater, which wasn't looking much better. He hadn't considered that he wouldn't have access to a washer or dryer in his hasty move to the decaying bookstore apartment, and he definitely hadn't had any desire to haul all his shit three blocks south to the sketchy-looking laundromat with the flickering lights and the stringent smell of too much bleach.

He picked at the wool hem of his sweater, trying to pull it all the way back over the hint of his favorite thrifted Teenage Mutant Ninja Turtles T-shirt. "So sorry to put you all out."

"Not put out," Mathais said. "Concerned."

"Don't be."

Mathais blinked, raw hurt shining in his eyes at Bastian's bitter tone.

And Bastian knew he should apologize, but every word got stuck, leaving bitter residue at the back of his molars. He didn't mean to be like this. Didn't mean to stress out his friends, or act like a jerk, or make them hate him even more than he already hated himself, but sometimes, he just . . .

Sometimes he felt like it was impossible to remember how to function like a half-way decent human being.

"Last I checked," Mathais said, running a hand through his hair, "most monetary-related rebellions involve drugs. Alcohol. Buying a trunkful of fireworks and exploding them on some rich dude's lawn."

Bastian exhaled, relief coursing through his veins. "Taking notes," he said. It meant *I'm sorry.*

"Not buying entire bookstores," Mathais stressed, shooting him a rueful look. It meant *you're forgiven.* They walked down the hall and past a group of girls taping flyers to the long stretch of red metal lockers. TRIVIA NIGHT SATURDAY! they read. A couple of girls looked up and stared as they passed. Bastian looked back down at his feet.

"Or cars," Mathais added. "Dorian bought a car."

"I'm aware. Did you also tell *him* he should have invested in explosives?"

"Touché."

By the time they made it out of the building, Mathais had thankfully given up on the guilt speech and moved on to a play-by-play of the latest football game. Bastian followed him from the A building foyer to the beautifully manicured lawns of Preston Academy. The tree line was visible from the middle of the quad— thick evergreens, scraggly bushes, mountaintops that cut into the cloud-covered sky—but Preston made sure not to allow even a hint of wildness to creep onto their grounds. The majority of their students were not an inspired bunch. They were carefully curated cardboard cutouts descended from carefully curated cardboard-cutout parents. Wildness was offensive.

Growing up, Bastian and Dorian had been enrolled in a dozen schools by age thirteen. Bastian had *loved* it. Traveling the world gave him anonymity. People rarely remembered his name, which meant he only ever had to exist as a background character, a passerby, a blip in the lives around him.

Then their artist mother had settled in Portland on the advice of her meddling sister who was worried about the boys growing up without friends, without social lives, without things like homecoming and prom.

Bastian did not want things like homecoming and prom.

Turns out Dorian did. Turns out Dorian wanted things like Knowledge Bowl, and Science Olympiad, and to be future president of the student government.

So they stayed in Portland, and their mom enrolled them at Preston, and Dorian smiled and made friends and went to homecoming and prom, and Bastian did his best to stay under the radar.

And then she'd died.

And Aunt Bri had decided to buy them a whole-ass townhouse because *It's best for you to have stability, why don't you finish up high school in Portland, and then you can both go to college, and I'll sell the place.*

Aka, I don't want to deal with you. I'll just throw some money at the problem; that will make it go away.

Bastian couldn't exactly complain—going to live with her sounded like its own kind of hell—but sometimes he really wished they'd been whisked away somewhere new. Somewhere no one stared at him in the hallways.

They made it into French at the height of Mathais's story, just as his voice reached peak volume while regaling Bastian with the dramatic tale of the quarterback of the opposing team being taken down by none other than Mathais himself. Professor Dane shot a scathing glare in their direction, Mathais saluted him, and Bastian cringed, making his way toward the only two seats available at the very back of the class.

He opened his book, slumped in his chair, and let his thoughts wander toward the dusty bookstore, the hole in the window, the mounds of moldy serial novels, weather-beaten paperbacks, and lonely hardcovers that waited for him. And a cat. A snarly, matted cat. What was he going to do with a cat?

Bastian's nose wrinkled. Feed him. Water him. Pet him? Maybe. Wash him? Definitely. Bookstore cats were *a thing*. This could totally work in his favor if Bastian made him presentable enough to not scare away potential customers.

He pulled out his pack of gum as Professor Dane started scribbling on the whiteboard in front of the class, punctuating each word with a pointillistic smack of his dry-erase marker.

Slipping the gum into his mouth, Bastian flattened the wrapper on the edge of the desk and peeled off the sticky silver with his fingernail, trying to ignore the twinge of his shoulder from a phantom ache that never really went away. He'd regained full range of motion since the car accident—the only sign of the shattered ribs and collarbone he'd sustained was a long line of ropey scar tissue chest to neck and a couple metal screws that he'd been informed would definitely set off airport detectors—but the raw, aching hurt of it seemed to be permanently etched in his memory. *You were lucky,* everyone told him. *It could have been so much worse.*

It *should* have been so much worse.

It should have been him who died.

He forced his hands back to the gum wrapper, peeled another long strip of silver off, and pressed it to the shiny lacquered desk. He needed to call Riley's brother and get an estimate on rehabbing the store. He needed to get someone in to fix the broken window ASAP, but that meant another phone call, which *ugh*. Bastian shuddered. He definitely needed to start sorting the thousands of books with far more vigor. He'd see if Mathais would help, because six feet of pure football muscle was going to go a lot further in hauling books off of high shelves than he and Riley were going to manage on their own. Then he could dust. Or vacuum. Did hardwood floors need vacuuming? He had no idea.

"Mr. Barnes!"

Bastian blinked. Dane stood, one hand on his hip, eyes peering over his wire-rimmed glasses, frown painting his face. "Sorry," Bastian murmured. He could feel his cheeks heating already—the girl in front of him had turned around and was staring. Jasmine Batawi. Cheer captain, active member of the student government, current valedictorian of their class, and on-again, off-again girlfriend of Dorian.

Bastian offered her a weak grin.

Mathais kicked the leg of his desk. "Page twenty-three," he hissed.

Bastian looked down at his book. A boy in a fedora was jauntily handing a baguette to a girl with braided hair. There was a list of prepositions. This was review. This was stuff he should be able to do in his sleep.

Another classmate turned and stared at him.

"Moving on," Dane said after a hideously uncomfortable pause while Bastian grit his teeth, tried to come up with something to say, and failed miserably. "Pay attention, Mr. Barnes."

Bastian managed a small nod as Jasmine threw her hand up in the air and listed off a dozen prepositions and contractions, barely coming up for air.

By the time the bell rang, he'd done nothing but press his entire gum wrapper's worth of silver onto the desk.

As they filed out of class, Dane handed back the tests they'd taken last week. The bright-red Sharpie bled through each packet all the way to the back. There was no anonymity here. Bastian snagged his test, the bloody *F* crumpled under his grip as he forced it deep into his backpack.

"How'd you do?" Mathais asked.

His voice sounded a little too bland and monotonous for him to be entirely disinterested. This was a test too. Bastian refused to look at him.

"Look, I can help you study . . ."

Bastian tried to suck in a breath, but it wouldn't come. His throat tightened, his chest hurt, he couldn't swallow, everything was too hot—

"Just talk to Dane. It's only been a year since the accident, he'll understand!"

"Not a big deal," Bastian managed to get out, but he sounded like he was about to cry. It was a stupid test. It was whatever. Bastian didn't care; he really, really didn't.

You do, his brain whispered.

His hands clawed around his backpack straps. He didn't want to be here. He didn't want to be anywhere. Jasmine turned around, eyes landing on him, and he just wanted everyone to stop looking at him.

Mathais sighed. "Whatever. Come on. Indian buffet time!"

Standing date, every Friday afternoon, they'd pile into Dorian's car, drive downtown, eat until they couldn't move.

There wasn't enough spit in Bastian's mouth to swallow. "Bathroom," he mumbled, veering left as they made it out of the classroom. "Meet you outside."

He didn't wait for a confirmation from Mathais, just bolted down the hall, threw open the bathroom door, slammed himself into a stall, and pressed the heels of his hands against his eyes.

Breathe.

You're failing.

Count.

Everyone hates you.

Think about those breathing meditation shorts on YouTube—boxes expanding, shrinking, expanding, shrinking—

You should have been the one to die.

Bastian flinched. He dropped his hands, curled them into fists, and squeezed as tightly as he could, until his fingernails bit into his palms.

Someone else walked into the bathroom, and the sink cut on. Bastian sucked in a breath and held it as long as he could, then tried to carefully let it out. Andrea—his therapist—told him that panic attacks were a grief response, that he needed to breathe and allow himself space to be upset, that he should call her if he needed, and all of this was normal, but he hated himself, he hated himself . . . .

His heart was smacking against his chest so hard it hurt.

The sink cut off.

The person left the bathroom.

"I hate you," Bastian whispered to himself. His eyes fell on the small silvery bruise at the base of his thumb—a remnant from the accident that had never faded. Bastian swallowed hard, twisted a finger in his bracelet, and started yanking at it until the twine burned his skin. He took a deep breath. "I hate you," he murmured again. Let his breath out.

This wasn't what Andrea meant when she told him to count.

He pulled the bracelet tighter.

I hate you, I hate you, I hate you.

              ᚼᚼᚼᚼᚼᚼᚼᚼᚼᚼ

The parking lot of Preston was filled with noise as students gathered around cars worth more than apartments. Bastian gripped his backpack tighter and forced himself forward, eyes at his feet. His skin still felt too prickly and hot, but at least he was breathing now and not seconds away from crying.

A particularly garish, sparkling green Lotus roared out of a parking stall, zooming so close to Bastian it kicked up gravel at his feet.

"Watch it, pretty boy!" the driver called, smirking out his window and flipping him off.

Bastian grit his teeth. Greer Morgan—of the infamous Morgan family who'd donated so much to Preston over the years that they now had the auditorium, the library, and the football stadium named after them—was an asshole. Had always been an asshole. Would always be an asshole. And spent way too much of his time trying to get a rise out of Bastian for the sole purpose of irritating Dorian (who had, after a drag race fiasco that had almost ended with a dozen members of the Preston student government splashed across news headlines, made it widely known that he wanted nothing to do with Greer).

Bastian had gotten very used to ignoring him, but right now, hot on the heels of the bathroom panic attack, he found himself curling inward, heat slithering down the back of his neck as he tried to come up with something witty to say, failed, hated himself for not coming up with something witty to say, hated himself more—

Greer gunned it, tearing down the gravel drive and out the gate.

Bastian swallowed hard. He picked his way through the crowd until coming to Riley, Mathais, and Dorian, who were all standing next to a brand-new Audi A8—its pristine body a glossy black so clean that Bastian could see his face reflected back.

He could see Dorian's face too—eyes horribly sad, mouth a straight line etched so deep he looked carved from stone.

Usually, it was easy to tell the twins apart—Dorian wore his smile like a best friend and his uniform like someone born to sway the opinions of the masses. His dark-brown hair was clean-cut on the sides, long enough on top to soften his face. His nose was the nose of royalty—carved marble, straight and proud and true.

Bastian's hair was mussy and long enough that he could tuck it behind his ears. It was not styled, not clean-cut, not attention grabbing. His face was thinner than Dorian's. More severe. His nose was crooked at the top from an unfortunate incident two years ago involving a rusted-out wheelbarrow with a flat tire, a pothole, and Mathais.

Dorian was the friendly twin who everyone talked to.

Bastian was quiet. Vaguely threatening in a cornered animal sort of way. Unapproachable, unless he was standing next to Dorian.

"Your stuff is gone," Dorian hissed. The way he said *stuff* implied a curse word.

"You owe me Indian food and a ride home, but I'm not participating in this," Riley said cheerily, yanking open the door of the Audi and tucking herself inside. Mathais gave Bastian an apologetic shrug, then followed her. A cluster of girls walked by them, one of them pausing to wave. Dorian gave her a big smile and shouted, "You all going to Trivia Night?" He waited for their wildly affirmative response before turning back to Bastian, eyes going flinty hard again. "What do you think you're doing?"

Bastian forced his eyes up to Dorian's. "Can we not do this right now?" he asked. He was a live wire, sound was too loud, breeze was too prickly, sun was too bright—

"Where are you living?"

Bastian's teeth clenched. "The streets."

Dorian's eyes narrowed. "Oh, come on. I came back from a meeting last night and your room was empty. Everything gone. Even Mom's awful Maserati poster. Everything. The bed. Towels. The stupid coffee grinder!"

The way he said *stupid* implied an even worse curse word.

"I promise to buy you a new coffee grinder."

"That's not . . ." Dorian sucked in a deep breath and pressed the heel of his hand to his forehead. "You can't just leave."

The back window of the Audi rolled down, and Riley stuck her head out. "You guys done yet? I'm hungry."

Bastian shook his head. "Bookstore has an apartment," he mumbled. "I'm fine."

"You are so far from fine—"

"Indian buffet"—Riley said, completely ignoring their antics—"closes at three. She pointed at the garishly large face of her watch wrapped around her wrist by a bright-blue crocheted band. "Twenty minutes, boys. I'm hungry."

"Twenty minutes," Bastian repeated to Dorian. "Better go."

Dorian's jaw clenched. "We're not done—"

Bastian opened the door and climbed in, squeezing next to Mathais, leaving the front seat empty. His nausea grew. He wiped his palms against his jeans and forced himself to relax. The door was right there. He could see the handle, the lock, the window. He'd been letting Dorian drive him for the last month, which Andrea had informed him was amazing progress considering he'd spent five months refusing to set foot inside a car.

Didn't feel amazing. Felt like he was going to throw up.

"You coming?" Bastian ground out, hoping that his voice sounded anywhere near the vicinity of normal.

Riley threw a fake punch at Mathais. Mathais caught her fist and turned it into a high five. Riley laughed.

Dorian's eyes squeezed closed, and for a single moment, he looked like he was finally going to lose it, throw a *real* punch, scream and yell, and act like a normal human being.

He didn't. He let out a long sigh, dug in his pocket for the keys, then sank into the driver's seat.

The car rumbled to life, and Bastian's stomach sank even lower. He eased his hand toward the handle, letting it hover just shy of the metal. It was pointless. If they got hit, there wouldn't be time to escape; there was no throwing open the door midaccident and leaving. He forced his hand back down. Dorian caught his eyes in the rearview mirror.

Bastian looked back out the side window, Dorian pulled the car out of the lot, and Bastian concentrated on breathing.

CHAPTER FOUR

Portland, Oregon

The air conditioner kicked on as Bastian made it up the stairs and into the apartment. He threw his backpack down on the scraped-up hardwood floor and surveyed the space. Like in the store beneath him, random pieces of old and dusty furniture had been left in the rooms. A kitchen table—top weathered, wood eaten away by decades of beverages set down without a coaster. A desk in the bedroom that had once been rehabbed with too many coats of paint—now the drawers had swollen with the humidity, and the paint stuck so hard they were impossible to pull open. A step stool in the kitchen with a missing wood plank—useless.

Despite Dorian's indignation, he'd really only hauled out a couple of things from the townhouse they'd previously shared, and a bed frame wasn't one of them. His mattress sat pushed against the far wall of the bedroom, rumpled and forlorn next to the desk. The air-conditioning unit chugged away, pulling the Portland wet out of the room and replacing it with chilled, dry air.

Bastian followed the sound and threw himself belly first on the mattress.

He had homework to do. He couldn't afford to fail another test just because he was too tired to concentrate, but all he wanted was to sleep, to not dream, to feel like a person again, not some mangled fuckup whose brother could barely look at him.

Bastian squeezed his eyes closed and took in a shuddering breath, sorting through the memories of the buffet.

Riley laughing.

Mathais competing with himself to see how many gulab jamun he could cram in his mouth before choking on syrup.

Dorian cramming naan in his face while methodically highlighting large swathes of his planner and discussing his upcoming Knowledge Bowl tournament, Science Olympiad championship, and the Student Government Trivia Night he was heading up. Loudly. To no one.

Bastian had been mostly silent, but he didn't think they'd noticed. It wasn't any different than normal. No one had sensed that he was holding himself together with the single piece of twine looped around his wrist.

Groaning, Bastian rolled over to his back.

He could tackle French homework tonight. Email Mr. Dane and beg for some extra credit. A lot of extra credit. Enough to put him above an F for the class because the last thing he needed was a physical letter from Preston showing up at the townhouse informing Dorian, professional interceptor of school-related letters, how much he'd fucked up.

He closed his eyes.

The hum of the air conditioner buzzed; the sounds of the city faded . . . .

The endless expanse of gray extended in front of him, glassy water shivering underneath every step he took. Bastian swore, tangling his fingers in his bracelet and then pulling tight enough for it to bite at his skin. "Wake up," he ground out.

This wasn't what he meant by wanting sleep.

"Come on, come on," he hissed, giving up on the bracelet entirely and digging his nails deep into the skin of his wrist.

If he breathed in too sharply, he smelled gasoline.

If he breathed in too sharply, his collarbone burned.

Bastian shuddered.

He could walk for as long as he wanted, but he never arrived anywhere. He could stay still, but then the cold permeated his entire body, seeping through his feet, to his joints, all the way up to the back of his throat.

This was the recurring nightmare that had been haunting him for the past year. Sometimes there were weeks when it disappeared; sometimes it was every night that the cold wrapped around him, tugging at his limbs, screaming in his ears.

Then he woke up, sweating, gasping, unable to shake the feeling of wrongness from behind his eyes.

In the worst version of the dream—the kind that hooked claws into his skin and pulled until he jerked himself awake, shivering and sweating—he didn't hear the screaming. He only heard himself murmuring "*Mom.*"

Scowling, Bastian dropped his hands to his sides. Trying to wake up never worked.

His bare feet sloshed through the water. "Name," the hollow voice whispered. "Name and location of death . . ."

In his last dream, a door had appeared right in front of him, etched into the gray fog by warm, glowing light. He'd walked around, but nothing lay behind it but more ghostly gray. He tried to open it, but there was no knob, no handle, only the slightly rough surface of what felt like concrete.

He'd started talking to Andrea about it in their last few sessions, and she said this, just like his panic attacks, was a classic case of post-traumatic stress disorder associated with grief response. She'd smiled at him. Given him a book to read. He tried to trust her because that was what he was supposed to do. The book said things like *post-traumatic stress disorder is a mental health condition that is triggered by a terrifying event*. It said things like *the most common events leading to the development of PTSD include combat exposure, physical assault, and being threatened with a weapon*. It said things like *the grieving process is important and different for everyone*.

He didn't want to grieve. He wanted to forget. Move on. Be normal, be unnoticeable, be ordinary, not that kid people whispered about as he moved through the hallways at school.

Andrea also said he should embrace the nightmares. That he was rational enough inside them that he could try to affect some sort of change because lucid dreaming was a legitimate thing. This could help him come to terms with his guilt.

So he tried that, too, because he was supposed to.

It didn't work.

Fuck, it was cold here. Bastian huffed a breath into his hands, then tucked them deep into his pockets and kept walking. The water lapped over his feet, the bitter chill leeching up his legs. There were no doors anywhere—just black water and gray fog as far as he could see.

A long time ago, he'd liked the color gray. A couple of years back, right after they'd moved to Portland, his mom had rented a little gray beach house outside Seaside. They'd spent a couple of weeks there over the summer. He remembered Dorian, curled up on the couch in the living room doing puzzles. He remembered sand, and water, and the smell of salt, and the way his mom had helped him hobble into the bathroom to clean his foot when he cut it on a jut of rock. She'd smiled and tilted her head, her long brown curls falling over her shoulder. He remembered looking at gray walls as she wiped the blood away. He remembered her humming quietly, the stupid chorus to a song that had been on the radio way too frequently that summer.

He remembered the way her voice dropped, low and melodic as she said *I love you*.

Bastian stopped. The door was right there in front of him, appearing out of nowhere—like it had always been there and he just hadn't stopped to notice. This time it was a burnished, golden wood.

He pushed against it. Nothing happened.

The whispers started up: *why, why, why, why*, tumbling through his head. It was Dorian's voice this time. Dorian's pleading. Bastian pressed his hands against his ears as hard as he could, but the sound didn't stop. It was inside him. He pushed harder at the door with his shoulder, and nothing happened; he kicked at the door, and nothing happened; he tore a hand from his ear and punched his fist into the wood hard enough that his knuckles tore.

The wood didn't crack, but it flickered for a second, going filmy. A shadow moved behind it, slightly taller than Bastian.

Before Bastian could move, it shifted back to wood again, solid and unyielding.

"I hate you!" Bastian yelled, punching it again. "I *hate* you!"

Hate you, echoed up and down the lonely space.

His fingers were numb with cold now. He wanted to wake up and stop thinking about Dorian, about the beach, about anything that reminded him of who he used to be, but he couldn't. The nightmare would end when the nightmare wanted to end.

The skin on his knuckles split and left a smear of rust on the door. In the distance, water burbled.

Bastian sank down, tucked his head against his knees, and waited to wake up.

"Name and location of death," someone whispered.

CHAPTER FIVE

Styx

An ache radiated through his chest, and Zan turned his head up, taking a long breath of air so thin it barely had any oxygen left at all. His fingertips were turning blue, his entire body felt like it was shaking apart, and the peaks of snowy mountaintops stretched out as far as he could see.

He was still at least a day's hike to the peak. The man he'd been with had bragged about this ascent. Mount Annapurna, with more than twice the death rate of Everest, had been his life's goal.

Unfortunately, it was the last life's goal he had. An avalanche had buried him and his team, leaving him to wander Styx for hours as his oxygen ran out on Earth.

Then, the memory had been alive. The harsh wind that ripped across the mountain face had bitten into Zan's cheeks and ripped at the skin of his hands. A bright-red tent below him had rippled and boomed, a bloody stain against the white of everything else around them.

The other climbers had been laughing, discussing tomorrow's

ascent, how they'd finally reach the peak.

Now? The memory was dead, like all the memories he had from the souls who had passed on. Nothing but the frozen figures of the men below and a silence so loud it made his ears ring.

He blinked slowly, a desperate tiredness falling over him like the world's worst blanket.

It was time to go.

Scrubbing a hand over his eyes, Zan considered his options. The Ferryman had stolen death from him just like he'd stolen life: plucking Zan from the Asopos before his lungs collapsed meant that Zan hadn't had the time to walk through his own mind. He didn't have access to his own memories. He would never see his family again.

He still had a collection of scenes from Greece, though, remembered by the souls he'd escorted over the years. Sometimes he wandered sparkling white city streets that had been built over villages like his own. Sometimes he went back to dip a hand in the sea and let the sun bake the salt onto his skin until it cracked.

It wasn't the same as home, but at least he'd be warm.

He forced himself up on stiffened legs, but before he could get any farther, the call of Styx roared in his ears. Some poor soul was waiting for him.

Sighing, Zan unzipped the red fabric that should have led inside the tent, but instead opened to the warm, golden light of his office.

No one was there. Instead, the door warped behind him, thinning out enough for him to see a boy standing there but solidifying back to wood again before he could step through. Zan stepped closer as it flickered again, faded, revealed the boy, stabilized again.

Zan recognized him immediately. He was Zan's age but a couple of inches shorter. He never made it fully into the office, instead he was caught somewhere close enough to life that the door wouldn't open. He'd been getting stuck here for months, fading away completely before he could get in.

"Name and location of death?" Zan asked, even though he knew the chances of the boy hearing him were low.

The door morphed back into transparency, and he watched as the boy raised his hands, hammering against it. A scowl tugged at his lips, and he opened his mouth, yelling something that Zan couldn't hear.

Zan didn't know what it looked like from his side. He could only access dead memories, not anything that close to life. He reached out, one finger stretching toward the curl of the boy's fist. "Who are you?" he whispered.

The other boy sank down, tucking his chin to his knees. Before long, he began to fade, graying out and dissolving to ash. The door snapped back into cold, hard cement and didn't flicker again.

Zan waited, hand pressed against the concrete for a long minute. He could almost imagine the warmth left behind. Zan wasn't supposed to feel anything toward the souls he had to deliver, but if this one was still mostly alive?

Zan always found himself hoping that he wouldn't come back.

He walked back to his desk and sat down in the chair, surveying the office. The dying souls who showed up in his office relived memories as Zan led them toward death. After the Ferryman ate them, Zan had continued access to the memories; he could wander through them as often as he liked. He slept in them, ate in them, survived in them.

And he returned to his office whenever a soul arrived.

The entirety of the small space was filled with knickknacks that no one would ever miss, things stolen from dead memories. Most were small—a glass marble, a single pearl earring, a butter-yellow silk ribbon. Books, and books, and books. He leaned back in his plum-colored armchair—a much harder theft to manage as he'd had to drag it by himself across an entire wing of the Buckingham Palace—and sighed. No matter how many things Zan collected, this would never be home. It was exactly six large steps from the center of the room to any of the walls.

Big enough to sit in. Small enough to lose his mind.

Zan opened his laptop and pulled up a game of *FreeCell*, scowling as he watched the pixilated cards deal out on the screen.

It had been 499 years since he'd buried himself in the banks of the Asopos.

The deal was almost up.

CHAPTER SIX

Portland, Oregon

Bastian paced, trying to shuck the sticky vestiges of nightmare that clung to his skin. The dream was an insidious thing, crawling inside him, skittering through every nerve. It always took him ages to calm down when he woke—even when he followed every one of Andrea's breathing techniques, it took hours before the sound of lapping water faded completely.

Stopping in front of the air conditioner, Bastian nudged the switch off. He needed to save money if he was going to hire Riley's brother.

He chewed on his lower lip.

He needed to call Riley's brother.

There had been a used bookstore when they'd lived in New York—about two miles from their apartment. Bastian biked over there every single day after school. Hung around so much that the little old lady who owned the place knew him by name and stocked cinnamon mints up front—just for him. Dorian had never seen the appeal of the place, but Bastian? He could lose himself for hours pulling books from shelves, reading first chapters, looking for the next gem to add to his ever-growing collection of pulpy and not-so-pulpy fantasy novels.

He wanted that feeling again.

Owning a bookstore at eighteen was ridiculous.

Opening a bookstore at eighteen was even more ridiculous.

Actually supporting himself enough to keep the electricity on by selling books at the bookstore was the most ridiculous of all.

But the idea of thousands of books below him rotting away was downright depressing.

He fumbled his phone out of his pocket, swallowed down his anxiety, and thumbed to the number Riley had plugged in: *Joon the reno master CALL HIM BASH*

Bastian hastily edited out all but the *Joon* part of the contact, then hit the call button before he could wuss out completely.

Joon turned out to be nothing like Riley—no dramatics, no crazy sarcasm, just curt, straightforward, all business. He agreed to come out the next day to check things out and give him an estimate, so Bastian promised to be at the store at eight o'clock in the morning to open the place and let him poke around. Even though he knew Bastian was supposed to be in school, Joon seemed pretty invested in keeping their dealings to strict business hours.

Bastian didn't have a clue what to anticipate in terms of the cost of renovating an entire storefront, but he figured it was going to be expensive. Very expensive. Blow-through-the-rest-of-the-life-insurance-money-and-then-be-unable-to-feed-himself expensive.

But when he hung up the phone and wiped his sweaty palms against his jeans, that deep-down flickering want inside him had grown. It was becoming impossible to ignore.

ᘖᘖᘖᘖᘖᘖᘖᘖᘖ

Hardwood floor installation: $18,000

Interior painting: $10,000

Roof: Good shape. No repairs necessary.

Window replacement: $20,000

Lighting

Plumbing

A/C repairs

More.

Bastian winced as he scanned the handwritten scrawl on the yellow legal pad that Joon had shoved his way. "So this is all . . . it all has to be done?"

Joon stared at him.

Bastian's cheeks flamed. "You look like Riley when you do that," he mumbled, looking back down at the paper. "All scary. Like I'm being an idiot."

"We're related," Joon said, completely monotone, still staring.

"Right. Uh . . ." Bastian scanned the sheet again. Total estimate: $90,000. And that was cheap. That was friend-discounted. That was *way better than it could have been*, according to Joon.

Bastian had enough money still sitting in the savings account, but he'd have almost nothing left when all was said and done. "Okay, so . . . I guess . . ."

"You need time to think it over?"

No. Because then he'd second-guess everything and would be right back to square one—failing high school while living in a run-down bookstore with no exit plan. "No," Bastian murmured. He set the legal pad on the carpeted front counter. A plume of dust rose. "When do we start?"

Joon blinked. Crossed his arms. "When's your opening date?"

Bastian shuffled his feet. He didn't have an opening date. He was functioning day by day right now; the idea of planning something that far in advance was enough to make him want to vomit. "Uh, January sixth," he said, throwing out a completely arbitrary number far, far in the future.

"Mmm," Joon hummed. "All right, that's fast but doable. Going to take me a week to get my team together. You need to have the place cleaned out by then."

"Cleaned out . . . where . . ."

Sighing, Joon reached over and took his pad back. "Look, get my sister in here, other friends. You do have friends don't you?"

Sort of. Probably wouldn't after forcing them into even more hard labor for nothing. Bastian frowned.

"Get them in here, get the books boxed and lined against the walls. Move the bookcases over too. We'll throw some tarps over them and work around it all. Not a big deal, kid."

Bastian's cheeks heated. He rubbed at the back of his neck and tried not to sound totally and completely petulant. "Don't call me kid."

He sounded totally and completely petulant.

"Call me when that's done," Joon said, ignoring him. "I'll shoot you an invoice. Then you can pick samples. Paint colors. Whatever you want. We'll get it done."

"Okay."

Joon nodded and walked toward the door.

"Thanks," Bastian added.

Joon shot him a thumbs-up with no smile. "No problem." Then he shoved the door open and let himself out to the street.

Bastian sighed. He pulled a stool out from behind the counter and sat down.

Meow, the feral cat whined, popping out from behind the awful velvet curtain and trotting over to him.

"You going to help move books?" Bastian asked.

Meow.

"Fair enough. You sticking around at least?"

Meow.

"So you need a name."

The cat sat down and started cleaning its whiskers.

"Book?"

The cat glared at him.

"Yeah, that's pathetic. Kang the Conqueror?"

The cat glared harder.

"Okay, okay, no supervillains. Ummm . . ." He cycled through favorite movies, shows, books . . . nothing. "I guess we'll just stick with Cat for now?"

The cat looked back down and kept cleaning its whiskers.

"I know. I suck. Sorry."

Meow, Cat said one more time, then trotted away.

CHAPTER SEVEN

Styx

"**N**ame and location of death."

The girl standing in front of his desk watched him, eyes wide. She looked to be a few years older than Zan, with long blonde hair that was matted with blood and dirt, and a thick bruise circling her neck. It squirmed beneath her skin, a twisting blot of blue, purple, and silver.

Marked then. Close enough to death that the Ferryman had almost grasped her without Zan's help, but something must have dragged her soul from the brink.

Zan's stomach twisted. He hated escorting younger people for obvious reasons, but there was also a sick desperation that jolted through him every time someone close to his age wandered into the office.

He missed talking to people.

He missed feeling human.

"Name and location of death?" Zan asked again, forcing his eyes back to the screen.

The girl mumbled an answer, Zan typed it down, then he grabbed the key ring from his desk and handed it to her. When she selected one, the gray wall of concrete across from Zan's desk wavered and morphed into hundreds of strands filled with tinkling rainbow beads. He tried to take the girl's hand, but she pulled away, refusing to look at him.

Zan's stomach sank further.

She led him through the beads, into a jumbled memory of neon and noise. The room was dark, the air smelled like incense, pot, and that cool mustiness of a space deep underground. A woman stood on a stage far in front of them—hands clutched tightly around a microphone, eyes squeezed closed as she belted out angry lyrics to a song Zan had never heard.

The girl pushed through the crowds, and Zan had no choice but to follow her.

"It's loud in here!" he yelled.

She didn't answer.

Zan shrugged, then tried again. "Cool band!"

She pushed toward a group of people in the front corner. They all embraced her, laughed with her, danced with her, lived with her.

Zan swallowed hard, watching their love. He closed his eyes and let himself sway into a clump of bodies at his right, wrist brushing against the sharp hip of another boy with glitter streaked down his chest. Sometimes, if he tried really hard, he could almost pretend that he was real again.

But the boy didn't look at him—was stuck in the predetermined loop of the memory, alcohol-laden eyes hooked on someone else.

The memory began to gray around them, edges of the far brick wall wavering like a desert mirage.

The barrier.

Swallowing, Zan pushed into the fray and grabbed the girl's hand, pulling her toward the fading edges of the club. She tried to fight him, yanking her wrist away and then taking off through the crowd, but the rest of the memory was solid, and it wasn't hard for Zan to give chase. He cornered her in the bathrooms, nausea crawling up his throat as she pushed herself as far into the corner as she could.

"It's okay," he tried.

She swore at him, hissing like a feral animal.

Zan's fingernails cut into his palms. "I have to . . . I . . . it's going to be okay."

It wasn't going to be. It never was—this was by far the worst part of the job. The part where he smiled and *lied*.

The wall behind her started fuzzing out as the barrier crept closer. She jerked forward in surprise when it began to give way.

"I'm sorry," Zan told her quietly. He stepped forward, trying to gently nudge her back.

"It's a dream!" she shrieked at him, spitting, and kicking, but the wall dissolved, and it was too late.

It was always too late.

Styx swirled around them soaking their feet, and the Ferryman rose up from the depths, oily beads of black coalescing into a sharp beak, razor scythes, serrated claws, feral teeth.

The girl was crying now, sobbing openly, pleading for Zan to save her.

Zan squeezed his eyes closed, trying to swallow down bile as he heard the crunch of the Ferryman biting down. A sickening slurping rose above the sound of the water.

"She did not pay," the Ferryman leered moments later.

Zan knew how much a single soul was worth in obols, in guilders, in pennies. It wasn't much, but occasionally it was enough to keep the monster sated. "I can't help that," he said shakily, still not opening his eyes. "That's not . . . I can't do anything about that—"

"There is less pain if they pay."

The words washed over Zan, not angry, not full of any emotion at all. Just a statement. He gave a short nod, still refusing to look. Then he turned and pushed back into the memory, picking up the set of keys the girl had dropped as he forced her through the barrier. He twisted them in his fingers as he walked through the dead air of the now-quiet underground club.

Zan paused, one finger reaching out and tracing the curve of his collarbone. It came away wet with sweat and golden glitter. He'd never move again—the only living memories belonged to people who were human.

And Zan was not human.

Humans didn't force people to their deaths. Humans didn't deliver them to vicious gods and ignore them when they cried.

He was just as much a monster as the Ferryman.

A horrible ache rose in his throat, making it hard to swallow. Zan stalked back to the office, beads swishing behind him as he picked through the keys. The door was still wavering when he found the one he was looking for, and as he held it up, the door flickered, stuck between brightly colored beads and cement for a moment before morphing to red clay.

Zan walked out onto the banks of the Asopos.

This wasn't his river. This was from a memory only a few years ago, from an elderly man with relatives in Greece. Here, sickly trees were caught in the sway of the wind, the sun beat down overhead, and the muddy clay that Zan had sunk his body into had baked into stone-hard ground. Here, the river was a noxious purple, stained from pollutants being dumped upstream. The man had told him all about it—ranting about how the tourist beaches were closed when he'd visited, and he'd complained to the staff at the resort because that is something he should have been informed of before paying top dollar, and the entire experience was a waste of his time, how was he supposed to reconnect with his roots if the entire godforsaken land was uninhabitable?

And Zan had tried to listen, but the words had washed over him, background noise in comparison to the horror he'd felt at seeing how his home had changed.

He toed off his shoes and socks, the soles of his bare feet burning on the hot ground. The water wasn't much better, shallow and so warmed by the sun that it was tepid at best. It was still, not lapping at his skin or rolling toward shore. He pushed through it, wading until it came up to his chest. Then he ducked beneath the water and started counting.

One. Two. Three—

Beams of sun splintered beneath the surface, fragments of light illuminating specks of dirt and rock that had been churned up by the waves when they'd been alive. There was no sign of life—no fish, no tadpoles, not even the slick of algae-coated rocks.

Forty-one. Forty-two.

Zan blinked as the acidity started to burn his eyes. He slowly exhaled, arms carving swathes around his body as he tried to push himself lower. The mud was softer here, and he forced his feet in, letting the clay hold him down just as it had done so many years ago.

The girl had been so scared.

And Zan had forced her anyway.

One hundred fifty-eight. One hundred fifty-nine. One hundred sixty.

A bubble escaped his nose, freezing in front of his eyes. His head hurt. There was horrible pressure behind his eyes, his chest was caving in, he needed to breathe, he needed to, breathe, he—

The world tilted sideways as his vision spotted, white stars blooming behind his eyes. He needed—

The memory popped away, and Zan fell to the floor of his office, sucking in a horrible, rasping breath. He was soaked through, shivering so violently he could feel his teeth clacking together. His sinuses were a mass of pain, his chest full of knives. He curled in on himself, pressing his forehead against his knees and wrapping his arms around his body.

Monsters didn't feel like this, did they?

Monsters didn't know love, they didn't know grief, and they didn't know *fear*.

Water dripped from his nose as he shook, and Zan squeezed his eyes closed, focusing on the burn of his lungs and the sluggish, cottony ache of his heart.

CHAPTER EIGHT

Portland, Oregon

His therapist's office was in a tiny strip mall off Willamette Avenue. It sat between a pet supply store and a bead gallery that Bastian was pretty sure was actually a drug front.

The court-appointed sessions with Andrea had been mandated last year because he was a minor, but he'd turned eighteen only a couple months after the accident and had been showing up less and less ever since. Dorian had a separate therapist, and they'd both been assigned to what Bastian liked to refer to as "couples counseling" with a third once a month, but those sessions were completely useless. Dorian had moved on with his life. Therapy wasn't going to make them a normal family again.

Bastian sighed. It was starting to mist, but he kept standing on the sidewalk, watching Andrea's door. Usually Dorian dropped him off, but Bastian had skipped school again for another brief meeting with Joon, had ignored every single one of Dorian's increasingly frustrated texts, and had opted to walk it. In hindsight, stupid. He only had his sweatshirt to zip over the scratchy wool of his uniform sweater, and the October wind was bitter and already tinged with winter.

He didn't know what he was going to say to her today. Even though the hallway dream hadn't reappeared over the last week, he still hadn't slept. The constant dust being kicked up in the store made his throat scratchy and sore, he hadn't paid for heat yet despite the sudden turn of weather, and his stomach was in a constant state of nausea-inducing anxiety because Dorian kept texting him about *college*, *applications*, and his *future*.

Andrea would home in on every bit of this and push at him until he either gave in and spilled his guts or snapped at her—both of which would provoke enough anxiety to lose more sleep, starting a vicious cycle of self-deprecation and misery.

A girl wearing a wildly floral skirt—and enough bangle bracelets that she jingled with every step—disappeared into the bead shop. Bastian popped a piece of gum into his mouth, cinnamon flavor bursting over his tongue. He checked his phone. 2:13 p.m. Two minutes. Sighing, he pulled open the glass door and entered the little sitting room outside Andrea's office. He sat down on the checkered couch, pulled over a *National Geographic* with a rabid-looking rhinoceros on the cover, and read exactly two paragraphs on the grieving process of African elephants before the office door opened.

"So good to see you, Bastian!"

Bastian set the magazine down. "Hey." He followed Andrea in and sank down in the brown leather armchair in the corner. She sat down directly across from him in a matching chair, though hers was dark blue, and the leather was worn thin on the arms. Her glasses were bright orange and clashed horribly with her garishly patterned peacock feather shirt. It made his head hurt.

"Tea?" she asked.

"No."

"That kind of day?" She smiled at him, then picked up her own mug—salmon pink with black-and-white polka dots that clashed even more with the rest of her ensemble. The words *I will probably spill this* were scrawled on it in cursive font.

Bastian shrugged. There was an unlit candle that smelled like pine, a giant sparkling geode, and a box of tissues on the table next to him. He wondered if Dorian cried in therapy. Bastian didn't. His finger wandered to the cuff of his sleeve and pushed up underneath, rubbing at the silvery bruise on his thumb. It still hadn't gone away, and the skin was smoother there—almost like the scarred skin around his collarbone.

Andrea's eyes flicked down to his hands. He stopped rubbing.

"All right," she said. "Where would you like to start today?"

"Week was good," he mumbled. "I'm fine."

"It's okay to not be fine," she said mildly.

Bastian looked back down at the floor. "Never mind."

She was completely unaffected by his nonanswer, just grabbed a legal pad that was leaning up against the base of her chair and pulled a pen from somewhere in the mass of kinky curls that haloed her face. Then she fixed him with an interested stare and didn't say anything else.

"Moved into the store," he finally muttered, trying to break the awkward silence. He hated when she did this—stared at him until he broke. It always worked.

He hated that too.

"The bookstore," she clarified.

"Right."

"How did your brother react?"

"I don't know. We haven't really talked. He's angry. Don't

know why, now he gets the whole townhouse to himself. Seems like a great deal on his end."

"Not having to live with you?"

He snuck a glance at her. She was watching him intently, hardly moving at all.

The townhouse was rarely a focal point of their conversations. In a rare display of consensus, both Dorian and Bastian found it to be completely stifling and oppressive after their mom's death, but had agreed to stay at their aunt's insistence. But as the weeks went on, it got harder and harder to look at Dorian. As Bastian's arm healed, as the cast came off, as the bruises faded to nothing on Dorian's face, as they pretended to live this life where they got up in the morning and went to school like normal teenagers, it became too much.

Because nothing was familiar anymore.

Because a year ago, Bastian had ruined everything.

Andrea still wasn't saying anything, so Bastian focused his attention on the stupid-looking geode. The rock was as big as his head with dozens of purple striations running through it, polished to a perfect shine. He pressed a finger against the center where it was still rough. His skin caught against the glittering crystals.

"Would you like to talk about the store?" Andrea asked, finally giving in. "Or we can talk more about Dorian."

"The store is the store, and Dorian is an asshole."

"I think Dorian is trying his hardest," she said gently.

"Yeah. Whatever. I know."

She kept watching him. Bastian's fingers twitched, and for a second, he wished he'd let her make him a cup of tea. At least then he'd have something for his hands to do. "I had another panic attack at school," he finally said, pulling his hand back from the geode and forcing them down into his lap. "I tried to breathe. It didn't help."

Her eyes softened.

He looked back down at his lap, so he didn't have to look at her.

"Was there something that triggered the attack?" she asked.

He picked at his jeans. "Failed a test," he mumbled. "Wasn't a big deal."

"It doesn't have to be a big deal to be upsetting," she said.

"Yeah, I know."

He wanted to itch at the mark on his thumb again, but he didn't want her scratching that into her pad along with whatever else she was going to write down later.

"And what happened after?" Andrea asked.

Bastian grit his teeth. "Uh, I pulled my shit together, and I went to lunch with my friends." His voice sounded harsh, angry. He didn't want to talk about this, he shouldn't have brought it up at all—

"Did Dorian drive you there?" Andrea asked.

And there it was. He didn't want to talk about it at all because it always led here. Always. And like a stupid idiot, he walked right into it.

"Yeah, and it was fine," Bastian ground out. "Nothing happened." *Except you couldn't breathe, and you kept your hand on the door, and you about hyperventilated at every stoplight because you could hear screeching brakes, shattering glass, screaming—*

Andrea smiled. "Bastian, you got into a car, and you let Dorian drive you right on the heels of a panic attack. That's an incredible step!"

Truly incredible, Bastian thought grimly. He forced himself back to chewing his gum and relaxing his jaw. "Can we just talk about the bookstore instead?"

"I'd love to make some space for your success—"

Bastian groaned. "I'm *fine*. Really."

"Mmm," Andrea hummed.

Her pen started tapping against her notebook for a second as she considered, and Bastian was sure she wasn't going to let him drop it this easily, certain she was going to press him more, but—

"I'd love to hear about your store," she said. "I'd also like to use some time to try a few other coping mechanisms that might help future attacks."

Bastian blinked in surprise. He didn't want to save time for coping mechanism talk, but the fact that she'd dropped the car thing so easily was a relief. So Bastian talked about the amount of money it cost to renovate a three-thousand-square-foot building, and how right now, he was feeding Cat stale pieces of doughnut that he'd bought half off next door but was going to hit the pet store on his way out of here and buy real cat food, and Andrea walked him through another breathing technique— this one tracing the lines of his fingers—and when the session ran out, they scheduled another appointment in a week that he might or might not decide to show up to. Then she led him out of the office.

There was another man sitting on the checkered couch, reading the same *National Geographic* that Bastian had picked up when he'd gotten there an hour ago. Bastian wondered if he'd read far enough to find out that elephants have a generalized response to death and show grief even toward deceased creatures that are not their own kind.

"Goodbye, Bastian," Andrea called after him.

He waved over his shoulder, then pushed his way out of the office.

Where Dorian was waiting in the Audi.

CHAPTER NINE

Portland, Oregon

"Was not expecting you," Bastian said. He hesitated, but the sky rumbled with thunder, and rain started sheeting down. Grimacing, Bastian yanked open the passenger door and sank down into the seat, kicking his feet up on the dash. His Chucks left stripes of mud against the pristine plastic.

"Why are you like this?" Dorian groaned.

The car was parked. There was no rumble of engine underneath him, but Bastian's fingers still tightened on the door. He forced a breath out and stared at Dorian like there was nothing wrong. Dorian leaned over and rifled through the glove box, coming up with a handful of single-use packs of antibacterial wipes. He clicked it closed again.

"Feet down," he ordered, throwing them at Bastian.

Bastian did not put his feet down.

Dorian's hands closed around the wheel of the car, knuckles white. He let out a deep breath, took another, let that out too. The tightly coiled anger leeched from his body.

Just like that.

Bastian hated how easy it was for him.

Dorian reached over and turned the car on. The engine growled to life.

Bastian yanked his feet down and threw his hand up against the side of the door before he even realized he was moving.

"Sorry," Dorian murmured carefully, like he was trying to calm a spooked horse. He slowly lifted his hands off the steering wheel as if to say *we aren't going anywhere yet.*

Bastian winced, pulled his hand back down to his lap, looped a finger through his bracelet, and started tugging at it until the twine bit into him.

"We need to talk about you moving out," Dorian finally said. The lines of his jaw tightened ever so slightly—the only indication that he was frustrated.

"Obviously," Bastian muttered.

"Bash—" Dorian squeezed his eyes closed, then did another one of his deep breath things he probably learned in therapy— one of those deep breath things that magically *worked* for him. He ripped open one of the antibacterial wipes, reaching over Bastian to wipe up the mud on the dashboard. "I got home from school last week, and you were gone. And you won't answer my texts, and you missed our therapy session again, and you'll hardly even look at me at school, and every time I try to talk about it you just . . . you do what you always do."

"Which is?"

"Run. Change the subject. Ignore it."

Bastian let go of the bracelet and dropped his hands to pick at the hem of his sweatshirt. The ghost on the front of it peeked out from behind a giant red NO symbol. There was buttercup-yellow paint splattered across that—the same buttercup-yellow that their kitchen had been painted when they'd still lived in the house on Burnside, before the accident. Mom had been wearing this sweatshirt when they'd painted, found it at the thrift store that week, forced them all into a *Ghostbusters* marathon as the kitchen walls were drying.

"Buying some crumbling property is *not* what you were supposed to do with the money."

Scowling, Bastian kept picking at the worn hem, watching the fabric strain further over his fingers.

"It was money for school. For—"

"It was for *me*," Bastian hissed. "It wasn't for school. There was nothing it was specifically designated for; there were no hidden stipulations or strings attached."

"Yeah, but that's what she intended it to be. You ever think about how lucky we are to be *alive*? How shocked the doctors were . . ." He shook his head. His fingers tap, tap, tapped against the steering wheel. "We got a second chance, Bash. Don't waste that just because you're trying to make some sort of rebellious statement."

Bastian could feel the heat rising to his cheeks and ears. He knew *exactly* how lucky he was to be alive. Dorian was never in any danger. Dorian was bruised but crawled out of the car on his own. He's the one who called 911 first.

Bastian would remember that moment forever—the way everything around him faded away. How quiet, lapping water surrounded him, and an oily black shadow curled around him, brushing against the base of his thumb—

Then the air had flooded into his lungs so quickly he was sick, and all he knew was horrible pain, piercing sirens, the acrid smell of vomit, the presence of dozens of paramedics all shouting around him, and the throbbing, pulsing ache of what would become the small silver bruise that never faded.

Bastian was the one they dragged from the smashed wreckage of the car, resuscitated when his heart stopped beating, resuscitated again when his heart couldn't keep up. Bastian was the one in surgery as they repaired his collarbone, drained his lungs, and fought to keep him alive.

And for what?

Bastian bit the inside of his cheek as hard as he could, tasting the blood that rose to the surface. He wondered what Dorian would do if he threw open the door and left. If he started kicking the dash as hard as he could. If he punched him straight in the nose.

Probably tear open another antibacterial wipe, carefully dab the blood off his face, and deep breathe some more.

"She didn't *intend* anything," Bastian finally said. He dropped his sweatshirt hem and went back to the bracelet, pulling it around, and around, and around his wrist. "She died. She's gone. Forever. And that's not the sort of thing you anticipate enough to plan this shit. Not at forty-two. Jesus. Fuck. I mean . . ." He didn't know what he meant. He didn't know how to fill the gaping hole in his chest that had been eating at him for almost a year. He'd tried stuffing it full of her, her sweatshirt, her Maserati poster, her coffee grinder, *her*, but nothing ever worked.

His foot knocked against the glove box, and it clicked open, revealing a neatly zipped leather case full of neatly organized insurance papers and the stash of wipes. Bastian leaned forward and grabbed one of the wipes, ripped it open, balled it up, and threw it at Dorian's face.

Dorian didn't even flinch, just picked it up and stuffed it in the plastic bag he kept in the center console.

"Stop it," he said quietly.

"No. You wanted to talk about this so bad, let's talk about it.

I bought a bookstore. I'm failing high school. I'm a mess, I'm not moving on, I'm not healing or whatever bullshit the therapists tell us we need to do."

"You're failing?" Dorian threw his head back and squeezed his eyes closed. "Christ."

Christ was the worst curse word Dorian used in public.

Bastian grit his teeth. "It's not a big deal."

"You're smart."

"Wow, thanks," Bastian drawled.

"There's no . . . is it that you're not turning in assignments? Or you don't understand? We can help if you don't understand the material. Mathais is already fluent in French, Riley's on the valedictorian list right behind Jasmine and me—"

Bastian forced his hands to his sides. His fingers curled to fists. "I understand the material fine. I have no interest in your help."

"At least move back in. Mistakes happen. We can sell the bookstore back, just—"

"The bookstore was not a mistake," Bastian growled.

"Bash—"

He'd rather face a lightning bolt straight to his brain than this. Bastian threw the passenger door open and climbed out of the car to the sound of thunder in the distance. Rain spattered around him, instantly soaking his shoes. "Later."

"Wait, no, Bash!"

Bastian ignored him. There was a bus stop a block from here. It was a major hub. He could suck it up, force his way onto the 22 down to the store. It *probably* wouldn't crash; he *probably* wouldn't die.

Fuck. Andrea told him to celebrate his "success"—what better way than having a complete breakdown on a bus?

He drew in a shaky breath and started walking.

He'd make it home. Then he'd lock himself in the store, and he'd pet Cat, and he'd start going through the piles of newly dusted books, and he'd find something to read, and he would not think about school, or Dorian, or what his mom would say if she could see the bookstore.

(She'd love it. She'd love it just like he loved it. She'd understand.)

The car pulled up next to him, and Dorian rolled the window down. "Bash, come on, get in the car. It's going to storm."

"You're driving on the wrong side of the road, asshole," Bastian muttered, still walking. "I'll take the bus." He shoved his hands deep in his pockets. He could see two people sitting inside the little terminal. Another was standing, staring at the map. Normal people. People who rode buses all the time. People who didn't die on buses. His heart kicked against his chest.

"Bash," Dorian insisted.

Bastian had almost made it to the edge of the street. A bus came around the corner, hiss of exhaust loud in the air. He forced his feet forward. A car pulled into the lot and honked furiously at Dorian, who was still easing the Audi down the wrong side of the street. Dorian gave him a politely apologetic wave but kept slowly inching forward next to Bastian, pulling in so close to the curb the tires rubbed at the cement.

"Please," Dorian pleaded. "I lost her too."

One foot. Two foot. One foot. Bastian groaned and turned back toward Dorian, who had one hand on the wheel, one arm hanging out the window, gripping the side of the car like he was going to be able to steer it out of oncoming traffic with nothing but the strength of a single, poorly toned bicep.

"Now I'm losing you."

Bastian's mouth was drier than dust. The rain fell harder, dripping from his hair to his eyes.

Dorian sighed, pulling his arm back in the car and then wrapping his hand around the wheel. "Can you text me when you make it home?" he asked, finally giving in.

Bastian hated the way regret rose instantly in his throat, the way he so badly wanted Dorian to just keep trying. He hated how even though their faces were the same, everything else was different. He hated that a year ago, he'd been driving, and Dorian had been looking out the window, and his mom had been messing with the radio, and then everything had stopped. Severed. Ended in the space of seconds.

The wind picked up around them, and the clouds rolled in even darker. Bastian flipped the hood of his sweatshirt up. It was soggy with rain. "Yeah," he muttered, then turned from the Audi and kept walking.

Eventually, he heard the Audi pull out behind him and watched from the corner of his eye as Dorian drove back toward campus. The rain poured harder. Bastian reached the bus stop and ducked underneath the overhang, shuffling between a mass of other sopping wet people. His throat was dry and scratchy, his arms and neck itchy. Bastian tried to swallow and focus on the bus schedule printed out beneath the glass.

He needed the number 22. Following the route with his eyes, Bastian ticked off blocks. Thirteen. Only two stops between here and the bookstore. Probably ten minutes, twenty tops. He'd step on the bus and flash his student ID and find a seat and sit down and close his eyes and breathe like Dorian breathed, and then it would be over.

The whooshing sound of hydraulic brakes hissed, and Bastian tore his eyes away from the map to see the bus turning the corner and pulling into the stop.

The people around him pushed forward, surging toward the door as it creaked open.

Everything was too hot, too scratchy, too loud. Sound narrowed down to nothing but his heartbeat, furious and frantic in his ears.

Bastian forced himself to take a single step forward, watching as all the normal people filed in, swiped their cards, took their seats.

His palms were sweating, and he couldn't get enough air, and a wave of heat rushed through him, burning all the way to his eyes, and shit, *shit*, he didn't have a bathroom to hide in this time. He was literally going to start crying right here in the middle of the street because he couldn't get on a fucking bus.

He tried to step forward again, but his feet wouldn't move. His entire body was rigid. Paralyzed.

The last of the perfectly normal people got on the perfectly normal bus.

The door creaked closed.

Bastian sucked in a shaky breath, rubbed furiously at his eyes, then stepped back out into the rain.

CHAPTER TEN

Styx

The tunnel was the same as it always was—cloudy gray all around, the mirrored black water underneath his feet. He looked down, watching his reflection as the glassy surface cracked his face, sending pieces rippling and disappearing far into the distance.

He was still wearing his mom's old sweatshirt and his black Chucks, but everything was faded, color warping and leeching as he watched. Blinking, he carded through his memories from the day. Therapy. Dorian. Bus. Failure, failure, *failure*.

His teeth clenched, and he shook his head.

Walk. Bookstore. He remembered making it in the building, petting Cat, then heading up the creaking stairs to the little apartment. He remembered looking at the Mas on the wall. Remembered stripping the sweatshirt off, then balling it up and throwing it at the poster as hard as he could. Remembered it softly bouncing off.

Remembered a wave of exhaustion. Falling onto the bed. Squeezing his eyes closed and wishing desperately he could breathe without the weight of her death threatening to drown him.

Therapy. Dorian. Walk. Bookstore. *Nightmare.*

The cold was seeping through his shoes, so Bastian started walking. The air was so thick with electricity, the hairs at the back of his neck stood straight up and his sweatshirt prickled at his skin. He could hear the sound of more water in the distance, faint, but rhythmic in its quiet growl. He kept walking, but the door didn't appear.

All he wanted was sleep. Regular, normal, close-your-eyes-and-rest sleep. "Stop it," Bastian pleaded, rubbing at the gray splotch on his . . .

On his wrist. It had spread to his wrist.

Bastian watched it curiously as it warped, graying, fading, then becoming clear again, and slowly growing.

Bastian squeezed his eyes closed, grit his teeth, and snagged at the skin of his neck with his fingernails, pinching as hard as he could. "Wake up, Bash. Wake up."

Wake up, wake up, wake up, wake up, the walls sang.

He opened his eyes. The door stood in front of him, a glowing line of light running along the underside of the cement. He pressed the palm of his hand against it.

And his mouth dropped open in shock as it creaked open, cement catching for a single second before revealing a tiny, cramped office.

The room was octagonal and small, with no other doors or exits. The hardwood floors glowed gold, and the perimeter of the space was framed by dozens of bookshelves, all in varying heights, shapes, colors, and sizes. They held battered books, but they also held empty picture frames, torn maps, chipped seashells, rocks, feathers, coins, buttons. Broken things.

"Name and location of death," a bored-sounding voice called.

Bastian tore his eyes away from the shredded head of a doll whose mouth had been stitched in a crimson scream. A boy sat in the center of the room, surrounded by a desk far bigger than he was. He didn't look up. He had one knee pulled to his chest as he hunched over a battered laptop, stickered with sparkling stars. He wore a neon-green windbreaker that looked like it was straight out of an '80s after-school special. It was brighter than anything else in the room. Dark curls fell over the black plastic frames of his glasses as his fingers started moving, the *clack* of a keyboard loose with age filling the small space. He looked up.

"Oh," he said. "It's you." His voice was calm and quiet. It barely rolled above the faint sound of water. "I was hoping . . ." He shook his head, looking back to his laptop. "Never mind."

He sounded almost sad.

Bastian opened his mouth to say something, to say anything, but his voice caught in his throat. This was the voice in his dreams; this was the boy who'd been haunting him since the moment he woke up in the hospital, and this entire situation?

He couldn't wait to see how Andrea picked it apart in a session. Dreaming of ghostly hallways and haunting voices was one thing, but constructing an entire human being who was looking at him with a combination of confusion and sadness?

That was getting to be a bit much.

Bastian scowled. The cement door was still warm underneath his palm. He pushed it open farther and took another step forward. "Who the hell are you?" he grunted.

The boy looked up, dark-green eyes glowing in the warm light. His head quirked to the side, and he leaned back in his chair, pushing his glasses up on his nose. "I'm here to guide you across the River Styx."

Bastian barked a laugh. It echoed too loudly, bouncing back

and forth between them. "Well, *this* is totally normal," he muttered to himself. "Your brain isn't screwed at all."

"It's not a dream," the other boy said somberly. "I'm the servant of the Ferryman, and I need your name and location of death. Because you are supposed to be dead."

Bastian swallowed. He lifted his hand and watched as his fingers began to crumble to dust.

He tried to take another step.

The dream dissolved.

CHAPTER ELEVEN

Styx

Zan blinked, watching the soul flicker out of existence.

Again.

A twist of relief caught in his throat for just a second, quickly replaced with gut-twisting fear as his eyes flicked back to the computer screen. The soul had stepped through the door. The program had loaded.

It flashed once, then an error message popped up.

Soul detection error

Press Continue to manually enter data

Press Cancel to quit

Zan smashed the Cancel button as quickly as he could. That particular error wasn't completely unheard of—Styx was traveled by only the souls who were unable to make the cross from life to death without a little push, and occasionally there were a couple of particularly hardheaded individuals who refused entirely. Miraculous recoveries, near-death experiences.

It had been a dozen years since he'd had one, though. They

always put the Ferryman in a foul mood. Once a soul was marked for death, he got greedy, and this one?

This one had been evading capture for far too long, and now that he'd officially stepped through the door . . .

The screen flashed black as the program closed out, then the laptop started humming as the operating system rebooted.

Zan swallowed his anxiety and reached across the desk, pulling a battered deck of cards toward himself. He tapped them out, shuffled a few times, and dealt out a manual game of solitaire, then slumped forward on the table. He wound one hand tight in the dark curls that constantly fell into his eyes and pulled tight until he could feel a bite of pain.

The computer screen flashed.

Error report sent, it read.

Zan's heart was beating too fast, and he couldn't suck a breath in. He hadn't been quick enough. If he didn't do his job, he didn't earn his freedom. Simple deal. Toddler terms.

Error reports meant he needed to *get out of here* and give the Ferryman time to cool off.

He forced his eyes back open and yanked at the top drawer of the desk, pulling out an enormous set of metal-toothed keys. He flipped through thousands, watching as each individual key flicked out of existence the moment he decided it was not the one he needed. He finally settled on one made of thick steel with a handle wrapped in tiny threads. It looked like it was made of rebar. He quickly held it to the door, watching it swirl.

Moments later, he stepped out onto the ledge of an unfinished construction project, three hundred feet in the air.

Huaibei City, China. Pingshan Power Plant.

The door faded behind him, and Zan sighed in relief, quickly darting across the ledge until he came to the very middle of the curve. The Ferryman was only able to reach into the edges of memories, where souls passed over, where they brushed against Styx. Zan was far enough into this one that he wouldn't be able to seep in. That didn't make Zan any less nervous. Any less afraid.

Zan squeezed his eyes closed. He remembered his mother praying in their small kitchen, the pages of her book fluttering in the dry wind. They'd fallen open to a page covered in swooping ink figures. The Ferryman, painted in slashing strokes, rippling waves of water in the background that shone so liquid black they looked like the paint hadn't had time to dry, skulls at his feet, emaciated bodies bent in supplication, and his two-pronged scythe hanging above his head.

Thousands of years may have morphed the Ferryman into a kindly servant of Death in all the storybooks, but Zan knew the truth. He was just as much a god as Hades was. And he was even more vicious.

Sinking down on his haunches, Zan caught his balance with splayed fingers. He lowered himself down onto the cement ledge, feet dangling over the side, kicking against the concrete. *Thump. Thump. Thump.* This memory wasn't very old. When he'd first come—with a grizzled construction worker—the wind had whipped around him so fast that they'd had to hunch to keep their footing. Now, there was no more movement, no more scent, no more sound. Up here, there was nothing but the stinging, biting cold of wind that no longer blew. It was similar to Mount Annapurna in the eerie stillness of being so high, but there was no view of mountaintops, only the twin of the tower directly across from him—the hyperbolic shape curving up toward the clouds. He'd never seen the facility in working condition—only had this single memory of it, before it had ever come alive.

When Zan was really lonely, when it got so bad he started

thinking about seeking out the Ferryman just to have someone who'd listen to him speak, he'd let go entirely and fall as long as he could. It was a different kind of pain than lying at the bottom of the Asopos, a different kind of fear than the burning cold of the mountain—this was a swooping terror that felt almost like freedom.

He never hit the bottom before blinking back into the office. Zan wasn't trying to die; he was just trying to *feel*.

He looked up at the sky. The boy would come back. If he'd made it into Zan's office, then he was getting closer to death, not farther. So he would come back, and Zan would bring him over, and the Ferryman would forgive him.

It wasn't Zan's fault.

It wasn't.

The dark shape of a sparrow hawk was paused in midflight between him and the gray sky. Zan took a deep breath and reached up, making a circle of his index finger and thumb. He caught the bird between them. Sometimes Zan would visit, would cup his hands around his mouth and screech at it.

The hawk never answered, just stayed frozen, wings out-stretched on whatever jet stream he'd found when the memory had first been born.

CHAPTER TWELVE

Portland, Oregon

The doughnut shop was busy. Bash fidgeted in line, gritting his teeth and shifting the two bags of groceries he held between hands.

Coffee.

All he needed was coffee.

His head was pounding. He wasn't sure if it was from the nightmare, or that after waking, he hadn't slept the rest of the night—only that even though he'd already spent his morning and part of the afternoon gulping coffee while watching the flooring guys stain the hardwood, he still couldn't keep his eyes open.

The line moved forward.

He listened to a man dressed in a perfectly pressed business suit yelling about the poor doughnut selection.

He listened to a woman ask for three Boston creams, six maple bars, and one rainbow sprinkle.

He tapped his hands against his legs and moved up one more spot. *You are supposed to be dead.*

He listened to the blue-haired teenager behind the counter yell to the back for someone to start another pot of coffee.

His phone buzzed in his pocket, and he ignored it, because the odds of it being Dorian asking him why he'd skipped school again were far too astronomically high to chance.

There was a college kid standing in front of him with a bright-green backpack. It reminded Bastian of the neon-green windbreaker that the boy in the nightmare had worn. His eyes fluttered closed.

That boy had been lanky and long—taller than Bastian. The glasses he'd worn had perched awkwardly on his nose, like the frames were too big for his face. He'd looked tired. Had sounded so, so sad.

Bastian couldn't remember another time in his life that he'd been aware enough in a dream to remember every single detail. This boy had been too real.

You are supposed to be dead.

By the time he got to the counter, the pot of coffee was completely empty so he had to wait while the new one brewed, and the cashier said, "Would you like to try an apple fritter with that?" and Bastian did not, he really did not, all he wanted was coffee, but he found himself mumbling "Sure" because maybe the cashier had to ask that, maybe they had to sell a certain amount of doughnuts by a certain time or they'd get in trouble, which was so stupid.

Totally stupid.

He was anxiety-spiraling.

Also totally stupid.

The cashier handed him a doughnut, and Bastian thanked her even though he'd been nauseous and shaky all morning from the dream and there was no way he was eating it.

His phone buzzed again. He ignored it again.

When he finally had his plain black coffee in one hand—largest size available—and the apple fritter in the other, he exited the shop, dodging out of the way of a group of girls who were laughing so loudly it made his head pound.

When he got back to the bookstore, the lights were all on.

Bastian groaned, then forced the door open with one shoulder, looking down in horror at the doorknob that was now wrapped in jingling bells.

There was only one person who would find that funny.

"Riley!" Bastian shouted.

No answer.

Heaving an enormous sigh, he kicked the door closed, scowling as the bells jingled again with an obnoxiously cheery sound. "Riley Kim, why are there bells on my door?"

There was a scuffling from the back office, then Riley appeared, looking entirely too pleased with herself. "It's homey!"

"I very specifically did not ask you to make my bookstore *homey*."

"Also cheerful. Makes people happy. Does double duty and alerts you to possibly having a customer to help!"

Bastian glared at her. "I don't have customers to help."

She shrugged. "Future problems, Bash." She turned and cupped her hands to her mouth. "Mathais! Get out here!"

"Why are you here?" Bastian grumbled. He tried to drink his coffee, but one of the bags of groceries he was holding shifted on his elbow, the cup jerked toward his mouth, and he ended up with a mouthful of scalding-hot liquid, causing him to curse, sputter, and spill the same scalding-hot liquid over his hand, leading him to curse and sputter some more. His head kept pounding. He squeezed his eyes closed, but everything went grayish, like the hallway. It was nauseating. He forced them back open again.

"Graceful," Riley called.

Bastian carefully eased the bag to the ground, then set the

paper cup down on the counter, wiped his hand against his pants. He flipped her off as Mathais came around the corner, a stack of books clutched in his hands.

"Did you know that you've got signed first edition copies of stuff here?" he asked, not looking up. He had the top book flipped open, eyes poring over the text. It was incredible that he was able to walk around the chaotic mess of books still piled all over the floor.

"Hello to you too," Bastian grumbled.

"Seriously! Did you know?"

"Nope."

"There's other stuff too. A signed Murakami. A bunch of super-old-looking Hemingway. I put some stuff on the desk in your office for you to look at. *Your office.* So weird. Sounds like something I'd say to my dad. Anyway, so much poetry, Bash, so much."

"Aren't you guys supposed to be in school?" Bastian asked.

"Friendly today, aren't we?" Riley piped up from behind a bookcase.

Mathais frowned as his eyes came to the end of the page he was on. He closed the book, set it on the floor, then opened the next book in his stack. He still hadn't looked at Bastian. "Oh, Riley and I got out of last period early. No football today on account of our awe-inspiring win on Friday. Coach was so excited he about shit his pants. And Riley had nothing better to do because her life is boring—"

"Hey!" Riley shouted.

"—and I have nothing better to do because my life is boring too. Figured we'd come help! Your door was open. We didn't know you weren't around. By the way, it stinks in here."

"Lock your door!" Riley shouted. "You're going to get murdered in your sleep!"

Sighing, Bastian picked up his bags. "Flooring guys just left an hour ago. New polish." He gestured at the floor. "That's the smell.

I gotta bring this stuff upstairs," he said. "Don't . . ." he paused, thinking. *Hang more bells on the door? Leave?* Sighing, Bastian settled on a shrug. "Just be careful. Some of the bookcases are super unstable without stuff on their shelves."

"Noted, boss," Mathais snarked, giving a salute and a grin.

Bastian turned and headed for the stairs. Cat followed him up and watched him expectedly as he unpacked milk, cereal, cans of chili and SpaghettiOs, and a dozen cans of cat food. Bastian pulled out one of the plastic plates he'd bought last week, opened a can, dumped it on the plate, and put it on the floor. Cat gave a contented little chirp before diving in.

"Better than doughnuts?" Bastian asked.

Cat didn't answer.

By the time he made it back downstairs, Riley and Mathais were arguing over a key ring full of different paint swatches that Joon had dropped off yesterday. Bastian swiped it out from under them, smacked the cash register six times to finally get it open, and dropped them inside. "Mine," he said.

"Yeah, but who amongst us has quality taste?" Riley asked.

"Not you," Mathais said.

She stuck out her tongue, then turned back to Bastian. "You need a name."

Bastian's eyebrows rose.

"For the store. I assume you aren't keeping Calderaldeblurble Collectibles because that's old, and stodgy, and dumb."

Bastian's eyebrows rose further. "What?"

"You know." She rolled her eyes. "Caviar. Caldecott. Carboxylation. Dude with stupid long name who owned the place before you."

"In what world is Carboxylation easier to remember than Cavendish?"

"In a world where I show up to chemistry class and actually pay attention, thank you very much. Name, Bash. You need a new one."

"I'll figure it out," Bastian said.

"Figure it out faster. Joon said he was moving on an expedited schedule for you. That means all-nighters."

"How is this your business?"

"Because he's my brother, and you're my friend—"

"And Riley takes immense pleasure in inserting herself in other people's lives," Mathais said, eyes back on the stack of books. "Poetry," he said, passing a book to Bastian. "Tennyson. Do you like Tennyson? Probably. Very dramatic. Like you."

"Excuse me?"

"Put that in the poetry stack," Mathais ordered.

"I don't have a poetry stack!"

Mathais pointed toward a couple of heaping boxes stacked precariously near the first of the bookcases. "You do now."

Bastian opened his mouth to respond, but suddenly Cat raced down the stairs, threw himself up on the counter, and shot straight into Bastian's coffee cup, which cartoon-toppled from the ledge onto the hardwood floor, splashing muddy-brown liquid all over his shoes.

Bastian squeezed his eyes closed again, got the same nauseating grayness, threw his hands down on the counter, and tried not to scream.

"Ewwwww," Riley said, taking a step back as she eyed Cat distrustfully. "You still haven't gotten rid of that thing?"

"All I wanted was coffee," Bastian moaned.

Cat batted at his face, then strutted back and forth on the counter.

This distraction had finally shaken Mathais from his book fixation, and he set the stack down, crept forward, and rubbed his pointer finger and thumb together like an absolute idiot. "Here, kitty kitty, here, kitty kitty—"

"Scratch him," Bastian muttered toward Cat.

Cat didn't scratch him. He ignored Mathais completely and headbutted Bastian in the arm with as much force as he'd hit the cup. Useless. "You're the worst," Bastian said.

"If he bites you, you'll probably get infected and die in agony," Mathais said very matter-of-factly. "Feral cats carry disease."

"Now who's being dramatic?"

Mathais reached into his pocket and pulled out his buzzing phone. His eyes flicked over the screen. "Dorian parked."

"No," Bastian said. "Absolutely not. I didn't invite any of you here!"

"Kinda did," Mathais said. "Couple days ago you said 'Riley, please help me, I'm a baby and don't know how to move a bookshelf by myself.' Ergo, we were invited. And . . . well . . ." He looked almost apologetic. "Dorian really wanted to come?"

Bastian's ears were ringing. He wasn't ready for Dorian to see this, and he definitely wasn't in the mood for another lecture.

"He's getting out of his car," Mathais remarked.

Bastian threw himself off the counter, walked over to the door, and flipped the deadbolt on it right as Dorian stepped up. "No soliciting!" he said through the glass.

Dorian had the absolute gall to smile at him, raise one hand, and politely knock.

"Come on, man," Mathais said.

Riley eyed him, one eyebrow arched. "If you guys don't work this out soon, I'm finding new friends."

Bastian said nothing, just glared daggers at Dorian, who politely rapped on the door again, smile growing ever so slightly more forced.

Cat gave another hideous meow, hopped on the ground, and trotted over to Bastian where he started winding in and out between his legs.

"Bash," Riley ordered.

Cat rose up on his hind legs and started scratching the glass of the door like a dog.

"Et tu, Brute?" Bastian moaned. Whatever. It didn't matter anyway. At least if they were all here, he'd stand no chance of falling asleep and having the stupid dream.

"I hate you all," Bastian muttered as he unlocked the door and nudged Cat out of the way with one foot. Then he gave a sarcastic salute. "I'll be in the office."

"Don't be like that," Dorian called, closing the door gently behind him.

It jingled again. Bastian's mouth pressed so tightly in a line his teeth hurt. "It's fine. I hear I have first edition copies to go through. Easy money, or something." He turned and walked back to the office, not looking back, not even when Riley said, "It's a really cool space," and Mathais said, "It fits him," and Dorian said, much, much softer than the other two, but not quiet enough for Bastian to ignore, "It reminds me of Mom."

CHAPTER THIRTEEN

Portland, Oregon

Despite his reluctance to have anyone around, the gang had all been surprisingly helpful for the rest of the evening. More than half of the bookshelves had been emptied, their contents stacked orderly along the far back wall of the store. Riley had done the most complaining of the bunch, shucking off her uniform sweater and skirt within the first few minutes of touching the dusty books, trading them for a pair of Bastian's old sweatpants and a T-shirt, then pulling a pair of knitting needles from her backpack and settling in the corner. She was content to bark orders at the boys while she held court, knitting needles clacking as a deep-burgundy scarf grew.

Bastian didn't mind. She held a bizarre amount of knowledge about obscure authors and was able to direct most of their finds toward specific genre-labeled piles. One step closer to a real store.

He and Mathais took the back half of the store. Mathais stuck in his earbuds and worked in silence—the muted chatter of Dorian and Riley arguing about something that sounded suspiciously like the Student Government Trivia Night floating around them. Bastian really hoped he wasn't about to get dragged to that. The only thing worse than showing up at school and trying to avoid attention was showing up at a school-sponsored, Dorian-and-the-perfect-student-government-planned event and trying to avoid attention.

It wasn't possible.

And he was always miserable.

By the time Riley, Mathais, and Dorian finally left the store, it was dark outside, and the roaring bass of the club was vibrating through the walls. Bastian waved them all off, locked the door behind them, then turned and walked back to the office to deal with the small pile of accumulated first editions they'd found over the course of the afternoon.

Bastian grabbed the small stack and sank down into the dusty couch with them. Cat jumped up next to him, walked back and forth across his lap a dozen times, then settled, purring so loudly that Bastian could almost forget about the obnoxious thumping bass from next door.

He didn't know the first thing about pricing books, so he pulled out his phone and searched through eBay, looking for matches to the couple of books that Mathais had found. A few were priced in the fifty-dollar range. Nothing wildly exciting, no hidden million Riley-dollars, but these were only a couple of books. He was sure he'd find more if he spent some serious time digging.

Bastian searched other used bookstore websites and scrolled through pages. His stomach was doing that fluttery, nervous thing. Excitement?

His arm flared in pain.

Bastian cursed, dropping the phone and then pulling his arm to his chest. The silvery bruise was shiny in the fluorescent overhead light. He rubbed his eyes. He was exhausted, he wasn't sleeping, it was probably totally nothing, just a bruise that kept getting bumped so it wouldn't fade.

Except, just like in his dream last night, it had spread.

He traced the shape of it, from the base of his thumb all the way underneath the piece of twine he'd tied around his wrist.

Bastian paused, studying the bracelet.

His mom used to loop the strands around their wrists when they were children. *Wishing bracelets*, she called them. Three wishes for three knots. When the bracelet fell off, the wishes would come true.

I wish for Mom back, he'd whispered a year ago, stupidly reenacting the ritual like it would actually do anything.

Knot.

I wish for Dorian to forgive me.

Knot.

I wish it had been me.

Knot.

Wincing, Bastian worked a finger underneath the twine and rubbed at the bruise. The pain had faded as quickly as it had come. Now his arm was all prickly, like it had been asleep, and he was coaxing blood back into flowing. He yawned and laid his head back on the couch. The light above his head started buzzing.

Bastian closed his eyes.

CHAPTER FOURTEEN

Styx

The black water stretched out in front of him, and there was nothing but the sound of his own breath in his ears.

"Not again," he murmured.

Not, not, the fog whispered around him, sending his voice back and forth down a space that never ended.

The darkness curled around his jeans, snagging vapor fingers around his ankles. Bastian started to walk. It followed him, growing, pulling more firmly. He shook his leg, but it didn't dissipate, just massed around him until it was a solid, writhing thing, growing bigger and bigger with every second.

Bastian swallowed down the prickling fear that was skittering up his arms to the back of his neck and started to jog.

The black came faster and faster, so he started to run, but it didn't stop. It pooled along in the cold water, shining like oil and turning everything behind him into a liquid, inky river. He frantically looked everywhere, trying to find the door, the sheet of concrete, where was it, where was it, *where was it.* Darkness tugged at his lips and snaked into his mouth and down his throat, and there it was, right there, the outline of a door glowing in the orange light—

Bastian tumbled through, sprawling face-first on the golden hardwood of the little office he'd dreamed of a week ago.

"Nice landing."

Bastian pushed himself up to his knees, gasping for breath. He could still taste the oily bitterness of the black. The desk was still there. The laptop full of stars was still there. The boy with the curls and bored-looking face was still there, only this time he didn't look so sad; he looked determined.

"Name and location of death?" he demanded, studying Bastian intently.

You are supposed to be dead. Bastian swallowed. Hard. The boy had different glasses, enormous circular frames that caused the green of his eyes to look even brighter. Bastian's entire body was too hot, then too cold. His palms were starting to sweat. "Leave me alone," he grunted, hoping he sounded tough.

He didn't. He sounded stupidly nervous, and it made him want to hit things.

The boy's eyes narrowed, unimpressed. "You're stubborn, and I get it, but you've got to understand that this is my job."

Tearing his gaze away, Bastian looked at the desk. There was a small pile of sea glass piled in the corner—foggy greens, blues, and purples. The hardwood floor shone golden brown, and the whole place smelled vaguely of incense and aged paper.

It was so vivid. *Real.*

"So I'm really going to need a name and location of death, it's the rules and all . . ." His voice trailed off. "You're marked," he murmured cryptically, eyes dropping to Bastian's arm.

Bastian looked down. The silvery bruise was there, more

prominent in the orange light. His hand was tingling, all pinpricks and needles. He shook it and swallowed hard. "I'm not dead."

The boy pushed back from the desk, chair squeaking against the hardwood. He stood up. "Of course you are," he mumbled. "He touched you. And if you were that close . . . why didn't you just cross? I don't understand why he didn't take you then, I just . . ." He tangled his hands in his hair for a second, pulling hard as his face scrunched up. "He knows you're here. We need to move, because if he finds out you're here, and I didn't bring you *again* . . ."

He spoke faster now, words tinged with nervousness, voice fading into an indecipherable slur of frantic monologue that Bastian couldn't make out. Then suddenly he straightened. Dropped his arms against his sides and looked back at Bastian. "Name," he said firmly.

"Bastian Barnes," Bastian said. He blinked in surprise, not sure why he'd said it.

"Great," the boy said. "Bastian Barnes." He slowed around Bastian's name, mouth rounding out the vowels in a way that was almost musical.

Bastian shook his head. This was just a lucid dream, like Andrea said. Control it. Fueled by guilt, spun out of his subconscious that refused to accept that he was still alive. This place was a dream; this boy was a *dream*.

Nothing more.

Bastian pinched the skin of his wrist between his fingernails, trying to shock himself out of this place and wake up, but of course, nothing happened.

"Bastian Barnes," the boy murmured again, leaning over the laptop and typing. "I hate to keep pushing, but it's kind of my job, and you already escaped once, and I'll be in trouble, I mean, you definitely don't want *him* coming after you, I'm the better option, I guess both options suck, but—"

"I'm not dead," Bastian said, interrupting the hyperactive stream of complete gibberish. "And you're nothing but a nightmare." He turned back to the door.

It had disappeared. There was nothing but a blank wall of concrete, no sign of the darkness that had followed him. Anger was bubbling inside him, thick and awful. He was so tired of dreaming, so tired of being haunted by grief, or guilt, or whatever it was that Andrea kept peppering him about in therapy. So damn tired. Squeezing his eyes closed, Bastian hauled back, then slammed his fist into the wall as hard as he could.

The dream didn't dissolve, the wall didn't flicker or move; the only thing that happened was that his knuckles split again, in the same place as last time, leaving another smear of coppery blood across the gray concrete.

"Stop bleeding on my door!" the boy behind him sputtered.

Bastian turned. "I want to wake up."

The boy stared at him incredulously. "Okay, first, stop punching things. It's not . . . it won't help anything, and all you're doing is making a mess of my office, and it's not like I have anything else around here, so I'd prefer it if you just . . . didn't do that, yeah? Secondly, look, Bastian? You go by Bastian?"

Before Bastian could open his mouth and tell him to fuck off, the boy plowed on again.

"Bastian, look, uh, thing is . . . I'm really supposed to log you in first. Rules and all that. I get in trouble otherwise, and I know you think you've got it rough, but trust me, things could be a whole lot worse, so . . . location of death? *Please?*"

Bastian very much wanted to punch more things, all the things, just to make a point. But his knuckles were sore. And he was exhausted. And he was definitely, absolutely, very much not dead.

He'd know if he was. He'd be grateful for it.

It would solve a whole slew of issues.

"Not dead," he repeated. The bookcase next to the cement wall held another pile of sea glass. Bastian stepped over and picked up one of the larger rocks, turning it over in his hand. It was foggy purple.

The boy didn't answer, just chewed on his lower lip as though thinking long and hard about what he wanted to say next. When nothing materialized, Bastian looked back down at the piece of glass. It was milky in the middle, clearer on the outer edges. It had one side that was sharper than the others, and he ran his finger along the edge, feeling it bite into skin.

"Okay. Let's go slow. I'm Zan," the boy said, breaking the silence. He didn't offer a hand. He wrapped his arms around his chest and studied Bastian with a vicious intensity.

Bastian's eyes narrowed. He set the glass back down.

Sighing, Zan tugged the top drawer of the desk open and pulled out a set of keys. They flickered in Bastian's vision, in and out and in again. It made his eyes hurt, like he'd stared too long at one of those twisting black-and-white optical illusions. Every time he thought he'd focused on the shape of a key, it was gone again.

"I'm not a dream," Zan said. He popped the drawer closed, key ring jingling in his hand. Then he stepped toward Bastian and carefully reached out, wrapping his fingers gently around Bastian's wrist and studying the silvery mark.

"Most of the time, people just die," he said, eyes flicking up to Bastian's. His voice was different now. Pitched lower, full of bitterness. "Sometimes they get stuck, though. End up here. In between."

Bastian looked down at his other hand, knuckles sticky with blood that hadn't dried. *The River Styx*, Zan had said in the last dream. "Uh huh," he murmured. "Makes total sense."

Zan looked up, nodding. His fingers twisted in the key ring, over and over. "So that's where I come in. I get to bring you over."

"I'm going to count to three, and I'm going to wake up."

"Sure," Zan sighed, leaning against his desk. "Okay."

Bastian closed his eyes. Counted. *One. Two. Three.*

Nothing happened.

"Or," Zan said, jingling the keys. "We go somewhere. Anywhere you want. Dealer's choice. Pick a happy memory."

Bastian grit his teeth. This was a dream. A really awful, ridiculously ornamented, unbelievably self-flagellating dream. He stepped toward the second bookshelf, inspecting the contents. There was a metal padlock there, the kind that they had on all the lockers at Preston. This one was scarred and rust-pocked with age.

Zan walked around the desk and over to the bookshelf and picked up the lock. "Pulled that from a bridge in London," he smiled weakly. "It's a love lock."

Bastian froze.

"Super cool really," Zan continued, completely oblivious. "Couples . . . or . . . people who love each other bring padlocks to this bridge and lock them all, and it's some statement of their bond. An affirmation? It's kind of like calling down a favor to the gods if you think about it. I liked the idea, so I took one." Zan carefully placed it back on the bookshelf, in between a pile of mismatched buttons and a waxy, misshapen rainbow-colored candle.

Bastian still hadn't moved.

Eight years ago, Mom had pulled him and Dorian along for a spur-of-the-moment "exploration trip" around the country. Caused them to miss school and end up a year behind. They'd wound up in Wyoming at one point, staying in a run-down hotel in the middle of nowhere. A small jogging path ran alongside the hotel, and they'd walked it one morning—him and Dorian and Mom—until they came to a section lined by a jagged chain-link fence that stretched over the freeway. The fence was littered with locks, flowers, key chains. He and Dorian had been up ahead, eagerly plotting their evening at the hotel: pool, vending machine snacks, more pool, more vending machine snacks.

Mom had stopped and called them over.

Pulled a lock out of her bag.

Bastian still had no idea why she had it, or where she'd gotten it, but he remembered so clearly the sound the lock made as it clicked into place.

This place will remember us, she'd laughed.

And Bastian and Dorian had rolled their eyes and kept walking, plotting, living.

Bastian scowled. He was not dead.

This was stupid. His subconscious was clearly dredging up memories he'd buried long ago; it was a horrible, horrible nightmare, and he was *done*. "Get out of my head," he growled, reaching out for the second shelf, and swept everything off it. Dozens of buttons scattered over the polished wood floor. A tiny crystal fox shattered next to his foot. Little shards of glass sparkled in the dim glow of Zan's lamp.

Zan's hands tangled comically in his hair for a second as he took in the destruction. Then he turned on Bastian, eyes flashing in anger. He tried to snag Bastian's arm in his grip.

Bastian ducked out of his way.

"Stop it," Zan hissed. "You have to come. There are rules!" He reached out again, fingers brushing against Bastian's wrist.

Bastian pulled back. His arm burned, his teeth were chattering, the cold was leeching into his bones, and he wanted to wake up. "Wake up," he said. "Wake up, wake up, wake up . . ."

Zan's mouth was a single straight slash. "We are on Styx," he said, like it was rote mechanics, like he'd said it a million times. "Think of a happy place. Your happiest memory." The keys in his hand jingled as he reached toward Bastian. "And choose a key."

Bastian closed his eyes. "You're a nightmare," he said, voice shaking. His stomach ached, his eyes burned, he felt like he was about to cry.

"Key," Zan repeated, thrusting the ring in Bastian's face. "I have to bring you. Just choose!"

Bastian didn't want to pick a key. He took a step back. His boots hit the cement wall. He turned around and pushed against it, willing it to be a door, wishing for it to be a stupid, fucking door. His head was muzzy, stuffed full of cotton. He could taste ash in his throat. He held up one hand and watched it crumble to dust. His wrist went next, arm, shoulder—

CHAPTER FIFTEEN

Styx

"No," Zan whimpered as Bastian faded right before his eyes. "No, no, no, no—" He grabbed the keys and threw them at the wall. They hit with a clatter, and the door flickered from wood, to metal, to moss, to bone, and finally back to cement as the ring fell to the floor.

Zan sank down with them, back pressed against his desk. He watched the edges of the room, eyes flicking back and forth from the bases of all of the bookshelves, waiting for the Ferryman to creep up from the floors.

Long minutes passed as adrenaline flooded his system. His heart raced, he sucked in shallow breaths that couldn't quite fill his lungs, and time ticked, and—

Nothing.

Zan tipped his head back, knocking against the desk. The pieces from his bookshelves that Bastian had angrily thrown lay scattered around the hardwood. He reached out and picked up a pearl button, rubbing his finger along the smooth edges.

Bastian Barnes.

A soul out of time.

And Zan had decided to rattle on about love locks instead of yanking him straight to the Ferryman because Zan had no common sense.

"No," Zan said quietly to himself. Because truthfully?

He rattled on about love locks because he didn't want to deliver Bastian's soul.

Because even though Bastian was convinced this was all a nightmare, he'd still looked at Zan like he was something real. He'd listened like Zan was *real*.

Zan closed his eyes and listened to the lulling water, so calm against the rapid, terrified beating of his own heart.

CHAPTER SIXTEEN

Portland, Oregon

Thump. Thump. Thump. Thump. Thump.

Bastian cracked his eyes open, trying to regain his bearings. He was in the bookstore office. On the horrible couch. Back pressed against the aging frame, body curled around Cat, who raised his head and gave a very dissatisfied chirp at the sudden movement.

Thump. Thump. Thump. Thump. Thump.

Someone was beating down the front door.

Bastian groaned, shoved Cat off, then pushed himself up. His cell phone clattered to the ground.

He was cold, stiff, and the dream was still thick enough to taste at the back of his throat. His entire body hurt because sleeping on a decades-old couch with barely any stuffing left was a bad call, and his throat hurt because the smell of freshly polished wood was still rank enough to burn with every breath. If he closed his eyes, he could see the awful rusted lock, feel the crunch of the crystal fox underneath his foot. He could hear the boy's voice saying *Bastian,* the sound of the word ever slightly too round, the barest hint of an accent he couldn't quite place. Bastian shook his head, trying to jar loose the image of the boy with the green eyes.

Zan.

It was a nightmare. It *had* to be a nightmare, a weird, déjà vu–type experience. Bastian really wasn't the type to be dreaming about pretty boys with pretty eyes *who were convinced he was supposed to be dead*—

He scrubbed his eyes, then stalked to the front of the store.

"Bash Barnes, let me in!" Dorian yelled, pounding the door again for good measure.

The Audi was idling against the sidewalk behind him, and he clutched an umbrella between his fingers, protecting his uniform pants from the drizzling rain.

Bastian grit his teeth and combed a hand through his extremely grimy hair. Wincing, he threw the deadbolt on the door and stepped out of the way as Dorian stepped in, politely brandishing his umbrella toward the street and leaving it outdoors, rather than spattering rain all over the inside of the store.

"You weren't answering your phone. I tried to text you last night, and you didn't answer, so I tried to call you this morning and . . . you weren't answering your phone, Bash, I can't do this. I can't . . . not after . . ." He swallowed hard, forcing both hands into the pockets of his khakis. "If you're going to live on your own in the middle of the city, you have to answer me when I call. Just so I know you're alive!"

"I'm fine," Bastian muttered.

Dorian swallowed. The line of his jaw moved incrementally as he chewed at the inside of his cheek. "Then answer your phone."

"It died," Bastian lied. "Forgot to charge it." He'd been too busy dreaming himself an entire world complete with an annoying, chattering boy named Zan, who clearly agreed with him that Bastian should have been the one to die. *Way to go, subconscious. You win this round.*

"First hour starts in two minutes," Dorian said with a pained expression. "You didn't show at school again yesterday, and I let it go but *please*, Bash. Please try?"

School yesterday . . . he didn't show . . . so . . .

Bastian blinked. He'd lost an entire day to a nightmare? Crossing his arms, Bastian pinned Dorian with a glare and tried to suppress his growing anxiety.

"I didn't go to school because I wasn't feeling well."

"Bash, are you sick—"

"You're not my adult," Bastian scoffed. "You don't need to worry about me, or hold my hand when crossing the street, or tuck me in at night."

"Bash—"

"Why are you here?"

Dorian let out a long breath. "Because I know you won't take a bus or a taxi, so I'll drive you."

Bastian gritted his teeth and flexed his hand. There was a phantom ache from punching the wall in his dream. The ache was imagined like Zan had been imagined. It wasn't real.

Dorian's mouth pressed to a straight line. He sighed, then stepped forward and reached across the counter, plucking a single floor swatch up from where Bastian had set it near the register. He looked down at the matching new floor. "It looks nice," he murmured.

It did look nice. With the morning light coming through the enormous windows, the bronzed, warm-looking wood glowed. It was almost the same color as Cat's fur.

It was almost the same color as Zan's office. Bastian shuddered and picked at his wishing bracelet.

Dorian ran his hand along a bookcase. "I've got . . ." He cleared his throat. "I've got a meeting after school, but if you needed help later with the books I could probably swing by?"

It was another peace offering of sorts, but the nightmare wedged at the back of Bastian's throat before he could answer. Bastian blinked, then took a step backward. "That's okay."

"No, I mean it." Dorian cocked his head at the sound of a car honking outside, then looked straight at Bastian. "It's comforting, right? The smell of books? I know you used to be super into this stuff with Mom, and I never really got it, but I guess . . ." He shrugged uncomfortably. "I guess I can see the appeal."

Bastian frowned. This *was* a thing he'd shared with Mom. Antiquing and thrifting through the many cities they'd lived in, walking streets looking for stores wedged in unlikely spaces. Dorian had always been the more analytical of the three—had been happiest with his robotics club, and Knowledge Bowl team, and the dozens of other extracurriculars that he'd been purposely accruing over the years for the sole purpose of getting into the University of Michigan premed program—his dream school. The few times he'd tagged along, he'd gotten so fidgety at the lazy way Bastian and their mom idled through dust-covered stores that he'd quickly proclaimed it *your thing* and tried his best not to secure an invitation to one of their many expeditions.

Bastian had never really explained to him how much he loved the smell of paper.

About how being surrounded by stories felt safer than being surrounded by himself.

About how sometimes when he closed his eyes, he saw his mom upside down, strapped in the car seat next to him, blood dripping into her eyes, mouth moving in the shape of a scream, but if he tried really hard, he remembered the way she loved libraries instead.

The way she planned trips to them in every city they visited and collected editions of her favorites in every language she could get her hands on. She had six different editions in six different languages of *The Little Prince* because it was her favorite. Two of them were signed.

They were sold, put up for auction along with everything else she'd owned, the money split evenly into the two accounts saved for him and Dorian.

"Bash," Dorian said, eyes flicking down to his shoes for a second, tips of his ears going pink. It was only a moment of indecision, then he looked straight back up with his perfect smile showing off his perfect teeth. "Just let me give you a ride."

"I'm fine."

"No. You aren't. And you don't have to talk to me about it, but please don't fail out of Preston. She wouldn't have wanted that."

Bastian stared at him for a long time. Cat meowed from behind him and started winding around his feet. Dorian took a hesitant step backward.

"I need my sweater," Bastian finally mumbled. "Don't go walking around the store in your muddy shoes."

Dorian's shoes weren't muddy. They were immaculate despite the rain, probably just as clean as the day he'd taken them out of the box, because cleaning his shoes daily was the kind of thing Dorian did.

He nodded anyway, then leaned against the front counter to wait.

Bastian turned and took the stairs two at a time. Cat followed him up. Bastian needed more than a sweater—his pants were creased and full of cat hair, he hadn't showered in two days, and he smelled like sweat and dust. He stopped by the bathroom and brushed his teeth, trying to scrub the taste of the ashy dream away. His backpack was sitting next to the wall exactly where he'd dropped it three days ago, slumped and sloped, crumpled pieces of paper spilling from its insides. He was pretty sure he had an English paper due today. He was also pretty sure he had a chem test this week. He was absolutely sure that he hadn't written the paper, studied for the exam, or done any of the variety of assignments he'd been given over the last couple of weeks.

Sighing, Bastian grabbed his rumpled sweater from a pile in the corner. He paused. The silver had crawled up the base of his thumb, wrapped around his wrist, and extended toward his elbow—swirls of color spidering out over his skin. It didn't shimmer like it did in the dream. It looked almost corpse-like.

CHAPTER SEVENTEEN

Portland, Oregon

"**N**o."

"You can't say no, it's a school event," Riley said, hanging over the lip of her seat and peering owlishly at Bastian's school desk. There was a carved-out heart at the top right corner, with the initials J+M etched into the center. She pulled out her pencil and started scribbling, covering the entire heart in graphite. "Rich parents to gawk at. Swanky mansion owned by swanky, rich donor dude to make fun of. And obviously trivia, where you can watch me own the rest of the student body. What's not to love?"

Bastian tried to shove her off his desk, but she remained shockingly unmovable despite her small frame. This was what he got for showing up to school. He'd managed a week straight of classes after Dorian started picking him up in the mornings—gave Joon a key to the store so he could start on the rest of the renovation while Bastian slumped over a desk and half-heartedly paid attention to annoying teachers—but now he was suffering the consequences.

"Six o'clock," she muttered, the *O* popping from her deep-purple painted lips. She finished off the heart with a dramatically swirled arrow, then started scrawling letters at its point. "Who doesn't like trivia?"

"Me."

"Come on, student gov has been working for months on this. Aka President Dorian has been working for months on this. He's so proud. Support him."

"No way," Bastian said, eyeing the garish banner that was tacked across the front of their French class. Trivia Night Saturday!, it read in green sparkle paint. Go Eagles!

"And you're coming too," she said, turning and flicking her pencil at Mathais who was sitting at the next desk over. It bounced harmlessly off his knee. "Vassie will be there."

"Stop trying to set me up with your weird friends," Mathais said, eyes straight on the board, refusing to look at Riley.

"And Dorian will be there," she added. "Obviously."

"Why exactly would you think that was a positive in my book?" Bastian asked incredulously.

"Because no matter how much the two of you pretend you hate each other, I know the truth. You're totally codependent. Like, ridiculously codependent. Remember in tenth grade when you got split into different math classes, and he went marching straight into the office to demand they switch him to yours, and you went marching straight into the office to demand they switch you into his like five minutes later, and then you were still in different classes, but they wouldn't switch you back again, and you both complained every day for six effing months over it?"

"That was before," Bastian muttered.

"Yeah. Whatever. He's been driving you to school in the mornings, don't think we don't see. It's cute. Happy little Barnes boys. Anyway, he has to do a whole announcement thing. You can throw paper airplanes at him. Or pencils." She reached out with her shoe and pulled her pencil back over to her. Picked it up. Threw it right back at Mathais, who batted it out of the air.

"Catlike reflexes," Mathais grinned.

Riley pulled her knee to her chest and rolled her eyes. "It'll be great," she said to Bastian. She toed her pencil back again, then leaned over his desk and returned to scribbling.

There was nothing that sounded more miserable than being stuck with his all-too-preppy classmates in whatever Preston alumni mansion the student government had selected for the evening. Not when he had a perfectly good book and Cat waiting for him at home.

"I'm helping you remodel your store. You owe me." She took her hand away, the words *PARTY POOPER* now standing in stark contrast against the desk.

"Nice."

"You owe me, Bash . . . ."

"Truth," Mathais said, not looking over.

"Traitor," Bastian hissed.

The last of the students filed in as the bell rang. Professor Dane stood; Riley gave Bastian's desk a hard kick, whispered "Tonight," then turned around in her seat.

Bastian looked back down at his desk. She'd pressed the pencil down so hard there were curds of graphite surrounding each letter. He brushed them off. The words smudged.

For the rest of class, Professor Dane fired off conjugates, Riley twirled a long piece of her hair around one finger, Mathais raised his hand at every question, and Bastian did his absolute best to nap with his eyes open.

He didn't need school. Or a degree. He had a vacant bookstore to waste time in and the leftover insurance money to pay for at least six months' worth of electricity. Six months was more than enough time to open the store, sell some books, and pay the bills, right?

God, his head hurt. Bastian scratched at the base of his thumb, then traced the blooming bruise that circled his wrist.

ꙮꙮꙮꙮꙮꙮꙮꙮꙮ

Dorian had to work on trivia party setup after school, so he dropped them all off at the bookstore on his way out to the mansion.

Bastian spent a good fifteen minutes trying to explain to Riley that only assholes owned mansions and therefore he had no interest in showing up, but she just stuck her nose up and said, "Only assholes are named Sebastian, too, so what's your point?"

He had to agree that it was a fair assessment.

Then she badgered him about loyalty and friendship and values until Cat entered the argument and swiped Bastian's forearm for no reason at all—promptly ending any and all discussion as Bastian yelped and started bleeding all over the new hardwood floor.

Now, he sat back against the register, one knee pulled to his chest, arm held out, bloody scratch marks still oozing. Mathais spun circles on an old stool they'd found, and Riley sifted through the old file cabinet in the back office, looking for a first aid kit that almost certainly did not exist.

"There's definitely no kit!" Riley shouted from behind the curtain.

"Did you check the desk?" Mathais called.

"There's definitely no kit," Bastian repeated under his breath. "I'm fine." He wiped his arm against his T-shirt, leaving darkened splotches across the dark-green fabric.

Groaning dramatically, Riley walked back out to the main floor. "That thing probably has rabies."

"Looks pretty alive to me."

"Yep," Mathais agreed. "Definitely nothing wrong with that cat. Took one look at Bash and said no way. Smart. I say keep him around."

"He likes me," Bastian muttered, which was true. Cat had been perfectly friendly with him up until the point that Riley yammered and wildly gesticulated so much that Bastian about forced her out of the store.

So much noise. He'd have scratched someone too.

"Saw the ledger on the desk," Riley said, bouncing back out of the office. "No wonder they shut this place down. Pitiful. He didn't have a single week where net profit exceeded one hundred dollars."

"Look at you and that Econ class paying off," Mathais said.

"I'm just saying," Riley said primly. "I could do better."

Bastian rolled his eyes. "So sad for you that it's my store."

"You bought this place to mope. And catch rabies."

"Fight, fight, fight," Mathais chanted.

Pushing himself up off the floor, Bastian shot him a withering glare. "Don't you have homework to do?" he asked.

Mathais looked guiltily down at the array of textbooks, notepads, highlighters, and brightly colored Post-it notes he'd splayed across the countertop. "Yes," he sighed. "So do you."

"Not interested."

"They're going to kick you out, you know," Riley sniffed. She pushed herself up on the counter with both hands and peered at Mathais's French homework. "Slacker," she said. "You're supposed to be rewriting those as entire sentences. Not just the incorrect verbs."

Mathais coldly pulled his notebook back and flipped it closed.

Flipping her hair over her shoulder, Riley stalked over to the corner where her swollen messenger bag of homework, knitting needles, and three balls of variegated yarn sat abandoned from where she'd left it earlier. "Call pest control," she called, sitting down and pulling out her half-finished scarf. "At least get rid of the cat."

"The cat stays. Customers love that stuff. As the French say, *je ne sais quoi*!" Bastian called back.

Mathais grinned and threw his hand up. Bastian air high-fived him, then headed toward the back of the store where he started moving books back onto shelves. The back bathroom was torn apart as Joon's guys ripped up plumbing, but it was supposed to be done in the next two days. Windows were coming in next week. Branding needed to happen—Riley was on him about choosing a name, and he knew that eventually he'd have to figure out a sign, and business cards, and all the little details—but he'd get to that.

"Don't get too involved!" Riley shouted back to him. "We're leaving soon!"

For Trivia Night. That he'd woefully agreed to because Riley knew how to push every one of his buttons and get him to agree to just about anything.

He'd known her since ninth grade, since she'd moved from Baltimore and introduced herself as Riley Kim, and he'd moved from New York and introduced himself as Sebastian. Since she said, *Sebastian's too preppy. I'm calling you Bash.*

Since Bastian had decided that made her perfect.

He grabbed a pile of books and carted them back up to the front of the store.

"Crap, we really need to go," Mathais said. He looked at his phone, then closed each textbook, filed each notebook, and stuffed them all inside his backpack.

"Come on," Riley said, snapping her fingers and pointing at Bastian. "Show on the road, and all that! You can shower at my place." She carefully wound up her yarn and packed it in her bag.

"I'm fine here," he said. "I can meet you guys."

She cocked her head. "Bash Barnes, you have never been fine. But at least you used to be happy."

He froze. She knew him in the before, and she knew him in the after, and she knew all the things missing. Sometimes he couldn't stand it. *You are supposed to be dead.* Bastian swallowed around ash clogging his throat. His vision narrowed, and for a second, he swore he could see the shadowy gray fog rising up behind his eyes.

"Uber's here," Mathais announced, breaking the spell.

Bastian blinked. Riley's nose was scrunched as she stared at him curiously.

"You okay?" she asked.

Bastian looked out the window. A man walked by wearing an enormous backpack and carrying two ski poles. He waved at them.

Life was still life. Chaotic, and miserable, and sad, and weird. Bastian cleared his throat. "I'm fine," he murmured. He looked at the tiny Honda Accord that had pulled up to the side of the street. The Uber driver inside was looking at his phone. The car would barely fit all three of them, and it would absolutely crumble into nothingness in a crash.

"Seriously, just come with me," Riley said. "My mom will drive us there."

"I'll walk," Bastian said.

"It's like three miles!" Riley exclaimed.

Mathais paused, one hand on the knob of the door. "I can go with you," he offered. "I'm up for walking."

"Nah, I'll catch up with you guys."

Shrugging, Mathais opened the door. The bells jingled. "All right," he called over his shoulder.

"You better show up," Riley ordered.

Bastian flashed her a thumbs-up and closed the door behind them, doing his best to contain his shudder at the sound of the car doors opening, then slamming closed.

CHAPTER EIGHTEEN

Portland, Oregon

The walkway of 1300 Oakmont Terrace was paved in white sparkling stone—the kind of stone that said *this place is very important*, the kind of stone that said *dress code required*. Last year, Trivia Night had been held at a rustic-chic warehouse downtown on the water and was coordinated by the family of a graduating senior. This year? Bastian was pretty sure the place was owned by an alumnus who didn't even have kids at Preston anymore.

Bastian looked down at his worn T-shirt, the D.A.R.E logo splashed across the front in glow-in-the-dark white. Vintage. Thrift store find. His favorite.

Not 1300 Oakmont Terrace appropriate.

Riley wasn't 1300 Oakmont Terrace appropriate either, though she managed to pull off rich artiste aesthetic with her mismatched orange flannel pants, pinstripe vest, knee-high leopard-print boots, and hand-knit fingerless gloves. Despite the distinct lack of uniform, she still looked like she fit in.

"This is ridiculous," Bastian said as soon as she walked up. He watched her mom drive off in their tiny brown Corolla. It didn't fit in either.

"You'll have fun."

"Sure."

"Seriously! Dorian and Mathais can cover philosophy and all things French. Mathais has sports. I've got science. Okay, let's be honest, I've got everything. You've got books and . . . old stuff."

"Seems like you guys will be fine without me," Bastian said.

"Us guys don't have weirdly specific knowledge of 1980s pop culture," Mathais murmured, stepping up behind her. "Nice shirt."

"I tried," Bastian said dryly.

Mathais shrugged, then turned toward a chorus of boys screaming "Matty-boy!" that sprang up across the lawn.

"I'll find you guys inside," he said with a wave, then jogged over to the clump of football players eagerly awaiting his presence.

Sometimes Bastian didn't know how they'd become friends at all. Then Mathais would fall into one of his hyper fixation modes and spend weeks forcing them all to listen to his exuberant monologues extolling the virtues of meter and prose of random classical writers. He was a football player because he was enormous, but at heart he was a poet. He was just as at home in Bastian's bookstore as Bastian was.

Bastian watched Mathais disappear into the crowd of athletes, then followed Riley up the walkway, dodging other groups of Preston Academy students and warily keeping an eye out for Dorian, who was sure to swoop in and forbid him entry without wrapping a tie tight enough to choke himself with around his throat.

He yawned and itched at his wrist. It kept throbbing, pulsing with his heartbeat. His head was muzzy, and his eyes kept closing. All he wanted was a nap. He wondered if Oakmont Terrace had a wet bar. A hidden stash of very expensive liquor reserved for men in twill suits and dress socks, the kind with the little embroidered diamonds.

He was willing to try about anything at this point to get an actual night's sleep.

"Riles!" A girl at the front door exclaimed, trotting over on her three-inch heels and then wrapping her arms around Riley.

Jasmine Badawi.

Bastian internally groaned. It wasn't like he hated her or anything, but she knew Dorian better than most people did, which meant she acted like she knew *Bastian* better than most people did, and all in all, being around her just tended to be awkward and weird.

"Jaz!" Riley exclaimed right back. She returned the hug just as enthusiastically.

"I'm supposed to ask for your tickets and all—"

"Here!" Riley procured two pieces of black matte cardstock from the lining of her vest and handed them over.

Bastian could barely see the glint of the golden embossed lettering:

Preston Academy
Trivia Night

"Why do we have to have tickets when we're obviously members of the student body?" he mumbled.

"He's cranky," Riley said, rolling her eyes toward Jasmine and laughing like it was an inside joke.

Bastian wanted to say something snarky, or witty, or anything at all, but Jasmine had already moved on.

"Dorian's inside," she said, waving toward the clipboard sitting next to her. "If you were looking."

He wasn't, but he eyed the board anyway.

Dorian Barnes was checked off. So was Greer Morgan.

"Your parents coming?" Jasmine asked.

Bastian looked over at Riley, whose mouth twitched.

"Do they ever?"

The answer to that was no, but it was more complicated than it sounded. Her parents both worked full-time jobs, blue-collar jobs like Joon—far from the lawyer, programmer, doctor families that frequented Preston's alumni list. Riley was the sort of person who wasn't supposed to belong at Preston. Her tuition was drawn from the Equitable Experience Fund, Preston's fancy way of saying "scholarships for people who shouldn't be here." Riley still managed to fit herself right in because she was using the place as a stepping stone into any college she wanted, but even though her parents were the most supportive people Bastian had ever met, they avoided these events because they made them uncomfortable.

Bastian really liked Mr. and Mrs. Kim.

"Well, mine are somewhere inside," Jasmine said. "I swear, half the adults are already trashed. You'd never know it. But they are." Someone let out a loud whooping sound across the lawn, and Jasmine's eyes narrowed. "I don't even know why he came," she muttered. "Speaking of trashed."

Bastian didn't have to turn around to know exactly who she was talking about.

"Greer's easy enough to avoid," Riley said with a shrug.

"Ugh." Jasmine leaned closer to Riley, eyes still on the lawn. "Someone told me he raided his dad's liquor stash and showed up loaded. He's *going* to get himself expelled, and I'm *not* going down with him."

Both girls turned and watched as Greer led a group of boys around the back of the mansion. Bastian stood, awkwardly picking at his fingernails and wishing they could just go inside.

"Oh! Wristbands!" Jasmine announced, jerking him back to

reality. She reached into a little tin pail set up behind her and pulled out two blue bands. "Hand?" she asked Bastian, watching him through mascara-thick lashes.

He awkwardly stuck his wrist out and let her wrap the band around. It got caught on his bracelet, which he tugged out of the way.

"Oh my gosh, what did you do?" Jasmine exclaimed, navy-blue fingernails tracing the bruise after she pressed the sticky side of the band down.

Bastian yanked his hand back and stuck it in his pocket, refusing to feel bad at the wounded look Jasmine gave him.

Riley didn't seem to notice, just stuck out her own wrist.

"I'll catch you later?" Jasmine asked as she released Riley.

"Obvs!" Riley announced, loud enough that Bastian was certain the entire student body heard.

"Obvs," he repeated quietly, following her inside.

She very deftly smashed a leopard-print boot down on his shoe.

The inside of the mansion was no less brazen than the outside. An enormous chandelier lit the marble entryway; droplets of rainbows reflected in a scatter of stars that speckled the winding staircase. There was a jazz band playing somewhere deeper inside, and the sound of glasses clinking and people chatting upstairs. Riley ignored both and tugged him down the hall, following the calligraphic scrawl of signs that read TRIVIA ROOM, and THIS WAY, and ALMOST THERE.

Eventually, they came to a private home auditorium that had been decorated in golden sparkle and black draped fabrics. It was louder in here—less rich, less prestigious, more high school. He thought he saw Greer nestled against a dark corner alcove. Riley looped arms with Bastian and dragged him along to the very front table, the table where Dorian perched on one silver filigree stool holding court to a gaggle of girls who were batting their eye-lashes far more vigorously than Jasmine.

Riley very loudly greeted all the girls while Bastian tried to sneak into a chair. Dorian looked over, grin growing. "You came!" He wedged his way out of the group and sank down in a seat next to Bastian. "What do you think?"

Bastian eyed the stage at the front of the room. A single mic sat in the middle. At the edge of the stage there was a small table with a laptop that was rigged to project to the movie screen. It looked considerably less suave than the rest of the mansion. This was the only part that looked like it was actually coordinated by students. "Cool," he said, because Dorian was looking at him expectedly.

"Really didn't expect you to show," Dorian said, tugging at his tie.

Bastian picked at the blue band. "I was dragged."

"I mean, you still didn't have to. For me or whatever."

"Wasn't for you."

"Oh." Dorian's smile grew more forced. "Yeah, okay."

Bastian picked harder, until the sticky threads of the band started to tear. He didn't mean it like that, but he didn't know how else to talk to Dorian. Sometime in the last year, they'd frayed just as surely as the band around his wrist. It was more than the accident. It was Bastian trying to regain mobility of his shattered collarbone. Bastian waking up in the middle of the night, gasping and sweating and terrified. Bastian walking into the tiny kitchen of the townhouse for a glass of water and finding Dorian there, too, also haunted, also not okay.

For a few weeks, he thought that they'd be able to use this shared grief to move past it together. Soon though, Bastian was the only one in the kitchen at night. Dorian was sleeping. One of them was healing, and one of them was left behind.

The fracture grew.

Dorian went back to school and smiled, and laughed, and signed up for even more clubs. Bastian's grades slipped, he fell asleep in class, he found himself in the bathroom in the middle of a period barely able to breathe around the phantom smell of gasoline, hugging his arms around his chest, trying to keep himself from shaking apart.

The fracture became something he no longer knew how to fix.

"Heyo!" Mathais announced, bounding in out of nowhere and snagging the chair next to Dorian. He slammed down two drinks in fancy copper cups on the table hard enough that they sloshed over. "Team Falcon a go?"

Dorian's eyes lit up.

Bastian chewed on his lower lip, then reached over and grabbed one of the mugs, sniffing hesitantly. All he could smell was ginger. He hated ginger. He pushed it back with a grimace.

"Falcon?" Riley asked, joining the table. "Pathetic. I want a different name." There was a glass vase on the table filled with gold-flecked marbles and black roses, with a rhinestone-encrusted number 3 on it. She reached across and plucked a rose out, then began shredding the petals.

Bastian watched one float lazily to the floor.

"Vote," Mathais said. "All in favor?"

Dorian raised his hand. Riley shredded another rose. Bastian didn't move.

"Tie," Riley said. "New name."

"Bastian doesn't count, he wasn't voting."

"Were you voting?" she asked, fixing him with a glare.

"Not particularly."

She flicked a petal at him, but it only made it far enough to settle on the table. "Vote."

Bastian groaned. "One vote for Team I Don't Care."

"God, you're the worst," she said as Mathais and Dorian high-fived. Mathais scrawled *TEAM FALCON* on a big piece of black cardstock, then fixed it in an empty skewer that was sticking out of the vase.

Maddie Adams, vice president of the student government and wearer of khaki uniform pants that had been ironed even stiffer than Dorian's, picked up a microphone and started explaining the trivia rules. A couple of guys from the football team passed around whiteboards and dry-erase markers. One of them stopped at their table and fist-bumped Mathais.

A few servers dressed in black and white made their rounds, passing out more sodas, water, and what looked like fake champagne. Maddie tapped against the mic again, then started the game.

Bastian didn't listen. He turned his head. The crowd that was surrounding Greer had dissipated. Greer caught his eye and raised his own glass, an actual glass, filled with actual clear liquid that was almost certainly alcohol. Greer smirked. Bastian looked away.

The tables were mostly separated by typical teenage affiliations. The sports kids. The Knowledge Bowl/Science Olympiad table that definitely had a leg up on this entire evening. The theater kids.

His eyes narrowed. The theater table didn't have a vase full of golden marbles. Their vase was full of foggy purple sea glass.

For a terrifying, lurching moment, Bastian wasn't sure if he was awake or asleep.

"Bash?"

He blinked. Riley was staring at him. Mathais was sucking down his ginger ale. Dorian looked constipated, which was his general thinking face. Bastian grabbed one of the water bottles and cracked it open. "What?"

"First question. Come on, pay attention, we could win this if you focus!"

"Winner gets Seahawks tickets," Mathais confirmed, like that was a motivating factor.

"I don't know what part of me you think screams I-want-to-win-Seahawks-tickets," Bastian said.

"Winner *wins*," Riley stressed, like that was a motivating factor also.

"Thirty seconds!" Maddie cheerfully announced.

Riley gave a pained moan. "Come on, Bash, who was the first author to win both the Hugo and Nebula Awards! I say Herbert. Confirm? Come on!"

Bastian leveled her with a glare. "Bold of you to think I read."

"You own a bookstore. *Answer!*"

He was starting to feel sick again—weird, and nauseous, and head-spinny. Maybe if he messed with them, they'd stop relying on him for answers. He tried to give an I-know-what-I'm-talking-about-looking shrug. "It's not Herbert. It's Ursula Le Guin."

Riley frantically scribbled onto the whiteboard up until the point that Maddie blew an obnoxiously loud air horn. She stuck the board up in the air. There was a wild array of answers, from their own Le Guin to Shakespeare, which was stunningly incorrect.

"Tables two and five take points!" Maddie called. "The correct answer is Frank Herbert!"

Riley's eyes narrowed, and her knuckles whitened as her hands tightened to fists.

Dorian said, "It's okay. First question. We've got the rest."

"I swear to god, Bastian, if you threw that on purpose I will strangle you," Riley hissed.

"I don't have any idea what you're talking about," Bastian said angelically, trying to ignore the way his stomach was twisting.

Mathais snorted into his mug.

"It's fine, guys!" Dorian clapped his hands together at an excruciatingly loud volume for the two winning tables.

"We got this, guys," Bastian deadpanned. His head really hurt. He looked back over at the theater table where the sea glass vase sat. It held only golden marbles. *Fuck, what was happening?* He rubbed his eyes and drank down the rest of his water bottle.

The applause died down, and Maddie shouted out the next question.

Between the four of them, Mathais and Riley proved most useful. Dorian spent most of his time between tables, socializing with anyone who so much as glanced in his direction. Bastian spent all his time trying to stay awake. By the end of the hour, they were surprisingly tied for third place, behind the members of the Science Olympiad team and the theater kids.

Bastian laid his head in his arms. The room tilted underneath him. He squeezed his eyes closed and started counting his breaths, twisting his wishing bracelet over and over. Trying to ground himself the way Andrea always told him to.

"Bash! Are you drunk?" Mathais reached over and grabbed his water from his hands, sniffing suspiciously.

Riley was waving the whiteboard in front of his face again. "Where did Prince William and Kate Middleton first meet? Quick!"

Bastian swallowed. Now his arm was falling asleep. "Olive Garden," he said.

She dropped the whiteboard and tried to smack him, but Bastian managed to duck away.

"A football game," Mathais said the same moment Dorian exclaimed, "I think it was college!" Then leaned over and grabbed the board.

The air horn blew, their table lost, Maddie announced the winners, the room broke into the same sort of easygoing chaos as the halls between bells.

"Yay," Bastian said and offered a watery smile to the gang. Riley's eyes narrowed.

A hand came down on Bastian's shoulder.

"Hey, Bash," Greer crooned, leaning close enough that his lips brushed against the shell of Bastian's ear.

Bastian shrugged him off. "What do you want?"

"Saw you eyeing me."

"I wasn't . . ." Bastian scowled, pushing himself up off the table and sinking back in his chair. "Whatever," he muttered.

Mathais mumbled something about needing another drink as Greer's eyebrow quirked. Dorian eyed them suspiciously but stood up from the table, wandering up toward the front of the stage to confer with Maddie about something. Greer stepped up closer and leaned his forearms against the table, conveniently blocking Riley from the conversation.

"Asshole," she muttered, leaning past his arm and grabbing Bastian's hand.

"It's fine, Riley," Bastian mumbled.

Greer laughed. "See?" he said, flashing her a grin. "It's fine."

Riley's eyes narrowed.

Bastian pulled his hand back and mouthed *I'm fine* at her, not because he particularly wanted to talk to Greer, but because he was really tired of everyone treating him like he needed his hand held everywhere he went, and God, his head hurt—

Riley huffed a curse but pushed off her chair, too, and followed Mathais.

Like Dorian, Greer was also decked from head to toe in his Preston uniform, but where it made Dorian look like a pretentious prick, it made Greer look downright dangerous. It cut across his already sharp edges and whittled him down to nothing but a sharp-toothed smile and flinty black eyes.

"After-party," he said. Not a question. A demand.

Greer's after-parties were famous. His father held Hollywood connections, and his current stepmother (number six . . . or maybe seven, Bastian had no interest in keeping count) was a supermodel who wasn't much older than Greer and who had lots of friends with access to lots of drugs.

"You're coming, Barnes." He leaned closer, snagging Bastian's hand and rubbing his thumb over the loop of bruise-colored skin. "Ouch."

Bastian tugged his hand back. "We'll see," he mumbled.

"No. You are. Hey, hey, heard you got a new place. A cool place. A private place."

"You're not invited."

"You wound me."

"And you sound like a Bond villain."

Greer barked a laugh. "Fair enough. Keep your secrets." He reached into his pocket and drew out a gleaming flask. "Top off your drink?"

Bastian glared at him. He wanted to sleep, *really sleep*, he wanted everyone to stop talking to him, to leave him alone.

Greer held out the flask.

Bastian's nerves were live wires, buzzing and sparking. He just wanted to stop feeling anything at all. Reaching forward, he snagged the flask out of Greer's hand, tipped his head back, gulped down something so smooth it barely burned at all.

"Niceeee," Greer drawled.

He sounded far away. The liquor coated Bastian's throat, warm and heavy as he swallowed. *This is fine*, he thought. Totally normal.

Not at all fucked up, Andrea would be so proud, Dorian . . .

Bastian winced as he pulled the lip of the flask away from his mouth. The metal was cool in his hand as he handed it back.

Greer grabbed it, fingers brushing against Bastian's. He took a long drink, then grinned down at Bastian. His teeth looked like fangs.

"You're more fun than your prissy brother," he said casually.

Heat flared in Bastian's cheeks, and he bit down hard on the inside of his cheek. The room was swaying, and maybe Zan was right. Maybe Dorian should have been the only one left alive.

His eyes flickered closed, he could hear screaming, there were medics over him yelling something about heart rate, blood pressure, dropping—

"Come on," Greer said loudly, throwing an arm around Bastian's shoulder and wrapping it tight around him.

Bastian blinked his eyes open. He sucked in a deep breath. Trivia Night. Party. Mansion.

Greer smelled like sweat and so much cologne it burned Bastian's nostrils.

"Come on," Greer said again. "Girls. Boys. Models. Beer, whiskey, scotch"—he tapped the pocket with the flask—"the good stuff. Other things. You want powders or pills?"

Bastian wanted Greer to go away. His head pounded, and he swallowed hard around a tongue that felt too big for his mouth. Greer was graying, fading out, becoming ghostly and *wrong*.

"You don't look so good, buddy," Greer said, tugging Bastian even closer.

Bastian couldn't breathe. There was something wispy black dancing at the corners of his vision. "Not interested," he managed.

"How about explosions? Fireworks? Something for everyone. I'll drive you, babe."

"I said no."

Greer's sneer deepened. "Oh, right. You don't do *cars*."

Bastian threw himself up from the table and shook his head free. The blackness at his vision crowded him, dancing just out of sight, making everything around him start to waver like it was bathed in the single light bulb of the nightmare hallway. "No," he said again. Somewhere, Dorian was yelling his name. Somewhere, a flickering light danced in front of him.

He pushed off from the table, stumbled, fell—

CHAPTER NINETEEN

Styx

Bastian opened his eyes.

The mirrored black water stretched before him, hollow splashing echoing in his ears. His head was full of wasps buzzing in time with the pulse of his heart. There was no sign of Dorian, or Greer, or any part of Trivia Night. Fear slithered down his back.

What was real?

A fraying tendril of black wrapped around his ankle.

His heart kicked against his chest, and Bastian didn't turn to see if the darkness was there, just took off, water splashing around his ankles as he ran. The door was right there this time, shiny chalk outline, cracked open ever so slightly so he could see light beyond it.

He pushed through, slammed it closed behind him, and turned to find Zan at the desk, staring up at him, mouth open.

Bastian's hands started to shake. He clenched them to fists and forced them behind his back.

"Hi," Zan said. "Long time no see." He cocked his head and scowled petulantly.

He did not sound friendly.

Bastian looked at his feet. "Why am I here?" he murmured. "I wasn't sleeping. I was at a school thing, I'm—"

"We're going to forgo the location of death," Zan interrupted, closing the keyboard. "Do you have any idea how much trouble I'm in?"

Bastian frowned.

"Clearly not," Zan went on, pacing back and forth behind the desk. "He's furious, I'm walking on eggs around here trying to avoid him, you're making my life a living hell. Or . . . lack of life, I suppose."

Bastian opened his mouth and closed it again. Cocked his head. "Walking on eggs?" he finally asked.

Zan didn't stop pacing. "Eggs. Yes. Things are delicate here, and you've gone and ruined it."

"Egg . . . shells?" Bastian asked. This was ridiculous. His heart was still slamming against his chest, his palms were sweating, and none of this made sense. "Eggshells," he said again, more confidently this time. "Walking on eggshells means you're being careful. Walking on eggs just means you're an idiot."

Zan's scowl grew. "Know-it-all," he muttered, coming to a halt by the desk again and glaring at Bastian.

"Sorry," Bastian offered.

"Are you, though?"

He wasn't. Wiping his hands against his pants, Bastian wandered over to one of the bookshelves, trying for nonchalance, failing miserably. His hands wouldn't stop shaking. There was no sign of glass on the floor from where he'd shattered the crystal fox during the last dream. A little pile of sea glass perched in front of a dozen leather-bound volumes with golden Greek letters embossed on the spine. He picked up the large purple piece he'd seen last time and turned it over in his fingers. It looked just like the pieces that he'd seen in the vase at Trivia Night.

He pocketed it. Zan watched him the entire time, lips pursed tight but not saying anything.

Bastian crossed his arms and leaned against the shelf. The awful headache that had been building since that afternoon had suddenly disappeared. "So how do I get back?" he murmured.

"To . . ."

"To my life. How do I stop dreaming this place? How do I wake up?"

"Not a dream," Zan said. He stepped out from behind the desk. The weird, shadowy keys were clenched in one hand. "Thought we covered that."

"*You* covered that. And made no sense."

"You are particularly asinine, so I'm not surprised. Does anything make sense to you?"

Bastian stuck out a foot as Zan passed and grinned in satisfaction as the other boy stumbled, righting himself at the last moment by reaching out and smacking a hand onto another bookcase, which shook loose a pile of change. The coins fell to the ground, metal smacking against the hardwood in tinny harmonium.

"Whoops," Bastian said.

Zan glared at him. "Think of a happy place. Your happiest memory."

"You asked me that last time."

Zan's fingers crawled through the keys. Bastian tried to keep his eyes on them, but they flicked by so fast he couldn't seem to focus. "I ask that every time," he muttered. "Styx isn't a dream. It's a place full of memories. It's where people get stuck when they can't quite die. They pick a memory, and I lead them through it. You're stuck. You're supposed to be dead. I'm supposed to lead you."

"To death," Bastian said. It was supposed to be a joke, but his words sounded hollow.

"I'm the tour guide," Zan said with a little nod. "I'll lead you to the Ferryman."

"Ferryman?"

Zan gave a broken laugh. "You're impossible." He shook his head. "Charon. At least that's what all the books call him." His eyes drifted up toward one of the bookcases.

Bastian tried to follow his glance but couldn't make out what he was staring at. Another pile of buttons? The burnished gold wristwatch? Or the super-thick black leather book with no inscription on the binding?

"I know him as the Ferryman," Zan said, shaking his head and looking back at Bastian. "This is his territory. He is Death."

"I thought Hades was Death."

Zan's jaw tightened. "Souls who die belong to Hades. Souls who get stuck trying to cross the river . . . those belong to the Ferryman."

"Funny how that never made it into any of the textbooks," Bastian said petulantly.

Zan threw up his hands in frustration. "You asked!" he exclaimed. "I'm telling you what I know."

"So why are you here?" Bastian asked. "If he's a god, and he's taking souls and whatever, what does that make you?"

Zan cringed. "A self-sabotaging disaster?" He shrugged miserably. "I made a deal and now? I'm fulfilling my end of our agreement. Five hundred years cataloging souls, and then I get to go free. I'm almost done, except you keep disappearing until I can bring you over. And last time the program logged you"—

he motioned toward the laptop—"so unfortunately that's it. You're in the system. It's time to go." He held out the key ring.

Bastian looked past him to the desk. The laptop sat there, next to a textbook written in another language. Maybe Greek? Something Cyrillic. There was a deck of cards dealt for solitaire. There were no other sounds but Zan's breathing and the quiet trickle of water coming from somewhere behind the walls. Bastian chewed on his lower lip. He could sit here and fight about it, or he could play along.

Bastian reached forward and tore a key free from the ring, metal warm in his grasp. The teeth were tiny bits of green-tinged copper; the handle was twined with metal worked to look like leafed branches. It was the fanciest key he'd ever seen.

Zan plucked the key from Bastian's hands and held it to the block of cement at Bastian's back. "Interesting," he murmured.

The cement warped, vines twisted up it, and the door cracked open.

CHAPTER TWENTY

Styx

Bastian stepped out onto a forest floor spongy with bright-green moss. He tipped his head back and took a deep breath of damp air that smelled musty like mud and sweet like rotting wood. The trees surrounding them grew so high and clustered so tightly together they split the sun, causing it to fragment into pieces that spun on top of the moss—a kaleidoscope of light. He could barely see the blue of the sky.

Stepping forward, Bastian pressed his palm against the bark of the nearest tree. It was rough and cold, too far in shadow to be warmed by the sun.

"So where are we?" Zan asked.

Bastian didn't answer, just started walking through the trees. He remembered this. He remembered this forest, this hike, this *day*.

He took a deep, shuddering breath. He wasn't dying. He. Wasn't. Dying. This was only his subconscious. He'd been here so it made sense that he'd dream of here except . . .

The tree felt so alive. The dappled sunlight sparkled on the ground so clearly. This was more than a dream. This was reliving a memory so specific it was hard to imagine it not being real.

Pushing the heels of his hands to his eyes, he took a deep breath. He forced himself to move, retracing the invisible path of memory, heading to a place he hadn't been back to since before his mom died.

He picked his way over deadened logs, shoes sinking deep into mud as the forest floor sloped down. Zan tromped along behind him, making enough noise to scare away every animal within a ten-mile radius until finally he stumbled, snagged a hand around a small sapling, and uprooted the entire thing.

Bastian grit his teeth. He didn't know if he was more desperate for Zan to disappear and leave him alone, or more terrified of what might happen if he did. "Do you *mind?*"

Zan stood slowly, brushing dirt off of his pants. He looked mournfully at his green windbreaker that now had a giant stripe of mud down one arm. "I wasn't dressed for hiking."

Clenching his teeth so hard they hurt, Bastian took a deep breath in through his nose, letting it out through his mouth. *Disappear*, he thought. *Leave me alone, don't be real, don't be real, don't be real.*

Zan kicked at a patch of oyster mushrooms attached to a stump. They sloughed off sadly, crumbling to the moss below.

Bastian pulled to an abrupt halt and turned on him. "Look, full offense, we're standing in what is one of the few last memories I have of . . ." He swallowed, feeling his cheeks heat up. "We are standing in a good memory. It's *my* dream. I don't need company. We're in the middle of an enormous state park. Go. Somewhere. Else."

"Not going to happen," Zan said. "You've already escaped twice. Kind of have to escort you personally. I'd say sorry, but . . ."

He shrugged apologetically and looked at Bastian's shoes. "I'm not. Not really. It's in the job description and all."

Bastian's hands clenched to fists at his sides. He could keep moving and try to ignore Zan's constant noise. He could sit down and refuse to move until he woke up. *What if you never wake up again*, the voice inside his head chided. *What if you are dead.*

Bastian shivered. "Whatever," he finally muttered, turning and carefully picking his way over fallen branches again.

Zan followed.

The sun speckled the trees in front of them as birds sang overhead.

⊏⊐⊏⊐⊏⊐⊏⊐⊏⊐⊏⊐

A small abandoned logging camp sat right up against a creek. The logging equipment was rust covered; creeping branches crawled through holes and tightened, pulling the pieces closer and closer toward the ground. The creek was calm—water barely moving with the current—and Bastian grabbed a stick and hunched down beside it, drawing figure eights in the water as it lapped at the wood.

His mother was near here. If he waited in this spot, then maybe he'd see her again. Hug her. Tell her how much he missed her.

Tiny shadows of tadpoles emerged in the swirling mud. Bastian smiled. Zan was somewhere behind him, picking his way through the hollowed-out underbelly of a yellow piece of logging machinery and actually giving him space. The water rippled, and something splashed downstream.

It was almost peaceful.

This forest was about an hour south of Portland, a place that they'd drive on the weekends—him, Dorian, and their mother. It started as a thing he hated, a family activity forced upon them by her and her girlfriend-of-the-month Lindsay. Once a week, they'd pile into the car and drive up to Rainier, his mother smiling big and bright, Lindsay being obnoxiously cheery next to her, filling the car with inane and insufferable chatter.

After they'd split up, their mother kept going, kept dragging them. It became a quieter trip. Something he and Dorian actually looked forward to, though they'd never said so.

Bastian wished they'd said so.

He blinked and looked down at the water. His stick had been submerged and still for so long that more of the tadpoles had come out and were swimming lazily around the swollen wood.

"Shit!" Zan exclaimed.

Bastian pulled the stick out of the water and turned, glaring.

"Sharp," Zan said, sucking a finger into his mouth and motioning toward a jagged hunk of machinery.

"Hope your tetanus shot is up to date," Bastian deadpanned.

"This is the wonder of Styx," Zan returned. "You're already mostly dead. Nothing can physically hurt you."

"Being *actually* dead can."

Zan huffed a laugh. "Sure."

A cool breeze riffled through the trees, and Bastian closed his eyes, listening to the quiet rub of leaves, the soft tapping of branches. It was summer in this memory; everything was quieter, muffled by green. When fall came, the dry crackling of leaves would take over. Winter was sharp—nothing but withered branches and frozen bark. Dorian made some comment once when they were younger about how the sound of a forest changed depending on what season you were in. Winter was frigidly quiet. Fall was loud—crinkly and sharp. During summer, the leaves whispered. They'd both been crouched in the shadow of an enormous tree, Dorian dragging a stick through the dirt and leaving mandala patterns, Bastian with his head thrown back, letting the rough bark tangle in his hair.

He'd laughed. Told Dorian he was stupid.

Dorian was right, though.

A rock skipped across the stream, causing the water to ripple out and disrupt every bit of calm there was. It only made three hops before sinking.

Bastian looked up. Zan stood near him with a palm full of stones. "This isn't a truce," Bastian said. He dropped his stick and wiped his hand against his jeans, leaving a single streak of river mud across the denim.

"I don't need a truce. I need to do my job. You don't have to like me."

"I *don't* like you."

"Fine." Zan picked up another rock and flicked his wrist. This one only skipped twice.

Bastian bit back a curse as the bruise near his thumb flared to life, burning so hot he bit back a gasp.

"That's his mark, you know," Zan said sadly. "It's Styx, calling you. You're not supposed to be in the world of the living anymore, and it's just going to keep dragging you back here because you're meant for death. You've seen it before, right? Heard the water?"

Bastian's stomach twisted uncomfortably as he thought back to that moment after the accident. The oily black brushing against the base of his thumb.

The searing heat faded as he rubbed his wrist. Bastian looked down at the bruise.

Dreams did not *mark* you.

"We have to go," Zan said, pushing at his lopsided glasses frames before they tumbled from his nose. Black plastic frames again—but these ones were rectangular.

Bastian stared hard at him, at the faint spattering of freckles across the bridge of his nose that blended almost entirely into his olive skin. He had a silvery crescent scar that started at the corner of his left eye and traveled all the way down to the top of his cheekbone. It looked like a moon.

Zan held out a hand to pull Bastian up.

Bastian shook his head. "Not yet." He looked back out over the creek, furious at himself. His eyes were starting to water.

Zan crossed his arms. "Yeah, about that . . . I can't really trust you won't fade again. You got your memory. It's time."

Bastian squeezed his eyes closed. "My mom's about to come out from one of those hiking trails behind us," he mumbled. The words were rushed, fast, tripping over themselves as they tumbled from his mouth. "I haven't seen her since she died . . . since . . . look, I know this isn't real, and you're a dream or whatever so you probably don't understand the concept of love, but I miss her. I want to see her again. So just shut up, okay? Just give me five minutes. *Fuck.*" He scrubbed his eyes, then looked back down at the water. A single tadpole had come back out and was circling his stick.

"Oh," Zan said quietly.

The wind picked up through the tree, leaving dimples and crests across the water. Zan crouched down next to him. He studied Bastian, mouth curled in thought, eyes filled with something that looked an awful lot like pity. "I miss my mom too," he finally said.

Bastian tore his eyes away. The awful, burning fear that he was about to start crying was gone, but it was quickly being replaced by irritation. He didn't need to sit here having a heart-to-heart with the boy haunting his dreams. Scowling, he picked up his own stone and settled it between thumb and forefinger. Then he hurled it to the stream and watched it skip five times. "Beat that," he muttered.

Zan's eyes narrowed in thought for a moment, then his lips

quirked into a half grin, shattering the seriousness of his face. He surveyed the ground and pulled another rock up, sharp corners jutting out but perfectly flat on top. When he let it fly, it only skipped twice before plunking back down.

Bastian snorted. "You're terrible."

"It's not like I've been practicing!" Zan said indignantly.

"Here." Bastian found another stone and released it across the water. This one skipped six times, leaving smaller and smaller echo rings as it traveled. The tadpoles were all gone now; there was nothing but calm water lapping at the bank so gently that not even sediment was disturbed. "You need to curl your fingers more. Like this." He scooped up another rock and handed it over, then reached across and forced Zan's fingers around it.

Zan froze, smile disappearing entirely, eyes suddenly wary as he yanked his hand away.

Heat rose in Bastian's cheeks, and he shot up, taking his own step back as sudden, inexplicable humiliation flushed through him. It figured. Even his stupid dreams didn't want to be anywhere near him. "Whatever," he muttered.

Zan blinked furiously. "I'm sorry, I . . ."

The sun disappeared behind the clouds, and coldness set in, seeping into Bastian's bones.

"I . . ." The rock Zan had been clutching fell to the ground. The line of his jaw had gone sharp and tight. "This is . . ." he murmured. "This is bad."

What? Bastian tried to say, but the words pooled at the back of his throat, solid enough to swallow. He tried to let go of the stone he was holding, but his fingers disintegrated, becoming ash that floated away. He couldn't feel anything. He looked down, and there was nothing there.

CHAPTER
TWENTY-ONE

Styx

Bastian's mouth opened, lips almost moving in the shape of a *no*, then he faded away.

Zan looked down at the rock in his hand, then across the stream, where there was no longer any breeze and no longer any current at all. He hurled the rock as hard as he could, watching as it immediately sank in the dead water. He picked up another rock, hurled that too. Another. Another. Then he tangled his hands in his hair, opened his mouth, and screamed until his chest heaved and his lungs burned.

The sound echoed for only a second, quickly leaving him with nothing but silence—no more hawks, no more trees rustling, no more anything. He was used to it, the hollow popping of his ears, the desperate desire for noise of any kind. The only sounds were the ones he made, and it never got any easier. Zan sucked in a deep breath and slowly dropped his hands back to his sides, wiping his palms against his pants and leaving streaks of dirt. He pushed himself up from the bank of the stream, shoved his glasses back up his nose, and wandered down the bank.

He should have been faster. He shouldn't have listened to Bastian's stupid plea to see his dead mother; Zan should have yanked him to the back of the memory where the roar of Styx always waited. And now?

He couldn't keep hiding. He was going to have to explain himself.

Heart pounding against the cage of his chest, Zan pushed farther inward. The forest grew denser here, leaves underfoot sinking every step. The sky was dark gray, clouds frozen above him. The needles on the trees took on a grayish hue. Zan rubbed the back of his neck and walked all the way until the memory stopped.

The edges of it were fuzzy, cloudlike, whispered shapes of almosts beyond a gray mist. He could hear the rush of Styx. The boundary was malleable—Zan could push and watch it mold around his fingertips—but there was a point where an unbearable cold started to seep through his bones. If he kept pressing, he'd break through to the water. That was the Ferryman's domain.

Zan chewed on his lower lip and pivoted, refusing to cross over. He followed the line of the gray edge north, counting his steps, staying close enough to the barrier that the Ferryman could find him if he really wanted to speak. A few minutes later, he passed a fawn standing between two large trees, sunlight speckling its back. Zan walked toward it and held his hand underneath its nose.

There was warmth there, a single puff of breath frozen in time.

He ran a hand down its back, letting the coarse hair rub against the palm of his hand as he scanned the trees surrounding them.

There. Back about fifty feet, hidden by a copse of brambly thorns, stood its mother.

A fallen tree lay between the fawn and the deer, and Zan moved for it, sitting down in a divot between two branches, letting the silence grow.

Zan rifled through the leaves and picked up a stick, then hurled it as far as he could, aiming just left of the mother deer. It smashed against the underbrush, two inches from her face. She didn't blink.

He grinned, but it was a sick, rictus thing. Zan rubbed his hand against his mouth, trying to erase it.

The edge of the memory pulsed, then inky black darkness rolled in, seeping over rotting logs, curling around trunks of trees.

"It was a mistake," Zan murmured, rooting for another stick. He threw that too. It broke the blackness, causing wisps of dark to curl up in the air, but it was only a momentary lapse. Soon it was swirling around Zan's legs, staining the denim of his jeans. "I'm not breaking the bargain."

The darkness kept coming, pooling near the mother of the fawn until it was larger than she was, until it was the shape of an enormous black stag. "No?" the Ferryman asked. The shape of the single syllable looked wrong in the mouth of a deer.

Zan shivered. "No."

"You owe me his soul."

"I know."

"You grow weak. He was not supposed to live."

Zan frowned. It wasn't his fault that Bastian kept disappearing before he could bring him over. He was trying. He'd done everything right. *Except log him*, his mind whispered. *You didn't log his name. You wanted to keep him. To talk to him. He lost his mother too. You wanted to feel human.* Zan toed at the black dirt. The smell of woody rot dissipated, and the smell of salt water rushed to take its place, clinging to the lining of his nose. "It's just one soul," he murmured.

The stag reared up, black hooves smearing to pincher claws, fangs sliding from the curve of its mouth, and Zan flinched back, fear sliding down his back like ice. "I didn't mean that," he said quickly, words tumbling from his mouth in panic. "I know it's important, it's my job, I didn't mean—"

"Do not think to play with me, Alexander," the stag boomed. "He is not a plaything. He is *mine*."

Zan shuddered. "I'm not playing," he said meekly. "I'll fix it—"

"Will you? Or are you ready for me to taste your soul? Slurp it from your body, devour the flavor of your fear."

Zan tried to shake his head, but his entire body had gone cold and still.

"Nothing waits for you on the other side of death," the stag growled. "Not your family. Not your home. Not another chance."

"I know," Zan whispered.

"I do not think you do. Because I feel as though I have been quite generous with you, yet here you sit. Breaking our deal."

Zan flinched, looking back down to the ground. "I'm sorry," he murmured. "I'll bring him. Next time. I promise."

The Ferryman stared at him, beady black eyes sparkling with barely contained fury. Then he nodded, black dripping from his form until there was nothing but a dark shadow staining the forest floor where he'd stood. Zan squeezed his eyes closed.

When he opened them, he'd faded back to his office, sitting on the floor, spine pressed against one of the swollen bookcases. This was nothing. His deal was almost up, and he wasn't about to sacrifice it all for one stupid boy.

One boy who said his name.

One boy who looked at him like he was *real*.

Zan shook his head hard. He wouldn't give Bastian time to fade again, and he'd deliver him to the Ferryman just like he'd delivered a million other souls.

Zan tucked his head against his knees, pulled in a shuddering breath, and tried to forget the memory of Bastian's fingers closing around his own.

CHAPTER TWENTY-TWO

Portland, Oregon

Bastian's head throbbed.

It was the only thing he registered at first—awful, jabbing fire above his right temple and a corresponding pulsing in his wrist. He blinked, wincing at the light and the noise that began filtering through the pain.

He was lying on a table covered in stars.

No.

Glitter.

Groaning, Bastian pushed himself up, his vision swimming as he took in the theater room, the loud banter of high school kids, and a very concerned-looking Riley hovering in front of him.

"Bash?" she asked, reaching out carefully.

He jerked back. The bruise on his wrist flared in pain, and he looked down to see that the corpse-like hue had spread farther, spider-webbing out toward the crook of his elbow. He could still smell the sweet pine scent of the forest. He could still hear the plunk of the rocks and the sound of Zan's voice, quiet and determined.

Worse, there was an awful ache in his chest, a hole that throbbed with every beat of his heart, because he'd missed her. He'd missed seeing his mom walking out of the woods from a much smaller path, her brown hair pulled tightly out of her eyes, her backpack snug around her shoulders. He remembered her holding tight to a small book on mushroom identification. She'd had an enormous Puffball tucked into the crook of her right arm, and a smile splitting across her face.

He'd been so close, but he'd missed her.

He'd woken up too soon.

". . . back up, give him space," someone said behind him. Bastian shook his head, turning to see Dorian pushing through the crowd and then shoving Greer out of the way. Greer had a smarmy-looking grin plastered to his face. The flask of scotch they'd shared had completely disappeared. A couple of adults streamed by him—Bastian recognized Jasmine's father but none of the others.

"Bash—" Dorian said, reaching the table and grabbing Bastian's arm.

". . . 'm fine," Bastian mumbled. The room swayed, and he grabbed the table edge. Riley moved closer, sat down next to him, wrapped her arm around his shoulders. "Water?" she asked Dorian.

"Water!" Dorian announced to the crowd.

A woman in a black, sequined gown kneeled next to Bastian and pressed the back of her hand hard against his forehead.

Bastian tried to yank away, but Riley held him steady. "Fine," he mumbled again. Heat was rising in his chest, there was a lump in his throat that was impossible to swallow around, he could feel the impending panic attack shaking through him, threatening to take hold any second.

Something pressed into his thigh as he leaned back against the table, and Bastian shoved a hand in his pocket, already knowing what was there before his fingers fully closed around it.

A piece of sea glass from Zan's shelf. Smooth. Purple. *Real.*

He needed to get out of here.

Shoving himself up from the table and dislodging himself from the hands of the woman, Bastian skirted around the table. "Just got dizzy," he mumbled, rubbing his eyes. "Uh . . . sorry . . ."

". . . has he been drinking?" Jasmine's father asked, voice booming through the space. "Has anyone seen alcohol?"

The rest of the room was starting to quiet—kids were backing up, lining the perimeter, no one wanting to be involved.

All were staring right at Bastian.

"I haven't been . . ." Bastian started to protest, but he snapped his mouth closed again, because he had. Greer had given him a sip of whatever was in the flask, and maybe he'd spiked it with something? Maybe he was hallucinating?

Except he'd had this dream before, so many times, and there was glass in his pocket, *there was glass in his pocket*—

Bastian pressed a hand to his forehead and squeezed his eyes closed, trying to gain his equilibrium back. There was something wrong with him, something inside him was broken, he needed to *get out of here.*

The woman in the dress had picked up one of the copper mugs that Mathais had and was sniffing it suspiciously.

"We're not drinking," Dorian insisted. "He's sick—" He moved next to Bastian and tried to grab his arm again.

Bastian yanked it out of the way. His entire arm was on fire.

"You're marked," Zan had said.

He could feel tears pricking at his eyes and wouldn't that be the kicker. To break down crying in the middle of Trivia Night in front of the entire school.

"How are you feeling . . . Sebastian? Right?" Jasmine's dad asked.

"Just need air," Bastian mumbled. "I'm fine, I'm sorry—"

Her dad's eyes crinkled at the edges, then he turned away from their table and announced, "Clear a path, kiddo needs some air!"

Bastian was now *kiddo*. He was going to cry in front of the school, and be labeled kiddo in front of the school, and possibly have a panic attack over his dead mother in front of the school, and God, he hated himself.

If only he'd looked both ways, if only he'd taken his foot off the gas, if only he hadn't been driving, if only he hadn't been born—

"Bash," Riley said, interrupting his spiral.

"I'm fine," he mumbled again, for what felt like the hundredth time. He shoved away from the table, stumbling only slightly.

Riley followed, close at his heels. "I'm coming with you," she hissed.

"I'm fine, just . . . outside . . ." Words were getting stuck on his tongue, and his mouth tasted bitter and stale, like Greer's scotch.

Dorian called after them, but Riley yelled at him to stay put, and Bastian didn't turn around. By the time they'd made it to the hall, he could hear Jasmine's dad's voice booming through the room, announcing another round of trivia. Like nothing out of the ordinary had happened.

One of the servers stopped them on the way out, asking if he was okay. Riley made up some excuse about not enough food through clenched teeth, and they let them by.

Outside was quieter—the tinkled laughter of the adults filtered from the open balconies that ringed the mansion, but the only person actually outdoors was a woman in an emerald-green cocktail dress, lazily smoking a cigarette. Riley steered him the opposite way, toward the side of the house, stopping between two perfectly pruned trees.

"You can go back," Bastian said, wiping his eyes. His wrist was throbbing, and his hands were starting to shake, and he couldn't breathe, he couldn't suck in a breath, he needed to be alone—

"What's going on?" she said, turning an accusing glare at him. "I was watching you. You were fine. Then Greer came over and was talking to you, and you fell over. What did he give you? I swear I'll kill him—"

"Wasn't Greer," Bastian managed to bite out. He sucked in a breath and held it, willing himself to calm down.

His heart was racing in his ears.

"If it wasn't Greer, then what's going on? Are you okay? I'll call my parents, they can take us to the hospital or something, I don't know Bash, you're freaking me out."

"Do not," Bastian managed, swallowing convulsively, "call your parents." He toed at the ground with his shoe and focused on keeping his breaths even. He didn't want to get her parents involved. He didn't want to have to try and explain this—that his nightmares were getting stronger and stronger. That he was losing time. That he was going crazy. "Sorry," he settled on.

"You're *not* okay, don't try to pretend this is normal, *God*, Bash."

Bastian grit his teeth. He already knew this wasn't normal; he didn't need Riley of all people reminding him. "It was too hot in there. I just got dizzy. I'm fine," he reiterated, but a flicker of guilt crawled up the back of his throat.

"Sure." Riley looked over his shoulder and gave a little wave. A moment later, Dorian and Mathais crowded into their shadowed space. Mathais's face was full of concern. Dorian's was full of terror.

"What happened?" he asked as he stepped way too close to Bastian, wrapped his hands around Bastian's head, and pressed their foreheads together.

They used to do this when they were kids. One would get hurt, the other would close in, hands pressed to ears, close enough so they could hear each other's heartbeats.

"Don't do that," Bastian muttered, yanking back again.

Dorian's hands dropped to his sides, terror in his eyes replaced by anger. "You scared us," he barked. "I don't know what's going on, but you need a doctor. We need to call 911, Riley—"

Liquid anger flooded his veins. All he wanted was to be *left alone*. Not this. Not Riley worrying, and Dorian freaking out, and everyone looking at him. All he wanted was to disappear. Bastian crossed his arms, dug his feet into the dirt, and refused to budge an inch. "I'm fine," he forced out. "Stop worrying about everything."

"Worrying about everything?" Dorian's voice went even higher, and he drew himself up to full height, anger now evident in the taut line of his spine. "Of course I'm worrying about everything! First, it's slacking off in school, then it's skipping school entirely, now it's passing out in the middle of Trivia Night and pretending it's all fine? *You're not fine.* I don't know what's happening, and you . . . you just don't *care*! You know you're failing three classes, right? Do you know that they're talking about expulsion? You don't do you, why would you, the letters are coming to our apartment. The apartment you apparently no longer live in. So I'm sitting there, cleaning up your messes—"

"Guys," Mathais said, trying to edge forward.

Dorian threw his hand up, so tense and angry that Mathais froze in his spot. "I'm cleaning up your messes," he repeated. "Constantly. Do you have any idea what that's like? I'm trying to get out of here too, Bastian, I've got my own stuff going on. Grades, college applications, trying to keep breathing, living, not thinking about *her*. I *know* it sucks. I was there too!"

And you walked away, Bastian thought. *I wasn't ever supposed to.*

"You're wasting your life—"

"Don't," Bastian growled. There was something flickering at his vision again, something black, and oily, and foul. He tried to force it back, but his head was starting to swim. He didn't want to do this. He didn't know if the dream was about to take over again or if he was actually dying.

"Don't what? Grieve? She was *my mom too!*"

"Guys!" Mathais barked.

Dorian buried his head in his hands and let out a desperate-sounding laugh. He slowly looked up again, dropped his hands to his sides. His hair was no longer perfectly combed. It stuck up at odd angles, impossibly mussed. He looked like he was about to start crying.

"Sorry," he said, turning to Mathais. His voice wavered for a moment, like there was going to be more, but he finally offered a small wounded shrug. "I have to get back. It's not fair for me to leave Maddie on her own." He chewed on his lip, staring straight at Bastian. Like a switch flipped, he combed his hair back with his fingers and straightened his tie. "Wait for me," he said, voice back in total control. "I'll give you a ride home. I just need to go talk to Maddie first." Then he turned and headed back into the mansion.

Mathais and Riley eyed each other. Mathais spoke first. "I'll go with him. Uh . . . text me?" Riley gave him a thumbs-up, and he awkwardly jogged after Dorian.

After a long, uncomfortable silence, Riley finally nudged Bastian. "You have to let him in at some point."

"Why?" Bastian muttered.

"This is ridiculous. You're struggling, and he *cares*. He misses you, he feels like he's being totally left out, he's angry, he's sad, he's feeling all the same stuff, and you're supposed to be his friend. You're supposed to be his *brother*."

A flicker of guilt lit in Bastian's stomach. He shook his head. "He's fine. He's perfect, he's got all this," Bastian said, waving his arm toward the mansion. "It's not my fault he's got a problem with me and won't drop it."

Her jaw clenched. "*You're* the problem, Bash," she finally said. "You're destroying us."

Then she turned on him too, picked her way across the lawn, and disappeared around the bend.

This was what he wanted. To be left alone. So why did he feel like he was going to be sick?

Bastian forced a trembling hand into his pocket. He pulled out his pack of gum. He tucked a piece under his tongue and folded up the wrapper, smaller, smaller, smaller until it could no longer be creased. He dropped it in the dirt next to the wrinkled trunk of a dogwood.

His phone buzzed.

Greer [9:18 PM]: Hey babe. I've got better drugs than scotch. You name the time and place

Bastian stared at the message for a moment, then deleted it and shoved his phone back into his pocket. He opened and closed his fingers a few times. The flaring pain in his arm had leeched out, and everything was now icy cold.

Bastian stepped out onto the walkway and looked back at the mansion. The woman in the green dress had disappeared. He could hear the muted sounds of the jazz band echoing out to the street.

Swallowing hard, Bastian turned, stalking away from the mansion and back to the street. It was starting to mist, and it was a three-mile walk, but he wasn't waiting for Dorian.

He pulled out the piece of glass from his pocket. It was murky purple—big enough to fill the palm of his hand.

Real.

Bastian pulled up the hood of his sweatshirt and sucked in a long breath, shivering as the rain started soaking through his clothes.

CHAPTER TWENTY-THREE

Styx

A woman holding tight to a faux crocodile-skin purse stepped out of the hallway the next morning. Her blue-white hair was still bound up in curlers, and every wrinkle on her skin was caked with age.

"Where is Eugene?" she asked, eyes filmy with cataracts but filled with hope.

"Name and location of death?" Zan asked.

Her mouth crinkled at the edges. "Florence Lewis," she said after some thought. "Bristol."

He typed in her name and picked up the keys, stepping out from behind the desk. "Think of a happy place. Your happiest memory."

He held out the keys. She shakily reached for them, palsied fingers landing on a standard-looking apartment key. The number 2387 was embossed on the top, the silver faded with age.

As soon as she touched it, the cement wall wavered, then changed to an apartment door, the same 2387 painted on the front.

"Eugene?" she called, twisting the knob and walking through.

Zan followed her through and stood against the wall as she walked up to a man in a rocking chair holding a bawling infant. For a long time, she did nothing but cry.

"Are you lonely?" Zan asked after the man in the chair stood and walked to the other side of the room, and Florence didn't follow.

She looked up but didn't meet his eyes. Her milky, cataract-filled eyes still shone with unshed tears. "Never," she said.

Zan shuffled between his feet, stupidly hoping she'd actually meet his eyes, but just like everyone else, she avoided looking at him.

"I had a love," she continued sadly, motioning toward the man with one gnarled and liver-spotted hand. "You can never be lonely when you love."

You probably don't understand the concept of love. That's what Bastian had said, what he'd yelled at him in the middle of a forest so dappled with warm sunlight Zan had wanted to bottle it up and take it with him.

It felt like there were rocks in his throat as Zan swallowed.

He *did* understand it. He'd loved his family. He'd loved his mother so hard he sacrificed himself to a monster to save her, and what was that if not tangible, desperate *love*.

"If you are going to kill me, I am ready," the woman said, tearing him from his thoughts.

But here he was, delivering souls to a god who delighted in fear, who sucked life like marrow from bones, who laughed as humans cried. And Zan had done it for 499 years without question because he selfishly wanted to live again.

So maybe Bastian was right. Maybe he'd lost the ability to love long ago. Maybe he was just as much a monster as the Ferryman.

The memory warped and rippled, the kitchen sink disappearing into a wall of fog. Zan didn't say anything, just held out his hand.

Florence nodded, pulling two quarters from her pockets and then placing them in the palm of her hand.

A believer then. This would be easier that way. She wouldn't feel pain. The Ferryman had always promised that those that paid wouldn't suffer.

As Zan pushed through the wall, he was suddenly awash with some awful impulse, some terrible desire to prove himself still human, still capable of feeling love. The cold ate at his limbs as the blackened river flowed by. She let go of his hand first, stepping into the water. It lapped at her skirts, causing them to balloon up before soaking through.

Zan didn't look away.

The Ferryman rose up from the banks of the Styx, whisps of black shooting tendrils around the woman's waist, her neck, her wrists.

Zan didn't look away.

The black drew together, forming a human skull, teeth sharp like fangs, boned fingers clutching a single, sharpened scythe.

Zan's breath tightened in his chest, panic buzzing through his body so loudly his ears rang. He tried not to move, tried not to turn attention to himself, but still, the Ferryman's head quirked, grinning at him.

Zan blinked furiously, eyes watering as the woman raised a hand.

You did this, he thought wildly. *You did this, and you deserve to watch the consequences, you did this—*

The Ferryman let out a low growl, long tongue darting out as he lapped between her fingers. The silvery flash of coins disappeared.

There was a moment of perfect silence so complete Zan felt his ears pop and the dizzying slosh of his equilibrium collapsing.

Then the black roared up from the river, all claws and teeth, tearing at the woman's clothes, sucking the skin from her body, the muscles from her bones, and the light from behind her eyes.

It was over faster than she could scream, all that was left was the billowing fabric of her skirts vanishing beneath the surface of the choppy black water.

And the Ferryman rose, empty eye sockets of his void black skull fixing back on Zan.

Zan ran, pushing back through the barrier, back through the apartment, back into his office where his laptop sat, open, still blinking on the spreadsheet where he'd logged Florence's information. His heart was in his throat, pounding so hard and loud he was surprised the entire room wasn't shaking.

She didn't feel pain, he thought frantically, trying to distill the swirling, terrified mess of his brain into something palatable. *She didn't feel any pain, she paid him, and she didn't scream, she said she was ready to die—*

"She said she was ready to die."

Zan flinched back at his own voice, surprised he'd spoken the words aloud. He grit his teeth, suddenly furious at himself. He'd been doing this for lifetimes; he didn't deserve to feel *bad*. He didn't get to sit here having a moral crisis about how the Ferryman chose to collect his souls, not when he'd never once allowed himself to watch, not when he'd never once allowed himself to think about *how*.

But it was worse.

It was so much worse than he'd ever allowed himself to imagine. She'd offered up the coins so gently, and still, the attack was merciless. Zan closed his eyes, but he could only see the gentle acceptance of her face turning to terror in the space of a single second.

She didn't feel it. She couldn't have felt it, it was too fast, but—

He—

You did this.

Falling into his chair, Zan slammed his laptop closed and sank over the desk, burying his head in his arms.

Maybe Bastian would come back today.

Maybe he wouldn't.

Maybe Zan shouldn't be hoping some boy who'd reached out and touched him was going to show up again in his office, because he was either going to have to cart him off to the river or get his own soul viciously yanked out of his body, and both options were *horrific*.

Zan dropped the keys back on the desk with a shudder, then wandered the perimeter of the office, fingers brushing along the edges of the shelves. He stopped in front of a pair of tortoiseshell glasses, lenses so thick they could stand up even with the earpieces tucked in.

He could go visit the '70s bar again and get drunk on crème de menthe. Or the tiny underground Cuban bar in Florida or the little bistro in Paris that sat in the shadow of the Eiffel Tower.

He could go bury himself in the Asopos again, or jump off a building, or sit on top of Everest until his skin flaked and burned from the cold.

There was the lodge in the Alps with the hot chocolate that he hated, where the snow was frozen in the midst of falling so thickly it looked like a winter wonderland. There was the Orient Express, except the memory was confined to only the dining car, and for supposed luxury, the food was iffy at best. There were football games, and cruise ships, and islands, and forests, and casinos, and spas, and classrooms, and suburban houses, and on, and on, and none of it was *his*.

Zan reached past the glasses and tugged a red-spined book out from behind them. Volume clutched in his hand, he picked the keys back up, forced one off the ring, and stepped up to the door.

He walked through to the Metropolitan Museum of Art, inside the Mastaba Tomb of Perneb. This memory fuzzed at the edges along the perimeter of the tomb, so Zan had never been outside it, only walked the tiny corridors a hundred times, brushing his fingers along the hieroglyphs so carefully etched into the walls. A security guard stood there, both hands behind his back, and a stern look frozen on his face.

There was an offering table deep inside, with a small area for Perneb's spirit to pass through so he could continue living forever in the afterlife.

As someone who'd wandered the afterlife for hundreds of years, Zan could have told him that it wasn't all that exciting.

Zan leaned up against the back wall. There were six other people in the exhibit with him. A mother with two children—one boy far too young to be trusted not to touch things, the other boy with a surly looking frown on his face. There was one man with a Mets cap on. Another guard—a woman in a black pantsuit uniform—stood in the corner, her Metropolitan Museum of Art badge catching the dim light and flickering gold, her eyes narrowed and focused on the child too young to be trusted. Another man with a graying beard and angry eyes stood near her. He had on a watch, one of those fancy ones that people had started wearing a couple of years ago. It showed the year, date, time, and exercise mileage. It said January 5, 2016. It said 12:46 p.m. It said 7 seconds. It said 16.4 miles run.

The mother had a small leather backpack on—small enough that it had made it through security with no problem. Zan pushed himself off the wall, walked over, unzipped it, then rifled through until he found what he was looking for.

Fig Newtons.

He'd discovered these completely by accident somewhere

between iteration ten and iteration fifty of this particular memory. He'd gotten bored and decided to go rifling through the pockets and bags of everyone here. The mother had baby wipes, hand sanitizer, a wallet filled with membership cards to various museums and grocery stores, and a pack of Fig Newtons.

He'd initially plucked the bag from her purse out of curiosity. His mother used to make sweet cakes filled with fig paste. They were the best in the village. She'd pack them up in paper and sell them at the market in the afternoons. His younger brothers and sisters ran from stall to stall, buying sweets and little toys with whatever pocket change they'd saved up over the week. Zan did not. He sat sullenly behind the booth with his mother, handing over sweet cake after sweet cake as the villagers ordered, wondering if his father would come back for them or if they were going to be stuck there, doomed to never leave the town, forced into a lifetime of dusty feet and sunbaked skin.

The bag crinkled as Zan tore it open and pulled out a cookie. He bit into it and closed his eyes. They were stale. They tasted nothing like fresh fig paste—there was too much sugar, too much preservative—but he tried to pretend they tasted like home.

Sometimes he thought of his mother every single day, the pain so fresh he wanted to rip his own skin off to get away.

Sometimes he went days. Weeks. Months drifting through time and space as memories fuzzed into nothingness around him. And then he'd claw himself awake one day, anxiety thrumming in his veins, because if he could lose her for that long, could a year go by? Two? Would there be a day she vanished completely?

Zan would frantically rush through every memory he could find that held remnants of her, gathering them tightly to his chest, and refusing to let go, because if he forgot the way she loved him, then—

You probably don't understand the concept of love.

The cookie tasted like ash. Zan let it drop to the ground, wiped the palm of his hand against another man's shirt, then crinkled the bag closed and stuck it right between two blocks carved with depictions of men carrying goats.

The hazy nothingness of the end of the memory stood just a few feet from the place where the arch opened into the rest of the museum. He stared at it, inching closer and closer, until the shock of the icy cold caused him to give in and step back again. About a decade ago, a teenage boy had taken him to another memory within the Met—another floor devoted to an exhibit of paper cranes. They'd hung from the ceiling, from the walls, been scattered across the floor. When he was with the boy, the brush of wind from the door opening and closing caused some of them to slowly flap their wings.

He'd led that boy to his death just like he'd led thousands of others.

Just like he'd lead Bastian.

Because he had to.

CHAPTER TWENTY-FOUR

Portland, Oregon

"I'm sorry."

Bastian's eyebrows rose as he shoved the last of the *Z* authors into place. He stood up and brushed his hands on his pants. "What?"

"I'm sorry. For what I said. At the party."

Bastian blinked at her.

Riley frowned, looking up at him from where she sat surrounded by note cards, highlighters, notebooks, and textbooks. Cat slept next to her, sprawled out in the single bar of sunlight coming in through the window. Ever since Bastian had forced Cat through a sink bath (causing yowling, swearing, another bloody gash down the side of one arm, and the loss of a perfectly good towel that was now shredded), they'd made a wary sort of peace.

"You're not destroying us," she continued with a huff of exasperation. "I didn't mean that. I was upset, and you scared us, and I don't know. It just slipped out. But I swear I didn't mean it."

Wincing, Bastian fought not to pick at his bracelet. "It's fine," he mumbled. "I get it."

"You don't, because you blame yourself for everything, and I just need you to know that it was a terrible thing to say, and you can be mad at me over it."

"I'm not mad at you, Riley," Bastian said, finally giving in to the urge and rubbing at the twine.

"Good," she said, closing the massive chemistry textbook she'd been painstakingly plastering with tiny sticky notes. "Moving on. We need to talk about the name. For the bookstore. We've been over this, but you keep avoiding it."

Shrugging, Bastian walked over to the front of the store, relieved that she'd dropped the awkward apology and gone back to her regularly scheduled Riley-level bossiness. The countertop was bare now—no dusty Persian rug, no janky cash register that refused to open. He was supposed to be investing in some new point-of-sale system, but that meant research, and he wasn't anywhere near opening the store, so he still had time. Probably. "I'm working on it," he said.

Riley shot him an unimpressed glare. "Look, I'm not busting my ass for you to sit there and pretend like you don't care."

"You're sitting on the floor studying," Bastian said. "Not helping me."

"We've got a major test in chem, you should be sitting on the floor studying too. Regardless, I am helping. Give me your phone."

"No."

"Bash Barnes, I'll call Dorian!"

Bastian snorted. "What a threat."

"Fine, I'll call my mom and tell her you're coming over for dinner."

That was a threat. Riley's mom would spend an entire day prepping, then spend the entire meal peppering him with questions about schoolwork, his love life, Dorian, his love life again, on and on until he'd excuse himself from the table, ignore Riley's knowing look, and hide in the bathroom for fifteen minutes just to breathe. Then he'd have to reappear and try his hardest to be gracious, because he liked her. He really, really did. And besides Andrea? She was the closest thing to a mom he had.

He handed over his phone.

She snagged it right out of his hand and started typing. "Renee," she said, giving it back. "Grad student at Portland State. Graphic design. Just send her a text. She told me she'd be in the studio all day so go over now, tell her what you want, get it done."

"How do you know a grad student at PSU?"

"I'm full of surprises," she said.

"Riley . . ."

Riley picked up a highlighter and threw it at him. It skidded across the countertop, all the way to the edge where it hung, delicately balanced. "Her sister's a grade below us. And we're in business law together, she's really cute, and we have our final project together, so I've been working at her house. Now, be nice to Renee, or I'll kick your ass."

Bastian rolled his eyes, pushed his phone into his pocket, picked up the highlighter, and tossed it back to her. "I'll call her."

"No, you'll go over right now. I know you, Bash. You'll never call her because you'll pick up your phone and go all oh-no-phones-are-scary."

"I called Joon," Bastian muttered.

"Yeah, after like a week." She grabbed her phone again, thumbs texting wildly. "There. Renee's expecting you. In an hour."

Bastian groaned. "You're the worst."

"I'll lock up when I leave," Riley said, beaming at him.

Sighing, Bastian grabbed his backpack from behind the counter and started for the door. She was right. It *did* have to get done. He'd just . . . planned on procrastinating a little more. Like another week. Or month. Or something.

"Say hi for me!" Riley shouted after him.

Bastian gave her a salute, then headed out into the rain.

ᘓᘓᘓᘓᘓᘓᘓᘓᘓᘓ

Renee's studio wasn't so much a studio as it was a very large class-room space that was also shared by a very large number of art students. She was a perky girl with purple hair, patchy rainbow stockings, and lumpy corduroy overalls that looked like she'd sewn them herself.

"Hey! You're Bastian!" Renee stuck out a hand and shot him a toothy grin.

Bastian hated meeting new people. He awkwardly held his hand out, she shook it vigorously, and he mumbled something about how she could call him Bash. She led him over to a table and plopped down on a stool, one knee crossed, one shoe pushing against the table. The stool tipped back on only two legs. Bastian was impressed that she was managing to stay balanced at all.

"So Riley said you're opening a store!"

"I guess," Bastian said, then, because that wasn't really a con-clusive answer, he said, "Yeah, I'm opening a store."

Her smile grew. "Cool! How'd you manage that? You're a kid, right?"

He had a sudden and inexplicable urge to leave. "Family business," he managed to mutter, even though that wasn't in the slightest bit true.

"So you need a sign," Renee said, completely oblivious to his discomfort. "A logo. Branding. All that jazz!"

Bastian nodded.

"Sweet. I just got this deck," she said, taking out a small box that looked a little like a tarot deck. It was labeled *Who Are You*. "They're fun! They'll help me tell a little bit about you, and we'll go from there!"

Bastian didn't know how her learning about who he was was going to benefit anyone, but he found himself nodding again.

She started dealing out cards two at a time. A student at the end of the table looked over at them with curiosity. "Okay so, pick one, okay? Relaxed or disciplined?"

Bastian didn't know. Both? Neither? Fifty percent? He pointed at the disciplined card; she smiled, and it disappeared into her deck. He immediately felt like he'd made a wrong choice, but before he could change his mind, she pushed another two cards toward him.

"Curious or certain?"

He didn't know how those even fit together. "Curious I guess?"

The card disappeared.

"Niche or mass market?"

It went on for what felt like ages, and by the time they'd reached the end of the deck, Bastian felt like he knew himself even less than he'd previously thought. His hands were sweating. He wiped them on his jeans and wished he'd just made Riley deal with this. He'd trust her to pick a logo. She was cool like that.

"Sweet, yeah?" Renee said.

"Yeah," Bastian echoed.

"All right, so. You got any ideas already? Name? Color?"

Now she was asking? "Umm…" He picked at his thumbnail. "I was thinking Fox."

"Like orange?"

"Oh, yeah, I mean, orange for the color I guess. But the name. Fox Books."

"Fox Books," she murmured, scribbling it in the corner of her margins. "Any particular reason?"

"It's from a book," he said. "*The Little Prince*." His cheeks were heating up. He'd had the idea last night when sorting through another enormous pile of books. *The Little Prince* had toppled out into his hands. It was an older edition and in French. Not signed, not like his mom's but . . .

Renee was watching him, head tilted slightly, pen tapping against her lips.

This was a stupid idea, and he should keep it Cavendish. Stodgy, old, inconspicuous. He opened his mouth again but couldn't manage to say that.

"Very cool, very cool," Renee finally said. "All right, I know it's a rush job, but lucky for you, semester's ending and I don't have a final project yet. Ergo, I'm using this. That's cool, right? I'll get you mock-ups by next week, if so."

"Yeah, okay, I guess," Bastian said because what else was he going to say? No?

She pulled over a large notebook, opened it, then bent her head and started drawing.

Bastian cleared his throat. "Did you need anything else?"

"Oh!" Renee looked back up and smiled. "Nope! Unless you have any other suggestions?"

He shrugged awkwardly.

"Okay! Riley gave me your email, so I'll send them over when I'm finished," she said, then turned back to her paper and ignored him completely.

"Sure," Bastian said, pushing himself away from the table. The guy at the end of the table looked up again, then quickly turned back down to his work. The door to the studio opened with a bang, and a group of art students poured in, chatting wildly about some big project. Bastian slipped by in the chaos, pushing his hands in his pockets and ducking his head.

CHAPTER TWENTY-FIVE

Portland, Oregon

Joon was at the store ordering around a bunch of burly men when Bastian got back from the studio. "Plumbing," he called to Bastian. "Water's all off so don't use the toilets. Cool?"

Bastian nodded and gave him a wave as he headed up the stairs.

He grabbed a box of Froot Loops from the kitchenette and walked down the hall, pulling out a handful of sugared loops and chewing slowly. His phone buzzed once, Riley asking how the meeting with Renee went. He sent off a quick text telling her it was fine, then sat down at his desk and powered on his laptop, grabbing another Froot Loop between his fingers and popping it in his mouth as he waited.

The screen flashed on.

He chewed on his lower lip for a second before typing *River Styx*.

There was a slew of historical articles, speculative articles, and wiki pages devoted to the other side. There were other names: Spirit Road. Burial Road. Corpse Way. Funeral Road. The idea had been around forever—a clearly defined path to convey corpses from church to cemetery to avoid spirits returning to haunt the living. It didn't seem to hint toward purgatory so much as a road to travel to keep the dead, well . . . dead.

Bastian skimmed numerous articles citing everything from medieval church rites to witchy rituals used to call spirits back to the living before he found a decades-old-looking blog with a black background, lime-green typeface, and little dancing skeletons that scrolled across the top of the screen. Some fake string music played out his speakers. It sounded like it was supposed to be something that might have once been played by a symphony but had been forced into a midi computer file and sounded less like string instruments and more like the dying call of a duck.

Charon and the Corpse Road.

He read about Charon the Ferryman and his coin toll. This was not new information.

He read about crossing the river, about the Greek heroes Aeneas, Orpheus, Psyche, Heracles, and more. They all ventured into the underworld and returned (relatively) unscathed.

This was not new information either.

Bastian started skimming as the fake strings faded out and molded into a new song, a quieter song, a song that caused goose bumps to pimple all over his arms.

He read that the Ferryman was not just a figure in Greek mythology. He and his likeness showed up in cultures all over the world, spanning millennia. Sometimes he wanted a coin. Sometimes he wanted a kiss. Sometimes he was the one escorting the souls; sometimes he was the one eating the souls; sometimes he was the Ferryman.

He read that sometimes the Ferryman had a human with him. A soul bound into servitude. A secretary who kept tally of all of the souls crossing over.

The human asked two questions.

Name and location of death.

He read that sometimes souls were marked, a gray-smudged fingerprint, a slivered moon-shaped bruise, a silvery streak that grew and grew because the Ferryman kept track of every soul he was owed, and he *always* came to collect.

Bastian slammed the laptop closed as the music began to swell. The song continued for a couple of seconds after, before the computer went to sleep. Even after it faded, he swore he could hear it echoing in the tiny bedroom.

He looked down at his arm. The gray bruise was still there, marbling up his elbow. He flexed his fingers. They were cold and hard to move. Bastian shook his head, pulled his phone out, and tried to focus enough to scroll through his email. The letters fuzzed in and out of his vision. Everything faded around him.

Bastian slumped over his desk and closed his eyes.

CHAPTER TWENTY-SIX

Styx

The door was right in front of him, starkly outlined in the yellow light. It had never appeared this easily before. Bastian frowned, then pushed it open.

Zan sat with his back against a crooked-looking bookshelf, surrounded by pairs of glasses—plastic frames, wire frames, Coke-bottle lenses, long beaded chains. His head tilted so far to the left, he looked like he was about to fall out of the chair, and a manic energy filled his eyes. "Welcome," he called, throwing up his hands and smacking them together in mock joy. "Ready to die?"

He looked awful—eyes red around the rims, dark curls wild and tangled. "Bad day?" Bastian asked carefully.

Zan pushed at the pile of glasses and pulled up a pair of gold-rimmed aviators, forcing them over his nose.

They made him look even worse.

"Bad life," Zan said. He flicked the sunglasses from his nose and rifled around the pile, pulling up an unassuming pair of silver frames. They looked like the sort of glasses an aging engineer would wear. Zan put them on.

Bastian walked over, stopping right where his shadow over-took Zan's body. He sank down to his haunches and poked at the pile of frames. "What's with the glasses?"

"Did you know that the earliest pair of historically documented glasses was in thirteenth-century Italy? The lenses were glass-blown. Set in wood frames. There were no temples." He tapped at the plastic set snug around his left ear. "None of these. Instead, they'd hold them on their face."

He paused, looking at Bastian expectantly.

"Is there a point to this story?"

Sighing, Zan's eyes dropped back down to his lap. "There's been disputed evidence of magnification all the way back to hieroglyphs. Before. But mass production really started up with the invention of the printing presses. People wanted to read. Humans are always striving for that, you know? That next step. Learning. Higher-level stuff. Our advanced cortex doesn't allow us to wallow for long. Anyway. They figured out magnification, but study of optics took a while. Optics. It's from a Greek word. *Optiké*. The Greeks are the ones who studied light and vision that way. You owe us."

"Chatty today," Bastian murmured. He wasn't sure what to do. Peppy, let-me-log-your-death-location Zan was annoying, but this was painful. He sounded like Bastian felt on the heels of a panic attack. Scared and anxious, like he couldn't catch a breath. Bastian cleared his throat. "I hardly think the entire universe revolves around the Greeks. I'd be willing to bet that the Eastern world had plenty of their own studies going on."

"Fair enough," Zan murmured. He rifled through the pile, pulling up a battered-looking metal frame that no longer held any lenses. The frames were large and perfectly round. Zan held them up to his face. "I had eyeglasses growing up. Like these."

None of this was explaining why he was sitting mournfully in a pile of glasses, but Bastian stayed quiet.

"Still couldn't see very well," Zan pressed on. "They weren't that advanced. But they helped. They've come a long way now. I can't exactly march out and get a prescription. But I like taking them out of memories. Trying them on. Messing with the lenses to figure out just how much I can see."

"So . . . you steal them."

"It's not really stealing. The memory is old. It no longer exists. I could take something one day, go back another day, it would be there ready to take again. Constantly repopulating or whatever. And I can't move anything big. I mean . . . I guess I could drag whatever I wanted back, but there isn't room here." He waved his hand nonchalantly around, fingers graceful with every flick of his wrist. "Nowhere to put stuff."

Bastian slowly looked around. He'd seen the packed bookcases the last few times he'd been here, noticed the knickknacks, pieces of clutter, bits of broken things littering the shelves. It was sadder now, knowing that these were pieces of other people's memories. Bits of their pasts.

Bastian wondered if his own memories were now at Zan's disposal. If the forest was now Zan's, if Zan could just steal pieces from his life. Bastian didn't know how he felt about that. It was weirdly personal, but also hurt his brain to try to think his way through too much. If it was a memory, it wasn't a tangible place he could go back to, so did it matter if things disappeared?

"Can you put things back in memories?" he mused. "Like, things that never belonged there in the first place?"

Zan's brow drew together. "I . . . I guess I've never tried." His eyes flicked up, clearly considering the question. "I think that if the memories are already dead, it wouldn't do anything."

"But what about memories that are still alive?"

"I don't . . . I guess . . ." he stuttered to a halt, like the very idea had caused his brain to completely derail.

Bastian chewed his lower lip, not voicing his next question. Would it work the other way? Could he bring something from the real world *here*?

Then again, beyond bringing in an arsenal of weapons, knocking Zan out, and fighting a mythological god for his life, there probably wasn't much point.

"So this is where you live?" Bastian asked, pushing himself up from the floor and striding to the shelf near the concrete wall. There was an entire encyclopedia set at eye level. There was another entire encyclopedia set lower than that, this one written in French.

"Essentially," Zan said.

"Where do you sleep? Eat? Do anything other than sit at a desk and document people's deaths?"

"Oh." Zan set down the old frames and pushed the silver ones more firmly on his nose. "In the memories. Whatever I lead people through, I keep. File them away. I can go back in them at any time."

Somewhere far away, Bastian could hear the faint sound of water. If this was real, if he was going to take Zan's words as truths and believe it, then—

Bastian blinked a few times, trying to find his footing in a world that had suddenly turned on its axis as the realization hit him hard enough to make him take a step back.

He believed Zan.

And if he believed Zan, then he couldn't keep pretending this was just a dream, and if he couldn't keep pretending this was a dream, what the hell was he supposed to tell everyone outside of

Styx? *Sorry I keep passing out, it's just that I wasn't really supposed to live after the accident last year, so this spirit boy is trying to drag my soul to the mythical Ferryman. Big oops on my part. Next time I'll die when I'm supposed to.*

Yeah. That was going to go over great.

The water sound grew louder. Bastian rubbed his ears.

There was a little green box ringed with polished wood sitting above the encyclopedias. He picked it up, jarring the lid. A tinkling song rang from it for a moment as he fumbled it back closed. "So you live in other people's lives?" he asked.

Zan's mouth twitched. "Essentially."

"That's . . . weird."

His mouth twitched again, before settling into a firm line. "Essentially," he repeated.

Bastian set the box back on the shelf next to a tarnished silver frame with a picture of a stern-looking family, all in stiff, formal dresses, all with sour faces. "Bet you get lots of cool stories, though."

Zan slowly stood up. He gently pushed the pile of glasses into the corner with his shoe. "Huh?"

"Stories. From the people in the memories. You ever go exploring? Look for famous people? Talk to like . . . I don't know . . . Tolkien? Dickens?"

"That's famous people? Dead white men who wrote crappy books? You realize that the Greeks *pioneered* the novel?"

Heat rose to Bastian's cheeks, and his eyes dropped to the floor. "I mean . . . whoever," he grumbled. "Someone else?"

Shaking his head, Zan reached down and started shoveling handfuls of glasses into the bottom shelf of the bookcase behind him. "There's no one to talk to. Once the souls cross Styx, the memories freeze."

"My forest wasn't frozen."

"Because you were in it."

Bastian swallowed. "So when I wake up . . ."

"Everything stops. I can run around all I want, but there's nothing there. No weather. No rippling rivers. No people moving, talking, breathing, *living*."

Bastian tried to imagine what it must be like to spend an eternity in a place where the only other people to converse with were dead or dying—only around for moments. What it must be like to live in other people's minds, surrounded by nothingness.

It was horrible.

"I've already served 499 years," Zan continued. "I'm almost done. Don't feel too bad for me."

"Then what happens?"

Zan smiled, a true smile, the sort that made his eyes light up. "Freedom," he whispered. "I get to live out the rest of my life wherever I want. I could go home. I mean, it wouldn't really be there anymore, but I could still go back."

"But only if you lead me to death."

Zan froze. He looked up, jaw tight and brow furrowed.

"You get freedom, if you lead me to the Ferryman, right? That's what you kept talking about last time, how we had to go because he was going to be mad. So you don't get freedom if you let me live."

Zan's face shuttered, and he nodded. "You're not going to live. You're messing everything up just by existing. So I have to."

Bastian combed his fingers through his hair and sank back against the bookshelf. "So why didn't you kill me? Last time."

Zan rubbed at the back of his neck, and his eyes dropped to the floor. "Mistake," he mumbled.

"But why?"

"You wanted to wait for your mom."

"Yeah, but if you're that close to whatever deal, and you're supposed to be killing people—"

"I don't kill anyone. I lead them. And for someone who wants to live, you're doing a really crappy job of convincing me to let you."

Bastian's eyebrow arched. "So I *can* convince you."

Zan looked up at him. His hands clenched and unclenched against his jeans. "Come on," he said, suddenly grabbing the keys from the desk. He took off the old pair of glasses and leaned over, grabbing the set of black plastic frames that Bastian had first seen him wearing. Then he stretched out his hand. "I want to show you something."

Prickling nervousness crawled up Bastian's spine. *Show you something* could mean *hey, look at this super cool memory that you're going to love*, or it could mean *time to die, sucker*. He eyed the other boy suspiciously, but Zan just waited, hand unwavering.

Before he could think better of it, Bastian slotted his fingers in Zan's and followed him through the door.

CHAPTER
TWENTY-SEVEN

Styx

Bastian didn't particularly have a problem with heights. He'd walked bridges that spanned over dams, climbed mountains to rocky outlooks, even climbed to the roof of the Preston Academy main building one afternoon with Riley just to see if they could.

This, though? The top of a pillar of concrete so high he was in the clouds, the ledge so narrow he barely had room for both feet?

This wasn't heights. This was a death wish.

There was no sound, no wind, not a single motion from anywhere around him. Bastian immediately hunched down low, but that didn't help—his ears popped, and the vertigo was getting worse with each ragged inhalation of his breath.

"Come on," Zan said, slowly lowering himself to the lip of the concrete and sitting. "Trust me." His feet dangled over the edge.

Bastian absolutely did not trust him. Bastian was going to officially die this time. He'd screwed up, taunted the Ferryman's stupid servant, and now instead of reliving his own memories, he was going to fall off the side of some ridiculous skyscraper, and then he was going to die, and—

Zan reached out and patted the space next to himself. Then he looked up at Bastian and winked.

He *winked*.

No, first Bastian was going to wrap his hand around Zan's ankle and pull him down too. Then they were *both* going to die.

"You good?" Zan said, full-on cocky grin splashed across his face.

"I hate you," Bastian muttered. He carefully lowered himself too, gripping the concrete as hard as he could between his fingers. His stomach swooped again, but he slowly sat. Crossed his legs. Planted himself firmly in the middle of the ledge and refused to move any closer. "Are you suicidal?" he asked.

"This is Pingshan," Zan answered.

Which wasn't an answer. He was clearly suicidal.

Bastian let out a slow breath and watched Zan. He was looking out over the horizon, stupid smile pasted on his stupid face.

"We're in Huaibei City, China," Zan clarified. "This was supposed to be a nuclear power facility. I assume it is, but all I've got is . . ." He motioned around them, toward the scaffolding that wrapped around the tower across from them. He tilted his head, watching the thick clouds. "If you look carefully," he said, eyes narrowing, ". . . there." His grin grew as he pointed.

Bastian managed to flick his eyes up without the vertigo getting worse. There was some kind of bird flying over them.

"Hawk," Zan said quietly. His hand dropped, and he just watched. "She's stuck there. Never moves."

"That's horribly depressing."

"Yeah," Zan said, still smiling.

"You're weird," Bastian grumbled. "You're super fucked and

weird." He snuck a look over to Zan, who was watching him curiously, eyebrows quirked up.

"Thanks?"

"Not a compliment," Bastian breathed, after a beat too long.

"I'll take it as such anyway," Zan said loftily. "Super unfucked and not-weird people are creepy." He looked back up at the hawk.

Something was tying Bastian's stomach in knots, making the palms of his hands sweat. He watched Zan's profile, the sharp jut of his cheekbone, the soft curve of his jaw. He was sans disgustingly fluorescent windbreaker today—just wore a simple black T-shirt that hung loose on his small frame.

He forced his eyes back to the hawk. "Are you going to kill me now?" Bastian ground out.

Zan reached out and tapped him, surprising Bastian so much he scrabbled at the concrete.

"What the hell?" he bit out, heart hammering.

"Jumpy." Zan laughed. "Do we look like we're on a river? I'm not leading you. Yet."

It was that stupid *yet* that made Bastian hate him even more. "I want to go somewhere else," he said, inching further away, out of the reach of Zan's arms.

Zan looked at him. "Scared?"

"No. Shockingly close to pushing you off."

Zan looked back up at the hawk. "I wouldn't die, you know," he murmured. "It wouldn't work. I drink a gallon of whiskey? Wake up at my desk like nothing happened. Throw myself off a cruise ship and drown in the ocean? Wake up at my desk like nothing happened. Jump off a building? Wake up at my desk like nothing happened. There is literally no situation I can put myself in that actually causes me harm."

Bastian tangled his fingers in his bracelet, looping it around and around his wrist. "So you spend your time here trying to die," he said.

"No," Zan murmured, staring off into the distance. "I spend my time trying to remember what it felt like to be alive."

Bastian didn't know what to say to that. He tangled his fingers in his bracelet and looped it around and around his wrist, shivering. He didn't know why Zan wasn't taking him *now*, leading him to death like he was supposed to.

Zan finally shrugged. "Truce?" He slowly scooted closer and held out his hand.

Bastian eyed him warily. "So what are the rules?" he murmured. Zan cocked his head. "You said you can't push me off the building, I wouldn't die that way, so there are rules about . . . how it's done. How it happens."

Zan's lips pursed. "I'd lead you to the river," he said. "Deliver you to the Ferryman."

"Yeah, but *how*. Where's this fabled river?" Bastian looked down over the edge of the building and immediately regretted it when his stomach threatened to revolt.

Zan leaned back on his hands and sighed. "It's all around us," he said quietly. "Where memories fade. At the edges. We're surrounded by Styx. If you walk too far past where you remember, you'll see it."

Bastian swallowed hard. "So that's where you lead souls? Past the boundaries of their memories?"

Zan nodded. His eyes fluttered closed.

The silence grew so uncomfortable it itched under his skin. "It's my turn," he said. "My turn for a memory. Because no offense, this one sucks."

Zan cracked an eye open, brow furrowing. "You're that ready to die?" he asked.

Now it was Bastian's turn to wink. "Maybe I'm trying to remember what it feels like to live too." He reached out for the keys that lay next to Zan's thigh, rifling through them like he'd done the last time.

A brass key fell into his hand, splotched paint striping the teeth in blues, greens, maroons, grays, and a door appeared in the wall behind them. Bastian carefully swiveled around and held the key up, watching as the door flickered and melted away to glass. A bar lay across the middle, a jangling bell hung on the front, and a COME IN WE'RE OPEN sign hung haphazardly in the window.

Zan scratched at the back of his neck and smiled hesitantly, motioning for Bastian to go first.

CHAPTER TWENTY-EIGHT

Styx

They stepped out onto cement flooring, into a store that smelled of sickly sweet fabric softener and mildew. Zan blinked, scanning the place, trying to find what was here that made it worth remembering.

Next to him, Bastian grinned. "Value Village," he announced. "Dorian fucking hates it here."

"Dorian?" Zan asked.

"My brother."

"You have a brother?"

"Yup. I have a life too. You know nothing about me."

"I know you have terrible taste in memories," Zan muttered.

Bastian turned to him. "Give me a chance." He shoved his hands in his pockets and started walking toward the dozens of aisles filled with color-coded clothes.

Zan didn't know what he'd been expecting. A holiday party, a futebol game, a sandy beach anywhere in the world, something more exciting than a low-end thrift store with scratchy music playing too loudly over the speakers. He frowned, following Bastian as he took a sharp right and pushed through racks of used prom dresses.

The song playing through the speakers cut off, someone announced that all orange-tagged merchandise would be an additional 50 percent off until closing, the music started up again, and a soothing, acoustic rendition of "Walking in a Winter Wonderland" filtered all around them.

"Come on," Bastian said.

Zan pushed through the rest of the gauzy sequined dresses and found himself standing in an aisle filled with bruised bits and pieces—single candle holders missing their mates, vases with chipped lips, picture frames that wobbled on their single legs.

"Stuff!" Bastian exclaimed. He picked up a horrible olive-green dinner plate with a mustard-yellow flower splashed across the inside of it. "Stupid stuff. Disposable stuff. Stuff no one else wants, stuff no one will ever buy."

"Point?" Zan asked, eyes flicking up to Bastian's.

Bastian's were flinty-blue ice, but then his mouth quirked up nervously, and he gave an awkward little shrug.

"Thought you liked this sort of thing."

"I . . ."

Bastian set the dinner plate down and cringed. "It's cool if you don't. I just used to come here a bunch when my brother and I lived with . . ." His voice fell, and he looked down at his shoes, nervous grin disappearing into shadow. "My mom was a thrifter. She came from money, but she didn't like to spend it. I don't know, we used to come here and just mess around. Look for the most ridiculous things we could find. Sometimes we made a game of it, you know? Like a scavenger hunt? Sounds really dumb. But we'd decide on purple, satin, and round or something. Three descriptors. Then we'd set a ten-minute timer and spread out, all trying to find the most ridiculous thing that fit." He leaned against the display, jarring it slightly and causing the glass and porcelain to clink together. "I haven't been back since . . . anyway. I don't know. Thought you'd like it."

Zan gaped at him. He didn't know what to say. He'd never had anyone use a memory just because they thought he'd *like* a thing, but he'd also never had anyone return to Styx again and again, escape the Ferryman, keep on living.

This was dangerous. He needed to find the barrier right now, yank Bastian through it, and stop doing this.

"We can go somewhere else," Bastian said.

Zan tilted his head in thought, watching the other boy. His blue eyes had softened, looking almost nervous. The black hoodie he always wore was zipped up to his throat, and he kept worrying at a piece of string around his wrist.

He didn't look like the other souls Zan brought. He wasn't old; he wasn't caked in blood; he wasn't sickly pale.

He looked so alive it hurt. Zan sucked in a breath and shook his head. "No, this is great." He reached out and picked up a tiny cherub angel. Its cheeks were brushed peach; its wings were coated in glitter that came off all over his fingertips. It was hideously ugly. He put it back.

"Look," Bastian said, stepping sideways to the end of the aisle and pointing at a rotating pedestal. "Glasses."

And there were. It wasn't like a display rack in a normal store—this one was a jumble of color and fragments—earpieces sticking haphazardly out; sunglasses layered over reading glasses layered over swim goggles. It was ridiculous.

It was *perfect*.

Zan pulled off the pair of black frames he'd put on back at the office and reached out and grabbed a pair of hot-pink cat-eye glasses, forcing them over his nose. He couldn't help the smile as it spread across his face. "Thoughts?"

Bastian's eyebrows rose.

Pulling them off, he tucked them in his pocket for later. Then he pulled down a pair of elastic swim goggles with a polka dot child band snugged so tightly the lenses bowed toward each other. He worked the elastic out.

"Thought you needed them to *see*," Bastian said.

"Everyone needs a good pair of swim goggles," Zan said. "Never know when you're going to get thrown in the deep end of a pool."

"Many pools in your office?"

"I'm surrounded by Styx. The presence of water is implied." Hiding his grin, Zan pulled a pair of child sunglasses off the rack and threw them at Bastian.

He caught them, frowning down at the little plastic Minnie Mouse figurines affixed to the sides like they'd done something personally to offend him.

"On," Zan ordered.

"No."

"This was your idea. You have to play too."

"This was my idea, so we play by my rules. You don't have anyone else to talk to. Looks like I'm in charge."

"Low blow," Zan said. He peered around Bastian, scanning the store. A group of teenagers stood chatting near a couple of weathered rocking chairs. An old woman in a motorized scooter buzzed out of a lane containing toys and crafts. The music above them switched over to a rendition of "Jingle Bells" played entirely on synthesizer. He twisted around—there.

At the very back corner.

Dressing rooms.

Zan pointed a finger. "Green," he said.

Bastian cocked his head.

"Fur, and animal."

"What?" Bastian asked.

"Your game." Zan grinned. "You don't want to try on ridiculous-looking glasses, then find me something green, fur, animal. Meet at the dressing room in three minutes. Go!"

He didn't wait to see if Bastian moved, just took off, tripping over a woman's cart, which sent a mannequin with a green feather boa tumbling. Zan grabbed the boa, then kept going, knocking over a rack of shoes as he skidded down an aisle full of clocks.

A sage-green one sat on the end—embossed-leaf hand frozen against a scene with Pooh Bear and Piglet sitting on the end of a bridge. Zan grabbed that, too, then raced back to the dressing room.

Bastian was already there waiting for him, arms crossed, one foot kicked up against the back wall. A fuzzy green pair of cat ears dangled from his pointer finger. "How'd it go?" he asked, snarky smile playing at his lips.

"Shit," Zan muttered. He tossed the clock over.

Bastian caught it with one hand and looked it over. "Not awful for a first attempt," he said.

Zan tucked the green boa around his neck and turned to look in the mirror. He ran a hand through his curls, pushing them out of his eyes. The swim goggles had been a casualty in the run, slipping off the top of his head somewhere near the shoes, but he still had the cat-eyes and the black frames in his pocket. He took out the latter and forced them back over his nose. Bastian's face was clearer with this prescription but still smudgy. Zan took the glasses back off and wiped them against his polo shirt hem, then put them back on and turned back around again.

Better. Still smudgy, but now he could make out the speckling of gray in Bastian's icy-blue eyes. His cheeks were flushed with exertion, even though the run through the store hadn't been all that vigorous.

His skin was prickling, heat crawling up his spine, and Zan blinked, tearing his eyes away—

The pair of fuzzy cat ears hit him in the face, and Zan flinched in surprise, stumbling backward. "Oh my god," he sputtered, reaching down to pick them up from where they'd fallen on the floor with a muffled thump. "Do you actually have friends in real life? Truly? Because you are the most obnoxious—"

"Put them on," Bastian said with a grin. "Winner decides the penalties."

Zan rolled his eyes, but he pushed the ears on his head. The fuzzy band rubbed against his neck. "Happy?" he asked belligerently.

Bastian's mouth twisted as he chewed on his lower lip. He cocked his head, brow wrinkling as he considered something. His hand moved to his pocket, and he pulled out a pack of gum, easily sliding a silver-wrapped piece from the cardboard. He offered it to Zan.

Zan took it. Unwrapped it. Put it in his mouth.

His mouth filled with an awful, spicy burn, and he quickly spit it back into the foil. "Oh god." He coughed. "What *is* that?"

Bastian gave him a blank look. "Uh . . . gum? Cinnamon gum."

"Cinnamon?" Zan exclaimed.

"Yeah . . ."

"That's repulsive!"

Bastian blinked at him like he'd just said something completely ridiculous. "That's . . . you've never had cinnamon gum?"

"No."

"You've never had *cinnamon gum*?"

"I've lived 499 years on a dead river escorting dead people to a literal god of dead souls. It's not exactly a bountiful land of plenty. And this is disgusting. Truly disgusting."

Bastian's brow grew even more furrowed as if he were trying to parse this sudden turn of events but couldn't quite wrap his head around it. "It's cinnamon gum," he finally said meekly. "I don't know what you were expecting."

"Peppermint. That peppermint stuff people chew. That tastes good. The normal kind."

"Cinnamon is normal in America."

Zan looked primly at him. "Americans are awful. The worst."

"Fine. Whatever. My bad, so sorry I made you gag with the horror that is cinnamon flavoring." Bastian grabbed another piece from the pack, unwrapped it, and stuck it in his mouth where he made a very large show of moaning, chewing, throwing his head back, and being obnoxious as hell.

Zan rolled his eyes, crossed his arms, and glared at him until he stopped.

"So now what?" Bastian asked, not looking at all chastised.

"Your game," Zan said, pushing open the curtain and striding out into the thrift store. The mannequin was still toppled sideways. An employee was carefully setting shoes back into the rack they'd knocked down. Not a single person looked up at them despite the chaos they'd just caused.

"It's like we're not even here," Bastian said.

Shrugging, Zan led him around a rack of underwear. "We're not, really. They'll talk to you. They might talk to me. But it's mostly variants of the same conversation. Patterns of whatever happened when this was real. And once you leave, they'll freeze this way."

"Jesus." Bastian stopped and turned, looking Zan up and down. "And this is how you live. There's got to be something you could do. Take down the Ferryman? How do you kill a god? Let's look up how to kill a god. I'll help you. Do I get to live if I kill Death? Benefits for both of us here—"

"Don't say that," Zan said.

Bastian swallowed hard, cheeks flushing red. He looked down and went back to picking at the string on his wrist. "Yeah. Okay, fine. Whatever."

Sighing, Zan looked back over the store. His palms were starting to sweat, but he wasn't sure if it was Bastian's bringing up the Ferryman, or if he was nervous that Bastian was going to disappear.

Because unless Zan led him to the Ferryman, he *would* disappear. And the Ferryman wouldn't eat his soul, and Bastian would live when he was supposed to die, and Zan wouldn't earn his freedom, he'd just earn himself a nice painful death.

He was so close. To picking a place to settle in the real world, in real time, where he'd have a normal human life, the kind with friends, and lovers. The kind where he aged and died after *living*.

"Zan?" Bastian asked.

Zan blinked, realizing that his mouth had twisted in some sort of awful half grin half scowl. He forced himself to relax. He could wait one more visit to deliver him. He'd hide from the Ferryman in the memories until the next time Bastian came; he was good at doing that. He wouldn't have to explain himself. It would be okay. "Orange," he said slowly. "Picnic . . . and princess." His eyes flickered back up to Bastian's, and he sucked in a breath, trying not to get lost in blue. "We meet by the front door. Ready?"

Bastian blinked, took a step back, and chewed on his disgusting gum. He smiled too. "Set," he said.

"Go!" they both yelled, then took off in opposite directions.

Zan found a vinyl tablecloth stashed amid the outdoor toys and wrapped it around his waist. He found a tank top in the teen area with the word *Princess* bedazzled across the front that he yanked over his head. He was reaching for a battered croquet set packaged in clear plastic, a bright-orange ball visible from the outside, when everything went silent.

"Shit," he murmured, hand closing around the bag and pulling it out.

The music had stopped.

The people had stopped.

Everything was frozen.

Bastian was gone.

CHAPTER TWENTY-NINE

Portland, Oregon

He came to in halting, uneasy segments. First, the sensation of his hand against wood; next, the white-noise buzz of the light flickering overhead; next, the sound of the heavy bass from the club next door; next, the realization that he was sprawled out on his desk, cheek pressed to the hardwood, affixed by a disgustingly impressive amount of drool.

Bastian groaned, then blinked himself awake, vaguely aware that he was gripping something tight to his chest.

He pushed himself up slowly, wincing as the pounding in his head crested.

He slowly opened his fingers.

In the center of his palm, between his heart line and his love line, sat a tiny crystal fox, curled nose to tail. He'd pulled it from a shelf at Value Village in the dream, after Zan had said *orange*.

It looked almost exactly like the one Bastian had smashed in Zan's office.

CHAPTER THIRTY

Portland, Oregon

"I just think you should probably begin considering that this might be a nervous breakdown," Riley said, sitting down at the desk next to Bastian and flashing him the sort of look that said *there is no might, only definitely, you are* definitely *having a nervous breakdown.*

"Don't care," Bastian muttered, then turned his head.

"You're not sleeping. You're not turning in assignments, you're skipping class, obviously something's wrong!"

Bastian sighed. She didn't know the half of it. "I'm here, aren't I?" he murmured.

"Excuse me?"

"I'm not skipping class. I'm here."

"Wow, Bash, one day out of the whole week, congrats, I'll be sure to hand over your trophy later. It's a miracle they haven't expelled you, you know—"

Bastian closed his eyes again, tuning her out as she really got going on her Bastian-needs-an-education tangent. Facing this way, he could see the clock. Fifty-two minutes until history class ended, and lunch began. Fifty-three minutes until Dorian was inevitably on his back, trying to get him in the car, out to lunch, some place quiet and inconspicuous to "talk this out," *this* being Bastian and his terrible choices like falling asleep, losing time, and somehow missing four days of school.

Not that Bastian was planning on explaining *that* to Dorian.

Riley leaned over and smacked him on the head. "Listen to me, jerk. You want to be a washed-up druggie like Greer? Cause no offense, you don't exactly have the financial safety nets he does. You kind of blew it on the store, you're not in any position to barge in and pay off the teachers so you can get your degree."

Bastian glared at her. "I'm not Greer," he hissed.

She opened her mouth again, but before she could say another word, the bell rang and their history professor walked in, arms full of paper.

"Translation," he announced to the front of the class, followed by an intensely long monologue on the importance of translation in a historical context.

Bastian flipped through the packet and skimmed a few paragraphs.

"These are due after the break," Professor Amar announced.

Bastian sighed. They had a two-week break over the holidays, but he'd planned to spend it putting the finishing touches on the store. Not doing schoolwork. He took one of the paper packets as they were passed back and leaned back in his seat, pretending like he was listening but actually thinking about his fox that he'd nestled safely on his desk at the store, right next to the purple piece of glass. He thought about Zan and his piles of glasses and shelves full of books. He wondered if bringing items from dream to waking was possible, would it work the other way around?

ꛫꛫꛫꛫꛫꛫꛫꛫꛫꛫ

Dorian was waiting for him outside the classroom.

"Don't you have better things to do?" Bastian muttered, attempting to brush past him but stopping short as Dorian snagged his arm.

"Therapy," Dorian murmured, quiet enough that Bastian couldn't hear him over the chaos of the hallway between classes, but he could see the shape of the word on his lips.

"Not interested."

"Please. It's not just for me. We need to talk about things together—"

"Don't," Bastian said, yanking his arm free and walking. It didn't do any good. Dorian followed him and kept so tightly pressed against his shoulder that everyone else had no choice but to flow around them. A tangled jam forcing diversion from the path. Two brothers. No one else.

"I know you bought the bookstore for her," Dorian said.

"You don't know anything."

Dorian swallowed. "You remember how Mom and Aunt Bri were?"

Snorting, Bastian rolled his eyes. "Obviously. She hated that woman. And with good reason, Bri is a total b—"

"I know," Dorian said stiffly, cutting him off. "Look, I just . . ." He twisted the strap on his backpack, looking horribly uncomfortable. "My therapist," he started, then cleared his throat. "We've been talking a lot about relationships. And how . . . how it's really hard to get close to someone? Especially when you lose, well . . ."

Bastian did not like where this conversation was headed. He did not need to be discussing their mom in the middle of the hallway. "Can we talk about this late—"

"I don't want us to end up like them," Dorian said quickly.

"Like Mom and Aunt Bri. They hardly ever spoke, the last time we even saw the woman before Mom's death was when we were in kindergarten and she stayed with us for three days and just kept commenting about how Mom should get a real job, art was a hobby, not a business venture."

"Right," Bastian hedged, eyeing escape routes. He wasn't going to group therapy. He wasn't, he *wasn't*; the last time he went Dorian started crying, and he couldn't deal with that again because Dorian was perfect, Dorian wasn't supposed to *cry*—

Dorian reached out and grabbed his arm. Bastian barely kept himself from yanking back.

"I don't want you to disappear," Dorian said quietly. "Don't do that to me. I know therapy is scary, but I want to do it with you, I want you in my life. Okay?"

Bastian's entire stomach flipped so hard his lunch was threatening to come up. "I gotta go," he mumbled, fingers hooking into his backpack straps. He turned on his heel, so focused on escaping, he didn't notice Greer until he'd run smack into his chest.

"Hey, B," Greer grinned, reaching an arm out and looping it around Bastian's shoulders, pulling him close for a hug.

Bastian ducked free. "Don't call me that," he mumbled.

Greer's grin just grew, and he stepped back, twirling a circle in the middle of the hall. "End-of-year party next weekend!" Everyone stopped to look at him, to smile, to wave. Dorian was popular, but Greer was dangerous. That apparently made him even more desirable.

"Busy," Dorian said, forcing a smile.

"Too bad," Greer said. He wasn't looking at Dorian. He was still looking at Bastian. "Et tu?"

Bastian shrugged. "Maybe."

Dorian nudged against him, but Bastian ignored it.

"Come on, Bash," Dorian said.

Bastian ignored that too.

"Maybe's not good enough," Greer said. "I promised you a good time, I intend to live up to that!"

Gritting his teeth, Bastian tried to wave him off, but Greer stepped closer, getting right in his face. "Live a little," he advised.

Dorian hooked a finger in Bastian's backpack and dragged him past Greer. Wincing, Bastian mumbled something about texting him.

Thankfully, Greer didn't follow.

"Jerk," Dorian muttered toward Greer. He looked back at Bastian. "You're not going."

Fury and betrayal burned hot through Bastian's blood. He glared at Dorian. "The fact that you think I'm going to just go off with Greer somewhere and . . . what? Get trashed? Arrested? Thanks for the vote of fucking confidence."

"I'm . . . sorry." Dorian looked physically pained. "I didn't mean—"

The first warning bell rang, and the rush of students moving past them started to dwindle. "Everyone goes to his end-of-semester thing," Bastian said. "Everyone. Including Riley."

"Yeah, but she's just social, she's not there to *actually* party—"

"Just drop it."

Dorian flicked him a wounded look, then nodded. "Okay," he said quietly. He tugged at his tie. "I'll come by tomorrow after school," he added. "I've got one last final to study for tonight, but then I want to help. Okay?"

Bastian had no intention of actually letting him in the building, but he nodded just to get Dorian off his back. Dorian looked like he was going to say something else, but thankfully, he finally turned and walked back down the hall.

Bastian swore under his breath. He didn't need Greer. He didn't need parties, or alcohol, or drugs.

He pulled out his gum, and as an explosion of cinnamon flared, he remembered Zan in the thrift store.

The way his eyes had widened ever so slightly when Bastian showed him the rack of glasses. How a smile tugged at his lips. How he grabbed the most ridiculous pair of pink ones and stuck them on his face, and he looked ridiculous and adorable and didn't look at Bastian like he'd fucked up somehow, just looked at him like an equal, a friend, a . . .

Bastian's stomach was starting to turn flips again, but this time it wasn't nausea. It was something very different. He shoved the pack of gum back in his pocket.

He wanted to go back to Styx.

CHAPTER THIRTY-ONE

Styx

"We should stop meeting this way," Zan said, eyes flicking past Bastian's to the door. "If you want to live, that is."

Bastian eased the door closed behind him and watched as it turned back to slate-gray concrete. It was a mind fuck. Nothing really transformed; it was just a door one moment, a wall the next. It left a fuzzy, flickery weight behind his eyes, like there was something there that he just wasn't catching. "Skipped class," he said, tearing his eyes away from the wall. "Went back home. It's more fun here."

"If by fun, you mean dangerous, then sure, I guess," Zan said slowly. The pink cat-eye glasses he'd plucked from the thrift store during their last dream together fit snugly over his nose.

Shrugging, Bastian ran his fingers along the bruise. "I don't know," he said. "I was thinking about y—" He swallowed, cutting himself off. "Styx," he finished lamely. "Then this kind of went all itchy, and I just fell asleep."

"The mark," Zan said, voice hushed and full of concern.

Bastian pulled his sweatshirt sleeve down, covering it completely. "Not a big deal." He walked around the desk and pulled Zan's laptop to him. Zan didn't stop him.

"So how's life?" Zan asked after a long moment.

"In a general sense?" Bastian answered. "How's the world? Is it still standing? Have there been any shocking societal collapses of note? Or *how's life* specific to me?"

Zan finally flashed a small grin. "Specific to you," he said. "I'd imagine that if there were a societal collapse, this room would be filled with a lot more people."

"Specific to me, shit sucks." Bastian opened the laptop. "Does that actually happen? War or something bring a ton of people through here? Do you have a busy season?"

"Morbid."

Rolling his eyes, Bastian watched the screen flicker then settle on a bright-green screen. A cascading deck of cards filled the screen, bouncing at all the corners. Bastian started at it in disbelief for a moment before throwing an accusatory glare toward Zan.

"Don't look at me that way," Zan said.

"*FreeCell?*"

"Not a lot of interdimensional options," Zan said with a rueful-looking shrug.

"You have the entire world at your fingertips! Go steal a TV! A Nintendo! I don't know, someone's got to have a legitimate gaming system in one of their memories, pick up *Animal Crossing*."

Zan's mouth twisted. "What's *Animal Crossing*?"

"What's . . . *Animal Crossing*?"

"Yeah. And who do I play it with?" He quirked one eyebrow.

"Yourself. *Animal Crossing* is literally a by-yourself game. How do you not know that?"

Zan pursed his lips. His nose crinkled. A single curl lay on top of his pink cat-eye glasses. "*Literally*," he said, massively overenunciating the word just to mock Bastian, "I live in *hell*."

Bastian crossed his arms, unimpressed. "Get a Switch," he ordered.

"A what?"

"Switch. Nintendo. Little thing. Look, I'll find you one. I've got memories of a game store somewhere, we'll go. I promise it's more entertaining than *FreeCell*. Gimme the keys."

"A Switch," Zan murmured. He watched Bastian, startlingly green eyes studying him with intensity. "Okay."

Okay. *Okay*. Bastian found himself smiling. "Okay." He tore his gaze away and pulled out the desk drawer with the keys. He started picking through them, a tinkling sound of metal hitting metal filling the office.

"Focus," Zan said. "On the memory you want. It takes practice to get them right."

"Yeah, yeah, I did it just fine with Value Village," Bastian said. *Green*, his mind said. *Green, gold, warm, smile, Zan, Zan, Zan*—

"Bastian?"

Bastian forced his stupid brain back to game store. Only game store. Nothing else. Dominick's. Tiny shop next to an equally tiny bodega across the street in front of the downtown bus station. Should have everything he needed.

Bastian plucked a key and tossed it to Zan, who held it to the cement. The wall flickered and blurred to bright yellow.

They stepped through.

"Grimy," Zan said, brushing his hands on his pants and wrinkling his nose.

Bastian took in the small store—the dirty windows, the ceiling with the water stains, the faded carpeting that looked like it was decades old. The musty smell of the dragon's blood incense that the owner burned all day and night had seeped into everything. "Guy who owns the place isn't exactly the best at cleaning," Bastian said. "Spends most of his time running *Magic* tournaments in the back room."

"*Magic?*" Zan asked.

Bastian snuck a look at him. "Another game," he said slowly. "It's fun. I can teach you that, too, but it's two player, so . . ."

Zan smiled. "Okay!"

"Be right with you!" the owner called from behind a curtain in the back of the store.

Bastian stepped up to the glass display, watching the curtain the entire time. His stomach fluttered unpleasantly. "Is this going to hurt him in real life?" he asked.

"Huh?"

"The guy who owns this place. He's really nice. I feel bad stealing—"

"Didn't take you for such a rule follower." Zan grinned. "It won't hurt him. Memory already happened. I could go steal the *Mona Lisa* right now, and tomorrow it would be straight back in the memory, like I'd never touched it."

"So you could steal it again?"

Zan quirked a grin. "If I wanted a thousand *Mona Lisas*, I could have a thousand *Mona Lisas*, but between you and me, that painting is *ugly*. And, you know. Limited space."

"All right," Bastian said. He *believed* Zan, but his palms were still sweating. He'd never stolen anything. He wasn't a thief. "All right," he said again, under his breath this time.

He wiped his hands on his pants. The consoles were all stacked neatly inside the display case, their boxes advertised in yellow, black, pink. There was a huge marble chessboard out on a table, so he picked it up.

Zan watched with interest.

Bastian raised it above his head, squeezed his eyes closed—

Dropped it on top of the display, which immediately shattered, sending glass shards flying everywhere. "Okay," he hissed, snatching the Switch and a couple of games. "We gotta go, we gotta go—" He grabbed Zan's hand and pulled him back toward the door, but Zan was just laughing, cracking up, tears streaming from his eyes.

"What?" Bastian exclaimed. "Come on!"

Zan allowed himself to be pulled back, the door opened, and they tumbled back into the warmth of the office, box clutched tightly underneath Bastian's arm.

Zan was still laughing. "Oh my god," he said, hunching over, hands on his knees, gasping for breath.

"What's so funny?" Bastian growled.

"You! There was a door! On the display case! They slide open, dummy! And you . . ." He threw his head back and gasped in another breath. "You . . . you go and . . . you pick up a chessboard and smash the thing . . . just . . . smash . . . crash!" He pulled his glasses off and rubbed his eyes. "Shit!"

"So glad you find this entertaining," Bastian muttered. His cheeks were flushed red, his heart was still beating too fast, so much adrenaline was rushing through him that his hands shook. "You could have said something," he muttered. "Mentioned the sliding door thingy, stopped me, or something." He started working at the tape on the box. "Ungrateful."

Zan swore again, still trying to control himself. "That was just . . . that was something else."

"So you've said," Bastian grumbled. He unpacked the Switch as Zan sank down in the back corner, wiping his eyes with the back of his hand, still laughing. Bastian scowled. "Stop it."

"Hilarious," Zan said, throwing his head back. "You are hilarious."

"I can still take this back," Bastian threatened.

"Oh really? And smash it back through the case?"

Bastian tried to glare at him but found it impossible to be mad. It *was* ridiculous. And now that the adrenaline was starting to fade, he could see the humor. Now that the door was closed, now that he held the little box with the Switch, he realized just how completely asinine that decision had been. Smash it with a marble chessboard. Worst idea ever. Heaving a sigh, he sat down next to Zan and powered on the device.

Zan calmed down immediately and shifted closer as the screen flickered on.

"Wow," he said.

Bastian snuck a glance at him. His eyes were huge. The NINTENDO logo reflected in his glasses.

Bastian looked back down at the game and fought to hide a smile. "It's not much," he said. "I mean, we can find you some other stuff at some point, a TV, or, I don't know, do you have Wi-Fi here? I mean—"

Zan reached past him and toggled one of the buttons. "Wow," he said again. "This is super cool." He leaned closer. They both hunched over the tiny screen, setting up a tiny village. Their cheeks almost touched.

Bastian's hands finally stopped shaking, but his heartbeat didn't slow.

CHAPTER THIRTY-TWO

Portland, Oregon

"**D**o you believe in purgatory?"

Andrea looked at Bastian over the rim of her bright-pink coffee mug. She didn't smile, but her brow knight together as she considered the question. "In a religious sense? Or spiritual?"

"Aren't they the same?"

"No," she said, carefully setting down her mug. "I don't think they are."

"All right, fine, do you believe in purgatory in a religious sense, *or* a spiritual sense?"

"Hmmm. I suppose I haven't given it much thought, to be honest, Bastian. I grew up in a heavily religious family but have distanced myself from the church. A long time ago, I believed in a black and white as heaven and hell. I suppose that includes purgatory, in a waiting-to-be-judged sense." She paused, lips pursing. Then asked, "How do *you* feel about purgatory?"

"So you don't," Bastian said, ignoring her last question.

"Where is this coming from?"

"Maybe I grew up in a heavily religious family but *haven't* distanced myself from the church."

Her eyebrows rose, and she picked up her mug again, sipping slowly while waiting for him to give a real answer.

"The dream is getting weirder," he finally said. "There's another person there. Says it's an in-between space like purgatory. Calls it Styx."

"Like the river."

"Like the river," Bastian nodded.

"And you believe them?" Andrea asked mildly.

Bastian chewed on his lower lip. There was I'm-having-a-recurring-nightmare crazy, and there was I'm-having-a-recurring-nightmare-and-I-think-it-might-be-real crazy. He knew which category he fell into, but he wasn't entirely sure he needed Andrea aware of it.

Then again, he was talking more in this session than he'd talked in the entire last year because he couldn't stop thinking about Zan, and he had to tell *someone*, so she was probably already on high alert. "I believe him a little, yeah," he finally admitted.

"Does that scare you?" she asked.

"Don't baby me. I just want to know if you think there is . . . there might be . . ." His fingers clenched the arm of the sofa, nails leaving divots against the wood. "I don't know. A space that exists in between life and death, I guess. An in-between."

"Purgatory."

"Right."

"I think you're grappling with some large issues, and I wonder if this is related to—"

"Whatever, never mind," Bastian interrupted. He forced his hand to relax and dropped it to his lap like everything was fine, like he wasn't filled with so much nervous anxiety he was about to explode, like revealing this part of the dream wasn't like revealing a part of his soul. He shouldn't have brought it up in the first place. He didn't know what he'd expected.

"Dorian's applying to college," he said, because talking any more about Styx was not an option, and because he needed to give Andrea something mundane so she wouldn't try to relate this all back to trauma.

"That's wonderful," she said. "How does that make you feel?"

It made him feel worthless when she asked the same question to every single statement he uttered. "Good for him," he said, managing to keep the bitterness from his voice. Most of it. He eyed the bookshelf behind her chair. It was stuffed with texts full of boring-looking medical titles.

"Are you hoping to apply as well?" she asked. Her tone implied that she didn't care, that she would support Bastian in whatever decision he made. Bastian had no such illusions. She was an adult, and all adults had this stupid, preconceived notion that success came only from a shitload of debt and a little piece of paper with your name scrawled across it.

"Nope," he said. "I've got the bookstore."

She smiled at him. "How's the renovation?"

"Almost done," Bastian said.

She asked him more questions about the store. He talked. Told her about Cat, about the box full of signed *Star Trek* serials he'd found stashed in between a hundred cookbooks, about the stupid little bell Riley had put on the door.

She didn't ask about the dream again.

That was good.

When he got back to the store that evening, he had an email from Renee with three attachments.

Tried some stuff with your top font choices and color schemes. I did the designs with The Little Prince in mind. -Renee

Something jagged caught in Bastian's throat as he scrolled the designs. He tried to swallow, but his mouth was too dry. He wiped his prickling eyes.

The Little Prince may have been his mom's favorite book, but for a long time, it was his too. Now that he was looking at Renee's work, it seemed impossible that he ever would have considered anything else as inspiration.

Bastian expanded the first graphic and sat back in his chair. His arm was starting to ache; cold seeped through his fingers. He was so tired. He let his eyes follow the simple black-and-orange lines of the logo.

Fox Books, it read. There was a simple fox in the bottom right corner, its bushy tail winding up and over the letters to twine with the B.

Sentimental.

Bastian leaned forward on the desk, leaned his head on his arms, and peeked at the little crystal fox he'd stolen from Styx.

He looked back at the logo. It was perfect.

CHAPTER THIRTY-THREE

Styx

"Hey," Bastian said, stepping out of the hallway and into Zan's office.

"Hey," Zan said, leaning back in his chair and watching Bastian with a cocky grin. His glasses were askew on his nose—regular black plastic frames this time. He wore an orange sweatshirt with a roaring tiger in the middle. It said *Castleford Tigers* in faded, cracked lettering.

"Nice sweatshirt," Bastian said.

"Went back to your thrift shop. Debated between this and a pink sequined dress. This seemed more practical." His grin grew.

Bastian tried to ignore the sudden warmth in his cheeks. "Boring memory to waste your time in," he said, looking anywhere but at Zan. He pushed a hand in his pocket, fingers brushing against crystal.

It worked.

He could hear his heart beating wildly in his ears as adrenaline burst through him. Bastian drew out the little crystal fox. "This is for you," he said, setting it at the corner of Zan's desk.

Zan eyed it. "Okay . . . ?"

Bastian picked at his bracelet, suddenly flustered. "I found it when we were in the thrift store together, but I woke up before I could give it to you. I broke yours. The first time I was here. Wanted to replace it. I woke up with it in my hand and realized that if I was bringing stuff back to life with me . . . maybe it could go the other way?"

It worked! the little voice inside his head screamed.

Zan picked it up, cradling it in his hand. The light from the office caught on the brushed orange tail, causing the crystal to sparkle. "Conscientious," Zan murmured. He pushed back from the desk and set it at the top of the back bookshelf, a satisfied grin spreading across his face. "I love it. Thank you."

Bastian picked at his bracelet, suddenly extremely nervous. No matter how many stupid crystal foxes he brought, Zan was going to have to lead him to death. He had to. It was his *job*. He wasn't going to skip out on his deal just for one stupid teenager who was supposed to die and had already eked out a year's worth of life he wasn't ever supposed to have.

"Where to, today?" Zan asked.

"Do people ever die when I'm here?" Bastian asked suddenly.

Zan's eyebrows rose.

"I mean, you know. You're supposed to guide souls and all. Do people show up, and then you aren't here, and then you don't guide them, and then you get in trouble?"

Snorting, Zan opened the laptop and turned it toward Bastian. A spreadsheet was pulled up—names and locations of deaths listed neat and orderly down the columns. It looked so mundane, uncomfortably like the Excel spreadsheet Bastian had been keeping filled with book titles as he found them.

"See?" Zan asked.

Bastian leaned forward, reading the names.

"Not very many show up here," Zan clarified. "Plenty of people die the normal way. Go straight to Hades, or Heaven, or nowhere . . . whatever they believe in, I guess. Huh, you ever think about the philosophical ramifications of that? I mean, the people who show up on Styx show up here whether or not they worship the Greek gods. Different cultures, different beliefs, are the Greek gods the true gods, or do they just mold to fit whoever's coming through? Do people see the Ferryman, or do they just see whatever incarnation of death they believe in? Does the pantheon even exist?" His brow drew together.

"Uh, okay, didn't exactly mean to cause a religious crisis or anything—"

"Just weird," Zan confirmed, face relaxing again as he shrugged. "Never thought about it."

"And here you were thinking Americans were the ones with the egos. We have nothing on you Greeks." Bastian grinned. "Next time you see your Ferryman, you can ask him."

Zan's jaw clenched, and his eyes darted past Bastian, scanning the small room for a second. "Yeah, hard pass," he finally murmured. He swallowed hard, eyes flicking back to Bastian's. "Anyway, there aren't very many people who come through here. Most really do die. A few miraculous recovery folks slip by. For the most part, I get people in comas, or old people who just get stuck. And they're few and far between. So yeah, I guess someone could show up here while I'm with you, but barring global catastrophe, I think the odds are low."

Bastian reached out and scrolled through the list. Odds might be low, but after five hundred years, there were still more names than he could possibly read through. "But I'm not in a coma," he murmured. "So why do I keep coming back?"

Zan's nose wrinkled. "I don't know," he finally sighed. "There have been a couple of people before who flickered in a few times but not many. Not like this. And I . . ."

His eyes dropped again.

Caught them, Bastian's mind filled in. *Lead them to death. Always.* An uncomfortable weight sat in the pit of his stomach. "I thought you were going to get in trouble if you didn't bring me over," he said slowly. "So why haven't you?"

Zan's shoulders hunched. "Are you complaining?" he asked bitterly.

Rolling his eyes, Bastian looked straight at him. "Just trying to gauge how much time I have," he said, aiming for casual but coming off rough enough that Zan flinched. "For someone who made such a big deal about me screwing up your deal, you're not trying very hard."

Zan frowned. "I'll bring you," he mumbled, crossing his arms in front of his chest.

He sounded like he was trying to convince himself more than Bastian.

"When?" Bastian demanded.

There was no answer. Sighing, Bastian turned back toward the computer and kept scrolling names. "You have access to all the memories of these people?" he finally asked.

"Sure."

"Everything?"

Zan's face twisted in thought. "People gravitate toward their favorites. I've been all over the world. But no, not everything."

Bastian shut the laptop and hauled himself up on the table, legs kicking at the air. "Impress me."

Standing up, Zan leaned against the furthest bookshelf and picked up a dusty baseball. He turned it over and over between his palms. "I've been to six of the Seven Wonders. I'm still missing the Hanging Gardens, but it's only a matter of time. I was at the Dodgers game, the one in Atlanta where Hank Aaron beat Ruth's record. I only know those names because the woman who took me through the memory kept shouting them. I've seen Churchill speak. I met Nelson Mandela. I've been skiing in the Alps, snorkeling with dolphins off the Egyptian Riviera. Want me to keep going? I've been at the finish line of dozens of marathons. I've been in six different Olympic stadiums on five different continents. I've been in bars and apartments, museums and gardens decades before you were born." He finally stopped, taking a deep breath. "Impressed?"

Bastian stopped kicking his feet. The space between them had gone taut, full of tension.

Zan stepped forward, close enough that they were face to face. His face glowed gold in the flickering lamplight.

Bastian realized he was holding his breath. He slowly let it go. He was too hot—everything was electric between them.

Zan dropped the ball. It rolled past Bastian. Bastian didn't look after it; he couldn't tear his eyes away from Zan's.

"So where do you want to go?" Zan whispered.

Bastian let out his breath. "You choose," he said, trying to give a nonchalant-looking shrug. He watched the way Zan's throat moved as he swallowed. The hairs at the back of his neck prickled in anticipation.

"All right," Zan said. He flicked a key out, and the door turned to ornate wood. "Hope you—"

CHAPTER THIRTY-FOUR

Styx

Bastian's stomach lurched, pulling tight like they were falling, falling, falling. He stumbled forward, but Zan kept ahold of his hand, yanking him close enough that Bastian could feel the tension in his entire body. The warmth of the office had vanished—in its place was a frigid cold that crawled from his toes all the way up to the base of his neck. Bastian tried to breathe in, but his lungs were ice, cracked and desiccated.

The distant quiet lapping of water that he'd always heard inside the office was now a roar—swelling and falling in time with the beating of his heart. Bastian blinked furiously, trying to see anything beyond the muzzy black in front of his face.

"Don't," Zan said, voice hushed and nervous.

Bastian took a step forward. The ground underneath him was smooth, not dirt, not rock, something more slippery. It was cold, seeping through his shoes and wicking up his pants. Like the nightmare but worse. Faster.

Bastian blinked again, eyes finally focusing on a long blackened river that chugged by them both.

"Please, don't," Zan hissed. His grip tightened around Bastian's wrist.

The mark burned. Bastian gasped in pain, and the cold permeated his skin, freezing his heart, his blood, his lungs—"Bastian!" Zan yelled. His fingers clawed into Bastian's skin, and he yanked.

ᑲᑲᑲᑲᑲᑲᑲᑲᑲᑲ

Bastian's entire body disengaged. He'd been on roller coasters that left him feeling weak and nauseous—they had nothing on whatever this was.

He hunched over and pressed a fist to his mouth. He tried to suck in fresh air, but he ended up gagging instead, barely keeping himself from emptying his guts all over the beautifully polished marble floor they stood on.

"What was that?" he managed to spit out.

Zan stood over him, eyes flicking back and forth. His entire body was stiff, tight like a spring ready to burst free. Slowly, he relaxed, body uncoiling and eyes finding Bastian's. "The Ferryman," he said nervously. "That was . . . that was Styx. And the Ferryman was waiting."

Bastian pressed the heels of his hands into his eyes. The burn of the mark on his skin was fading, but when he looked down, he could see the silvery bruise still writhing underneath his skin. He didn't need to take off his sweatshirt to know that it was crawling toward his heart.

He could feel it.

The river was still loud in his ears, disorienting him. "Why?" he asked.

"I don't know," Zan said. "But I . . ." He looked away again, turned in a slow circle. "He didn't follow us," he said shakily. "We're far enough inside the memory, we're okay."

The *for now* was implied.

Bastian shuddered. Zan didn't sound confident, but Bastian had no choice but to trust him. He took another breath, slower this time. Let it all out. The nausea faded as quickly as it had come, but his limbs were still heavier than normal, and the pressure behind his eyes was still dizzying. "Where are we?" he asked, focusing on a single terra-cotta-colored diamond. It sparkled.

Zan let out another breath, then gave a shaky laugh. "Klementinum," he said. "Prague."

Bastian would have laughed if he wasn't concerned that he might still puke all over the shiny, polished floors. Klementinum. A historic library. That he'd been to with his mom, because his mom loved libraries more than she loved almost anything else. They'd only spent a half day in Prague—she'd caught a train into the city for the sole purpose of adding this library to her list of libraries she'd visited. Dorian had been with them. There was a selfie that Bastian had saved on his phone of the three of them at the top of one of the bell spires, laughing ridiculously. The rooms had all smelled like four-hundred-year-old books. It was incredible.

Now he was here again, trying, and clearly failing, to escape the echo of his dead mother.

"Bash?" Zan prodded.

Bastian straightened. The world had stopped completely spinning, and his mouth had stopped trying to salivate him to death. "Been here before," he said. "With my mom."

"Oh!" Zan's face brightened. "I love this place. The memory isn't very large"—he scuffed a shoe against the floor—"but we have this room. Full of theological texts . . ." He grabbed Bastian's hand and pulled him, ducking underneath a red velvet rope, stepping up to one of the many floor-to-ceiling bookshelves. "We can touch them."

He reached up and pulled down a book and an insane amount of dust.

"Wait," Bastian said, heart sinking. "You're not supposed to—"

"Don't worry, I won't drop a marble chessboard on anything." Zan sat down on the floor and carefully opened the text. "No one can see us. Memory is frozen. We can't hurt anything, we can't change anything, we can do anything we want to." He traced a finger along the curled ink of an enormous, medieval *M*. The page he'd opened to was written in a language Bastian was unfamiliar with, but the smell was there. The age, the paper, the must and dust and perfection that came from preserved books. Bastian crouched down next to him, heart pounding.

When he'd come with his mom, they'd been part of a tour group. No one was allowed near the books; they were only allowed to walk the strip of marble floor. They were allowed to look, not touch.

The nausea, sound of the river, panic lacing Zan's voice, all of it faded because this? This was magic.

Bastian reached out and brushed the pads of his fingers across the soft paper. He drew back quickly, cringing at the thought of destroying something so preserved.

"Rule follower," Zan taunted, but he relented, carefully closing the book and then leaning back on his hands. "This place makes me miss my mother."

Bastian turned his head.

"This," Zan said, motioning toward the library. "It's hundreds of years after she lived, and she really didn't care about books all that much but . . ." His eyes landed on a perfectly still woman, frozen in memory, not even the barest hint of breath caught in her chest. "There's a special collections room that houses stuff from first-century Greece. My mother . . . there was this slow renaissance of paganism in Greece while I was growing up. She believed in the pagan practices. Had this book with all these rituals, used to worship the old gods, all that stuff. So I would love to show her." He ducked his head. "I've never really talked about her to anyone. I don't have anyone to talk to, I guess. It's lonely, you know? My father left when I was a kid. Not left, left, but . . . went out to try and find a better place for us. We were supposed to follow. My country was all war, constant war, all over religion. Back and forth. People always dying." He scowled. "It was horrible. But he didn't come back. And I couldn't take care of everyone because I was about to get conscripted myself. We needed her."

His jaw clenched, and he cleared his throat. "I tried to get her to see a medic first. I really tried, but she kept fighting me, and when I finally dragged someone in, they said it was too late. She was coughing up blood, barely breathing, but she kept begging me to believe. Begging, Bastian. I can still hear it sometimes, the awful, rasping sounds she made at the end. So I found a ritual in her book. Figured if her gods actually existed, they'd help. In the end, it was grief and stupidity. Me on the banks of the Asopos River, suffocating in the mud, waiting for someone to answer." His face twisted up. "The Ferryman saved me." Zan gave a broken little laugh, then threw his head back, studying the frescoed ceiling. "Made me my deal. Saved my mother. She lived. I didn't."

Bastian's fingers curled in, nails biting into his palms. "That's a terrible deal."

"I know," Zan agreed. "I've had plenty of time to reflect, believe me, I know. No one should live this long. But I don't regret it. She was worth saving."

No one should live with this much loneliness, Bastian thought.

He looked up at the ceiling, at the frescoed men and women, their plump peach-colored cheeks, their silken extended arms. He tried to think of something to say but was unable to tear his mind away from the fact that Zan sacrificed himself for his mother, purposely, intentionally.

Unlike Bastian, who was clinging to a life he was never supposed to have.

"When did you come?" Zan asked, jarring Bastian out of his guilt spiral.

Bastian picked at the thread on his jeans. "Huh?"

"Here. This memory is a couple decades old. But when were you here?"

The thread snapped off. "Two years ago," he said, not meeting Zan's eyes. "With my mom and my brother. She loved books. Libraries, bookstores, anywhere that smelled like paper. Like this." He cracked a smile, but it hurt. "I love them too."

Zan watched him. "I'm sorry," he said quietly.

Bastian shrugged awkwardly and went back to picking at his jeans.

Sighing, Zan pulled the book toward himself. "You tired of melodrama?"

Bastian looked up.

"I kind of brought the mood down. Like, a lot. So . . ." Zan opened the book and rifled through the pages. "Let's do something fun."

Then he tore out a page of priceless, centuries-old paper.

Priceless. Centuries old. Bastian gave him a horrified, wounded look and tried to yank the book back.

"Oh, don't look at me like that," Zan said, holding him off. He crinkled the piece into a ball. "We can come back. You'll see. It will be perfect all over again. Just like new." He let fly the paper and gave a self-satisfied nod as it hit the woman at the display case right in the back of her head. "Come on!"

"Fuck," Bastian said, batting Zan's hands away and finally snatching the book out of his grasp. "Doesn't matter if it's perfect later. You're destroying priceless history now. That's . . ."

"Soulless?" Zan asked, flashing him a grin. "I can't be killed. I can't get in trouble. Definitely a little soulless." Then he launched himself up, grabbed the book, and took off running.

Bastian pushed himself off the floor and gave another scan of the building. Still, no one moved. It was just as dead as the abandoned nuclear reactor. The memory of his mother weighed heavy on his shoulders but watching Zan run through the building, shouts of glee echoing in the perfect acoustics of the space, he couldn't help but feel a strange sort of happiness. No one could see him. Judge him. Be angry at him. Grinning, Bastian sprinted after Zan, catching up within seconds and then tackling him to the ground. Zan yelped, then buried his knee into Bastian's gut, and Bastian wheezed in agony, doubling over and pressing his hands to his stomach.

"Unfair," he groaned, as Zan snatched the book back.

"Chaos, Bastian, chaos!" Zan shouted as he ran, tearing more pages out like an absolute madman.

Bastian stumbled to his feet and took off after him again, shoving him away from the book hard enough that Zan went sprawling across the marble floor. "Chaos, Zan," Bastian snarked back, picking up the book and then running in the other direction.

He swung around a frozen woman, dodged a group of touristy-looking people with pasty faces, threw up his fist and whooped, then veered around the corner and tucked into a small alcove behind an enormous yellowed globe. He swallowed around the sounds of his own gasping and tried to make himself small, invisible. His heart beat so loudly in his ears he was certain Zan could hear it.

There was nothing.

No sound.

Not a footstep, not the sound of a single boy breathing.

Bastian carefully peered around the corner.

"Gotcha," Zan yelped, exploding into view. He grabbed the book from Bastian's hands, threw it on the ground, then kicked it across the floor of the library. It smacked into the side of a pedestal holding a bust of some old, dead white man, slid down, and exploded yellowing pages everywhere.

"Oh my god," Bastian wheezed, bending over his knees and blinking spots from his vision.

Zan watched him, shoulders half raised in some sort of shrug, grin quirked.

"Destroyer of books," Bastian finally said, still breathing hard.

"Nice title," Zan said. "Makes me sound very powerful."

"You're looking at me like I'm supposed to high-five you or something."

"You are such a buzzkill."

"How do you even know the word buzzkill?"

"A dictionary. Stolen from the Library of Congress. I tore some pages from that too. You Americans have a strange grasp of language."

"We . . ." Bastian paused, parsing through the rest of that sentence. "You've been to the Library of Congress?"

"I've been to a couple of big libraries. Amazing really, what some people hold on to. It's the artists, really. You'd think it was the academics who kept these buildings as their top-tier memories, but it's really the artists. The dreamers. I've seen Bibliotheca. National Library of Spain. National Library of Belarus, of Russia . . ."

He held out a hand, ticking fingers off one by one. "The Vatican Library. Alexandria. Royal Library of Ebla, though that was a bit dusty. They were still excavating."

Bastian gaped at him. "You've been to all these places . . . and you're just ripping pages out of the books?"

Zan nudged him with his shoulder. "No. I promise you I was respectful for a while. A decade or so. After that?" His green eyes sparkled. "Gets boring. Gotta make my own entertainment. But I've brought a lot of them back. The bookcases in my office only hold so many things, so I cycle. I got bored in my first hundred years, so I picked up some languages, did some studying. History gets boring after a while. Repeats itself and so on. Now I mostly read for pleasure. Or for destruction. Either or, depending on the day."

Bastian tried to parse through this. Libraries. Endless libraries. Stealing endless books. The idea was so much better than he could imagine—so much better than his moldy, little bookstore. "How many languages do you speak?"

Cocking his head, Zan rubbed the back of his neck. "Seven, I think? Wait, no, eight. English, obviously, French, Italian, Mandarin, Turkish, Persian. I have a very basic knowledge of some Arabic. And Greek, although not in any dialect people are familiar with now. I suppose it would be easy enough to learn contemporary . . ." His face shuttered. "Not interested, though. Why? You?"

"English."

"How exciting."

"Yeah, fuck you. I've taken seven years of French, so there, you can count that too."

"*Merveilleux, quelle culture tu possèdes!*" Zan rattled off.

"*Tu n'ès pas aussi intelligent que tu le penses.* And your accent is *horrible.*"

Cracking a grin, Zan held his hands up in mock defeat. "Fair enough. Kind of hard when you don't have anyone to *actually converse with*."

"Point taken," Bastian conceded. "You get people from all over the world here?"

Zan nodded.

"So how do you speak to them?"

"Oh." Zan looked mildly curious. "I think it's just a general . . . dead river thing. I mean, we're not exactly following Earth rules or anything. They hear me how they want to hear me. And most of the time . . ." He frowned, looking sad again. "They don't really have any interest in listening to what I say anyway. Sometimes I wonder if it really matters that they understand me at all." He picked up another book and ripped out a page, crumpling it in the palm of his hand and then throwing it toward the center of the room.

Bastian watched it hit one of the frozen guests. He spun slowly, taking in the whole space again. There were no windows in the room—no sunlight to damage the books—only artfully painted walls to create the illusion of sun. The overhead lighting was dim as well, but the light directly over the statue fell on the book, highlighting the dark-brown leather. There were dust motes there, hanging in the spray of light, as perfectly still as the people around them. Bastian shuddered. "There's another room past this one," he said, tearing his gaze away from the stagnant air. "Old chapel or something. My mom was really into it when we were here." He turned and pointed toward a pair of ornate doors, wood polished to a glossy sheen.

Zan grabbed his arm. "No."

Bastian paused. "Not part of this memory?"

"Styx is behind that door," Zan confirmed, eyes going hard and flinty. "The man who this memory belongs to . . . that's where I brought him to die. That's where the Ferryman is waiting." He took a deep breath in, shaking his head as his face softened again. "There's better stuff in here anyway. Like this." He turned and shoved the enormous globe off the pedestal.

The crash was loud enough to vibrate in Bastian's shoes.

Bastian winced. "So destructive," he moaned.

Zan breathed out, eyes flickering with something like relief. "Everything else is boring," he said. Then he cupped his hands to his mouth. "Boring!"

This word boomed, too, so many times it was dizzying.

"Great acoustics," he stage-whispered.

"Clearly."

Zan reached into his pocket, drew out another piece of crumpled paper torn from a priceless artifact, and threw it at Bastian's face. "Come on!"

He took off toward the front of the hall again, nearly topping the woman over in his haste to get to the shelves stuffed with books. Bastian looked back to the doors. He remembered a small chapel back there, with an enormous organ, and rows upon rows of pews. His mother had sat there, looking up at the instrument, a bemused smile on her lips. They didn't go to church, but it sure felt a lot like prayer.

Another crash resounded through the hall, and Bastian looked to see Zan pulling down armfuls of books, destroying shelves, kicking pages and dust all over the place. Bastian cupped his hands to his mouth. "Stop!"

"Make me!" Zan yelled back.

Bastian groaned and ran after him. Zan threw books, Bastian picked them up and tried to jam them back on shelves, and they laughed until Bastian began to fade.

CHAPTER THIRTY-FIVE

Styx

The black seeped into the office, roiling underneath bookshelves, dripping from empty candlesticks, between glass beads, staining the floor.

Zan swallowed hard, setting down the Switch console and then carefully setting papers over it, hoping more than anything that the Ferryman wouldn't notice the animated game and ask about where it came from. Ask about Bastian.

It gelled slowly, oily beads clinging to the hardwood floor, climbing up the legs of the desk, leaking over the sides onto Zan's papers as they pulled together, forming first a gnarled hand, then a withered arm, billowing robes, paper-thin skin layered over black veins that wriggled. "He has not passed over," the Ferryman spat from the brittle bone jaw of a void-black skull.

Shuddering, Zan pushed away from the desk and slowly stood. "I'm trying," he said. His mouth was so dry, speaking the words was almost impossible. "The barrier . . . it . . ." He cleared his throat. He'd practiced the excuse over and over and still wasn't quite able to force through it. "The barrier is never close in his memories," Zan lied. "I can't bring him over until it thins."

"Lies," the Ferryman drawled, voice dripping with sweetness, orbital bones so liquid black they ate all the light in the room. "The barrier has never proven a problem before."

Zan swallowed hard.

"And yet you do not deliver his soul. Is our deal over, then?"

"No!" Zan's palms were starting to sweat, and he wiped at his pants for a moment, before shoving them deep into his pockets. The Ferryman stared at them still, the crinkles around his eyes deepening as he smiled.

Zan chewed on the inside of his cheek and forced himself to still.

"One hundred twenty-six years," the Ferryman said.

Zan nodded, feeling sick to his stomach. One hundred and twenty-six years was the longest anyone before Zan had lasted. It was a fact that the Ferryman liked to throw in Zan's face any-time Zan was feeling particularly belligerent or uncooperative. Everyone had broken. *Everyone.* There was not a single soul who had outlasted the Ferryman's bargain; they had all tried; they had all eventually given in to death. Zan was different. Zan was an anomaly.

Zan was so tired, but his will had always been strong. Until now.

"You are fascinated with this creature. This human."

"No."

"Yes. Yes, I think you are. Humans are so intriguing to me. They are desperate to speak, not so desperate to listen. They only want to be seen, to be heard, to have someone embrace them and tell them what a good person they are, what a good job they've done. You want this, too, but you are no longer human."

I am, Zan wanted to say, but his throat had closed. *I am all of those things.*

"You act like them, you think like them, but you are not them. You have lived too long. You are something out of time. Lost. Pathetic. You belong here with me."

The Ferryman's robes slithered along the floor, wisps of black congealing to form a bed of serpents at his feet. "You are special," the Ferryman said after some consideration. He stepped closer, leaving oily black footprints that smeared into the wood. "You alone have lasted long enough to become practiced at this job. You are quick, you are merciless, you lead the lost souls, and I take them."

The word *merciless* sank like a stone in Zan's gut. "You have to let me go," he pleaded. "You promised. You swore you'd let me go free if I reached the end—"

The Ferryman's eyes narrowed. "And I keep my promises. But only if you fulfill the bargain."

A drip of sweat gathered at the top of Zan's forehead and finally dropped, rolling down his nose. His glasses slid with it. He didn't push them up because he didn't want the Ferryman to see how his hands were starting to shake as a slow realization burbled to the surface. "You don't have anyone but me," he murmured.

The Ferryman undulated, black dripping down his weathered face and staining the floorboards. "What did you say?" he growled.

Zan tried to moisten his lips enough to speak. "You don't," he whispered. "No one worships the old gods anymore. No one has tried to call you. You have no one else but me. You can't kill me because you *need* me."

The Ferryman's mouth curled into a wicked smile. "You know *nothing,*" he hissed. He hooked a dripping hand into the collar of Zan's Tigers sweatshirt, pulling him close. His breath was foul and rotten. "There are always souls ready to serve. So tell me, Alexander. Will this boy be the reason you fail?"

Zan gulped. "No." The word was heavy, a steel ball, a terrible weight torn from inside his chest.

"He was supposed to die," the Ferryman said. "Do your job, or you are mine."

Zan gave a small nod. The Ferryman's smile grew, and he let go. The black lost its form, dripping from his fingers, his brow, his poison-tipped smile. It seeped under the floorboards and under the cement door. It was only when the last of the dregs were gone that Zan numbly pulled out his chair and sat at his desk. He opened the laptop. Pulled up the chart. His hand nudged against the Switch, and the tinny, synthesized music of the Nintendo game started playing, muted from underneath the stack of papers. He tried to focus his eyes on the thousands of names on the screen as he scrolled.

He couldn't.

It didn't matter what the Ferryman said, Zan knew he was right. There was no one else. No other soul willing to serve, no one able to guide souls to the river.

The epiphany was a hollow thing. At best, Zan would deliver Bastian just like he was supposed to and be set free. At worst? He stood up and walked to the back bookshelf, trying to force his shoulders to relax. He reached up and carefully took down the tiny crystal fox, holding it between his hands, letting his palms warm the glass before carrying it back to the desk. Sitting back down in his chair, Zan set the fox next to the laptop, then forced a shaking hand to the keyboard. Typed in Bastian Barnes under Name. Clicked the cursor to Location of Death. Watched it blink.

CHAPTER THIRTY-SIX

Portland, Oregon

Bastian leaned against the front window watching mayhem unfold on the street as car horns beeped and honked loud enough for hackles to rise. The Fastsigns truck clogged the street right in front of the store, and even though there was a person lethargically waving a flag at the end of the street, the usually empty lane was now filled to the brim with traffic.

He sighed. Dorian, Riley, and Mathais had all managed to have finals scheduled on the last day of classes. Bastian had lucked out and finished yesterday, leaving him free to watch the final touches of his store go up.

Another driver laid on the horn for a full seven seconds.

Bastian winced, wishing that this could go a little faster.

The Fastsigns guys didn't seem to care. One loitered outside smoking a cigarette; the other two slowly piled equipment out on the sidewalk.

Guy with the cigarette finally ground it out underneath his boot before turning toward the store. A moment later, the bells jingled.

"Mr. Barnes?"

Bastian pushed off from the window and walked to the front. "Yep."

"Be a couple hours, then we'll get out of your hair."

Gritting his teeth, Bastian gave him a tight nod. Everyone on this block was going to kill him.

"Cool," the guy said, then he walked back out the door.

Bastian circled the counter and pulled out the stool. He sat down on it—one foot propped on the top rung, the other on the floor. Slumping down over the counter, he surveyed the store.

So much had changed in so little time.

The floors were completely done. The entire place smelled less like dust and more like wood stain, which wasn't necessarily an improvement in an olfactory sense, but certainly looked nicer. The fiction section had been put back entirely to rights. There were still stacks of books on the floor butting up next to every bookshelf and winding their way around all of the walkways, but now they were there with purpose. Now they looked homey, not dilapidated.

Everything was brighter. The sun came in through the newly installed windows and illuminated the shining wood bookcases. The countertops had been wiped clean, and there was a brand-new register sitting at the front, though it was still in its box because Bastian was too scared of breaking it to even think about opening it up.

Bastian ran his fingers over the packing tape on the box, and his eyes caught on the tiny plastic container of business cards.

Fox Books
Used and Collectible Books | Portland, OR
(503) 823-4087 | hello@foxbooks.com

A tiny orange fox sat on the edge, his tail curling out around the letters of Fox Books. Renee's branding had turned out absolutely perfect.

A loud, raucous hammering started up right outside the door. Bastian sighed. He took out his phone and started texting.

Bastian [2:34 PM]: You out of class?

It took a couple minutes of listening to the ear-splitting drilling outside before his phone buzzed.

Riley [2:36 PM]: Now I am. What's up?

Bastian [2:36 PM]: Bored. Come over?

Riley [2:37 PM]: Is Dorian invited?

Bastian sighed, then kept typing.

Bastian [2:37 PM]: Yeah

Riley [2:37 PM]: Sweet, getting food, then on our way. BTW I rocked my Physics final obviously, thanks for asking, I'm DONE! Party time!

Bastian [2:38 PM]: Don't tell that to Dorian the prude

Riley [2:38 PM]: 😙 🎉 🍆

Bastian [2:38 PM]: You don't even like eggplants

Riley [2:38 PM]: 🍆 🍆 🍆 🍆

Bastian set down his phone and grinned. The drill started up again, so he pushed off the counter and headed to the back office in hopes of a little more quiet. Cat was hiding back there, too, and was all too happy to jump into Bastian's lap the moment he sank down on the couch.

His arm started to tingle. "No sleeping," Bastian murmured to Cat. "Just sitting."

Cat headbutted him in the chin.

Even with the noise from outside that still filtered in back here, Bastian was having a hard time keeping his eyes open. Lately, all he could think about was what Zan was doing. If he was playing

Animal Crossing instead of *FreeCell*. If he thought of Bastian like Bastian thought of him.

The bells on the door jingled, and Bastian blinked.

"Dude!" Riley yelled.

Bastian gave a quick headshake and looked down at his phone. Somehow, forty-five minutes had passed. He hadn't been sleeping, but he hadn't been awake. His arm was numb.

"Bash!" She yelled again.

He could hear the mumble of Dorian's voice alongside her and a burst of laughter from Mathais. Cat jumped off his lap. Bastian stood up and wandered out to the store.

"Last day of classes!" she complained. "And you're nowhere in sight!"

"To be fair, I didn't have any finals today," Bastian said. "Finished everything yesterday." And totally bombed them all. Bastian didn't want to think about what his report card was going to look like when it came.

"Still had class," Mathais said. "Last day of classes with no finals is the best. You probably had movies all day! You missed out, man." He held out a fist—Bastian bumped it.

Dorian gave him a terse nod, then grumpily stated, "I need puzzle books."

Before Bastian could answer, he disappeared around the corner of a shelf. Mathais heaved a groan, then followed him. Bastian could hear them walking toward the back of the store, mumbling in hushed voices the entire way.

"He's grumpy that you didn't show at school," Riley said. "But I told him he had to behave, because you actually sat for your finals, which, let's be honest, is more than any of us thought you'd do."

"How nice," Bastian said dryly.

She rolled her eyes. "You two are impossible."

Bastian ignored her. She stepped up to the counter.

"Are those . . ." Her eyes widened as she grabbed a card. "Oh wow. Wow. They look really good!"

"Thanks," he mumbled.

"I'm sorry, what was that?"

Bastian scowled. "Thanks. For crushing on some girl and blackmailing her sister into designing me a logo."

Riley kicked at him. "You are so ungrateful. I couldn't see the sign yet, your big, burly installation dudes were all blocking it! Does it look amazing?"

Shrugging, Bastian snagged the card back from her and pushed it into the container. "They're supposed to be done in an hour or so. You'll see it soon enough."

"And then you'll open?"

He looked down at his hands. The opening plan was iffy at best and relied entirely on one thing—one thing he hadn't yet shared with his friends or Dorian.

Not dying.

"After winter break," he said quietly. "Missing the holiday rush, which sucks. But I'm planning to open January sixth."

"Jeez, fast!" She exclaimed. "You've got to get employees, Bash! You need to interview people!"

"I don't," he muttered. "Not yet. Doubt we'll have that many customers."

"Yeah, but come January, you'll be in school during the day. You can't just open a couple of hours every afternoon. You'll need the all-day coverage, right?"

"Right . . ." Bastian hedged.

"So you'll need—"

"I'm working on it."

Riley's eyes narrowed. She leaned forward, elbows on the counter. Blowing a piece of hair out of her eyes, she fixed him with a suspicious stare. "How?"

"So . . . party tomorrow night?"

"Don't change the subject, jerk."

Bastian gave her a false smile. "Look, I'll let you know the store details when I figure it all out. Okay?"

She scowled at him but eventually shook her head and gave it up. "Party tomorrow night," she confirmed. Her eyes narrowed. "You actually going to go? Thought you hated Greer."

"Last time I checked, you hated him too."

Riley laughed. "Yeah, but I'm popular. Regular socialite and all. Gotta hobnob with the kiddos. Networking, Bash, networking." She backed off of the counter and pulled out her knitting needles. She'd finished the last scarf a few weeks ago and was now working on something that looked like a cross between a sock and an amorphous manatee.

Bastian sighed. He was so tired. Tired of feeling like he never fit in anywhere. With Zan, it was easy. In real life? Being him sucked.

"Come," Riley said. "Worst-case scenario, you're bored out of your mind, and you leave. I think you'll have fun, though."

He wouldn't even need Zan at that point. Dorian would kill him fast. "Dorian—"

"Bash, when have you ever done what Dorian wanted? He's crazy uptight about his early decision college stuff so cut him some slack."

"And you're not?"

Riley shrugged. "It's all done already. Pointless to worry when I can't change anything. Ergo, I'm going to show up at Greer's and watch our classmates make fools of themselves and hopefully find a cute girl to make out with. Come with me. Maybe you can kiss someone too." She gave him a devious grin.

Shaking his head, Bastian reached across the counter and grabbed his sweatshirt from where he'd thrown it earlier that day. "Not going," he muttered. "I'm going to have an amazing time reading a book and not watching a bunch of rich assholes get trashed while kissing random people." *Not when I'd rather be kissing Zan*, he thought, then froze. Where did that come from?

Bastian ran his tongue along his teeth, suddenly feeling like he was too hot for his skin. Kissing Zan. Now *there* was a conversation starter. *Hey, so I apparently already have my sights set on someone else. He's five hundred years old. Cute glasses though and snarky like you. You'd get along. You know. If he was living.*

Insert twenty curse words and a punch to the face here.

"You are boring," Riley said primly, interrupting Bastian's spiral into complete insanity.

"Yeah, well . . ." Bastian wriggled into the soft black of his Ghostbusters hoodie, trying to pull sense back into his stupid, stupid brain. "You have fun being a socialite."

"Who's being a socialite?" Dorian asked, stepping up next to them.

"Who do you think?" Bastian muttered.

Riley harumphed them both, then pushed off the counter and disappeared behind a wall of books. Dorian didn't move, just stood there, awkwardly playing with the collar of his shirt.

"What?" Bastian asked.

"I'm going to Mom's grave on Sunday morning," he said quietly. His eyes flicked up to Bastian's. "Come?"

Bastian couldn't breathe. Somewhere behind a bookcase, Riley and Mathais had engaged in a battle over which Marvel movie was the best Marvel movie.

"Bash?"

He forced his eyes back to Dorian who stood there, pink polo shirt collar flipped, keys dangling from his hand, hair mussed in exactly the carefully curated way girls liked hair to be mussed.

"I know you still won't . . ." Dorian's eyes flicked toward the car. "Look. We'll go slow. You can maybe . . . drive? A little? If you want? My therapist said it would be good for you—"

"No," Bastian said, suddenly furious that Dorian's therapist was discussing Bastian's well-being.

"Okay. I was hoping you'd come."

Bastian didn't want to. He *really* didn't want to. Their mother was buried at a god-awful cemetery in Oakland, California—chosen by her socialite grandmother who Bastian and Dorian had never even met and okayed by Aunt Bri. It was a ten-hour drive from Portland; the only time he'd been was for the funeral service, and all he could remember was the foggy feeling from the painkillers they'd given at the hospital, the sound of the coffin lowering, and the disgusting smell of the public restroom in the main building where he'd thrown up more than once.

He wasn't exactly keen on repeating any part of that experience, so he'd never been back. And no amount of Dorian's therapist's advice was going to change that.

"I can pick you up?" Dorian asked. "Sunday morning around six? From the store?"

He wasn't pleading, but he sounded hopeful.

"Okay," Bastian said, because Sunday was two days away. There was more than enough time to find an excuse not to go.

Riley cracked some joke about frost giants, and Mathais's booming laughter echoed through the store.

Dorian smiled, big and bright. "Thank you," he said.

Bastian's eyes slid past Dorian's out the window. "I want a doughnut. I'll be back."

He left Dorian at the counter and walked out the door. The hammering and drilling stopped. He looked up at the sign guys who'd just put up the last S.

Fox Books, the sign read. Renee's branding brought to life in glorious orange lettering.

"What do you think?" one of the sign guys called down.

Bastian thought it was perfect. He thought it was more than he ever could have hoped for, that it was a dream come true, that it made him want to *live*.

CHAPTER THIRTY-SEVEN

Portland, Oregon

Joon finished up the next day, and Bastian wrote him a check for the remaining balance. It felt good. Right. He was down to the very last dregs of his funds, which was concerning, but looking around the store, he was jittery and excited. It looked a little like his favorite bookstore growing up and a lot like a place he wanted to lose himself in.

He thought of Zan, running through the Klementinum, Zan with his dozens of memories of libraries, frozen in time.

Bring Zan through a memory of this. Show him while you still can.

That thought made Bastian's palms go sweaty.

He thanked Joon, waved him out the front door, then locked it. Cat wound around his ankles, meowing for food. Bastian groaned but headed up the stairs and grabbed a can of cat food. He popped it open, dumped it in a dish, and his phone buzzed.

New email from Preston Academy.

The world shuddered to a halt as Bastian opened it and stared at the screen.

English: F

French: F

History, chemistry, calculus: F, F, F. Even the psychology elective he'd taken as an easy way out had only garnered him a C.

He'd known he was failing. He'd known that he stopped trying, that he didn't care anymore, that he showed up to sit for the finals just because it made Dorian less stressy and therefore less likely to show up at the store after hours and throw a hissy fit.

But seeing it flash in front of him on the screen, the Courier typeface underneath the sharp cut of Preston letterhead, made him feel absolutely worthless.

Chewing his lip bloody, Bastian tried to ignore the way his stomach had suddenly dropped all the way to his toes. He clicked out of the link only to find another email from the dean front and center, laying out options for him going forward. Summer school after next semester. Work with a guidance counselor. Repeat senior year.

No.

Meow? Cat asked.

"Yeah," Bastian murmured. "I'm fucked."

If he was lucky, they'd sent the email the same day they sent the physical letters, which gave him a couple days head start on Dorian finding out. Pretend like he scraped by, everything was fine. Get the mail forwarded to the bookstore.

He studied the bruise crawling up his arm. No matter how bright Zan's smile, how sparkling green his eyes, Bastian was under no illusions that this was going to work out in his favor. Zan would eventually force him to the river. There was no good reason not to. Bastian was playing with borrowed time.

And it was stupid to be upset about it, because for so long he'd wanted this. For so long he'd been convinced that he should have been the one to die.

Swallowing down nausea, Bastian closed out the email and pulled up Riley's number.

Bastian [8:49 PM]: You leave yet?

Riley [8:53 PM]: Uh...for the party?

Bastian [8:53 PM]: Yeah

He needed to go somewhere. He needed noise, and chaos, and a place to disappear—he couldn't stand the silence of the bookstore anymore. The beautiful flooring and perfect business cards he'd been so in love with just moments ago suddenly felt so stupid and irresponsible. He couldn't even pass high school. And what the hell was *Dorian* of all people going to do with a bookstore when Bastian died?

Sell it again, just like Riley had suggested on the first day he'd shown her.

Everything he'd done was pointless.

Riley [8:55 PM]: Yeah, I left, wait, are you coming? BASH! People are already trashed, come judge them all with me

Cat meowed at his feet, but Bastian ignored him. He typed out a quick *on my way*, pushed himself up from his makeshift desk, grabbed his sweatshirt, and shrugged into it on his way down the stairs.

CHAPTER THIRTY-EIGHT

Portland, Oregon

The street was already vibrating with the low bass growl of the music when Bastian stepped up. It did nothing for the persistent headache that pounded behind his eyes, or the nausea that was churning in his gut.

Greer's townhouse was on a street lined with a dozen other perfect cookie-cutter townhouses. It was on a street that looked like it should be filled with lawyers, doctors, and other business types, except these houses were so new that no one else had even moved in yet. Rumor had it, his parents owned the entire block. Rumor had it, his parents were part of the Mafia. Rumor had it his parents were investing drug money into real estate, were investment tycoons, were best friends with Elon Musk, were using the townhomes as secret laboratories to illegally experiment on cute animals, were wanted by the FBI, were the FBI—

Rumor was more exciting than reality. Greer came from way too much money, and people with way too much money spent it on stupid shit.

"Bash!" Riley called from the front door. She eased out onto the step, Mathais following like a wounded puppy as he clutched an ice pack to his cheek. "Oh my god, I've never once seen you at a party by choice, this is awesome!"

Mathais stumbled over and high-fived Bastian. He lifted the ice pack, revealing an enormous purpling bruise across his cheekbone.

"What happened?" Bastian asked.

"Fight?" Mathais offered.

Riley rolled her eyes. "As if. He got hit in the face with the door."

"The *door*?"

"Wouldn't open," Mathais grunted.

"Aka he was determined to open it for a bunch of really drunk girls, only he'd also been drinking, and apparently didn't realize that the door pulled, not pushed, so he was pushing with all his might, took a step back, someone came through the door the right way, and it smacked him in the face."

Bastian eyed Mathais suspiciously. "How long have you been here?"

"Literally fifteen minutes," Riley said. "Apparently he pre-gamed with the football team."

Mathais moaned, swayed a little, then plopped down on the sidewalk and started gagging.

"Nice," Bastian said.

"He's going to go sleep it off in the car."

"Sounds safe."

"Yeah, well, I'm not driving him back right now. His dad will kill him. I called Dorian. I didn't tell him *you* were coming so maybe if you're nice, I'll keep that on the down-low or whatever it is I'm supposed to do while you pretend he doesn't exist."

Bastian grimaced over the sounds of Mathais still gagging.

"Thanks. See you inside?"

She flashed him a thumbs-up. "Don't pull a Mathais before I get back. I'll find you in a minute." She nudged Mathais with her boot. He managed to blearily flip her off from his hunched position over the concrete before forcing himself back up to his feet.

"Be back," she said cheerfully, prodding him along.

"Yep," Bastian said. He watched them wobble down the street, then stepped up to the front porch and pushed open the door.

The music was unbearably loud now.

He only recognized a couple of people from school. The rest were college students—some sporting PSU gear; others way too old to be still in high school. He pushed his way through the crowd into the kitchen where a clump of girls was mixing drinks. Someone pushed a red cup into his hands, and he looked down at the suspiciously pink liquid. Someone else bumped into him, and it sloshed over his fingers, sticky and syrupy, and smelling like vodka.

He took a sip.

Tasted like vodka too.

Bastian shuddered and drank more, ignoring the burn in his throat. The music changed, the beat dropped, and a crowd of people cheered. Bastian swallowed down the last of the disgusting juice, shoved his way to the back counter, and filled it again.

"Trying to die?"

Bastian flinched, barely keeping himself from spilling all over the front of his shirt. Greer leaned against the counter next to him, holding a glass filled with something caramel colored. His cheeks were flushed, and his eyes were so vibrant that Bastian couldn't look away.

Bastian took another swallow of pink, blinking owlishly.

237

"Trying to forget."

"Anything in particular?"

"Your face."

"Oooo drunk Bash is fun Bash." Greer grinned wickedly at him.

Someone else shoved between them, holding out a cup. Greer easily sidled out of the way just long enough for them to fill it, then stepped in even closer the moment they were gone.

The alcohol was already sitting warm in Bastian's belly, the frantic buzzing in his head finally settling, limbs finally going wonderfully loose. He didn't need to worry about grades, or Zan, or being a total failure when his entire body felt liquid. "You got something stronger?" he asked.

Greer's smile grew. He wrapped arm around Bastian's shoulders and pulled him close, guiding him out of the kitchen. "Roof," he said.

They walked out into the living room. The front door opened, and Bastian saw Riley step back in. Her eyes narrowed as she mouthed *you okay?* He nodded at her and waved as they walked past.

The flimsy metal stairs up to the roof started at the back landing of the townhouse and crept along the brick, zigzagging their way to the top. Bastian tucked himself in as close to the building as he could and climbed. There was no wind, just a muggy, humid heat, and suddenly all he could think about was Zan sitting at the top of his reactor, feet hanging down, eyes closed, head thrown back watching the dead sky.

"You coming?" Greer called.

The stairs clanged as Bastian forced one foot in front of the other, trying not to look down through the metal grates of the steps.

The actual roof was a flat expanse with a single shed on one end and an exhaust pipe right in the middle. It was high enough to see over the entire Portland State campus—high enough that Bastian kept his distance from the sides.

Half of the space was littered with the cardboard shells of fireworks that they'd probably exploded earlier. It still smelled vaguely of metallic gunpowder. Greer held up a finger to Bastian, then walked over to a group milling around the debris and announced something about the arrival of a keg.

The group dispersed. Bastian listened to the metal clang of the steps and purposely walked straight toward the middle of the roof and sat down against the exhaust pipe, splaying one leg out and curling an arm around the other while sipping at his disgusting drink.

Greer waited until the last of the teenagers had left before casually sauntering over with all the grace of a predatory cat.

Predictable.

He pulled a pack of cigarettes from one pocket, a lighter from the other. Lit the cigarette.

"You are being awfully sociable," he said, crouching down on his haunches. He reached out and plucked the red cup from Bastian's hands and set it down.

Bastian scowled. "Point?"

"More sociable than usual."

"You don't know my usual."

"I know that you've never come to a party of mine before. I know that you keep your head down in the hallways and you try your hardest not to be noticed. You're a mouse. Quiet, quiet, mouse." He inhaled once, then puffed a stream of cigarette smoke into the night. It hung paralyzed between the two for a moment before dissipating into the humid air.

"Not a mouse," Bastian said. He was trying not to slur his words. He'd only had two cups of the punch, but he remembered Riley saying that if you were aware of trying not to slur, then you were already drunk. Was he drunk? The gravel of the rooftop was mostly gray, but there were a couple of shiny pieces of granite mixed in. Bastian picked a white one up, rubbing his fingers along the sharp edge.

His fingers closed around Zan's, curling them around the stone.

Bastian blinked, letting the rock fall to the ground. Greer was still watching him. "Been a bad week," Bastian finally admitted.

Greer dug through the gravel and came up with his own rock, then threw it. Bastian watched it soar over the edge of the building and out of sight. He wondered if Greer knew how to skip rocks, then frowned, shaking his head like he could throw off the thought entirely.

"Girl troubles?" Greer mocked.

Bastian reached for his cup, but Greer knocked it over with his hand. Pink syrup spilled out over the rocks.

"That stuff is disgusting," Greer said.

Tipping his head back, Bastian looked up. More stars had winked their way out onto the night sky. Everything was the damp of an impending storm, even though there were no clouds. The smoke from Greer's cigarette curled toward the sky. Bastian shivered.

Greer offered the cigarette.

"Pass."

"You're the one who asked me for something stronger. You're the one who followed me up here." Greer smirked.

"A cigarette isn't stronger," Bastian snapped. He didn't know what he was thinking. In the grand scheme of all of his terrible decisions, this was right up there with one of the worst.

Greer nudged his knee.

Bastian opened his eyes. Greer had a flask in his hand, the same one from the night at the party.

"What's in it?" Bastian asked.

"Do you really care?" Greer unscrewed the cap. His cigarette hung lazily from the corner of his mouth, and he tugged it free to take a long drink. "No more bad week," he said.

Bastian watched him swallow. He slowly reached out and took the flask.

"Down the hatch," Greer murmured.

Bastian winced at the burn of whiskey as he drank, only stopping when Greer yanked the flask away from his fingers.

"Jesus," he scolded, but his voice was warm with something like respect.

Bastian just shrugged, then leaned back and watched the stars again. His mother loved the stars. She used to wake them up, drag them outside in the early hours before dawn just to watch the asteroid showers. She knew the constellations. He wished he knew the constellations.

Zan's laptop was full of stars.

He blinked his eyes open as Greer started to laugh.

"You're out of it," he said, mouth stretching over vowels, releasing each syllable slowly like syrup.

Bastian looked past him, toward the rippling stars in the sky. There were people on the roof again, and he frowned, but it wasn't easy; he had to focus every muscle on his face to make it feel right.

There were people on the roof again, and he'd lost time.

He had lost time, but he hadn't gone to Styx.

Bastian dragged in a breath, then another, then another as the world moved sluggishly around him. He picked up his hand, staring at it as he wiggled each finger. He couldn't help feeling like he had to move, to speak, to exist in a way that mattered, to be noticed and not forgotten. The sky was full of stars, but it was also full of blue, and black, and purple, and night, and darkness, and light, and beauty, and—

"I'm going to die," Bastian said, because it slipped from his mouth before he could stop it.

"We're all going to die, B," Greer said breezily.

Bastian stood. He walked to the edge of the roof, and stepped out onto the ledge, and put one foot in front of the other, like Zan on top of a reactor, one step at a time, all the way to the Ferryman.

He blinked, and Greer was pulling him back, laughing maniacally. Then he was kicking firework debris off the roof and watching the pieces flutter down, he was downstairs in the kitchen swallowing down more pink, he was in a hallway, pressed up against a girl wearing too much eyeliner, he was kissing her, he wished she had glasses, he wished she were *Zan*.

Time kept slipping through his fingers like sand, and Bastian didn't care.

He didn't care, he didn't care, *he didn't care*—

His phone wouldn't stop buzzing so he took it out of his pocket and threw it on the couch.

The girl kept following him around, and he liked that because even though she wore too much eyeliner, she was pretty, and her name was Averie, but with an *ie*, not a *y*, and he thought that was pretty too.

He told her so. She smiled and kissed him harder, and he liked that, he—

The music kept changing, faster and faster and faster, and Bastian didn't like to dance, but he thought Averie with an *ie* did, so he danced, and he thought Averie with an *ie* was kissing him, but it tasted like cigarette smoke so maybe it was just Greer, everything led back to Greer.

Was this happiness? Was this what he was supposed to feel? There was too much color, and motion, and sound, and life—

His arm was numb.

Riley was near him, and then Riley was clutching him, and then Riley was pulling him down another hallway and pushing him up against the wall, and it was hilarious that she was able to hold him there because she was tiny, he had six inches on her, there was no way—

". . . going to kill you . . ." she was saying.

She had some sort of shimmering gold dust brushed across her eyelids and cheeks, and the light kept hitting it every time she turned her head. Sparkle, sparkle, "sparkle," he murmured.

Something pinched his arm, and he looked down to find her fingers wrapped around his wrist, gold-painted fingernails digging in.

"This was supposed to be fun, this wasn't supposed to be Riley-takes-care-of-her-gang-of-drunk-boys," she hissed.

"Notdrunk," Bastian managed to slur.

"Hilarious," she deadpanned. She tried to drag him farther down the hall, toward the back door that would lead to the outside, and he did not want to be outside. Outside was not the fun-side. Inside was the fun-side. He was pretty sure he was laughing.

"Oh my god," she muttered, pulling harder.

He yanked his arm back, everything swayed, he barely caught himself against the wall before falling over. "'m fine," he said blearily.

"I'm getting Dorian."

"No, I'm . . . just . . . no failing this way. People like me now. I'm . . . good."

She rose up on the balls of her feet, got right in his face. "Bash Barnes, knock it off. Now!"

The gold shimmer softened her edges, but he couldn't miss the fury in her eyes. "No," he murmured, stepping sideways.

Her hand snaked out, faster than Bastian could track. She grabbed his wrist, trying to pull him toward her, and he tried to yank back, but her fingers had slipped underneath his bracelet, and the twine tore.

It wasn't slow motion, wasn't like the movies when there is one moment when everything is fine, and the next, heart-wrenching moment twists so slowly you almost think you have the power to take it all back.

It was just a piece of old string that finally snapped. And dropped to the floor.

Bastian was pretty sure he was still laughing, but there were razorblades in his lungs, scraping against his flesh with every breath.

"Shit," Riley said, hand going to her mouth. "I'm sorry . . . Bash—"

Bastian opened his mouth, and laughter poured out. It was nothing. It was a stupid bracelet, and it held no magic, because wishing bracelets were for children, he was so stupid, he was such a stupid idiot, and he couldn't stop laughing. There was nothing here for him. He didn't know why he'd been trying so hard for *this*.

His legs tangled, and he fell toward the wall again, but then someone else was there, someone who smelled like sulfur and bad decisions.

"Greer." Bastian grinned.

"Asshole," Riley said, shoving at him and trying to get closer to Bastian.

"Babe," Greer whispered in Bastian's ear.

Bastian's eyes slid past him, catching Riley's in the dim light of the hallway. "Go away," he said. Then he pushed up from the wall and spun, following Greer, lips pressing against Greer's, because he had nothing else.

But Zan—

He had *nothing else.*

CHAPTER THIRTY-NINE

Styx

The doorway stood in front of him, chalked lines on cement, light glowing from underneath the frame. It creaked open, revealing Zan at his desk, dark curls falling messily over his glasses, fingers clenched tight around the Nintendo. The screen lit the moment he saw Bastian, the moment his lips pulled into a smile.

Bastian wanted to cry. Breathing hurt. Grief was clogging his chest. He wanted to stop feeling, he wanted to stop—

"Bash?" Zan asked.

He couldn't do this.

Bastian sank down to the floor, legs splaying out in front of him. He screwed up. *Again.* He barked a sudden laugh, so broken and shattered he clapped a hand over his mouth before another could escape.

"Shit," Zan muttered. He hurried around the desk and crouched next to Bastian. "What's wrong?"

Bastian wondered if he'd passed out at the party like he'd passed out at Trivia Night. He wondered if anyone there would even care.

He dragged in a hiccupy-sounding breath. Fuck, now he was crying. "I'm ready," he whispered. "You can take me now, I'm ready."

Zan's entire face fell. He sank down on his knees. He didn't touch Bastian, just sat there, motionless and immovable.

"I failed," Bastian ground out. He rubbed his eyes and tried to suck in another breath. Everything hurt.

"You failed?" Zan finally asked quietly.

"School. High school. Life, too, I guess." He threw his head back again and gave another laugh-sob. "I couldn't take it, so I went to this party, and got trashed, and I'm a mess . . . I . . ." He scrubbed a hand over his eyes, willing them to stop burning. "I didn't want you to be just as disappointed in me as everyone else, but here I am."

Zan nudged him. "I'm not disappointed in you."

Bastian's hand went to his wrist, went to pick at his bracelet, but it was gone.

Gone.

Bastian dropped his hands to his lap and looked back to Zan with hooded eyes. "My bracelet broke," he stammered. "It was . . . fuck, it's so stupid. It was a tradition. With my mom. Three wishes, three knots, when it falls off, they come true. Except they never come true because it's something children believe in, not adults, and it's just so fucking stupid. But it . . ." He tucked his head back down and swallowed. His throat felt swollen and scratchy. He just wanted to see his mom again. He closed his arms around his knees and tried to stop crying. "Can I?" he pleaded. "See her just once? Before we go, can I see my mom one more time?"

Zan watched him, uncertainty flickering behind his eyes. Slowly, he pushed off from the floor and walked back over to the desk. He grabbed the keys and fiddled with the first couple. "I don't know if this is a good idea—"

"I just want to see her," Bastian said. He wiped his eyes and reached a shaking hand out, desperate to have the keys in his hand before he could change his mind.

Zan handed them over and cleared his throat. "I can't let you go alone. I'm sorry, I . . ." He bowed his head and scratched at the back of his neck.

Bastian's stomach sank. "It's okay," he said quickly, even though it wasn't. He didn't know how to explain all this to Zan. What failing meant. How he'd stolen this life from his mother and wasn't even *doing* anything with it. Bastian rubbed his eyes again. The back of his hand still came away wet. And he wanted to tell her he was sorry, and he wanted to hug her, and he didn't want to do any of it with Zan watching, but when had he ever gotten what he wanted?

"It's just not safe for you to be in there alone." His mouth had twisted into an apologetic grimace.

"I get it," Bastian mumbled. He took the key ring and flipped through, trying to settle his mind on a specific memory. It was hard. Every time he thought of her, something else crept in—the memory of him failing school, the memory of Greer's lips on his, the memory of booming music and bad decisions. Everything flit through his brain—every time he thought he caught a memory, it sank through the cracks like sand. The keys flashed in different colors and patterns. Finally he grabbed one, yanked it free. The cement door flickered in front of him, then morphed into one of driftwood planks, little shells, starfish, barnacles hooked to the crevices. Golden bits of glass hung from a pull handle, a broken bottle wind chime.

"I'm sorry," Zan apologized again, stepping up beside him. He held his hand out. Bastian lay the key ring into his open palm. Then he pushed open the door.

༼༽༼༽༼༽༼༽༼༽

They stepped out onto a beach full of pebbles in all colors—some as bright as the green of Zan's jacket, others in dull browns and grays and whites. Bastian twisted his head, looking at a hazy gray horizon, with the barest slice of moon hanging down below the clouds. The sound of lapping waves surrounded them, burying deep into Bastian's ears, vibrating through his entire body.

"Wow," Zan said, kneeling down and burying his hand.

Bastian cleared his throat. "Sea glass." There was a person far in the distance, stepping through the waves. It was dark enough that he could only see the shadowed silhouette. Despair threatened to overtake him again, and he swallowed down an awful sound trying to make its way up his throat.

The glass clacked together, spilling over Zan's fingers as he splayed them for purchase before standing up again. "It's beautiful. I have some from another beach, but I've never seen this much."

"It's garbage," Bastian mumbled. The figure moved again, walking farther away. His stomach twisted in knots. He wanted to go after her, but he was afraid. The waves kept lapping.

There was something terrifying about standing near a dark ocean lit only by a hint of moonlight. It was vast during the day, but it was all-encompassing at night. If he closed his eyes, he could imagine being swallowed, sucked down to some place darker than any dark he'd ever seen.

"Beautiful," Zan affirmed. He started walking toward the water.

"Tourist destination," Bastian said. He followed, the memory tugging him along and refusing to let go. He sniffed and cleared his throat. His voice still sounded scratchy and raw. "It really is just bits of garbage. Glass Beach. Created from years of dumping into a small coastal area an hour north of here. Eventually it all erodes. Softens. Turns into this."

They were getting closer to the woman in the water. This was a bad idea. He shouldn't be doing this with Zan here, he wasn't ready to see her, he wasn't ready to die after, he wasn't ready, he wasn't ready, he wasn't—

"Bastian!" His mother called. She threw her arms out and twirled in the waves. "It's freezing!"

Zan stepped back.

"Come on!" Bastian's mom called.

Bastian looked at Zan. Zan took another step back, then turned and walked back up the beach, glass clinking and falling into place around his every step.

Bastian slipped off his shoes. Rolled up his pants. Took a step into the water and flinched. It was frigid, cold enough that he was already losing feeling in his feet. He didn't know how she could stand it.

He remembered this night, her staring up at the moon, him watching the humped bluffs of the waves as they poked craggy heads out of the ocean, them walking back from the water amid the sparkling glass. He'd been only nine. Dorian was back at the beach house, drinking hot chocolate and working on a puzzle. He didn't like the sound of the ocean's roar at night. He wasn't a little wild like Bastian and their mother.

"Beautiful!" His mother shouted as he came to stand beside her. "Look at the way the clouds are rolling. A storm is coming!"

It was the same thing she'd shouted nine years ago.

She held out her hand; Bastian slipped his in it. She was warm. Alive.

"I missed you," Bastian whispered. His chest was tight again, his eyes wet.

"Don't you love watching storms?" she said, not in answer, but in echo.

His stomach sank, his throat closed, he tried to swallow against the disappointment. He knew this would happen—Zan had already told him, and he'd seen it in the thrift store. The memories were just echoes. She wouldn't come alive any more than she already was inside his head—but it hurt more than he'd expected. "Mom?"

She didn't say anything, just gripped his hand tighter. A wave crested and washed around their ankles. The water hit Bastian's pant legs, wicking up all the way to his knees. He shivered. There was a clicking sound behind him, but he didn't turn to watch Zan picking up pieces of glass. "Nothing's the same," he croaked. "Dorian misses you too, you know? We don't talk much. It's not like it used to be. I look at him and I see you. I think he feels the same way when he looks at me. And I don't know how to fix it."

His mom held a hand up, made a circle of her thumb and pointer finger, captured the moon between them. "See that, Bastian?" she said. A smile bloomed across her face. The moonlight caught on her cheeks, causing the warm ochre of her skin to shimmer. "Orion." She let go of the moon and pointed up, tracing a finger across the sky.

Bastian swallowed hard. "We're supposed to be in therapy together," he continued. "But I can't. With him there, I can't. It's too much. It was my fault, and I'm sorry, I can't watch him there, I can't wait for him to crumble, break down, agree. It was my fault, and I'm just . . ." He squeezed his eyes closed, she squeezed his hand tight again, she whispered *Taurus*, and her finger slid to the right in the sky.

"I'm sorry," he said. "I'm failing. I'm going to drop out of school. Try to . . . I bought a bookstore with your money. I know it was crazy, but I was going to try to open it because I didn't know what else to do. I didn't have anything else. And now it won't happen at all because I'm going to *die*, and Mom, I—"

He ground the heels of his hands into his eyes and took a shuddering breath. "I miss you."

Her smile grew. He was taller than her now, but she still looked down, dark eyes glassy. "Should we go find your brother?" she asked.

They could. He could follow her back out of the water, pick his way across the glass, wind back up to the small beach house they'd rented for a weekend getaway. He remembered it all—Dorian hunched over the table in the living room, painstakingly matching piece by piece of an entirely black-and-white puzzle, his mom making them more hot chocolate, them flipping on the TV and watching some stupid *Ninja Warrior* show, him curling into the warmth of her body.

Him happy.

Her hand slipped from his, and she turned. "Coming?" She started walking.

Bastian hugged himself tight, trying to keep from shaking apart. "Coming," he croaked. He didn't follow, though. Just watched until she rounded the bend of a sand dune and slipped from sight.

He stood there a long time, until he could breathe without sobbing. When the tears had finally stopped flowing down his cheeks, he carefully walked out of the ice-cold water and slipped back into his shoes. Zan stood from where he'd been crouched picking through pieces of glass.

"I'm sorry," he said.

Bastian flinched. It was the same kind of sorry he'd given his mother, filled with grief. "Don't," he said.

"All right."

"There's nothing left," Bastian said. "Of her. It's just this. It's what's in my head. I never . . . I never got to say goodbye."

Zan looked at him sadly. "I didn't say goodbye either. When I left. And it kills me."

Bastian drew in a shaky breath.

Zan held out a hand, palm facing up. A piece of purple sea glass sat there. "For you. Because it matches one I have."

There were thousands more just like them scattered across the beach, but Bastian reached out and closed Zan's fingers around the glass. "No, it doesn't." He gave a wordless shrug. "I stole yours. One of the first times I met you."

Zan's eyes widened. "Oh," he said. He shrugged and pocketed it. "Then it's one for me. Because it matches the one you stole."

Wiping his eyes again, Bastian looked up at the sky. "I'm ready," he said quietly.

Zan stepped up close to him and held out his hand.

Bastian took it, threading his fingers in Zan's, but Zan didn't move, just stared out at the booming waves.

"Are you ever going to bring me across the river?" Bastian asked quietly.

Zan's fingers squeezed tight. "I'd miss you too much if you were gone," he murmured.

Bastian tried to answer, but he was already fading away.

CHAPTER FORTY

Portland, Oregon

Bastian opened his eyes.

There was no gray hallway, no ocean, no Zan, no dream. Just real life: a scraggly crocheted blanket thrown on top of him, his cheek pressed against the cold tile of a bathroom floor.

His head was pounding miserably, his mouth was so dry he could barely swallow, and every breath he took sent waves of nausea squirming up his throat.

Bastian rolled over and forced himself up. He was still wearing his shoes, his pants, his T-shirt. His sweatshirt had disappeared. So had his phone, his wallet, and keys.

He hauled himself up by the throat of the pedestal sink and very pointedly avoided the mirror. He didn't need to see how awful he looked. He flicked the water on, splashed some into his face, combed fingers through his greasy hair, then pushed his way out of the bathroom and down the hall.

There were a few other stragglers slumped over couches, chairs, sleeping in corners of the rooms. Red plastic cups littered the floor.

He could no longer smell the ocean from Styx; he could only smell liquor and vomit.

He spotted his phone lying in a puddle of something disgusting on the coffee table, and he snagged it, wiping it against his jeans. Then he wandered into the kitchen.

"Rough night?"

Bastian blinked. Greer was there, leaning against the counter, messing with a Keurig that looked conspicuously shiny and was spitting coffee like it had never once worked a day in its life.

"You're awake," Bastian said.

"I know Sunday's lazy and all, but you're overstaying your welcome," Greer said snarkily, motioning toward the microwave. 2:55 flashed in vivid green.

Sunday.

Bastian screwed his eyes closed for a second, breathing deep through his nose.

Dorian had promised to pick Bastian up on Sunday.

Greer offered the mug. Bastian took it with a groan. He hadn't had any intention of actually going to the cemetery but blowing him off like this was awful. He tried to take a sip of coffee, but it burned his mouth.

"Congratulations. You didn't die," Greer commented, rifling through the cupboards.

"I . . ." Bastian's mouth opened, stuck in confusion. Zan's voice echoed inside his head. *I'd miss you too much if you were gone.*

"You were real hooked on that last night," Greer repeated, coming up with a box of Lucky Charms. "Wouldn't shut up about it." His voice pitched higher in a mocking imitation, "I'm going to die. *I'm going to die.*"

Bastian watched him pour the cereal dry into a bowl and

then start picking out the blue marshmallows one at a time, eating them from his fingers.

"I don't . . ."

"Don't remember, yeah, yeah," Greer said with a grin. "Told you I have the good shit."

"Fuck off," Bastian said. The words stuck in his throat before working their way loose.

Sighing, Greer pulled out another marshmallow and popped it in his mouth. "Not your enemy here, B."

"Don't call me that."

Greer cocked his head, eyebrows raised. "Had no issue with it last night, *babe*." He stressed this last bit and popped another marshmallow. The corners of his lips were turning blue. "So did it work?"

"Did what work?"

"This." Greer motioned toward him. "Getting fucking obliterated, man. You're more fun this way, morning meltdown and all. Even sloppy drunk, you're a good kisser."

Bastian flinched. "Not having a meltdown," he mumbled.

"Could have fooled me."

Bastian took a long sip of coffee, shuddering at the bitterness. "I need to go home."

"Cool." Greer grabbed his bowl with one hand, fished in his pocket with the other. He came up with a baggie full of pills. "Top you off first?"

Bastian set his mug on the table. "I'm out."

"Oh, don't go all boring on me now. You're finally letting loose! You get Averie's number? She's college, bro. She'll put out. This is fun. This is living!"

Bastian was already turning for the door.

"Drama queen!" Greer called after him.

Bastian didn't look for his sweatshirt, just took off, letting the door slam behind him. Rain was pouring, and the moment he stepped from under the stoop, he was instantly drenched.

He made it to a bus stop terminal. He had no intention of getting on one, but he'd wait out the rain here, then walk home. He took out his phone. There were half a dozen missed texts from Riley, everything from asking where he went, to promising to not tell Dorian, to apologizing for the bracelet.

Bastian was cold all over. He rubbed his wrist, missing the bite of twine.

There was one missed text from Dorian, from only a couple of minutes ago.

Dorian [3:24 PM]: You should have come

There was an image file attached—a picture of a marble gravestone and a single red rose.

Nothing else, no admonishment, no phone calls, no anger, no pity.

I'd miss you too much if you were gone.

Bastian stared at the message for a long time, as three buses came and went.

Bastian hit reply.

Bastian [3:36 PM]: I'm sorry

CHAPTER FORTY-ONE

Portland, Oregon

Bang. Bang. Bang.

Bastian looked up from his phone. There were people standing at the front door of the shop, and he winced, realizing that the Open/Go Away sign that Riley had jokingly bought him was hanging in the window, Open side facing out to the street.

He wasn't ready for customers.

He didn't even have a way for them to pay yet; the iPad he'd bought to hook up to the sales system and credit card reader was still sitting brand-new in the box—

Bang. Bang. Bang.

"Coming!" he yelled, throwing himself around the front counter and to the front door, where he froze in shock. A couple stood there—man and woman holding three oversized reusable grocery totes and smiling toothy grins at him through the glass.

He recognized them immediately: Riley's parents.

Bastian pulled the door open, completely confused. "Uh . . ."

"Riley told us you were living all alone, and Joon reported that he'd never actually been invited up to your apartment, and given the state of the store, he wouldn't be surprised if it was uninhabitable," Mrs. Kim declared as she pushed passed him.

Bastian's mouth dropped open, stuck on the word *reported*. He understood why Riley would be worried—after the weekend's rash of increasingly poor decisions, she was probably concerned he was dead. Joon, though? He didn't know how he was supposed to feel about his contractor tattling on him to his parents.

"Come in?" he finally managed to Mr. Kim who was still standing on the landing.

His smile grew bigger as he stepped through the door. "Can I?" he asked, already turning toward the stacks of books, clearly wanting to explore. Bastian nodded, still speechless.

"Refrigerator?" Mrs. Kim asked, then thrust two of the bags into Bastian's hands and picked up the third that Riley's dad had set by the counter. She stalked forward, not waiting for an answer, just immediately heading toward the stairs at the back of the building like she had some sixth sense for homing in on living spaces. Bastian followed her, anxiety twisting in his stomach as he frantically ran through what the upstairs apartment looked like. Was there laundry all over the floor? Had he done the dishes? The bathroom situation was a nightmare; if she went in there it was all over—

She pushed open the door at the top of the stairs and went straight to the kitchen where she proceeded to unload the contents of an entire grocery store on his counter, including a full set of pots and pans that Bastian immediately recognized as being from her own kitchen.

"I have a pot," he started.

"That is nice," she told him, already cutting into a package of pork. "So do I."

He watched in disbelief as she made quick work of an onion, mushrooms, and an entire cabbage. As soon as she had that all in a large pot, she forced him down at the table and brought him over a steaming mug of tea, ordering him to drink it all. He obeyed, because with Riley's mom, that was the only option.

Then, horrifyingly, she started on the dirty dishes in his sink, moved on to dusting the entire apartment with an embarrassingly old broom that she found tucked in a closet, then pulled on a pair of enormous yellow gloves, grabbed the second bag that was apparently full of cleaning supplies, and stalked into Bastian's bathroom.

"Please don't—"

"Drink your tea," she barked at him.

Bastian's head was still pounding from the party two nights ago, his brother was refusing to speak to him, and his best friend's mom was cleaning out his apartment. This wasn't the worst way he'd ever woken up (he'd reserve *that* for Greer's bathroom floor), but it definitely wasn't great. These were literally the only two adults in his life he actually liked, and here one of them was, sticking a hand down his disgusting toilet. He pulled his tea closer and forced himself to sip slowly, wincing at the way the heavy ginger burned its way down his throat instead of focusing on how he wanted to sink through the floor.

There was a gentle knock at his door, and Mr. Kim stepped in, joining him at the table.

"She insisted," he explained.

Bastian tried to meet his eyes, but where Riley's mom was all business, her dad was all emotion that he wore openly on his sleeve, and the kindness and concern Bastian saw there was enough to make him want to start crying.

"The store looks wonderful," her dad said.

"Joon is really good," Bastian mumbled into his cup.

"Yes, he is, but he wasn't the one to organize and sort through thousands of books. Riley told us how hard you've been working."

Bastian shrugged jerkily. "It wasn't that hard," he said, when it was clear that her dad was waiting for a response. The kitchen was rapidly filling with the mouth-watering scent of whatever Riley's mom was cooking, and after existing on canned SpaghettiOs, Pop-Tarts, and next door's doughnuts for weeks on end, it was hard to concentrate on anything else.

"Joon didn't go to college," her dad said.

Bastian's head snapped up, eyes narrowing. He hadn't explicitly said as much to Riley, but the failing grades weren't exactly a point in his favor. If she was out there leaking his business to her parents just so they'd come convince him to make better life choices—

"He just wasn't the sort for it," her dad continued. "We were disappointed at first. Eun considered locking him in his room until he changed his mind. But in the end, we knew he would be miserable. And he always did like working with his hands."

Bastian stared at a scratch that ran the length of the table and disappeared under the lip, right where his knee was starting to jiggle.

Her dad's fingers rapped a rhythmic pattern. "You have a very good setup here," he said. "Riley says you are working on a website too?"

"Yeah," Bastian said quietly.

Her dad nodded with approval. "Well, you just let us know if you ever need anything. I'll watch the store for you if you need an afternoon off. Eun will happily bring you food at any time. And when Riley leaves for school, she's going to go out of her mind without someone to take care of." He smiled.

Bastian raised his mug to his mouth before realizing he'd already drained it of tea. The implication was clear. Riley was leaving for college. And Bastian was invited over at any time because he wouldn't be.

Because they understood that he still wanted to be *here*.

The warm fluttering feeling in his chest was no longer due to just the ginger. "Sure," he said quietly, surprised to find he truly meant it.

Moments later, Riley's mom strode from the bathroom, a satisfied but determined look on her face. "This will take longer than expected," she announced.

Bastian's face burned.

"You two go work. Come back when the stew is done."

Which is how Bastian found himself following Riley's dad back down to the store, letting him help set up the brand-new sales system, and scanning dozens of practice transactions.

So you're ready when you're flooded with customers, her dad told him as he hauled a stack of books over and plopped them on the counter, demanding Bastian ring up every one.

Bastian caught himself actually smiling.

By the time they both went home (leaving Bastian with a fridge full of fresh stew and groceries, a sparkling-clean bathroom, and more orders to come visit for dinner at any time), it was well into the evening. Bastian locked up and walked back over to the counter, inspecting the shining wood. Now, he had a credit card reader and the small iPad programmed with the system he'd purchased. There was a stack of books still sitting next to that—as the day had drawn on, Riley's dad had gotten progressively punchier, and had started acting like dozens of different customers, training Bastian in the art of being friendly no matter what situation he found himself in. Bastian grabbed a pile, ready to sort them back into their homes, but one toppled to the ground first.

He crouched down, Cat curling around his ankles, and his hand closed around the binding, recognizing it immediately. *Le Petite Prince.* The same one he'd found weeks ago.

He picked it up and dusted it off.

His mother had read it to him over and over when he was a child. He had vibrant memories of Dorian curled up next to him in bed, both of them listening to the soothing lilt of her voice.

He wondered if Zan had ever read it.

His entire arm buzzed, then went numb.

Bastian shivered as he walked back up the stairs.

I'd miss you too much if you were gone.

He was suddenly exhausted—even the spicy smell of soup still flooding the apartment was not enough to keep him from his bed. He knew it was too much to hope for. That the small life he was carving out for himself wasn't going to last. But what if there was a chance . . .

I'd miss you too much if you were gone.

His arm started tingling, numbness creeping through his fingers, and Bastian curled his body around the book and tried to fix it firmly in his mind so he might bring it through.

CHAPTER
FORTY-TWO

Styx

Zan smiled. The car was bright red with a smooth leather interior, had *Jaguar* scrawled across the wheel, and sat perfectly still in the middle of the frozen street. In the original memory, it had been driven by a man whose face had gone jaundice sallow, and it rumbled something fierce underneath them as they drove down the Strip. Zan had been absolutely convinced something was wrong with it.

He sat in the driver's seat now, hands wrapped around the stiff leather wheel.

He chose this memory because cars were cool. Bastian would think this was cool.

And then you can kiss him, his traitor brain whispered.

Zan ignored that. "Cool, right?" he asked, looking over to Bastian.

Who promptly turned ghost pale, sucked in a breath, threw the door open, and tumbled out of the car.

"Ummm . . . not cool?" Zan frowned, trying to figure out where he'd gone wrong. Bastian had shown up in the office looking a thousand times better than the last time. His cheeks had been flushed red, he'd grinned, his hand was tucked inside his sweatshirt pocket holding something that looked suspiciously book-like. (Zan did not *ask* about the suspiciously book-like thing because Zan was too busy watching the way Bastian's eyes crinkled up at the corners the bigger his smile grew, which was totally normal and not at *all* a problem.)

He'd told Zan to choose a memory this time, and Zan had picked here: a festival showcasing vintage cars, because what better way to impress another boy than making him fall out of a vehicle in panic? "Are you okay?" Zan asked cautiously.

Bastian's jaw clenched and unclenched as he slowly stood up from the ground and looked around.

Outside Zan's window, a woman in a skintight skirt was dragging a little boy behind her. He had a chocolate ice-cream cone in one hand. A single drip had made it all the way down to the bottom of the cone and was beading there, ready to drop in the next moment, a moment that would never come.

Zan cleared his throat. "Detroit, 1960. Dream Cruise," he said, because he figured he should say something, *anything* to ease the look of absolute terror that painted Bastian's face. "Uh, it's a line of cars that starts in Detroit but drives out to an island so close to Canada you can see the border. In the memory, they were moving. We looped around and around. Got to listen to this guy for hours expound upon the wonders of the auto show they'd started at. Not the most fun but . . ."

Bastian was doing a lot of swallowing and breathing. The utter panic seemed to be easing, and he cautiously stepped forward. "Don't like cars," he murmured shakily.

Zan wanted to die. "Yeah, I . . . I can see that. We can go somewhere else."

"It's not a big deal," Bastian said. He shuddered, though, and rubbed his left shoulder.

"Let's go, anywhere, you choose, we can—"

"No." Bastian hesitantly crept forward. "It's frozen. The memory. Won't move, right?"

Zan nodded.

Reaching out, Bastian brushed a single finger along the shiny red hood. "Jaguar," he murmured.

Zan shrugged. "That's what it says on the wheel." He winced. "I don't actually know anything about cars," he admitted. "Just thought you might . . ." Zan faltered, suddenly completely unsure of what to do with his hands. He didn't know what he'd been thinking, and he clearly sucked at this because *Hey, Bastian, good to see you, glad you're not dead yet, come on, let's go sit in a memory that clearly induces panic so I can stop obsessing over the way you chew your lower lip when you're nervous, or the way your cheeks flush if I look at you too long, sound like fun?* was obviously not the way to win affection.

It wasn't the way to win anything at all.

Zan sighed. "We can seriously go anywhere," he said, pushing his glasses up on his nose and sneaking a look at Bastian.

Who was leaning in and . . . inspecting the console?

For someone who didn't like cars, he seemed awfully interested.

"I *used* to like cars," Bastian mumbled, answering the unspoken question. He leaned in and inspected the console. He reached in and wrapped his hand around the stick shift. "This is an XK120," he said.

Zan relaxed incrementally. "Is that . . . good?"

"Really good," Bastian murmured. His hand crept up the leather seat, pressing against the stitched grooves. "This one was manufactured in '53, I think. I loved this car. I wanted this car. You have any idea what this would cost right now?"

"Uh . . ."

"They sell for hundreds of thousands of dollars. There's only a couple dozen of these left. In the world."

"Fancy," Zan confirmed. He drummed his hands along the steering wheel for a second. He'd never driven a car, but he'd sat in a few of them. This *special* one didn't feel any different.

Bastian straightened, jaw tightening as he started chewing at his inner cheek like he always did when he was trying to figure out what to do. "Ijustwanttoseetheengine," he suddenly burst out. It came out as a whoosh of sound, consonants and vowels tumbling from his tongue and tangling at his feet. "Then we can go?"

Zan's mouth hung open for far too long. "Of course," he finally managed.

The way Bastian beamed made his entire body flush so hot he was pretty sure he was going to self-immolate. He shook his head hard, trying to pull himself together while Bastian circled around to the front of the car. Bastian tapped on the hood, then tapped again before Zan realized he was supposed to be popping it. It took him a minute to find the lever, and honestly, he was proud of himself that he'd managed it at all, but Bastian didn't give him any sign of approval, just ducked deep inside the front of the car.

Zan eased out of the driver's seat. He had a gnawing sense of unease, a clod of guilt thick enough to choke on wedged at the back of his throat, but he had no idea *why*. Bastian was bent over the front, hands already deep inside the aluminum belly, so Zan walked over to the boy with the cone and knocked it out of his hands. The ice cream landed on the pavement with an audible splat and started melting immediately.

It did nothing to sate his sudden irritation with himself.

Zan shucked off his orange Tiger sweatshirt, balled it up, and tossed it toward one of the many trees speckling the edge of the sidewalk. It fluttered out, then floated straight to the ground. There was no wind to make it dance. He walked back to the car.

"Hold this." Bastian thrust an oil-covered stick thing into Zan's hand, not even looking up.

Zan peered at it. It left dark-brown streaks across his palm. Suspicious. "What is it?"

"No basic car maintenance in purgatory?" Bastian asked.

His voice sounded hollowed out from underneath the hood. Zan frowned. Somewhere in here there was a witty retort, but he couldn't seem to think clearly enough to find it. This was not going according to plan.

Okay, he didn't have a plan.

Remember when you wanted to kiss Bastian? his brain whispered.

Yeah, before he had a total freak-out. Not now.

Remember when he faded last time, and you pretended like it didn't bother you for about two seconds, but it did, so you thought about him, and you went back to his thrift store, and you stole another green feather boa, and you wore it around the office for days even when that weird old man who died of a food poisoning–related incident told you that fake feathers are bad for the environment and it's people like you who are the reason the planet is facing imminent destruction?

He remembered.

He also remembered how he was supposed to be escorting Bastian to the Ferryman to finish the job and earn his life back.

Hard pass, his brain said. *Just kiss him. Better plan.*

Yeah, Zan thought hard back. *If he was A) not freaking out, and B) looking at me instead of the bowels of a stupid car.*

"Beautiful," Bastian murmured to the car. "The engine is the heart of a car."

Zan rolled his eyes.

"This guy knew what he was doing. Everything is absolutely

immaculate. I can't believe . . . I never thought I'd see . . . Dorian would flip. He'd absolutely flip. Fuck . . ." He devolved into some inane sort of mumbling.

Zan sighed. A bead of sweat started at the nape of his neck and dripped down beneath the collar of his T-shirt. He resisted the urge to rub at it. Off in the distance, he could see a frozen sparkle of water in the bright sunset. A perfect day. A perfect memory. There was a clump of people standing in the grass talking animatedly. A girl wore a coral-peach bikini. A boy had one hand wrapped around the back of her neck, and another wrapped around her waist. Their eyes were closed. His mouth was inches from hers.

The hood of the Jaguar slammed closed, and Bastian stepped up beside Zan. "Voyeur," he said.

Zan looked at him. Bastian's jaw was still tight, and his hands were balled fists at his sides, tightening, loosening, tightening again. He doubted that Bastian even realized he was doing it at all. He wanted to know everything, why the fear, why the nervousness, why the intense fixation on a hunk of metal, why, why, why. "Done ogling your car?" Zan asked, tearing his eyes away from Bastian's hands and looking back toward the water.

"Never thought I'd see one of those."

"You're welcome, I guess?" Another bead of sweat trickled down his neck, and Zan resisted the urge to wipe it away.

"Why'd you choose here?" Bastian asked. "If you don't like cars?" He was staring at the water too.

Shrugging, Zan started walking—away from the couple, toward the center of the island. Bastian followed. "It's pretty enough," Zan said. He was absolutely *not* admitting to hoping that Bastian would be impressed. "And there's a greenhouse in the middle that's nice. There are butterflies. Frozen butterflies, but . . . it's cool."

"You like books, right?"

The non sequitur was strange enough that Zan pulled up right in the middle of the street and stared. "What?"

Bastian's cheeks were flushed, but it was hot. Of course they were flushed. Zan watched him swallow, then pull something out of his sweatshirt pocket.

The bookish-looking object *was* a book. Zan cocked his head and studied Bastian curiously.

"I do," Bastian said. He winced. "I mean. Obviously, I do. I own a bookstore. Uh . . . did I tell you that? I didn't know if you had . . . I mean, of course you had reading material, I just . . ." He shrugged, looking painfully uncomfortable for a second.

Zan froze, heart somehow beating even faster.

"Whatever. I brought you this." Then he shoved a volume into Zan's hands.

It was small—a dusty-blue hardcover with *Le Petite Prince* embossed in gold. "Oh," Zan said. His palms were sweating, and now he was pretty sure his cheeks were just as flushed as Bastian's. "Oh, wow—"

"It's only a book," Bastian interrupted. "I mean, my mom used to read it to me . . . not that . . . okay, that's weird. But I like it, and it was originally written in French, and you said you speak French, and it's probably better that way. I can bring you the English version if you'd rather, though . . ."

"Babbling," Zan murmured, opening the book to a page with a picture of a lumpy-looking hat.

"I'm not babbling," Bastian sputtered indignantly.

"You are a little."

"I—"

"You like me," Zan said, a bright smile breaking free and stretching across his face. He looked back up at Bastian, watched his cheeks grow even redder.

"I don't . . . I mean . . ." Bastian's eyes skating from Zan's face down to his shoes, then to the book, then back down to shoes again.

"You brought me a book," Zan said. "That you love."

"I don't like you," Bastian muttered.

"Clearly."

"Do you always do this?" Bastian demanded. "Make things awkward?"

"Do you always do this?" Zan parroted back. "Change the subject when you're uncomfortable?" He wanted to run, jump, pump his fist, and scream. *Kiss him!* his brain responded.

"You . . . look, just take the book. Leave it in a memory, chuck it in the ocean, don't read it, read it, I don't care."

"Yes, you do."

"Gah!" Bastian threw his hands up in the air, then stomped off in the direction they'd been walking. "Come on. Show me some stupid butterflies."

"I'm not chucking it in the ocean!" Zan called after him. He followed, trying to force the grin from his face. It didn't fade easily.

It took ten minutes of walking to reach the enormous greenhouse. Zan and Bastian wove through the frozen throngs of people to reach the inside observatory. Hundreds of butterflies hung above them, all in midflight. Zan reached up and carefully brushed his fingers against one with blue wings. They came away coated in iridescent powder. When he shifted the book back to that hand, he left a single, shimmering thumbprint right near the word *Prince*.

"Thank you," he whispered.

Bastian snuck a glance at him. His cheeks were still flushed red, and he looked back down at his shoes, but his lips curled cautiously into a grin.

Zan slowly held out his hand.

Bastian slowly hooked his fingers through Zan's.

Then they walked quietly through the entire observatory, carefully whispered breaths sometimes reaching the delicate butterfly wings, causing them to just barely flutter. They looked like they were still flying. They looked like they were still alive.

CHAPTER FORTY-THREE

Portland, Oregon

Bastian opened his eyes.

Something wasn't right. He was in his bed, lying on his stomach, definitely in the apartment, but the air was too still. No matter how many times he blinked, small dust motes hung frozen in front of him. He poked at his pillow, and it moved with his finger, but didn't pop back when he drew his hand back.

Frozen. Like the dead memories.

Something was wrong. He was supposed to be back in real life, but something was wrong, but he didn't . . .

He could still feel the warmth of Zan's hand against his own. He wished he were back there, with Zan, in a forest of butterflies, walking through a world that was entirely theirs.

Bastian slowly rolled his head to the other side of the room. There were gray spots swimming at the edges of his vision.

He remembered Zan's smile, his laughter, the way his eyes brightened the moment Bastian handed over the book, the way he said *You like me*. Zan was different. Zan was someone who made

Bastian's heart pound and his hands sweat and his mouth go all dry and chalky. That hadn't happened before.

That was something terrifying, and exciting, and *new*.

Swallowing, Bastian fell back onto the mattress.

Somewhere, Cat was meowing.

Bastian waved him off. It was fine. Everything was fine.

CHAPTER FORTY-FOUR

Styx

Bastian stumbled forward into the hallway. The air was thick and gel-like—he pushed through it like it was water.

Sebastian, the walls called.

Bastian flinched. He hadn't spoken. They shouldn't be echoing anything at all.

Sebastian, Sebastian, Sebastian . . .

Little specks of dust floated in front of him, catching in his eyelashes, fogging up his vision. The farther he pushed, the more they rained down. He sucked in a breath and choked on the smell of ash.

Sebastian . . .

Bastian tried to run. He forced himself against the air, clawing for purchase in the never-ending gray of the dream. He could see the chalky outline of the door ahead, almost there, almost there—

Black snaked around his ankles and tugged.

"No," Bastian said. He tore himself free and threw his body at the wall, scrabbling at the door, turning the knob, tumbling into the office.

Zan jerked back from the desk, eyes wide. "You . . ." His eyes flicked toward the door, then he jumped up, circled the desk, and crouched near Bastian. He reached out and snagged Bastian's wrist, shoving up his sleeve. "It's getting worse," he said slowly. "He's angry."

Bastian looked down. There was no longer a mark snaking up his arm—now his entire arm was faded gray. "It's fine," he muttered.

Zan looked at the door again, brow furrowed, eyes nervous. "It's not *fine*," he hissed. "The larger that mark grows, the closer to death you get. The barrier will fade. He'll be able to get at you with or without my help. This isn't something to mess with—"

"Like you *messing with* turning me in?" Bastian yanked his sweatshirt sleeve back down, covering the mark entirely.

Zan shook his head. "I didn't . . . I . . ."

"You were supposed to turn me in forever ago," Bastian cut in. "Zan."

Zan wouldn't look at him.

"Zan, you have to."

"It's like you want to die," Zan mumbled, eyes squeezing closed.

Bastian felt the world rock around him nauseatingly, the awful weight of inevitability freezing him just as solid as the people in Zan's memories. "I don't want you to get in trouble," he whispered.

A long minute passed. Nothing happened, and eventually Zan rocked back on his feet and swallowed. "He's not here," he said, like he was trying to convince himself. "At least not now. So . . ." He rubbed the back of his neck. "Starting again. Hi."

Bastian shook his head, swallowing down the fear still licking at his nerves. He pushed off the floor. "Hi."

"You scared me."

"I scared me too."

Zan cocked his head. He stood up and reached out. Bastian took his hand and allowed himself to be pulled up.

"I don't want you to die," Zan whispered.

Bastian squeezed his eyes closed. The buzzing of his numb arm was spreading into his chest. He tried to flex his fingers, but they were slow to move. Pricks of bright pain shocked through the pads of his fingertips as the blood rushed back. "I'm not dead yet," he said, eyes fluttering back open. Zan watched him, nervousness sharpening his features.

"I'm not," Bastian said again, louder this time.

Zan scratched at the back of his neck. "Come on," he finally said, turning and then hauling himself up on the desk. He reached over it and pulled open the drawer.

Bastian's eyes slid past him to the book perched in the very corner of his desk.

Le Petite Prince. There was a bookmark tucked in the middle and a couple of dog-eared pages. "You're reading it," he murmured.

Zan's brow furrowed, and he looked back down at the book. "You gave it to me. Of course, I'm reading it."

Bastian's heart kicked in his chest. The numbness didn't matter, the cold didn't matter, Zan was here staring at him like he *meant* something. He sucked in a shaky breath and grinned. The strangeness of the hallway was already fading now that he was here in familiar territory—safe with Zan.

"Come on," Zan said, motioning for him to follow. He held the key to the door, and it shimmered, cement becoming brightly painted blue-and-red metal.

Bastian watched him ease the door open, then they stepped out into a carnival.

An enormous Ferris wheel stood at the end of the pier, paused midrotation. Each car was full of people, all smiles and teeth and cotton candy. It looked vaguely familiar, but he couldn't quite place—

"Navy Pier," Zan said, answering his unspoken question. "Chicago."

"Why here?" Bastian asked.

Instead of answering, Zan grabbed Bastian's hand and pulled him through a stagnant crowd of families all standing in line for slushies. His grip was solid and warm. Bastian's cheeks flushed, and he was suddenly more than a little grateful that they were in the dark.

He didn't let go.

Zan led them all the way to the back of the pier, then around the side of the building. It was far emptier here—there was nothing but a narrow line for cars to drive, a pile of empty shipping crates, and a woman in a neon-yellow windbreaker, frozen mid-jog. They walked around her and out to the very edge of the pier.

"Too many people over there," Zan explained. "What are they all here for? Cotton candy? Overpriced hot dogs? The boy who brought me here seemed unreasonably excited about fireworks. Never saw them, though. He started fading so I had to deliver him before they started." He shrugged uncomfortably.

Bastian didn't think he'd ever understand what it was like to lead someone to their death. How it worked. How terrible it must feel.

Heaving an enormous sigh, Zan sat down. "I don't like water," he said, like it made perfect sense to take Bastian out to the edge of an enormous body of it and plop down where the frozen peaks of the waves were close enough to bite at his toes.

"As in drinking? Swimming? Bathing?"

"As in oceans. Or rivers."

Bastian winced. Obviously. *Obviously*, he didn't like water, he'd been trapped on the river of death for five hundred years. "Sorry," he mumbled.

Zan didn't say anything.

Sitting down next to him, Bastian looked out over the deep blue. He'd never been to one of the Great Lakes. It was bigger than he realized—almost ocean-like. The water was frozen midlap at the pier, white tips brushing against the wood underneath them. The sky was murky gray with an ominous green tint, dark clouds frozen above them. The air around them was swollen with humidity, but also cold—the chill of a storm cutting in fast.

"Thought it was fair," Zan said, nudging Bastian. "You don't like cars, I don't like . . . this." He cleared his throat and shook his head. "So now we're one for one on terrible memories."

"The car wasn't terrible," Bastian murmured quietly, thinking of the sparkling engine, of butterfly wings brushing against his nose and cheeks. He nudged a rock with his toe and watched it skitter off the pier and plunk into the water.

"Keep thinking the more I force myself around water, the easier it will get," Zan said.

Bastian watched him swallow—the way the line of his throat rippled. The soft glow of a streetlight flickered across his nose and cheeks.

Zan swallowed. "I drowned myself to get to Styx."

Bastian didn't move.

"Weird thing, drowning. The human body fights so hard to keep living, but when it gives up, it's actually kind of peaceful. Burns to suck in water. But when you run out of air, you kind of . . . I don't know." He looked down at the waves and kicked his feet against the wood.

"When I smell gasoline, I panic," Bastian said, because this was a weight that had been dragging him down for months, because he trusted Zan. He wanted to give up the secret. To speak it to the dead memory and let it freeze here. "I won't get in a car unless my brother drives. Sometimes not even then. He bought this brand-new Audi with the inheritance money, and it's beautiful, but sometimes I sit down in it, and I can't breathe. Only thing I can hear is screaming, only thing I can smell is gasoline, and I can't get enough air, and it feels like I'm dying, and I . . . I can't do it. I don't know what's wrong with me, I just can't."

"Why?" Zan asked.

Bastian pulled his knees to his chest. He worked out a piece of gum and unwrapped it, hoping the burst of cinnamon would distract him. He blew a bubble. It snapped before it gained any shape at all. "I killed her," he said quietly. "My mom. I was driving. She was in the passenger seat, Dorian was in the back. We were going out to the woods, escaping the city. We were almost to the highway, and I stopped at a light. I wanted to drive because I loved to drive, and Dorian didn't care so much and . . ."

The gum already tasted stale in his mouth. Ashy. Bastian closed his eyes. "We'd barely made it out of the city. Not even to the highway. But I'd driven the route before. We went hiking every weekend, it wasn't a hard drive. We hit this stoplight. Storm had come through, power was out, it was blinking red. I waited my turn. Then drove. This truck came out of nowhere. Smashed into the passenger side. They told us later that she was dead on impact. I . . ." He shuddered and tucked his head, grabbed his wrist—

But his bracelet wasn't there to fidget with, to twirl, and pull, and distract himself with.

And his mom wasn't there because she was dead.

Dead.

"I didn't know that," Bastian whispered. "I didn't know she

was dead already. Everything hurt, I kept trying to scream, but I couldn't get any sound out." He pressed his forehead hard against the tops of his knees, wishing it hurt more than it did. "I haven't told anyone that. The screaming part. I didn't think it would be so hard to scream but . . ."

"I tried to scream too," Zan said. "But no one could hear. I was underwater."

Bastian felt his mouth twist into a sick grin. He turned his head to the side, carefully watching Zan. "Helpless," he murmured. "It makes you feel utterly helpless."

"Helpless," Zan agreed.

The silence between them grew again. Without the background noise, wind, or water, or people, it was too hollow. Hurt his ears. Bastian tucked his chin to the top of his knees.

"Where'd you get your scar?"

Zan cocked his head. "This?" he asked, pointing to the silvery crescent moon that cradled his left eye.

Bastian nodded.

"Stupid, really. I was just a kid. Some friends and I . . . look, there were orchards that surrounded our village. Peaches. Whole place smelled awful by summertime, that gross rot smell, but in the spring when they ripened, it was amazing. We'd sneak in, climb the trees, grab what we could."

He paused.

Bastian pulled his knees closer to his chest and hugged his arms around them. "And then?" he prodded.

"Stupid," Zan repeated. "It was the end of the season, and everything was already gone, but there were some way up top? And I was the skinniest kid but also the best climber. So they dared me to go up. So I did. And I got a bunch of peaches. And I fell out of the tree, the end."

Bastian's eyebrows rose. "You fell out of the tree, the end? There's got to be more than that."

Zan's nose wrinkled. "Okay, okay, I fell out of the tree and smashed my face into a rock and managed to not lose any teeth but gashed my eye open, and I screamed and cried, and the other boys had to haul me in to get stitched up by one of the medics, and I kept screaming and crying, and then no one would play with me anymore because I was a crybaby, it was humiliating, now tell me your dumbest injury, not my turn anymore."

A grin cracked across Bastian's face, and before he knew it, he was laughing.

"Not funny," Zan muttered.

"Kind of," Bastian said, chewing at his lower lip and trying to stop grinning. He'd just let out a horrible truth that had been eating away at his insides for the last half year, and Zan had the power to . . . flip the switch. End it. Accept him for what he'd done and move on. Bastian wanted to lean over, wrap a hand around the back of Zan's neck, kiss him, and never let go.

His grin grew, but he tried to hide it. "Uh, dumbest injury was definitely breaking my nose." He traced his pointer finger across the bridge of his nose, landing right on the small lump. "There was this rusted-up wheelbarrow that my friend and I found behind the grocery store. We thought it would be an awesome idea for me to get in it and for him to push. There was a hill . . . it didn't turn out so well."

"Stupid," Zan said with a smile.

"Hey, you asked for dumbest," Bastian said. He scooted closer to Zan. "Your turn. What's the weirdest memory someone lived before they died? That they showed you?"

Zan leaned back on his hands and looked up at the clouds. "I guess . . . oh, man. This high school kid came through here once.

That's what you call it now, right? High school? He was younger than me but not much . . ."

"High school." Bastian nodded.

"Right. He took me to a domino tournament. Did you know that they have those? It's super competitive, I guess. I don't know, I didn't know what they were until he brought me. So this was the world championship, and they were about to set off a million dominoes or some ridiculously high number. And this kid's job was to set the timer. That was his only job. And he did it, except he bumped into the entire end display. Set like . . . two hundred thousand dominoes off before they were supposed to go. Ruined the entire thing. It takes weeks to set them up apparently."

Bastian watched him, eyebrows raised. "That's not weird. That's just sad."

"Yeah. I guess."

"I thought people relived the best memories?"

Shrugging, Zan tipped his head back further. The streetlight caught the line of his neck now, all the way down to the collar of a black Ramones T-shirt. Bastian wondered if he'd gone back to the thrift store again. If he even knew who the Ramones were. Probably not, but the idea of Zan wandering through Bastian's memories no longer filled him with dread. It made his heart beat faster. Made him start to sweat, just a little, in that nervous, butterflies-in-stomach way. Made him *happy*.

"Sometimes people fixate, you know?" Zan continued. "I try to push for best memories, but every now and again, you get someone totally fixated on the worst moment of their lives. It's awful."

"Setting off a bunch of dominoes is hardly the worst moment of his life."

"I don't know. He seemed pretty upset."

"Huh. All right. Next. Hit me with another."

"Mmm. All right. There was this woman in her fifties who took me through this really shady dance club. I watched her get high on cocaine for a good hour before she died."

"Going out strong."

"Something like that."

Bastian cocked his head. "How do you even know what cocaine is, ancient Greek boy?"

"Hardly ancient. Ancient Greece is over a thousand years before me. And I know what cocaine is, I've seen a lot of memories. You Americans were all very into it about forty years ago. Don't know why. The high isn't all that great. Opium is better."

"The high . . . you've done cocaine? You've . . . *opium*?"

Zan grinned at him. "I promise you're not missing out. That whole 'drug use begets genius' is stupid. I know I'm not exactly a poster child for innocence here, but drugs just make people assholes."

"Huh." Bastian hugged his knees tighter. Thoughts of Greer flickered through his head, but he pushed them down guilty. Zan was right. Drugs *did* make people assholes.

It was growing colder. He thought that these were supposed to be frozen memories, unchanging, but apparently that didn't hold entirely true for weather patterns.

"Tell me about your bookstore," Zan said.

Bastian smiled. "I bought it from an old guy who was barely alive. Was just trying to piss off my brother."

"No you weren't."

Bastian snuck a glance at Zan. He was still staring out at the water, barest hint of a frown playing at his lips. "Yeah. I was."

"No. You love books. You love libraries. You knew the Klementinum, you freaked out when I even touched a book there. You bought the store because you wanted to."

Sighing, Bastian turned back to the water too. "Fine. I like books. I thought it would be cool. Own a bookstore, sleep between the pages, live with stories. Literally."

"Weird," Zan said.

"Yeah. A little."

"A lot."

"You know what—"

"I'm weird too. I like abandoned nuclear reactors, it's not a contest or anything. Just saying. Your version of weird involves books. I like that."

Bastian pursed his lips and made a sort of humming sound as he tried to parse that. "Fair enough," he finally said. "We're both weird."

Zan nodded. "How'd you buy the store?"

"Called the guy. Met him. Wrote him a check."

"I mean where'd you get the money. You have any lucrative side-businesses I should know about? Mob ties? Are you some rich guy's heir? Royalty?"

"An abandoned bookstore doesn't cost as much as you think it costs," Bastian muttered.

"Costs more than the average eighteen-year-old makes, I'd imagine."

Bastian shivered. "Life insurance," he said woodenly. "My mom came from money." There was a pinprick of light in the distance from a ferryboat. It cast a long strip of light across the black waves. "She didn't want it, but it was there. She was an artist, so we moved a lot when we were younger. She always had us in the most expensive private schools there were because it's what made her family happy, but she couldn't seem to put down roots no matter how hard she tried. Portland was the longest we'd ever stayed in one place. Five years. She loved it there. Open sky, forests, ocean air, everything you need to be free."

"It sounds wonderful."

Bastian tipped his head. "It's okay. When she died, it . . . I don't know. It's still the same city. Still the same trees, the same ocean, the same sky. Feels worse now, though. But she left us money, and I didn't know what else to do with it, so I bought a bookstore."

"I would like to see your bookstore," Zan said.

Bastian snuck another look at him, but Zan was still staring off into the distance.

"I would like to take you," he said quietly.

"It's cold," Zan said suddenly. "Are you cold? Was it this . . ." Zan's jaw tightened, and he pushed himself up and peered out over the water. "I thought . . ."

His voice was laced with concern, and his intense green eyes crinkled at the corners as he watched the horizon.

Bastian followed his gaze. Far in the distance, the water seemed to be rippling. He scratched absentmindedly at his arm.

"The barrier," Zan said, voice ratcheting up. "It moved . . . we . . . we need to go. We need to go *now*." He grabbed Bastian's hand and pulled him up.

The rippling was growing bigger, the wind began to blow, and right below them, a tendril of oily black snaked up over the concrete ledge of the pier.

"*Now*," Zan hissed. He thrust the keys into Bastian's hand. "Go. *Bastian, go!*"

Bastian closed his eyes and tried to think of a good memory but all he saw was fire, all he smelled was gasoline. He flinched away "I can't—"

"Think of something happy," Zan pleaded. "Wake up. Don't let him take you—"

CHAPTER FORTY-FIVE

Styx

The stoplight flashed to red. Bastian slowed down, foot on the brakes, one hand on the wheel, the other reaching for the radio, swatting Mom's hand out of the way. She laughed. He laughed too—

Gasping, Bastian threw himself back toward the window. This wasn't . . . he wasn't . . .

"No," he whispered.

"Owner of the car picks the tunes," his mom said, still smiling, thumbing the radio back to the awful country station that they all hated.

Even though he said nothing, he could hear his own words from the memory in his head. *Gross!*

"Gross," Dorian echoed in the back seat. "Come on. It's an hour to the hiking trails, I'm not listening to this the entire—"

"Folded wings that used to fly, they've all gone wherever they go . . ." his mom sang, putting so much fake twang behind the words it was painful.

How do you even know this song, Bastian's memory muttered.

"No," Bastian moaned again. His mom kept singing. Dorian kept groaning. Neither of them had any sort of reaction to his panic because they weren't seeing this Bastian. They were only a memory. "No, no, no, no—"

He spun around looking for Zan, but he wasn't there. He squeezed his eyes closed and thought *I'm done*, he thought *Wake up*, he thought *Get me out of here, get me out of here—*

It didn't work.

He was still here on I-5, not quite to I-84, the light was blinking, he would stop the car, he wouldn't press his foot to the gas, he could change it, it was going to be okay, he could keep his eyes closed and wait it out.

It was a nightmare.

It was the worst nightmare.

He clutched the wheel with a white-knuckled grip. His arm seared so hot he gasped.

He couldn't do this.

His mom laughed again, and Bastian knew she was flipping the station, turning around in her seat, flashing Dorian a thumbs-up.

In his other memories that he'd wandered with Zan, they'd always been able to leave. To walk away. To find the door and escape back to the office, at any time; all he needed was to get out of this car.

Bastian reached for the door handle and tried to flip it open.

The locks clicked down.

"It's a dream," he said, voice shaky and uncertain. "It's just a dream." He swallowed hard and forced his hands down from the steering wheel to his lap. He wouldn't drive the car. He wouldn't accelerate when it was his turn, he wouldn't be in the path of the truck, he wouldn't watch his mother die, he *wouldn't*.

His nails bit into the palms of his hands, and Bastian tried to take a breath in, but everything was the bad kind of hazy, and he tried to suck in another breath, but it wasn't coming. He couldn't breathe.

Darkness crept in through the windows, saturating his jeans, flowing to the bottom of the car, curling around his ankles.

The light blinked.

The cars crept forward.

Even though his hands were nowhere near the steering wheel, his car rolled to the front of the line.

Wake up, Bastian chanted in his head. *Wake up. Fuck, wake up, wake up, wake up now.*

His mom looked over and smiled. The oily black crept around her, too, eating every bit of her light, destroying her. He watched her face melt away, her fingers curl and disintegrate.

Bastian flinched back. "Mom," he pleaded. His hands were starting to shake, and he reached for the handle of the door again, frantically flipping it up and down, up and down—

The black coalesced, filling out in his mother's form, smiling at him through her lips and flashing him pointy, dripping fangs.

"Hello, Bastian."

Bastian bit back a scream and fumbled with the lock again, digging his fingernails down into it, pulling as hard as he could.

"You look unhappy," the Ferryman said, voice dripping with sarcasm.

"You're not real," Bastian said, kicking at the door, trying to scoot as far as he could away from the awful, liquid reach of the oily black creature. "Not real. You're not real. You're not—"

The Ferryman snagged Bastian's wrist, black wrapping around and around. Bastian desperately tried to yank himself free, but the Ferryman's hold was too tight.

"You are not supposed to be here," the Ferryman chided. "My guide has done a very poor job."

"Wasn't his fault," Bastian gasped, still trying to pull free. *Wake up*, he chanted inside his head. *Wake up, now, wake up, wake up*—

"It is very much his fault," the Ferryman said. Another oily appendage shot from Bastian's mother's chest and smacked into his chest, pressing him against the seat.

"You are afraid," the Ferryman murmured silkily.

Bastian squeezed his eyes closed. *Wake up.*

"I can feel your heart. Too fast. Like a rabbit. A rabbit that should be dead."

Bastian tried to pull away, but there was nowhere left to go.

The Ferryman's smile grew. Another ribbon of black escaped his mother's mouth and slowly crawled toward Bastian's thigh, coating him in darkness, rubbing against the top of his leg. Bastian knew what was about to happen, he went wild trying to yank his leg back and jerk free, he tried to stop it, he tried, he tried—

The Ferryman slammed into Bastian's thigh, forcing his foot down on the gas pedal. The car barreled to the middle of the intersection, the semi slammed into the disfigured shape of his mom, Dorian started shouting, Bastian's arm went ice cold, he smelled nothing but gasoline, he tried to scream—

CHAPTER FORTY-SIX

Styx

Zan was frantic.

He'd blinked, and Bastian was gone, but it wasn't the normal kind of gone, because now there was oily black mist rolling over the waves and solidifying in a Bastian-like shape right next to him.

It was time to run, but Zan couldn't move.

"Alexander," the Ferryman said through Bastian's lips, black dripping from his mouth and down his chin. He scooped his fingers through the viscous liquid as it puddled in his lap. Then he held them up, watching quizzically as it oozed down to his wrist.

Zan's fingernails were daggers in his thighs. "Where is he?"

"I've been searching for you."

"Where *is* he?"

The Ferryman opened Bastian's mouth and laughed, a horrible caricature of any noise that Bastian had ever made. His throat muscles moved like a snake—roiling up before convulsing back down.

Zan wanted to tear his eyes free, but he was afraid to look away.

"He is not dead," the Ferryman said viciously. "Not yet. I'm with him in a memory, Alexander." His long black fingers traced patterns into the dock, leaving oily smears. He swallowed again, skin undulating and rippling. "You like memories. You flit through them like a pretty songbird flits through the sky. You are stupid like a songbird too. You should have done your job."

Zan stiffened. "I've done it."

Cracking a disjointed-looking grin, the Ferryman sliced the black finger across his neck. "You have not."

"I've done everything else, I've brought them all to you, every single one, he's only one soul—"

"Is he worth this? You failing?" the Ferryman laughed wickedly. He leaned even closer, reaching a hand toward Zan's face.

Zan jerked his head away. His heart beat frantically, thudding against his chest so hard it was painful.

The Ferryman laughed and stretched his arm up, finger pointing toward a single seagull frozen above the choppy water. Its beak was open in the middle of a screech. "You cannot love him," he said.

"Please don't kill him," Zan forced out through lips white with tension.

"Humans are fickle things, Alexander. They don't live long enough to learn anything worthwhile, certainly not how to love."

Zan swallowed hard. "That's not what this is."

"Isn't it? You miss being human. You crave it. I know you wait for the ones who don't know the way yet, the ones who struggle toward finding me. I know you follow them, tug them back, let them wallow in their stupid, stupid memories. I know the way your heart beats faster when they speak. You miss it. You miss being human. But this one is no different. He belongs to me."

Forcing a breath out, Zan tried to keep himself still, to keep his voice from quavering. "Stop watching me. Leave me alone. I'll bring him, he'll come, just—"

"If I wanted him dead, I would eat him right now. He is shaking. He is scrabbling at the locks on the car. He is *scared*." He sucked in a horrible breath, tongue hissing in pleasure.

The hairs on the back of Zan's neck prickled, and he fought not to look away. "Why?" he whispered, throat closing around the word as soon as it was free.

The Ferryman's eyes glowed. "Does he know the price you will pay for this?"

Zan forced his eyes back to the Chicago skyline. The clouds had frozen again, dark and ominous. The chilled air bit his cheeks. The storm wasn't coming.

It was already here.

"Let him go," he murmured. "Please just let him go."

The Ferryman licked his lips, tongue darting out farther than should have been possible from a human body. Zan shuddered.

"Right now, his heart is beating faster than yours. His fingernails have cut gouges into the palms of his hands. When he wakes, there will be blood caked underneath them. I haven't even done anything yet. The light has not changed."

We were almost to the highway, the big one, Bastian had said. *Stopped at a light.*

Zan knew which memory Bastian was trapped in. He chewed on his lower lip hard enough to taste blood. "Let him go," he croaked.

"Not good enough."

Zan looked back at him, watched as another bead of black dripped from his lips to his chin. There was black oozing in his eyes now, almost ready to fall.

"I want to play a game."

Zan blinked. "What kind of game?" he whispered.

"The fun kind. The kind where we strike a new bargain, because I like you. *I like you*, Alexander." He reached out and pressed one finger to Zan's lips.

Zan fought to keep still.

"You were right, once. Not that long ago, I think." His head tilted, and his mouth parted, forcing Bastian's lips all wrong, showing too many oil-stained teeth. "You said I don't have other sacrifices, and you were right. No one has called to me since you, Alexander, no one respects the old gods anymore."

Zan's entire body went cold. "I'm almost free," he whispered.

"You have one month until the end of our deal, is that correct? Ample time to choose. I must have a servant, and if you leave . . . mmmm. Your boy has already become acquainted with Styx. You have already taught him the rules."

"No," Zan said, shaking his head.

The finger moved with him, leaving a wet smear over his mouth.

"His soul or yours. Another five hundred years. Will you save him like you saved your mother? Or this time . . . will you choose to save yourself?"

The black in his eyes finally oozed over, dripping down Bastian's cheeks, staining them foul. Zan couldn't watch any more. He looked back down at his hands.

"I'm waiting, Alexander. Or should I perhaps call you as he does. *Zan?*"

Zan tasted blood from where his teeth cut into his cheek. His hands were shaking. There were no more options; he'd made his choice that day in the forest with Bastian, the moment he let Bastian fade. "Okay," he whispered.

The Ferryman nodded. "One month," he sneered. "Will you tell him, or shall I?"

Zan shook his head hard, blinking furiously. "Don't," he forced out.

A grin sliced across Bastian's face, jagged and misshapen. It was a hideous caricature of what Bastian looked like—there was no more warmth from his smile, just deadened black eyes. "Or would you prefer he not know at all?"

Zan froze.

The Ferryman's head tilted, and he raised one of Bastian's hands, the skin on his fingers dripping off to reveal bone. "That can be arranged," he murmured. Then he dissolved, black mist pouring out over the water and disappearing from view. The husk of Bastian's body slumped down and crumbled to ash. The clouds lightened. The warmth of the summer evening slammed back.

Zan squeezed his eyes closed. When he opened them, he was back in the glow of his office, sitting at his desk.

His home.

He couldn't do this for another five hundred years. He *couldn't*.

Zan grabbed the laptop, ripped it from the power cable, and threw it across the room as hard as he could. It hit the bookshelf next to the cement wall, causing glass to shatter, stones to tumble, destroying bits and pieces of other people's lives.

CHAPTER FORTY-SEVEN

Portland, Oregon

Bastian gasped awake.

His eyes frantically took in his surroundings and cataloged everything they saw. He was tangled in his sheets. On his mattress. In the upstairs apartment bedroom of the bookstore. The little alarm clock he'd plugged in at the other end of the mattress read 7:58 p.m. His phone next to him flashed MONDAY when he bumped it with his forearm. He'd been in Styx for what felt like only hours, but he'd lost an entire day since Riley's parents had come into the bookstore.

His arm was on fire, and he shucked off his T-shirt, heart racing. The gray extended over his collarbone, slivers of it curling toward his heart.

He could still smell gasoline.

Scrubbing his eyes, he tried to calm his racing heart. He didn't know if Zan was okay, or if the Ferryman had taken him too. He needed to go back. He needed to make this right—if he was

296

supposed to die, then he should die. Zan deserved that much. Zan deserved a chance at life.

Bastian had already had his.

He closed his eyes and forced himself to breathe deeply. His arm tingled.

The dream wouldn't come.

"Fuck," he whispered, turning over and forcing his eyes closed again. Hallway. Door. Office. *Zan.*

It wasn't working, he couldn't sleep, the dream wasn't taking him.

Bastian sat up. He pressed the heels of his hands against his eyes and tried to ignore the horrible, shuddery way his breath sounded every time he sucked in another chestful of air.

CHAPTER FORTY-EIGHT

Portland, Oregon

"Do you need to come in, Bastian?" Andrea's voice on the other end of the line was calm, mellow, soothing.

Bastian slumped against the brick outside the bookstore. He didn't know where to go. He couldn't stay in the store; the whole place reeked of gasoline, so he grabbed his backpack. Grabbed his phone. Walked out the door.

Texted Greer.

Then crouched against the brick, head in his hands, breath coming in and out, too loud in his ears.

He didn't remember calling Andrea, but now his phone was pressed against his ear, and she was speaking to him like he was a feral animal that needed to be coaxed down.

He could still. Smell. Gasoline.

"I can't," he said. "I have . . . I need . . . I'm fine. It's okay, I'm fine." His mouth was full of sea glass tumbling, and he couldn't form words around the pieces. He still couldn't swallow right.

"Bastian, stay on the line with me."

There were too many pieces of glass caught underneath his tongue.

"Can you tell me what you're going to do next?" Andrea asked. "Walk me through it."

This was bad. This was really bad. Her walking him through actions was a coping mechanism she'd used back in the early days of therapy, during the bad days when he could barely get up and out of bed, when he could barely speak at all.

"I'm fine," he managed.

"That's nice. I'm glad you think so. Now tell me what you're going to do next for my own peace of mind?"

"I . . ." He scrubbed a hand through his hair and tried to focus, but his mind was buzzing, and he was trying too hard to hold onto a rapidly fraying thread that was barely stitching everything together. "Food," he said.

"Wonderful," Andrea assured. "What kind of food?"

"Umm . . ." Bastian tilted his head slightly toward the bookstore again. There was stew upstairs, left over from Mrs. Kim. He should get up. Go back inside. This was . . . he was fine, it—

Andrea was waiting for an answer; he didn't know what to say. He couldn't think. He couldn't breathe. He wanted to get off the phone with her, but what if he hung up and she called someone to track him down and made everything even worse than it already was? His eyes flicked up, taking in the illuminated sign for doughnuts. "Shop next door," he managed to grind out. "Coffee."

"Coffee is good, but it's not food." Andrea said. "Let's figure out a food plan."

He didn't want to figure out a food plan. The thought of food was making his throat close up and fill his mouth with too much saliva. He should have answered Andrea's question by now, but he didn't know how to.

"Bastian?"

"Yeah," he said. A car horn honked; he looked up to see a flam-boyantly sparkling green Lotus pulling up to the curb.

"Food?" she prompted.

"I'll go . . ." He stopped. He still didn't know where to go. He—

"B!" Greer shouted, putting the car in park and then hanging out the window.

"Bastian?" Andrea asked.

Bastian squeezed his eyes closed. "I'm okay," he murmured.

"I'd love to see you at the office tomorrow," Andrea said. "I have room."

"No, I'm okay." He swallowed. Forced his eyes up to Greer and held up one finger. One minute. Give him one minute. Until what?

Until he asked him for the sort of drugs that would knock him out, force him asleep, *make* him dream.

"Can I stay on the line with you while you find food?"

He sucked in a breath and tried to force every bit of uncertainty from his voice. "I'm okay. Just got a little panicky. Everything's fine now, my friend is here."

Greer tapped the horn three times, then smacked the side of his door with the palm of his hand.

Hurry up.

That meant hurry up.

"Please call me anytime you need," Andrea said. "And really, I'd love to see you sometime in the next few days if you can man-age. I know we have our normal scheduled time, but it sounds like it's been a hard day."

"I'll call you," Bastian said. Then he hung up.

He tucked his phone back into his pocket. He pushed up from

the sidewalk, forced himself away from the building, walked up to Greer's car.

"Got your text," Greer said with a snarky-looking grin. He peered around Bastian, eyeing the strip club. "Nice place."

"Yeah," Bastian murmured. His voice sounded hoarse. Wrong.

"You look high," Greer said.

"Not," Bastian said. A beam of purple-hued light from the club cut across the hood of Greer's car. Bastian had a sudden and inexplicable urge to touch it.

Greer patted the side of the car again. "Need a ride? Or want to hang out here? You can show me around your place."

He was still grinning like this was all a big joke.

"No," Bastian mumbled. "Actually, you said . . . a while ago . . . uh . . . do you have . . ."

Drugs make people assholes, Zan whispered in his ear.

Greer's grin faded. "Making me feel all used," he muttered, pushing himself up and then turning, hanging over the back of his seat. He rifled around for a moment before coming up with a dull blue backpack with a cheap brand name slapped on the front. The kind no one at Preston would be caught dead wearing. "What're you looking for? Ups, downs, turnarounds, everything in between, baby."

"I need sleep."

Greer frowned. "Boring."

"Something to knock me out," Bastian amended. "I just need something to . . ." he faltered, not sure what else to say.

Greer zipped open the front pocket of the backpack and rifled through a dozen plastic bags before pulling the smallest out. Inside were ten blue pills, circular, tiny, inconspicuous. He held it out. "Easy sleep," he said, smile curling. "No colors, no party. Just boom. Down. Like the *dead*."

Bastian shuddered. *Gasoline. Screaming. Red light blink, red light blink, red light blink.* "How much?" Bastian heard himself ask.

"Take them. On the house. One friend to another, wipe away that emotion, baby, be nothing."

Bastian's fingers closed around the bag, and he tucked it into his pocket. "Thanks," he grunted, then looked up at the sky. Clouds were rolling in fast and angry, blocking all the stars from view. A storm was coming. He watched Greer toss the backpack into the back seat of the car like there weren't thousands of dollars' worth of illegal substances housed inside it.

"Had fun at the party," Greer said. "Sure I can't come in? You're sweet when you're plastered."

Bastian took a step back. "Umm, yeah, sorry . . . I . . ." he murmured. Swallowing was still hard. A couple of college kids jostled past him, voices drunkenly loud. He watched them pull open the black door of Mirage and disappear. "Maybe next time," he managed, eyes flicking back to Greer before falling to the pavement.

Greer drew his hand through his hair and tilted his head back. "You're no fun."

Bastian shrugged uncomfortably. "Thanks," he finally managed. "For . . . you know."

"Don't take too many," Greer grunted. "Those are like animal tranquilizers. They'll take you *down.*"

It didn't sound as much a warning as it sounded a dare.

CHAPTER FORTY-NINE

Styx

Zan waited in his office, feet kicked up on his desk, fingers flicking the controls of the Switch, growing a garden of roses, an orchard of peaches, a row of perfectly tidy houses with perfectly cute animals. The volume was turned all the way up, but the music was boring, relaxing, monotonous.

He lost a fish.

And another.

Bastian didn't show up.

Zan tucked the Switch in the drawer and walked the octagonal perimeter of his office, feet treading a path worn into the wood from five hundred years of pacing. This was good. If he didn't show, then Zan wouldn't have to talk to him. And if Zan didn't talk to him, he wouldn't have to admit that there was a choice, that he was struggling, that he desperately wanted to live, and Bastian didn't deserve lifetimes of servitude, but *neither did he.*

Zan pulled out a volume of a Greek dictionary set he'd stolen from a Greek library a hundred years ago and ripped the pages out one by one by one because maybe if he tried hard enough, he could summon an outraged, book-loving boy here by sheer force.

Bastian didn't show up.

He gathered each piece of sea glass, shell, bead, and rock from the shelves around the office. Piled them all in the center of the room. Picked through them and sorted them by color. White. Gray. Brown. Purple.

Bastian didn't show up.

He opened the cement door to a speakeasy in Berlin with champagne in gold-dusted glasses, and whiskey so rich it tasted like syrup. A woman sat at the bar—fingers of one hand curled against the curve of her rich umber shoulder, her other hand cupping her chin as she leaned against the sleek surface of the bar. She wore a necklace of thick pearls around her throat. Zan reached up and snatched it free.

The string broke, the pearls scattered over the bar and down to the floor, rolling among the feet of frozen men and women.

There was nothing for him here.

Zan grabbed a martini glass from a laughing man and smashed it against the floor.

The Ferryman wouldn't have taken Bastian without Zan knowing, not when he'd made another bargain. It was a game. It was just a *game*.

"He has to come back," Zan whispered to himself. His throat ached with something worse than desperation.

He swiped his arm across an entire table, watching glasses and plates shatter on the floor, then walked back to the door— geometrically painted in orange and green. He held up the key and stepped back into his office.

Bastian didn't show up.

He sorted more colors. Green glass. Pink beads. Cream shells.

The door opened, and a little girl stepped out, clutching a tiny stuffed pig to her chest.

"Mom?" she asked, eyes blinking furiously, mouth quivering.

Zan's heart sank. These were the worst kind. These were the deaths that made him want to give up, to stop running, to call the Ferryman, to end it.

And Bastian . . . he couldn't make Bastian do this. He *couldn't*, he—

"I want my mom," she said, wiping her eyes with a fist caked in blood.

Zan sank down to her level and tangled his hands in his hair, pulling enough to feel the bite of his barely contained grief. "Think of a happy place," he said, voice rough like he'd forgotten how to speak. "Your happiest memory."

"Mom?" she asked again, higher pitched now, close to panic. She held her hand out in front of her, opening and closing it. Blood dripped to the warm wood floorboards. He could hear it.

"It's okay," he ground out. "She's here. Just . . . think of her? Okay? Think really hard?"

The girl clutched the pig tighter and started to sob.

Zan forced himself up for the keys. He pushed them into her tiny hands, and she didn't speak, she just cried, and he led her through the memory of a small bedroom where her mom sat on the floor singing a quiet song, and when Zan pulled her through the closet door, the sound of the river roared so loudly in his ears that he swayed, dizzy on his feet.

The Ferryman rose, and Zan watched as he started at her fingers, unraveling the bright white of her soul as she sobbed.

This was what he'd be resigning Bastian to. This, over, and over, and over again until Bastian gave in and let the Ferryman eat him too.

Because no one had lasted as long as Zan.

When he got back to the office, the sound of her last gasps for air still echoed all around him. He picked up a rock, a big one, the size of his fist, ringed with a vein of silvery crystal. He threw it as hard as he could against the door. The sound of it smashing against the cement wasn't loud enough to drown her out.

"I can't . . ." he whispered, sinking down to his knees and curling his spine, tucking his head. "I don't . . . I can't do this again . . . I can't stay here . . ." He sucked in a shaky breath and squeezed his eyes closed, fingers already reaching up for the key ring. He flicked through them fast, pulling one by rote memory, then he unlocked the door and stepped through into a little attic room over an Irish pub owned by the boy's uncle. In the original memory, the off-key sound of men and women singing "The Wild Rover" had leaked through the floorboards. Now there was only silence. A bed was pushed up against a wall covered in black mold, and the smell of barley beer and battered fish wafted up, and he didn't care because this had been home for that boy; this had been a place that he was loved and cherished, a place where his uncle had walked up the creaking stairs and pushed open the door and hugged him so tightly that tears sprung to the boy's eyes.

Zan's mother used to hug him that way too.

He threw himself onto the lumpy mattress of the bed.

Stuck to the side of the battered dresser, right in his line of sight, was a single notecard, oily black ink dripping down the paper. Zan reached out and slowly pulled it from the bruised wood.

28 days.

He balled it up and threw it across the room. It bounced off the far wall. Zan ripped off his glasses—the pink cat ones—and threw those too. He kept waiting for a sudden tug back to the office that would signal a soul showing up. He kept hoping it would be Bastian.

Nothing happened. Zan was alone.

CHAPTER FIFTY

Portland, Oregon

Dorian [8:21 PM]: Can I call?

Bastian frowned at his phone. The walls were flickering all around him, fuzzing out his vision in some weird, half-dream state. He'd taken the last of Greer's pills a couple of hours ago, and the edges of reality were blurring.

The drugs had knocked him out, but he hadn't been able to dream. Nothing was working.

Blinking heavily, Bastian looked at the date on his phone.

December 24, it read. Six days since the party. Five since Riley's parents in the bookstore. Three since Zan. Since the Ferryman. Since *gasoline*.

He shuddered. Then the last two days were completely lost to drugged sleep. He'd barely managed to get up and feed Cat when necessary; otherwise he'd been collapsed in bed, not moving.

There were dozens of missed messages from Riley, Mathais, and Dorian.

Bastian's head pounded, and his mouth tasted awful. His arm was completely numb.

He didn't know why the Ferryman didn't take him, why he wasn't dead, and all he could think was that it was Zan. That somehow Zan had convinced the monster to let him go at his own expense.

That he needed to get back into Styx, and he needed to *die*.

Bastian sucked in a breath, then dialed Dorian.

"That was fast," Dorian said on the other end of the line.

"I was available. You want to talk, talk."

"Bash . . ." Dorian said. There was a tapping sound in the background.

Bastian could picture him perfectly. Sitting at his desk, his fingers anxiously drilling away against the wood.

Dorian cleared his throat. "You disappeared. You wouldn't pick up your phone. You kept texting Riley that you were fine and to leave you alone, and we did, but God, Bash. This is fucked."

Bastian didn't think he'd ever heard Dorian say *fucked*. He was right, though. Bastian pulled his numb arm to his chest and rubbed at it, trying to coax life back. He didn't say anything.

"Riley told me you wouldn't leave the party. Said you were drugged up. Crazy. Kissing college girls, kissing *Greer*. And then you didn't come to the cemetery, and you apologized, and I thought that was a breakthrough or something until you disappeared. I still couldn't get a hold of you. I tried knocking at the bookstore, and there was no answer. Christ. *What is the matter with you?*"

Bastian squeezed his eyes closed and tangled his fingers in his hair, pulling hard. He didn't know what to say. He couldn't exactly tell Dorian that he was supposed to be dead, that somehow, he slipped under the radar, that there was a boy cursed to lead him to the Ferryman, that he was maybe, kind of, almost definitely in love with the boy cursed to lead him to the Ferryman.

That would all make him sound insane.

But he also didn't know how to tell Dorian that instead of opening the front door, he'd been so drugged up on pills like some washed-up loser that he hadn't even realized anyone was there.

Gripping the phone tighter, Bastian stood. He walked the length of the tiny bedroom above the stairs, turned ninety degrees, walked the width of the tiny bedroom above the stairs, turned. "Sorry," he said, after the silence had gone on for too long.

"I thought you just needed space. The bookstore. Me to stop following you around. I got the letter from Preston, you know. I know you failed your finals. They're going to hold you back."

Bastian stopped at the far end of the apartment and pressed his forehead against the wall. The paint felt sticky from the humidity.

Bastian imagined Dorian on the other end of the line, brow furrowing as he chewed on his lower lip—just like Bastian chewed his lower lip when he was nervous.

"Bash?" Dorian asked.

"Yeah. I know."

"So what have you been doing? Getting high? With Greer? You hate that guy, you always have."

Bastian shrugged, even though he knew Dorian couldn't see him. He was so tired. He still didn't know what drugs Greer had given him, but they left him feeling sluggish, made everything around him look bland and colorless.

It was kind of like waking up from Styx, only there were no Zan memories to temper the misery.

"I'm serious, what's wrong with you, Bash? What's going on? Please let us help."

"I'm sorry," Bastian repeated.

Dorian was silent for a long time. "The cemetery was terrible," he finally said.

Bastian pressed the palm of his hand against the wall too. Tilted his head until he could stare at his fingers, at the spot where the bracelet used to lay. "Okay."

"It sucked. Not enough trees, too much sunlight. She would have hated it. But I brought some roses because she liked roses and—"

"Orchids," Bastian murmured. "She liked orchids."

There was a pause, then, "Oh."

Sighing, Bastian pushed off from the wall and sat down at the edge of the stairs. Cat took this as an invitation to crawl into his lap. Bastian didn't mind. The store below was dark; the only thing he could see were the ghostly shadows playing along the edges of the shelves from the streetlight outside. "Sorry," he said again. For what? For knowing what flowers she liked, for getting wasted at a party he didn't even want to be at, for failing out of high school, for buying a bookstore, for crashing the car and killing their mother, for living when she didn't.

"I'm here. I'm alive," Bastian said quietly. "So, you can . . . I don't know. Do whatever. I'm fine."

"No."

The line went silent. Bastian could hear Dorian breathing. For a long moment, their breaths were perfectly in sync, but then Bastian realized what he was doing and forced them apart again.

"Our therapist said I should reach out," Dorian finally said. "Said it was okay if you didn't want to come with me to the cemetery, that it was your choice to make, that you were grieving in the way you needed to grieve, but that I was allowed to be upset over it. And I am. Upset over it. It was awful there with the hot sun and hardly any trees, and it was horrible seeing that single stone, and you . . . just . . ." His voice dropped off for a second, and he took a deep breath. "Bash, you should have been there."

The shadows flickered more, creeping up the stairs. An awful, itchy desperation crept down Bastian's spine.

"Bash?"

"Tacos," Bash managed to get out.

"Excuse me?" Dorian replied.

"Remember that taco stand? By campus?"

"Uh . . ."

"It was good. We used to go there." His fingers were tingling, and he closed his eyes. Dorian was irritating, and frustrating, and perfect, and sometimes Bastian hated him so much he wanted to scream, but they were brothers.

For so long, Bastian had tried to pretend that didn't matter.

"With Mom," Dorian said quietly.

"Right."

"You . . ." His voice trailed off.

Cat meowed, and Bastian opened his eyes. A tendril of sunset snaked down the wall. "Can we meet there?" he murmured.

"All right," Dorian said.

"All right," Bastian echoed. He ducked his head, relief causing his voice to shake. "I can be there in thirty."

"I can pick you up—"

"No."

"Okay. I'll be there," Dorian said.

Bastian hung up. He grabbed his sweatshirt from the back of the desk chair, took his gum from the bedside table, and forced himself out of the apartment.

⌐⌐⌐⌐⌐⌐⌐⌐⌐

Tito's was a grungy Mexican taqueria that sat directly across from a bustling Mexican chain restaurant that was a campus staple due to their weekly rotation of alcoholic specials. Beyond the cheap drinks, Bastian could never figure out why the bulk of the college crowd went for the bland tables, stale chips, and crappy mariachi music when there was actual authenticity sitting directly under their noses, but he wasn't going to complain. There was no line here, and the metal tables that had been dragged outside for the night were entirely empty. Bastian and Dorian ordered, then picked a table as far from the noise and fluorescent lights of the college hangout as possible.

"This place hasn't changed," Dorian said, leaning back in his chair and studying Bastian.

His face was stone. It was impossible for Bastian to tell if he was disappointed, nervous, tired, or angry.

Bastian knew he should say something, but words were stuck in his throat.

Dorian's eyes dropped to his shoes. He sighed. "All right, well. I got into the University of Michigan," Dorian said. "Early decision. Thought you should know."

Bastian looked down at the table. The top of it was black metal crosshatched into diamonds just large enough that you could fit your fingers through. He poked his pointer finger through a single hole.

"Med school. It's the one I wanted. I got some scholarship money, but I'll put the rest of the inheritance money toward the rest of tuition. I'll be moving."

"To Michigan," Bastian said.

"Right. Riley and Mathais are still waiting on stuff. Won't know anything until February, but you know they're leaving too."

Bastian took a deep breath in, then let it slowly out his nose. "I know."

"It's okay. You can retake the year and catch up. It's not a problem, you'll make it work."

"I'm dropping out."

Dorian's eyes fluttered closed. "Bash—"

"I'm serious. I have the store. It's ready, I'll open it the first week of January." Bastian ground his teeth, nauseous at the lie. After everything they'd done, the store would never open. He'd be gone by then.

Dorian sucked in a deep breath. "Look, I can defer a year. I don't know, I can help you—"

"You're not going to defer a year. I'll be fine."

"You just . . ." Dorian chewed his lip. "Do you know anything about running a store?"

"No. I didn't know anything about buying a store either or renovating a store. I'll figure it out."

"Okay," he said, letting out a long sigh.

Bastian blinked in surprise. "Okay?"

Dorian offered a pained-looking grin. "It's not like I've ever stopped one of your weird ideas before. So okay. But you . . ." He leaned forward on his elbows. "Why did you go to that party, Bash?"

Bastian shook his head. "I was just trying to be normal," he murmured.

Dorian's eyes dropped down to the table. He watched Bastian pick at the grate for a long moment. "You don't have to be normal," he finally said. "You need to be you. And *you* isn't a partier. You like the forest. And the sky. And quiet places. And books."

"Yeah," Bastian said. He poked at the bottle of hot sauce sitting in the center of the table. "I guess." The hot sauce tipped over. He grabbed it before it hit the table, righted it, then went back to sticking his fingers through the holes.

"Talk to me," Dorian pleaded.

Sighing, Bastian closed his fingers in the grate and watched the tendons go white. "I . . . I've been having dreams." *Fuck*, this felt weird to admit to someone who wasn't Andrea. His jaw clenched.

"Really . . . vivid dreams, I guess. They're kind of taking over. Feel more real than this." He gestured miserably toward the table.

Dorian leaned over the table on his elbows and studied Bastian. "Okay," he said slowly.

"You don't believe me."

"No, you haven't said enough to believe or not to believe."

Pulling his finger out of the table grate with a pop, Bastian leaned back in his chair. He tried to keep Dorian's gaze but couldn't help looking back down at the table. This was still so personal, and weird, and he knew exactly how crazy he sounded. "Everything is different there," he mumbled. "I like that me a lot better than this one."

"Bash," Dorian started. His eyes flicked above Bastian's shoulder. The guy from behind the counter stepped up to the table and set down two trays full of fish, carnitas, carne asada, and chicken tacos. They'd ordered enough for a dozen people, but the waiter didn't even give them a sideways glance.

"You guys good?" he asked.

"Thank you," Dorian said. He waited until the guy had disappeared back inside the restaurant before talking again. "I like you this way," he said quietly. He grabbed a taco and took an enormous bite.

"No you don't," Bastian muttered. *Tell him, tell him, tell him* his brain chanted.

Dorian didn't say anything. Bastian reached across the table and picked up one of the tacos stuffed full of carnitas, studying it carefully. "The dream starts in this dark, endless space," he said. A drip of sauce curled down the outside of the taco shell. "The ground is covered in water. I walk through it. Sometimes for ages, sometimes not long at all, but eventually, there's a door. I push it open. And there's a boy waiting for me."

Dorian took another bite. "Okay."

Bastian swallowed hard. "He asks for my name and location of death."

Dorian's nose scrunched up, and his brow drew together.

"And he's real," Bastian plunged on, before he could lose the nerve. "Says I was supposed to die. That he needs to log me and take me to the Ferryman so my soul can pass over—"

"Have you talked to Andrea?" Dorian asked benignly.

Bastian grit his teeth. The taco shell was crumbling in his fingers. Grease leaked through the shell, staining his fingers orange. "Just listen," he muttered. "The accident that killed Mom? I was supposed to die too. I'm not supposed to be here."

Dorian put down his taco. His eyes softened. "That's what this is about? The guilt?"

Bastian forced himself to take a bite, but everything was sitting sour in his stomach. A truck drove by, two guys hanging out the window, three standing in the back trunk holding an enormous hand-painted sign that read FUCK EASTERN, GO VIKINGS while blasting the PSU fight song. Bastian watched them go by and waited until the last of the honking died down. "It's not a guilt thing," he said quietly. He pushed up his sleeve and extended his arm.

The entire limb had been gray and dead-looking for days but looking at it still gave Bastian that strange out-of-body experience of tilting, disorienting vertigo.

Dorian reached out and grabbed his wrist, pulling it closer. "What did you do?" he hissed.

Bastian fought the urge to pull away. "Nothing," he ground out, looking away as Dorian studied his arm. "The dreams started the week after the accident. When we were released from the hospital. When I woke up, I had a tiny fingerprint bruise right here." He leaned forward and tapped the inside of his wrist with one finger. "It wasn't bad at first, like one nightmare every couple of weeks, but lately, I don't know. It's been getting a lot worse. And the bruise has been growing."

Dorian's eyes widened, but he didn't look away from Bastian's arm. "It's moving," he whispered. "Underneath your skin, the color is moving."

"Yeah."

Dorian let go. He put his taco down and wiped his hands. He looked nauseous. "I don't understand."

"Me neither, really. I'm telling you, these dreams are real. The boy in the dream . . ." He cleared his throat. "Zan. Zan calls it Styx. Says I'm marked." He jabbed his arm. "For death. For the Ferryman." He laughed awkwardly. "I'm not going to escape it, I told you, I'm not supposed to be alive."

Dorian swallowed and squirmed in his seat a minute. Nervous. Unsure. "So like . . . in movies, you almost die, and you see the light, or you see your life flash behind your eyes or whatever. Then you come back. You're alive. But everyone around you is saying how you should have been dead. Near-death experience and all that."

"Point?"

"Just trying to . . . I don't know. Wrap my head around what you're telling me, I guess."

"You don't believe me."

"I didn't say that, I said I was trying to wrap my head around what you're telling me. It's called empathy. Participating in a conversation."

Bastian grunted and sat back in his chair. "I've met *him* too," he managed to say, barely suppressing a shudder. "The Ferryman."

"Ferryman," Dorian echoed.

"He's got Zan trapped in some sort of deal. Five hundred years of leading souls over, and then he gets to go free."

"Zan," Dorian echoed.

"Is this how to participate in a conversation too? Repeat whatever I say?"

Dorian's nose wrinkled, but he picked up his taco again and took another bite. "Right. So Zan . . . is some mythical god too? Leading souls?"

"No. He's human. Just cursed."

"Five hundred years . . ." Dorian murmured, chewing quietly. "Sounds lonely."

Bastian snuck a look at him. "Sounds *crazy*. I know."

"A little." Dorian finished chewing, then reached across the table and tapped Bastian's wrist once, right where his wishing bracelet used to lie. "Also sounds like something Mom would have believed in. That's good enough for me."

Bastian swallowed hard. Tears were pricking at his eyes, and he was not, he was definitely not, going to start crying in the middle of the taco stand with his brother watching, but Dorian . . .

Dorian understood.

It didn't matter if he believed; he understood.

Bastian breathed out through his mouth because his nose was getting all stuffed. He looked back down at the table and tried to pull himself together. The lone taco on his plate was getting soggy. Bastian poked at it with his finger until the meat slid out.

"Look." Dorian sucked in a shaky breath. "Life is messy, and awful, and tragic, and the last year has been all of those things and more, but there's good here too."

Bastian snuck a glance up. Dorian rubbed his eyes, then looked up at the sky, blinking furiously.

"You own a bookstore," he said quietly. "No"—he held up his hand as Bastian opened his mouth—"I mean you really own one now. It's not just some dusty storefront with mold issues and buckling floorboards that you bought in a fit of despair. You put work into it. It's your dream. A real dream. Not Styx, not death. Something living and growing. Just like you."

Chewing on his lower lip, Bastian reached across the table for a napkin and started shredding it. Little pieces of white paper speckled his plate.

"And I know I've been pushing you on the grades things, but if you don't . . . if you don't want to go to college, then at least fight for the store," Dorian said. "*Try.* I've got issues too. I know you think I've moved on or whatever, but I haven't, I won't, it's a part of both of us, and even if this is all real"—he gestured toward Bastian's arm—"are you seriously going to just let go? Take the easy way out? Leave me?"

His voice broke, and he pressed the heels of his hands hard into his eyes and drew in a shuddery breath. "Come to group like you used to," he said, voice muted from behind his hands. "Talk to Andrea. Talk to me. Talk to anyone. Just please don't spend your time waiting to die."

He dropped his hands back down and looked up at Bastian. His eyes were shiny. "Because you're worth it. Your friends think you're worth it." He looked down at the table. "I think you're worth it," he said quietly.

Bastian watched the ground. The Portland humidity was making him sweat, the smell of tacos was making him sick, his heart was pounding. He was trying. He wanted to live; he knew that now. He wanted Zan to make it out, he wanted his bookstore, and his friends, and his stupid feral cat, and his *brother*.

But if he didn't let Zan lead him over the river, then he was abandoning Zan to a fate he didn't deserve.

Bastian bit into his taco. It tasted like cardboard.

CHAPTER FIFTY-ONE

Styx

There was another note waiting for Zan the next day, pasted to the front of a little patisserie outside the French Market in New Orleans. He grabbed it—a ripped page from a Hello Kitty journal with black oil staining the pink paper. *27 days* was written in ink that bled through the page. He tore it to pieces, then stepped around the line of people waiting for beignets to snag himself an almond croissant and a bottle of water.

Another note, the day after that, stuck in between the pages of the book Bastian had given him. A library receipt from Baringo, Kenya, which had been scrawled over. *26 days.*

Zan didn't know what to do.

Every day, he found new ways to distract himself by bouncing from place to place—a futebol match in Brazil, a bachelor party in Las Vegas, a brasserie in Jakarta, a bougie nightclub in Sofia, Bulgaria.

None of them worked.

The display at a hockey game in Windsor read *22.*

The napkin under the cocktail glass of the woman at '80s night in Madrid had a phone number written on the paper made entirely of *19*s.

A child on a beach in Tokyo was frozen in the act of drawing an *11* in the sand.

He tried to track the Ferryman down. He forced through barriers wherever he could, waded out into the river, screamed as loud as he could, left his own notes, scribbled in the black volcanic sand of a beach in Hawaii, pushed together in sticks and stones in the middle of the Olympic National Forest. He took a pen from a tourist's backpack in the Mastaba Tomb and gouged out letters in the soft stone.

TALK TO ME.

The Ferryman didn't appear.

Time worked differently here. He'd never told Bastian that—never told him how sometimes it felt like moments and sometimes it felt like years between him appearing. He didn't think the Ferryman had control of it, but he was terrified that this was part of the game too. That the Ferryman would make him choose before Bastian appeared. That they'd never see each other again.

Zan hopped from place to place, frantically trying to feel something other than terror. He shoved people, hit people, positioned people in rows and knocked them over like dominoes; no one ever blinked, no one ever swallowed, no one ever moved.

He started avoiding the office, the walls of it closing in on him so tightly he couldn't breathe. He left notes. A scrawled message on the first page of *Le Petite Prince*, a note written on the spreadsheet in his laptop, fractured behind the broken screen—directions to specific memories for when Bastian came through. Specific memories for him to find and join Zan so they could talk, so he could explain himself, so that he could say goodbye.

He floated through the thrift store, crashing through the aisles, throwing casserole dishes, clocks, picture frames, upending the entire display of glasses and then smashing them underneath his feet.

Five hundred years, the voice in his head murmured on repeat. Was one life worth that?

Zan already knew the answer. He'd known it since the moment the Ferryman asked him to choose.

Yes.

CHAPTER FIFTY-TWO

Portland, Oregon

"Please stop that," Riley called over to Mathais, who was flipping the OPEN/GO AWAY sign back and forth in the window. He grinned over at her, then kept doing it even louder.

"God, you all are so immature," she muttered.

"You're the one who gave it to me," Bastian reminded her. "But yeah, hey Mathais, that's kind of defeating the point of a soft open. You're scaring away customers."

Mathais gave a heavily put-upon sigh and wandered around the corner, in search of Cat, leaving only Riley and Bastian, who was suddenly wildly uncomfortable.

They hadn't really spoken about the party, or his disappearance thereafter. And he knew that her sending her parents over was her way of showing concern and that she cared, but he still couldn't help feeling like somehow he'd finally pushed hard enough, cracked the friendship so far open that no amount of pushing was going to force it back together.

"Soft open," Riley muttered. "You go and buy a bookstore,

and suddenly you sound like a preppy kid with an MBA."

"Thanks?"

She rolled her eyes, then went rifling through her bag. "Here," she said a moment later. "Happy end of semester." She handed over a tiny tissue paper–wrapped gift.

Bastian took it hesitantly.

"Also, you can consider it an early birthday present."

"It counts for both?"

"The gift is for the end of the semester. The fact that I didn't make you an ugly scarf instead is for your birthday."

"Said with such love," Bastian mumbled.

"Just open it, jerk." Riley flipped him off, then went back to looking at her phone, peering over the screen of it every few seconds to check his progress.

He worked a finger underneath the tissue paper and pulled the package apart. A bright-orange woven strip fell out. It was about a half an inch wide and had a tiny silver fox charm woven into the middle of the strand. His palms were going sweaty.

"Give me your hand," Riley said.

Bastian looked back down, suddenly finding it hard to swallow.

Riley grabbed his wrist, pulled it toward her, and picked up the bracelet. "I'm sorry for breaking your other one. Dorian told me it was a mom thing, and I feel awful. So this isn't exactly the same, and I can't guarantee that this one won't break, too, but I can promise that if it does, I'll make you another. Cool?"

Bastian didn't know what to say. His eyes were all watery.

She wrapped the band around his wrist, then tied the knot once. "I wish for Bash Barnes to stop being an asshole," she intoned.

Bastian tried to yank his hand back, but she held firm. "That's not how it works," he said. His voice was too husky and low, and his tongue was too big for his mouth, and this was . . .

323

"*I'm* supposed to make the wishes," he managed to choke out.

"New rules," Riley said with a grin. "Four knots now. Maker of the bracelet gets the first wish. Owner of the bracelet gets the next three. Here." She tied another knot and looked pointedly at him.

"I don't . . ."

"You don't have to say it out loud, just go!"

Bastian looked back down at the bracelet. *I wish for the bookstore to work*, he thought.

"Yeah?" Riley asked.

Bastian nodded.

Chewing his lower lip, Bastian watched her pull a third knot tight. *I wish for Zan*, he thought, then shuddered. Every memory of Zan was tinged with the awful knowledge that his time was running out.

He swallowed hard.

Riley went to tie a fourth knot, but he reached out and stopped her. "Wait on that one," he said. "I can't decide."

She shrugged. "All right."

Bastian pulled his hand back and studied the bracelet. It was garishly orange and matched the bookstore sign. "Thank you," he managed.

Riley reached over the counter and smacked him on the head. "You're being an asshole already," she said. "Obviously my wish isn't working."

Bastian leaned back against the counter. "Doesn't work till they fall off. Naturally."

She rolled her eyes dramatically. "*Now* you tell me." She leaned over far enough that their shoulders brushed. "I'm sorry," she said quietly. "Now it's your turn."

Wincing, Bastian played with the tiny fox on the bracelet. "I'm sorry too," he said quietly.

The bells on the door jingled, and they both looked up from the counter as an older man and young boy entered.

"Welcome to Fox Books!" Riley announced with a wave. "Let us know if you need any help!"

They smiled at her, then disappeared around a corner.

"You're going to have to do that soon, you know," she said, eyeing Bastian. "I'm not always going to be here to be your super-attractive, socially not-awkward wing person."

"Noted," he said with a grin.

Mathais jogged up to the counter and high-fived them both. "Customers!" he said with his booming voice.

"We noticed," Riley said dryly.

"Where's Dorian?" Mathais asked.

Bastian rubbed at the new orange bracelet. Riley was amazing. "He's coming," he said, looking back up. "Got stuck at some meeting for student gov."

"It's December," Mathais said.

"Yeah, you tell him that. Not even Christmas break will keep him from the extracurriculars."

"As long as you're both here tomorrow night, birthday boys," Riley said. She stuck her phone in her bag and pushed off the counter. "PS, I'm not making you a cake. Someone else gets to be in charge of that."

"Not it," Mathais said.

"I have to make my own cake?" Bastian moaned.

Riley reached over the counter and mussed his hair. "Poor thing," she said.

They spent the afternoon like that, watching the occasional customer trickle in and celebrating every time. Riley bemoaned the fact that he kept screwing up the credit card reader and threatened to send her dad back, and Mathais bounced around the store like an overgrown golden retriever, following every person and doing his best to be helpful.

Bastian sold books and led customers through his store and occasionally leaned up against the corridors full of books and let himself smile.

He hadn't been this happy since before the accident.

Later that night, he lay in his bed, arm going numb. He forced his breathing to steady as he watched every shadow in his bedroom, looking for oily black.

It was okay if this was it. He was ready for Styx.

He looped his fingers underneath the new orange band and tugged gently, wishing for *Zan*.

CHAPTER FIFTY-THREE

Styx

Bastian opened his eyes.

Sebastian, the voice crooned, louder than usual, echoing through the empty hallway so loudly Bastian cringed. Tiny puffs of black licked up from the floor, curling into jagged claws.

The Ferryman.

Bastian tried to run, but the ground dissolved, and his feet were sucked down into pitch-black mud, and he couldn't move, couldn't tear away—

Sebastian . . .

A slick tendril of black looped around Bastian's neck and pulled.

He screamed, trying to tear away, heart beating frantically in his chest. "Zan!" Bastian yelled. "Zan!"

The Ferryman's grip tightened, liquid tendrils pouring out of the mud at Bastian's feet and crawling up his body, coating him in foul black, pressing into his mouth, his ears, his nose.

Bastian couldn't scream, he couldn't speak, he couldn't *breathe*.

"This is how Zan died," the Ferryman said, black lips brushing the shell of Bastian's ear. "Did he tell you of this? Of the way the mud caked around him, weighed him down? Did he tell you that he cried?"

Bastian tried to yank his head away, but the Ferryman held tight.

"He was braver than you. Has always been braver than you."

I know, Bastian tried to say, but the black poured in further, reaching down his throat.

"You are running out of time," he hissed. "Will you let him sacrifice it all?"

Bastian squeezed his eyes closed. He didn't know what that meant, he didn't want to die this way, he didn't want to die without seeing Zan one last time—

The Ferryman released him. Bastian fell forward onto his knees, fingernails clawing at the ground as he drew in a ragged, shallow breath.

He slowly looked up. The Ferryman stood there watching him, black coalescing until he had the skittering legs of a spider, the fangs of a viper, the head of a wolf. Black wept from his eyes.

"Are you worth it?"

He sank into the floor and disappeared.

Bastian sucked in another breath, one hand going to his throat. It was wet.

He pulled away and studied his fingers. Slimy black coated the tips.

The mud solidified until he was kneeling in an inch of tepid water.

Are you worth it? The space echoed.

He didn't know what that meant, only that he needed to get out of there right now and find Zan.

Bastian pushed off the floor and took off down the hall at a dead sprint, forcing his shaking legs forward until the door finally appeared. He shoved against it, forced it open, tumbled into the office.

Which was empty.

The only light was from the screen of the barely open laptop on the desk, the only sound the synthesized chirping music coming from the Nintendo Switch, which dangled from its power cable off the edge of the desk. The lamp in the corner had been shattered. Every bookcase had been pulled down, every book torn from the shelves, every one of the items Zan had collected for five hundred years was scattered across the room. Bastian stepped forward, and glass crunched under his feet. "Zan?" he whispered.

No one answered.

Bastian cautiously picked his way through the debris over to the desk. He pushed the laptop open further.

A spreadsheet was open, showing dates, names, locations.

Name and location of death.

Bastian scrolled through it, eyes scanning thousands of names.

The screen flickered. His ears popped. His hands were clammy, the temperature in the room was dropping just like the night on Navy Pier.

What if the Ferryman came back?

What if he took him this time, choked the life from him, snatched him away from everything, drowned him in black before he even got to say goodbye . . .

Bastian forced his shaking hands into his sweatshirt pocket. Sweat dripped down the back of his neck as he swallowed down nausea and fear. The cursor on the screen blinked on a single highlighted rectangle.

Name: Sebastian Barnes

Location: Are you afraid of heights?

Bastian looked up at the cement wall. The ring of keys sat there on the floor, abandoned.

The screen flickered again.

Are you worth it? the hallway called.

Bastian walked over to the keys, picked them up, thought as hard as he could about cement, and pipes, and a single, lone hawk.

He pulled a key, pressing it against the wall as a single curl of oily black trickled from underneath a toppled bookshelf.

Bastian stepped through the concrete door.

〰〰〰〰〰〰〰〰〰

There was no wind because the memory was still dead, but Bastian still sank down immediately to his hands and knees. He hated this place. "Zan!"

The height ate his words, swallowing them up almost before they'd even been voiced.

The second tower was directly across from him now, white cement curve of its body sharp against the ominous cloud-streaked sky. Bastian could pick out unfinished spots on it where thick metal rods stabbed through concrete, forming a skeleton for something that would never be finished.

"Bastian." Zan's voice shook as he stepped out from the shadow of an unfinished window.

"Hey," Bastian breathed, backing up until he pressed firmly against the wall, then slowly sliding down. He could still taste the foul black of the Ferryman at the back of his throat.

Zan rubbed his eyes. "I've been waiting, and waiting, and it's been so long. . .I just thought. . .I thought you were gone. That he took you." He bowed his head.

"He did," Bastian said. "In the Chicago memory. He stuck me in—"

"In the car crash."

Zan knew. Of course he knew. The Ferryman had probably thought it was absolutely hilarious. Bastian's legs kicked the edge of the building. "I tried to get back to Styx," he murmured. "But the dream wouldn't come."

Zan drew a hand through his hair. His glasses—the plain black frames this time—sat askew on his nose. He looked more harried than the last time Bastian had seen him.

"No one has ever stayed like you," Zan murmured. "I…" He cleared his throat. "All of this is my fault." His eyes danced furtively every way but Bastian's face. He picked at his fingernails. He was nervous about something; Bastian just didn't know what.

"I didn't think he'd follow me there," Zan said. "To the pier. I didn't think the barrier was that close, and I should have been more careful, it was my fault he found you—"

"It's not your fault I'm marked," Bastian said, eyes falling to the writhing gray of his arm. "You said it yourself, I should have died last summer. I'm already living on borrowed time."

Zan sucked in a breath. He finally looked over at Bastian. "I was so scared that you were gone forever, and I never even got to say goodbye."

Bastian blinked. His breath caught in his throat. "He found me outside your office," he finally admitted. "Right before I came here. He could have taken me right then, he could have taken me in the car, but he didn't. *Why?*"

Zan winced and drew back further.

"What did he mean when he asked me if I would let you sacrifice it all?" Bastian pressed.

Zan shook his head. "I don't know," he said.

It sounded like a lie. Bastian closed his eyes.

"I don't *know*," Zan said again, louder this time. More

insistent. "But I don't want to stay here. He can't get to the middle of memories. We're safe as long as we're far enough inside. So pick somewhere. I want to go somewhere alive."

Bastian looked up, eyes scanning the sky until he found the hawk. "And after, you'll take me to the river. This has to be goodbye."

Zan shook his head wildly. "No."

"Zan—"

"I don't want to talk about him," Zan said plainly, fixing Bastian with green eyes that glittered with flecks of gold. "I don't want to talk about the Ferryman, or sacrifice, or death, or even rivers. These are our memories right now. Not his."

Bastian's fingers tightened around the key ring. His stomach writhed in fear, his entire body was a taut stripe of tension, but Zan was right. If this was the end of everything, he wanted to make it count.

The pad of his thumb was already rubbing against the teeth of the key he wanted. "Do you like sunrises?" he finally asked. He held up a key and forced a smile.

Zan offered a shaky grin in response. Then he held out his hand.

᠌ܔܔܔܔܔܔܔܔܔܔ

The Super 8 motel sat at the end of a dead-end street, surrounded by nothing but broken-up sidewalk and tumbleweed. A dirt road led from it toward a small speckle of streetlights in the distance. They promised some semblance of life, but Bastian knew the only thing out there was an abandoned Quality theater and a run-down Walmart.

"Nice place," Zan said, stepping forward. "No sunrise though."

"Impatient."

The field in front of them was lit briefly by headlights. They watched a rusted-out pickup truck pull a U-turn in the hotel lot, then drive back toward the streetlights. "Buford, Wyoming," Bastian said. "Population 1."

"Awfully big hotel for one person."

Bastian shivered. It was still August, but the predawn temperatures already warned of winter. "Technically we're still outside of Buford," he said. "But just barely. It's a ghost town. My mom . . ."

He could still remember everything about that week. They'd driven from New York to Portland in her tiny Honda. The move across the country wasn't unanticipated. They'd stayed in New York too long; she'd gotten that itch to move. Dorian and Bastian could see it in her and had collectively begun packing their things before she even said a word.

The moving truck would arrive weeks before they would, carrying all their things.

She took a more circular route.

They slept in the car, in the parking lots of rest stops, national parks, and scenic overlooks. They hit Niagara, the Grand Canyon, Yellowstone, everywhere and anywhere that was supposed to be important. They hit other places too. Buford was on the list because it was in a county famous for rockhounding, and she had plans to hunt for sapphires.

They'd stayed at this little motel. The next morning, they woke up early and walked the jogging path. She'd hung a lock on the fence. *This place will remember us.*

She'd been so happy.

But this moment? The dark, the quiet, the just-before-dawn? This did not belong to her. This belonged to Bastian. He breathed in, smelling the dust of the small town that permeated this memory.

"I couldn't sleep," Bastian said. "I'd gotten used to the city, the cars, the people, the light pollution. But out in the middle of nowhere like this? There's so much quiet. And it had been so long since I'd really seen stars."

The SUPER 8 sign buzzed. Bastian looked up at it, then motioned for Zan to follow him. "Come on."

He took off toward the building, circling the perimeter until he came to an abandoned back lot. There was an escape ladder here—one of those old rickety black metal ones. Bastian reached up and pulled on it, wincing as the thing clanged and groaned on its way down.

"Really?" Zan asked.

Bastian just grinned, then started climbing. The ladder shook beneath him with every step, and the groaning got worse the higher he went. By the time he hit the second-floor windows, he heard Zan start up behind him, cautiously testing every step.

The ladder stopped midway between the third-story floor and the roof, so Bastian had to haul himself up the rest of the way. He waited at the top for Zan and stuck a hand out to help when he finally reached the last rung.

"Shit," Zan panted. "This better be a beautiful sunrise." He ignored Bastian's hand and pulled himself up, rolling over to his back as soon as he reached the roof. "I'm done," he said. "I'll see it from here, thanks."

"Three stories," Bastian said. "And you're winded?"

"You know all those people they find dead on Mount Everest?"

Bastian cocked his head. "Yes . . ."

"I've met a few. All highly motivated people. All people who like exercise. All very, very dead."

Rolling his eyes, Bastian turned and walked over to the east side of the building. The sky was freckled with bright stars. The hazy glow of *almost* flickered on the horizon, but there was no actual sunlight yet.

"Still no sunrise," Zan said, coming up behind him.

"Still impatient," Bastian replied. He sat down. The concrete was cold, so he drew his knees up and hugged them to his chest. Zan sat down next to him. Bastian had to fight back a smile. He reached for his gum. Held out a piece. Zan took it hesitantly.

"What do you think you'll do when you leave?"

Zan slowly crumpled the wrapper and stuck the piece in his mouth. "This is still disgusting," he said, but he kept chewing. "I thought we weren't talking about the Ferryman."

Bastian barely kept himself from shivering. "We're not," he said. "We're talking about you and what you'll do when you're free. Where will you go?"

"Not Buford," Zan said slowly.

It was clearly meant as a joke, but Zan's voice had tightened again. The twitchy nervousness was back. "Seriously," Bastian said. "Will you go back home?"

"I don't have a home."

"You've got anywhere in the world. You can't tell me you haven't thought about it."

"I have," Zan said. His fingernails scratched at the concrete rooftop.

Reaching out, Bastian laid his hand over Zan's. Zan stilled. Bastian leaned close—close enough that he could smell cinnamon. Close enough that Bastian could see the spattering of freckles across his nose, like the spattering of stars above them.

"I think I'd like Portland," Zan said quietly, eyes flicking up to Bastian's, green only barely visible in the dusky twilight.

Bastian stopped breathing. Warmth spread through him, *happiness*. No matter what happened, the Ferryman couldn't have this.

"You were supposed to be a dream," Bastian whispered, voice hollowed out.

Zan moved, pressing forward until their lips met.

Bastian closed his eyes and pulled Zan even closer until there was nothing but the taste of cinnamon, until there was no sound but the sound of his own heart beating in his ears.

A coyote howled, a long, piercing sound of loneliness.

Zan pulled away. "Not a dream," he murmured. "Real."

Bastian let go, sat back, and studied him. Zan's eyes were hooded and intense, his cheeks were flushed, his glasses were cock-eyed over the bridge of his nose, his hair was curling around the backs of his ears.

He was perfect.

Zan wriggled closer, then he lay down, back pressed against the cold concrete.

Bastian lay down, too, close enough that their heads brushed against each other. He pointed at a spot in the sky. "That's Ursa Major," he said, holding up a finger and tracing a line of stars.

Zan looked up and frowned, trying to follow Bastian's finger. "No it's not."

"Yeah, see, the stars form a W—"

"That's Cassiopeia. You took me to the top of a building to look at stars, and you don't even know what they are." He turned ever so slightly, grin growing until he was laughing.

Bastian scowled. His hand dropped. "I know the constellations," he muttered.

"No, no you really don't, oh my god, world's worst date."

"This isn't a date."

"You kissed me."

"Obviously a mistake!"

"Not a mistake," Zan said, still laughing, but rolling back over to his side. He reached out and grabbed Bastian's hand, holding it toward the sky.

Bastian thought briefly about yanking his arm free out of spite.

Zan traced his hand along the *W*. "Cassiopeia is the W. Named after a Greek queen. She was placed in the sky as a punishment after pissing off Poseidon. Then there's Ursa Major. You can figure out the Big Dipper, right?"

Bastian grunted. His hands were sweating, his heart was racing, and he felt utterly humiliated.

"Okay," Zan continued. "Those stars tell the story of Ursa Major the bear, and Ursa Minor the . . . baby bear."

"Lots of bears."

Zan snorted. "Okay, the snout is super pointed, but you can see the legs, right?"

Bastian squinted toward the sky. All he saw were stars that were rapidly fading as the sun began to rise. "Not really," he said.

Snorting, Zan dropped his hand. "Hopeless."

"It's dumb anyway."

"It's not. It's mythology."

"Like Styx."

"We're not talking about rivers," Zan chided. "Look, find Cassiopeia again."

"Okay." Bastian looked up, fuzzing his eyes just enough for the giant W to pop out.

"All right, Andromeda is right next door." Zan pointed up again, tracing a pattern.

Bastian couldn't follow his fingers, but he didn't say anything. He was close enough now that their shoulders were brushing. Close enough that he could feel every time Zan took a breath in.

"There is a quote in the book," Bastian said quietly. "One of my mom's favorites. Spoken by the Little Prince to the traveler he meets."

Zan nodded, dropping his hand to his side.

Bastian closed his eyes, the words he'd carried in his heart for so long rising easily to the surface. "'In one of the stars I shall be living. In one of them I shall be laughing. And so it will be as if all the stars were laughing, when you look at the sky at night.'" He peeked over at Zan who was watching him with hooded eyes. "You're my traveler," he said.

He didn't miss the way Zan's face fell.

"You're a sap," Zan said quickly. "I am not a traveler, and you are not a star."

"This has to end," Bastian murmured. The Ferryman's low hiss snaked through his mind. *You are running out of time.*

"It won't," Zan said, shaking his head. "Not yet."

The sky began to purple. If they kept watching, it would turn pink, and orange, and red, and bright, and beautiful, and Bastian had taken Zan here for this moment, but suddenly he wanted nothing more than to freeze time, to keep the stars and the heaviness of the night. His lips were still buzzing. He wanted to kiss Zan again. He wanted to live. To meet Zan in the real world, to show him everything.

The sun kept rising. Time kept moving. The memory was still alive.

"Sunrise," he said.

Zan hummed beside him.

They watched it paint the sky, stayed there long enough that the colors started to dull around them, all the way up until the memory began to fade.

"Please come back again," Zan whispered.

"Always," Bastian said. He held out one hand and watched his fingers slowly crumble to dust.

CHAPTER FIFTY-FOUR

Portland, Oregon

"So rad," Riley said, gold-flecked fingernails tapping away at the counter as she swiped the touch screen of the new point-of-sale console he'd finally (mostly) figured out.

"Rad," Mathais replied, in an I'm-clearly-mocking-you voice.

Riley rolled her eyes while Bastian continued flipping through a stack of unpriced comic books that Mathais had found stashed in a back corner. "I have no idea what any of these are," he said.

"But you're grinning anyway," Riley snarked. "What gives? You're happy."

"Sound the alarms!" Mathais bellowed. "Bash Barnes, happy! Apocalypse incoming, take cover now, all units are red!"

"Dumbass," Bastian said. He picked up one of the magazines and threw it at Mathais who caught it straight out of the air with a grin.

He *was* happy because he'd kissed Zan, and Zan had kissed back, and that was everything.

He was also terrified, because every moment here was ticking, grains of sand dropping silently in an hourglass he couldn't see.

Maybe the next time he dreamed, he'd kiss Zan again. Maybe the next time he dreamed, the Ferryman would be waiting, and everything would end.

He flinched away from that thought.

"Seriously," Riley said, not taking her eyes off the screen. "What gives? Please tell me you're not dating Greer or something."

"Eww," Mathais said, just as Bastian threw a comic book at her too. She didn't snatch it away quite so easily. It smacked into her nose, then dropped to the floor.

With a wounded moan, Riley turned on him. "Greer or weird college girl. Those are the only two people I've seen you with."

Bastian wet his lips. "So, ummm, I'm not hiring any extra workers," he said, trying to change the topic.

Riley flicked him a look that said *I know exactly what you are doing*, but she didn't press him on it. "Yeah. Dorian told us. High school dropout," she mocked.

Bastian grinned at her. She wasn't being antagonistic, just Riley.

"Look, I've got a ridiculous AP load next semester, but I can manage a couple afternoons of working," she said, fiddling with the register. "Paid obviously."

"Obviously," Bastian echoed. "No, look, I appreciate the offer, but I've got this covered. It's not going to blow up overnight, there won't be customers lining the street. I'm going to do it on my own for a bit. See how it goes. Can't be that difficult, right?"

Course, that was assuming he lasted long enough to try and that the Ferryman didn't show up tonight to rip his soul from his body.

Cat meowed at him. Bastian swallowed hard and reached down, scratching behind his ears.

The iPad whirred to life, then blinked furious red.

"Wasn't me!" Riley yelped, backing away with both hands up. "Bullshit," Bastian muttered. He hauled himself up and over the counter. VOID it flashed. He reached behind and pulled out the plug entirely, watching the screen go dead. "There, see? Easy."

"Going to do wonders for your accounting records," Riley snarked.

"You're the one who killed it, you know."

The door jingled, interrupting the start of what would be an impossible back-and-forth argument. Dorian stepped in, black peacoat clenched firmly around himself. He had a blue knit scarf tied around his throat, his own end-of-semester gift from Riley who'd somehow churned out an impressive number of truly hideous pieces of apparel over the last semester—lumpy socks, twisted scarves, oversized hats. She'd even started some sort of awful cardigan made of vomit-brown-looking yarn.

Bastian looked down at his orange bracelet and felt nothing but love for her.

His phone buzzed in his pocket. He pulled it out.

Greer [7:44 PM]: Hangout at my place later. Interested?

He ignored it.

"We ready?" Dorian asked, tugging at his scarf.

"Birthday boys!" Mathais announced, holding out his fist for Dorian to bump. Dorian did, then caught Bastian's eye.

"Happy birthday," he said quietly.

"Same," Bastian said back.

December 31. He'd made it to the end of the year.

They were going to get sushi takeout to celebrate, would come back to the bookstore and hang out for the night watching stupid Marvel movies and talking about the new year—planning for college, for bookstores, for life.

His phone buzzed again.

Greer [7:44 PM]: Free booze. Like I keep saying, you're fun when you're trashed

Riley waved at him. "Earth to Bash. You ready?"

He looked over at them, all standing by the door now, all bundled in boots, and coats, and hats. Even though it rarely snowed in Portland, this afternoon it had started coming down like crazy, coating the roads and the sidewalks with perfect powder.

"Coming," Bastian called.

Bastian [7:45 PM]: No thanks

He deleted the messages, blocked Greer's number, and shoved his phone in his pocket. He didn't need Greer when he had all *this*.

Then he grabbed his heavy jacket from the new coat hook he'd hammered in last night. Grabbed his keys. Followed his friends out the door.

CHAPTER FIFTY-FIVE

Styx

"I like the new one," Zan said, reaching over and brushing his fingers across the orange yarn around Bastian's wrist. "It's brighter. Happier."

Bastian stared out over the frozen overpass littered with rush hour traffic. They sat far above it all, legs swinging over the aluminum shelf of a billboard that read DON'T DRIVE LIKE A ROOSTER.

Bastian had no idea what it meant, or why this was someone's last memory, but he was more than happy to be sitting *anywhere* with Zan because the Ferryman hadn't been waiting for him when he'd entered Styx. He still had time. "It was a sort-of birthday gift," he said, looking back down at the bracelet.

"I didn't know it was your birthday!"

"Yep. A couple of nights ago. The big one nine. Everyone's favorite age."

"Ugh, you're officially older than me now. That's stupid."

"You've got five hundred years on me!"

Zan grinned. "Yeah, but time's frozen on Styx so you don't get to count years like that. Still eighteen. Always eighteen."

He frowned; fingers rubbed over the knot. "Three wishes, three knots, right?"

Bastian swallowed. "Right. Didn't make the last wish though. Not yet."

"Run out of ideas, oh wise, nineteen-year-old?"

Rolling his eyes, Bastian swatted at him. Zan ducked out of the way. The aluminum they sat on creaked and groaned.

"When did it all change?" Bastian asked, once they'd stabilized again.

Zan pulled his legs up and tucked his head on his knees, peering at Bastian.

"I mean . . . what made you keep me around?"

Wincing, Zan huffed a forced-sounding laugh. "You're a good kisser?" he offered.

A flush of warmth overtook him, and Bastian leaned over and kissed him hard. "Flattery will get you everywhere," he murmured, breath coming just a little faster as he settled himself back on the ledge. "But I'm serious. You risked everything for me. Why?"

Zan's face scrunched up. "Don't push me," he said in a tone clearly trying for levity but failing miserably. "I could still bring you over."

"Yes," Bastian agreed, even though the warmth of the kiss was fast fading, only to be replaced by burbling nausea. "And you still will. You have to. You know that, right? I'm not going to be the reason you lose your chance at life."

Zan shook his head, eyes squeezing closed. "It's fine," he said slowly. "I'm fine."

Leaning back on his hands, Bastian tilted his head toward Zan, watching him from the corner of his eye. "I used to say that in therapy all the time," he said. "I'm fine. You know what it always meant?"

He waited for an answer that didn't come. "It meant I wasn't," Bastian went on. "I wasn't fine. I needed help, I needed someone to see me and help."

Zan's fingers had curled around the ledge, knuckles bone white. He let out a strangled-sounding breath and looked up, cheekbones lit by the glowing sky. "I am, though," he said. "I promise."

Sighing, Bastian nudged him and held his arm out. "You tie it."

Zan looked over, nose wrinkling in confusion.

"You do it." Bastian shook his arm. "Tie the fourth knot. I have my wish."

Zan reached out and ran his fingers over the knot again. Then he picked up the two threads. "Is there like . . . something special you have to say?"

"Just tie it," Bastian said. "I'll do the rest."

Zan carefully knotted the bracelet, pulling tight.

Bastian thought about Zan. About dreaming. About what a future would look like if Zan could go free, and if Bastian could live.

Zan's hands were warm around his wrist. Bastian chewed his lower lip, forcing down the fear inside him that was threatening to eat him alive.

"I wish for you to kiss me again," he whispered, holding Zan's eyes.

Zan grinned, then surged up, lips meeting Bastian's. "I would have done that anyway," he said as he pulled away. "Wasted wish."

"Worth it," Bastian said.

Zan squeezed his hand. "I want you to show me your bookstore," he said.

Bastian pushed himself up. He extended his hand. Zan took it.

FOX BOOKS

The letters were brushed across the glass and painted in the same oranges as the door. It was a bright blotch on the busy street—Zan's eyes were drawn to it immediately in the gray misting rain, and all Zan could think was how wonderfully Bastian it looked. Hidden, but full of life. He glanced over at Bastian. "Wow," he said.

Bastian looked at the sidewalk. "It's not much," he warned. He pulled his hood up over his hair and turned his head to watch the line of oncoming traffic. A bus pulled away from the stop they were standing in front of. They only had to wait a few moments before the street cleared again. Bastian jogged across it.

Zan followed him, feet kicking up water.

The windows of the store were frosty with condensation. Zan stepped close as Bastian pulled out his key and turned it in the lock.

"It's really not much," Bastian warned again, pushing the door open and then stepping inside. A bell on the inside of the door jingled. "But it's mine."

The place was filled from bottom to top with books—books wedged into bookshelves, books stacked to Zan's height alongside bookshelves, books spilling over on top of bookshelves. There were wooden signs pointing the way to genres, hand painted with carefully calligraphed quotes. It smelled earthy, like paper and dust—exactly the way an old bookstore should smell.

"It's amazing," Zan said, because it was.

Everything here was electric, alive with possibility. If he closed his eyes, Zan could imagine living like this—among adventure, romance, and tragedy. Living with stories. He looked back at Bastian and could see the little lines in his brow, creases of nervousness. This was somehow more personal than kissing him had ever been.

"Cat is around here somewhere," Bastian said. He set his keys down on the counter next to the register.

"Cat?"

"Cat. Demon creature. Hellspawn. He's—"

A fluffy orange cat heaved itself up on the counter by Bastian. Bastian reached out a hand, and the cat headbutted him, then flicked his keys to the ground with one swoop of his paw.

"Hellspawn," Bastian repeated. He bent down to pick up his keys again, but Zan didn't miss the way he affectionately rubbed behind Cat's ears.

"He wants food," Bastian said.

"He lives here?"

"Yeah. Was kind of living here when I moved in. Didn't think it was fair to get rid of him. Pain in the ass, though."

Cat meowed again, and Bastian reached out to pet him. His hand missed. The echo had already turned, hopping down from the counter, not reacting to Bastian's movement at all. Playing out the path of the memory.

Bastian sighed and pushed his keys back in his pocket. "Wish you could actually be here. See it truly alive."

This was *alive*, Zan thought. The floor-to-ceiling windows let in enough light that he could see motes spinning slowly through the air. A boy on a bicycle sped by the window. Muted but heavy bass leaked in through the walls. Zan smiled. There was a little container of business cards by the register. Zan pulled one out. *Fox Books*, it read, in the same scrawl that was painted on the door. *Used and Collectible Books*. There was a phone number and an email address. Zan flipped it over. *Bastian Barnes, Owner* was written across the bottom edge—tiny white print against a matte black back.

"Souvenir?" Bastian asked.

"Sure," Zan said, pocketing the card. Then he reached into his other pocket and drew out a handful of things he'd pulled from the shelves in his office. Smooth skipping stones, a single white button, the pair of pink cat-eye glasses, and the rust-eaten love lock that Bastian had commented on during one of his first visits to Zan's office.

"What are you doing?" Bastian asked.

Zan smiled, because the moment Bastian had woken with a crystal fox in his palm pulled from a dead memory, the flickering flame of an idea had wedged tightly between Zan's ribs.

He would fill his office with pieces of Bastian, enough to remember him by, enough to get him through five hundred more years.

And he would fill Bastian's bookstore with pieces of himself.

Zan placed one of the stones next to the register and grabbed the rest of the stuff. "Stay there," he said, then wandered into the stacks of books. He deposited the glasses on a shelf filled with sheet music. Put another few rocks against the baseboards. Stashed bits and pieces of Styx throughout the bookstore, some in plain sight, some tucked so far away that he wasn't sure Bastian would ever find them all. When he was finally satisfied, he wandered back to the front of the store again where Bastian was still waiting as ordered.

Zan felt a spark of smug satisfaction over that.

"Did you just put garbage all over my store?" Bastian asked, but he was grinning.

"Totally," Zan confirmed. "Awful litter, customers are going to complain, you know how much I like chaos." He smiled at Bastian.

Bastian reached out and grabbed his hands, pulling him close. "I'll find them all," he whispered.

"I hope so," Zan said. He tipped his head, pressing his lips against Bastian's in an embarrassingly long kiss. When Bastian finally pulled away, he had a goofy-looking grin plastered on his face.

"Riley will be here in two hours," he said, face red. "You can meet her."

"She won't see me," Zan said.

"I know." His mouth pulled to a straight line, and he studied Zan intently. "But you could still see her. Dorian might come by too."

"You want me to meet your brother?" He could feel his stomach turning flips as he smiled. "Is he as much of an asshole as you?"

Bastian rolled his eyes. "Worse. Look, we can hang out here and wait for them. Or we can go somewhere else. Wherever else. Show me something amazing before I kick it."

It was just a joke, but Zan's smile vanished completely. He looked down at his shoes.

"Kidding," Bastian said a second too late. His smile had disappeared also.

A car horn honked outside. "You love it here," Zan murmured.

There was a long moment of silence, punctuated only by Cat's constant chewing. Then Bastian huffed a laugh. "Yeah. I do."

He blinked, and Zan watched the way his lashes moved. The air grew thick between them, every moment slowing so much that for a minute, Zan was certain the memory had died around them.

Bastian swallowed. "We don't have to stay here. I just wanted to . . ." He shrugged awkwardly. "My memories become yours, right? I know you're almost done on Styx, but now you can have a stale bookstore to wander around in when I'm not here. Read something. I know, you already have the Library of Congress, the Klementinum, and wherever else, so it's stupid—"

"This is better," Zan said. "They don't have *you*."

Bastian paused. Opened his mouth but shut it again, rubbing at his wrist. "You like doughnuts?" he finally asked.

It was clearly not what he'd intended on saying. Zan shrugged. "Not really."

"Do you like anything?"

"Figs."

Bastian made a disgusted sound, and Zan couldn't help his laugh that bubbled to the surface.

"Okay, well they have coffee," Bastian muttered, turning for the door. "Everyone likes coffee."

Zan followed Bastian outside and down the sidewalk, one shop over.

This store was lit by bright white, fluorescent lights. The floor was worn beige tile, the counters all had thick, retro bubble lettering in pink and brown that read SESAME DOUGHNUTS. The racks on all the walls held bagels, breads, and muffins. It smelled like yeast.

"There's a Krispy Kreme a block up that people go to," Bastian said. "Which is stupid. The Boston creams here are twice the size and half the price."

There was only a man wearing a bright-blue-and-green Seahawks hat in front of them. Zan heard him order a large black coffee and a dozen bagels.

Bastian walked around the edge of the counter. "I'll get coffee, you get doughnuts," he called. "Apple fritters and Boston creams!"

Zan pushed himself up on the counter, twirled his legs around, and popped over to the other side. He studied the cases. He had no clue what an apple fritter was, only that these all looked absolutely awful. "Here?" he asked, pointing at a case that contained doughnuts covered in sprinkles.

Bastian shook his head. "Over one!"

The girl behind the counter walked over to the muffins, completely oblivious to Zan.

Zan moved over to the next case. These doughnuts were labeled: Chocolate Frosted, Cinnamon Twist, Jelly, Glazed . . . he paused.

There was an empty row with a black label.

6 days.

Zan reached out and tried to tug the little plaque free, but it didn't budge.

"Come on," Bastian called.

Zan swallowed. He forced his eyes over to the next case, grabbed two of the apple fritters, and two Boston creams, then grabbed a strawberry-frosted one for himself. It would probably be terrible.

He hopped back over the counter.

Bastian handed him a paper cup filled with coffee. "I've got better memories with Riley than the bookstore," he said. "We'll come back. For now? It's your turn. Show me something amazing."

Zan took the cup, then held out his hand.

CHAPTER FIFTY-SIX

Styx

He blinked his eyes open, tangled in the sheets of his mattress, the bright sunlight cutting across his bedroom in a single buttery line.

He blinked, and he was on Styx.

He blinked his eyes open, and it was a slice of moonlight, crawling across the floor.

He blinked, and he was on Styx.

He blinked, and Cat was meowing, and his phone was buzzing, and he texted Riley and Mathais and Dorian that he was sick, texted them not to check in, texted them that he was okay.

He blinked, and he was losing more time, losing more life, he was on Styx, he was on Styx, he was on Styx, he was—

CHAPTER FIFTY-SEVEN

Styx

Zan took him to the Great Wall of China where they walked, sipping coffee stolen from the gift shop and eating pastries from a shop in Paris that Zan had found two decades ago—one that sold cookies stuffed with fig paste that almost tasted as good as his mother's.

Bastian drank his entire coffee in one go and stuck the empty cup inside the backpack of a hassled-looking mother clutching the grimy hands of two kids. Her mouth was open wide, her eyes frantic. A yard ahead, a toddler was frozen midrun. He took one bite of the fig cookie and grimaced.

"No?" Zan asked.

"Hard pass," Bastian answered. "Tastes awful." Bastian put the rest of that in her backpack too.

She had a key chain that dangled. It read 5.

When Bastian faded, Zan held on as long as he could until his fingers clenched tight around a fistful of ash.

Bastian took him to a hole-in-the-wall arcade that was a block away from the apartment he'd lived in in New York City. It was ten in the morning, empty except for a couple of school-age kids moving in strange ways on a dance platform in the far corner. Bastian broke into one of the machines by the back counter and pulled out hundreds of little gold coins. The manager yelled at the kids in the back for messing with the machines. Zan pulled them into an alcove between a machine labeled *Duck Hunt* and a machine labeled *Asteroids*. They kissed, they came out, the manager smiled at them and told them to have fun. They played something called *Pac-Man* and something called Skee-Ball. Zan's ball landed in a 4, then in a 3. They played something called *Centipede*. Bastian always won. Zan didn't mind.

When Bastian faded, Zan kissed him, closing his eyes as the press of their lips vanished to nothing but a memory.

Zan brought him to an underground club in Seoul, a festival in Rio de Janeiro, and a mountain in Geneva where Zan skied down, and Bastian watched. At the bottom of the hill, Bastian pulled Zan into his arms, and Zan looked at the snowflakes clustered on Bastian's lashes, and they didn't kiss, but their noses brushed.

"Will you ever drive again?" Zan asked, as they lay on a blanket, watching an air show that Bastian had remembered. The roar of the plane engines shook the ground around them, and they nestled so close their cheeks touched.

Bastian shook his head. "I don't know."

"Promise me you will?" Zan asked.

"I don't *know*," Bastian said again, harder this time. He looked down at his hands, entire body drawing to a sharp, dangerous line.

Zan turned and looked at him, eyes glassy and dark. "It wasn't your fault," he whispered.

Bastian's mouth opened, then closed again. He didn't answer.

Bastian took him to a waterfall named Multnomah that lay on the edge of a gorge separating Washington and Oregon. He wouldn't climb to the top—just stood on a bridge at the bottom and looked up into the frozen spray. In the crystal-clear stream below, there were thousands of coins.

"This all burned down about seven years ago," Bastian said. "Forest fire."

"Sad."

"Life."

"Pessimist."

"Pragmatist," Bastian corrected.

Zan's hand closed around a leftover gold arcade token in his windbreaker pocket. It said *2*. He took it out and tossed it over the bridge. It made the tiniest plink of noise as it hit the water.

"So they'll know we were here," Zan said when Bastian looked over at him curiously.

"Who?" Bastian asked.

Zan didn't have an answer.

They kissed again in Vietnam, on top of one of the giant boulders jutting out of Ha Long Bay. Bastian wrapped a hand around the back of Zan's neck and pulled him close and whispered "I love you" against his lips. Zan kissed him back and said "I love you too," and it was real, this was real, he was real.

When Bastian faded, Zan sunk down on his knees, tucked his head into his arms, and screamed.

"You should visit your mom," Zan said in Maine, standing on a rocky pier that extended just past an enormous lighthouse. A line of bright-red buoys bobbed in the water. Each had a big number *1*. "I mean in real life."

Bastian froze. "I don't need to stand over a gravestone to mourn," he said, voice strangled.

Zan considered this. Grief was a strange thing. Sometimes he woke up choking on it, fury and desperation carving the soft curves of his mother until she was unrecognizable. He missed her, and he didn't regret his sacrifice, but the hatred he had for the loss of his own life was razor sharp, painting all of his memories a little too vividly.

"I don't know if my mom is buried," he said. "I've never been allowed back in my own memories. I don't know how she died, how my siblings died, where they died, if any remnant even exists in the real world for me to find. I don't even know if *I'm* buried. Or what they did for me. Or if there was even a me to find."

Bastian didn't say anything, but he stepped closer.

"You should visit her," Zan finished lamely.

"And you should visit Greece," Bastian murmured. "When you get out of here. Really go visit."

The night air was thick with humidity. Every time Zan breathed in, he could feel the water deep in his chest. It was air, he was breathing air, but he suddenly felt like he was strangling, choking, dying just like he'd done five hundred years ago in the Asopos. He shuddered, then looked up at the sky. Found the Big Dipper. Worked his way out, eyes flicking along every star.

He watched the floating 1 buoy bob underneath a wave, then surface again with a pop.

"This is it," Zan said quietly. "This is our last night."

Bastian's head snapped down, brow creasing in confusion.

Zan swallowed hard. "He made me a deal," he admitted. He didn't wait for an answer, just plowed on, forcing out words he'd tried to practice for the weeks the Ferryman had been taunting him. "The night he took you in Chicago, he came and made me a deal. And I took it."

Bastian turned toward him, horror painting his face. "This is what you've been hiding?" he breathed. "*This* is what you've been too afraid to tell me?"

"It's my choice, and—"

"What was the deal?" Bastian shook his head, tiny movements at first but growing bigger and bigger. "Zan," he said, voice now strangled and harsh. "What did you do?"

Zan stuttered to a halt, hands half up like he was warding off an angry animal. "I. . .it. . ." He sucked in a breath, trying to order his thoughts. "He doesn't have anyone else," he said lowly. "Once my time is up, he doesn't have another servant."

"So what?" Bastian said, pressing his hands against his temples. "So what if he doesn't have a servant, that's not on you, you don't owe him—"

"It was you or me," Zan cut in. "One of us was going to be bound to him. Five hundred years. That was the deal."

Bastian rocked back on his heels like he'd been struck. "You . . ." His mouth worked around words that wouldn't form, his face drained of color. "You can't do that."

Zan hauled in a shaky breath. "It's my choice."

A deafening quiet grew as Bastian's eyes flashed icy blue. Then he threw his head back and shrieked. "Ferryman! Ferryman, come here! Take me! I'll serve you—"

"He can't reach us here," Zan said. "We're too far inside the memory." He swallowed hard, pushing on. "Bastian, you need to live. You have your bookstore, and your cat. You have people who love you. You can't give that up, not for me, not for anyone."

Bastian choked off a sob. "Don't do this," he pleaded.

"Thank you," Zan said. "For everything."

"You have to get out. It's your turn to *get out*. You have to meet Dorian. Meet Riley and Mathais, see Cat, see the store, not just in a memory. I *know* I have a life, but you deserve one too, oh my god, Zan, don't do this—"

Zan shoved his hand into the pocket of his windbreaker and

drew out the letter he'd spent hours on, the one the Ferryman had watched him write, black scythe gripped in one skeletal hand, rancid black dripping from his eyes as he smirked.

"It's for you," Zan croaked, trying to hand it over.

"No." Bastian stepped back, shaking his head.

Zan followed him, matching him step for step, until Bastian was a moment away from tumbling into the water. "Take it," he pleaded. "Please, take it, Bastian—"

The wind picked up, and bits of ash began to flake from Bastian's skin.

He was fading.

Panic bubbled up in Zan, the same frantic terror that he'd felt as the mud of the Asopos River closed over his mouth. "Bastian, please," he begged. "It's already done, don't leave like this."

Bastian reached out with a trembling hand as bits of his sweatshirt turned to dust. "Don't," he cried. "I'll come back. Tell him I'll come back, Zan, tell him it's supposed to be me—"

Zan jumped forward, forcing the letter into the pocket of Bastian's sweatshirt. Then he grabbed his hand and pulled him close, kissing him one last time. "Live for me," he whispered against Bastian's lips.

Bastian didn't answer, just crumbled to ash underneath Zan's fingertips.

Zan closed his eyes. This was it.

This was their end.

CHAPTER FIFTY-EIGHT

Styx

Styx: a space that exists in half dream, half death. Shadows that flicker at the edge of vision. A nightmare, a dream, an in-between.

Zan walked along the glass beach, the frozen shape of Bastian's mom at his back, frosted and softened bits of rock giving way beneath his feet with tiny plinks of sound. The ocean rippled beside him, glassy blue-green turning foggy and dark.

His head hurt from crying; his eyes were still red and sore. He rubbed them furiously and took another step forward, pressing against the ice-cold barrier.

The darkness clumped together bit by bit, pulling colors from everything around them until the landscape faded to gray, until the only thing left was a boy in golden-framed glasses, and a giant black stag.

"You never wanted him," Zan ground out. "You only wanted me."

Wisps of gray fog rose up around him, and oily black leaked from the stag's eyes. Zan watched it drip down, coating coarse hair.

"You have been my best," the Ferryman agreed placidly.

Zan tore his glasses off and threw them angrily, watching as they faded to the same gray as everything else. The stag blinked, big, watery eyes still dripping. His jaw curled up, revealing the dull incisors. He looked pleased. Like he knew he'd won.

Of course he'd won, Zan thought bitterly. He was the Ferryman. He was a god. And Zan never stood a chance.

"He will live," the Ferryman said. "And I accept your sacrifice."

Zan screwed up his face and forced his eyes up, struggling not to cry. His heart kicked in his chest, but he swallowed down his panic and reached out, brushing his hand across one pure black antler. "Five hundred years more," he whispered. "And then I go free."

"Mmm," the Ferryman hummed. "Do you think you will last this time?"

Zan thought of sunrises, of thrift stores, of monuments, of libraries. He thought of Bastian. He thought of love, of life, of being human. "Try me," he said, the words strong even as his hands began to shake.

The Ferryman laughed. "Oh, I will."

The stag dissolved; the stagnant beach popped back into existence.

Zan closed his eyes and listened to the sound of absolutely nothing.

CHAPTER FIFTY-NINE

Portland, Oregon

Bastian opened his eyes.

The sun was shining through his apartment window, leaving a slice of buttery light across his bed. Bastian's hand curled into a fist at his side, and he struggled to suck in a breath through his anger, and there was nothing but rage now, pure, unadulterated rage, and he rolled over and slammed his fist down as hard as he could on the bedside table.

Cat hissed at him.

Nothing else happened.

"No," he whispered. His other hand was curled inside the pocket of his sweatshirt, rough paper clenched between his fingers. Zan's envelope. Bastian held it up, but his eyes slid to his arm, the left arm, the arm with the bruise.

There was nothing there but healthy, normal, human skin.

"No," Bastian moaned. He squeezed his eyes closed and tried to picture the gray fog, the mirrored water, the door, tried to force himself back to sleep. "No, no, no, no—"

Nothing happened. No door appeared, no oily black snaked around his legs; there was absolutely nothing.

His phone buzzed. Bastian slowly reached for it and pulled it to himself.

Riley [9:13 AM]: Happy opening day! 😃 🎉 🎉

Bastian let out a wheezing sob as he looked at the date on his phone. January sixth. The arbitrary date he'd set months ago when he'd hired Joon. The date he never thought he'd get to.

The store was officially open. His life was officially starting. And as he pulled in a shuddering breath, he knew with a sinking heart and unflinching certainty that he was never going to see Zan again.

Meow, Cat said, stretching up and pawing at the bed.

"I can't," Bastian pleaded. This wasn't how it was supposed to end. Not like this—not with Zan a memory, a person he couldn't tell anyone about, a figment of his imagination that no one else would ever understand.

It wasn't fair.

He was supposed to be dead.

Meow.

Bastian pushed himself up. The letter crinkled as his fist tightened around it. "Coming," he said to Cat, voice scratchy with disuse.

Meow.

Bastian padded down the hall. Cat followed him.

His laptop was sitting on the table, next to a pile of signed books he'd found downstairs and intended to look up. Bastian ignored them and walked over to the fridge where he pulled out a single stale bagel and a jug of milk that smelled ever so slightly off.

He needed to go grocery shopping.

Meow.

His stomach churned. Bastian shut the fridge door and

grabbed a can of cat food from the counter. He opened it—rote, mechanical, without any emotion at all.

He couldn't do this.

Cat gave a happy chirp then started devouring his food. Bastian slowly walked over to the table and sank down in a chair. He pushed the books out of the way. Tore open the envelope.

Bastian,

I guess this is goodbye.

Bastian's hand started shaking. "No," he whispered.

I promise you, this was my choice. It was me or you and there was never an option. You didn't deserve to die. It was a shitty situation, you were dealt a crappy hand or whatever, but you still didn't deserve it. Move on, okay? You have friends, you have a brother, you have a life. And someday I'll have that too. It's still there on the table, part of the deal, so don't worry about me. I'm not dying. Just have more time to serve. It's okay. This is really okay.

Thank you for the forest. Thank you for the bookstore, and the arcade games, and the waterfall. Thank you for everything.

It was short, but these things always are in those books you love. And you love books. You love the romance of pages turning, the smell of paper, the promise of adventure.

I'm glad I met you. Just like the prince, I don't regret a single minute. You were right. I will be your traveler, and you will always, always be my star.

Love,

Zan

Bastian crumpled the page in his hand. Cat jumped up on the table and nudged Bastian's wrist with his nose.

Bastian just buried his head in his hands and sobbed.

CHAPTER SIXTY

Portland, Oregon

He opened the store that morning.

He opened the store the morning after that.

He sold off an arm's worth of Tolkien to a girl in a prep school uniform one week.

He sold three boxes worth of fiction to a man decked out in green-and-white Portland State garb the next week.

The first week of February, he took in six crates worth of pulp romance from a red-faced woman who claimed that her mother had an attic full of them and she didn't know where else to bring them.

Riley would totally call him a pushover later, but Bastian accepted them all. Smiled at her. Said "Thank you."

He didn't dream.

The bruise that had wrapped around his entire arm and reached for his heart didn't appear again.

He went to therapy, and Andrea told him he looked healthy, that he looked like he'd been sleeping well. Bastian didn't know what to say to that. He told her that he'd met someone, that they'd separated. She listened. There was a gaping wound inside him that didn't feel like it would ever close, but there was also something more. Something good.

Dorian and Riley and Mathais stopped in almost every day after school. They complained about classes, about tests, about professors who were trying to make them hate everything, about sports teams, and girls, and late-night study sessions that meant nothing because they were seniors. They were almost done.

Mrs. Kim brought him food once a week. She would drop it off, and he would eat off the leftovers for days, and it was a simple act filled with so much love that it made him want to cry.

Bastian kept trying to dream, but every morning he woke up, and colors were the right shade, there were no more oily shadows, no more sounds of water, no more fear, no more death.

No more Zan.

For months, Bastian opened Fox Books every morning, and for months, he balanced the register in the evening. It was working. It wasn't the high school to college to professional pipeline Dorian had devoted his life to, but it was perfectly Bastian. He'd opened a bookstore. He was actually making enough money to live. And with Riley's help, he was studying every night for the GED he'd take next month, which was its own kind of curse because now she walked around the shop holding her head high like she was the goddess of test prep.

He wondered what the Greek equivalent would be.

Zan would have known.

丮丮丮丮丮丮丮丮丮

Meow?

Cat hopped up beside Bastian at the register and inserted his very wet nose into Bastian's coffee.

"You are the worst," Bastian muttered. He reached out a hand and let Cat headbutt his way through Bastian's fingers.

The door swung open, and Riley strutted in, decked out in a horrible purple knit jumper and sparkly gold leggings.

"Sup." She pushed herself up on top of the counter and reached for his coffee. She snagged it and drank it all down, grimacing. "Gross," she said, crinkling the cup and tossing it in the bin. "At least try a latte."

"Maybe try buying your own," Bastian snarked back.

"Party tonight," Riley said. "Last one! It's classy, I swear. Jasmine's hosting, only the cool kids get to go. Aka us. No alcohol, no Greer, just a goodbye hangout. Come? Most people are heading out of town soon."

They were. Riley was leaving next week for a tiny liberal arts university in Southern California where she was going to double major in English and biology because she was always the over-achiever. Dorian was leaving in a couple of days for Michigan. Mathais would be staying in Portland and joining the ranks of the green-and-white PSU clan, but once his classes started, he wouldn't have as much time. He wouldn't be able to make it into the store more than once a week.

And Bastian was going to start interviewing employees in another month because the store was getting too busy for him to handle on his own.

Everything was changing.

"Come on, Mathais's coming, ergo weird cheerleader girl is coming—"

"Shelby."

"Weird cheerleader girl. He should have picked Vassie. She was perfect."

"Maybe he didn't want you plotting out his love life?"

"He's missing out," Riley said, nose in the air. "Anyway, Dorian's also going. He and Jasmine are back on I guess—"

"Dorian's back with Jasmine?"

"I know, right?" She drew conspiratorially closer. "Rumor has it, the day school got out he picked her up and took her back to the townhouse and—"

"Don't you dare finish that sentence," Bastian hissed. "Do not need to know."

"Just trying to keep you updated since you never hang out with us anymore, Mr. Bookstore Owner," she said perkily.

Bastian winced. "Update me on *anything* but that."

"All right, so party?"

You have friends, you have a brother, you have a life.

"All right," Bastian said.

"Come on, Bastian…" Riley blinked. "Wait. All right?"

Bastian shrugged. "Yeah. Okay. I'll go."

Riley was gaping at him like a stupid-looking fish. "Are you serious?"

"If this is going to cause your brain to go nuclear, I'll just stay here."

"No, no, no, this is great, Dorian is going to be absolutely— aww, man." She let out a string of curse words. "I owe Mathais ten dollars!"

"You *bet* on this?" Bastian's voice pitched higher. "Utter betrayal, Riley."

Shrugging almost apologetically, Riley leaned up against the counter, peering around the register. "Kind of? You have any mints?"

Bastian rolled his eyes. "Office."

Riley gave him a salute, then sauntered back like she owned the place, barely avoiding stepping on the toes of a kid who stepped up to the counter.

"What's up?" Bastian asked the girl.

She thrust up a pile of hefty fantasy tomes and stepped closer. "Found this behind one of the shelves," she said, setting a rusted lock up on the counter.

It was a metal padlock, the kind they had on all the lockers at Preston. This one was scarred and rust-pocked and immediately recognizable.

Bastian swallowed hard. He'd spent weeks after the final dream searching the store, looking for all traces Zan might have left, pulling rocks and buttons from behind books, scouring every corner.

He'd thought that he'd found everything.

"Didn't know if you were missing it," the girl said.

Bastian found himself smiling, even though it hurt. "A friend gave it to me," he said softly.

The girl cocked her head. Her pink glasses slid down her nose, and she pushed them up quickly. "Just these," she said, motioning to the books. Her hair was wound in intricate braids all over her head, purple-and-white clips holding them all in place. He guessed she was middle school age.

Bastian sorted through her books. "You like fantasy?" he asked, setting them all aside.

The girl's eyebrows knit together. "Uh . . . obviously." She crossed her arms and glared up at him, like she was daring him to make fun of her over it.

"Come here," Bastian said, circling around the desk. He led her back around the shelves and started pulling titles and shoving them into her arms, one book, three books, a dozen books.

"I can't pay for—"

"Oh, you can have them."

"Bastian!" Riley yelled suspiciously from the office.

Her eyes flicked nervously in that direction. Bastian held a finger to his lips.

"My store," he whispered dramatically. "My rules."

She gave him a grin. "I'm Robin," she said.

"Nice to meet you, Robin. I'm Bastian," he returned. He filled her arms with books, brought her back up to the front of the store, and helped her put them in a bag. She grabbed a business card.

"I love foxes," she said, taking the bag that he held out to her and dropping the card in.

"I do too," Bastian said. He leaned closer. "I also like magic," he whispered.

"Me too," she said with a grin, looking down at the bag full of books. "Thanks!"

The bag was heavy enough that she hobbled her way to the door. Bastian watched her make it out to the street, watched as an older woman joined and handed her a doughnut from next door.

"Softie," Riley muttered, coming up behind him.

You love books, Zan had written. *You love the romance of pages turning, the smell of paper, the promise of adventure.*

Bastian couldn't help smiling. He picked up the love lock, twirling it between his fingers.

He watched Robin through the window as she jammed part of the doughnut in her mouth. Cream leaked out the side of it. She wiped her hand on her skirt, then went digging into the bag he'd given her.

She pulled out a book.

He could just barely see the cover from the window.

The Little Prince.

CHAPTER SIXTY-ONE

Oakland, California

MOUNTAIN VIEW CEMETERY, the sign read, curling steel letters rising high above scraggly looking grounds. It was the place all the social-ites were buried, the place where the Barnes family that his mom had basically been disowned from had a dozen plots for a dozen deaths. There was a plot for Dorian. A plot for him. Planning for the future, courtesy of a rich asshole grandmother they'd barely met.

There were no trees around—the California sun lit the sky and beat down on the parched grass. Sweat trickled down the back of Bastian's neck.

Horrible place to spend eternity.

She would have hated it.

He walked in, hands shoved in his pockets, chewing his cinna-mon gum loud enough for it to pop and crackle. Dorian followed at his heels, a small potted orchid in his hands. He was almost completely silent.

According to the layout he'd looked up online, the row they

needed was as far from the front entrance as you could get. Bastian led the way for the first bit, but when the trail split into three, he paused.

"You should lead," Bastian grunted.

Dorian nodded. "That way," he said quietly, pointing straight forward.

They walked up the winding dirt trail, past gravestones with flowers and picture frames, toy cars, and teddy bears, faded fabric flowers, and little pots full of river rock until Dorian pulled to a halt.

The stone was large—gray marble, with a horrible imprint of her face that looked nothing like her. There were no items surrounding it. The grass was clipped short, but otherwise, there was no sign that anyone had ever been here at all.

In Loving Memory, the stone read.

Dorian carefully set the plant down, gently coaxing the purple orchid to brush against the headstone. Bastian sank down on his haunches, then reached a finger out, pressed a finger to the curled letter O, and traced the name.

A car drove up to one of the bigger plots near them—one with monster truck toys, and wind chimes, and flowers, and more. He watched a couple get out, watched them kneel in front of the stone and press an enormous rainbow-colored windmill into the dirt. They tucked their heads.

"Sometimes I just miss her so much," Dorian said, voice husky and low.

Bastian swallowed. "Same."

The woman nearby let out a sob. The man wrapped an arm around her and pulled her close.

There was no one else around.

Bastian pushed himself up from the dirt. There was a wrought iron fence surrounding the cemetery that he could see in the distance.

"Be back," he said, then started walking.

He missed his mom, but he also missed Zan. The way Zan would speak way too fast, the way he laughed, the stupid glasses he had, the ridiculous green feather boa. He missed watching the stars and running through frozen buildings.

Bastian passed more graves, marble stones reflecting sunlight and blinding him. The dirt road was chunked out in parts, and he kicked pebbles as he walked, listening to them scritch across the dirt.

The fence was black, barren, sharp edges jutting unforgivingly toward the blue sky. Bastian watched the road through it for a long time, but there wasn't a car in sight.

"I miss you," he finally said quietly, fishing out something in his sweatshirt.

He'd done his best to polish it, but the lock still had little pock-marks of orange rust. He'd barely been able to coax it open with the help of a couple sketchy YouTube videos and a knife. Stepping forward, Bastian looped it through one of the bars and clicked it closed.

"This place will remember us," he murmured.

The crunch of footsteps sounded from behind him, but Bastian didn't take his eyes off the lock.

"For Mom?" Dorian asked.

Bastian shook his head. "For a friend." He smiled. "Someone I hope to see again." Then he turned, catching Dorian's eye. "Ready?"

"Ready," Dorian said with a nod.

They walked back up the path, side by side. Bastian's phone buzzed, and he pulled it out.

Riley [8:43 AM]: Where are you guys? Dorian won't answer his phone

Bastian flashed the screen toward Dorian.

"I left my phone in the car," he said.

Bastian sighed.

Bastian [8:44 AM]: 10 hours out

Riley [8:45 AM]: I swear to god, Bastian, this is the last time we'll all be together, if you two don't show up to say goodbye I will never talk to you again, DO YOU UNDERSTAND?

The closer she got to leaving for college, the more demanding Riley had been about plotting his social calendar. It was something that would have once irritated him, but he found he didn't mind anymore. He actually liked the company.

Riley [8:46 AM]: TELL ME YOU UNDERSTAND. Meteors, Bash! WE PLANNED THIS A WEEK AGO. DO NOT MISS THIS! STARS! SHOOTING ROCKS! DID I MENTION, THE LAST TIME WE WILL ALL BE TOGETHER?!?!?!?!?!?

Riley [8:47 AM]: Wait, 10 hours? YOU'RE GOING TO BE LATE, WHERE ARE YOU???

Bastian [8:48 AM]: Leaving the cemetery now, just have to gas up. We'll be there before the meteor shower starts. Promise

Riley [8:49 AM]: You went to the cemetery? Dorian is with you? YOU WENT TOGETHER????

Bastian sent her a car emoji, a middle finger emoji, and an eggplant emoji for good measure. Then he tucked his phone in his pocket and scowled at Dorian. "Thanks for that."

Dorian shot him a rueful grin. "She likes you more than me. She'll be way more forgiving when we show up late."

"No one likes me more than you," Bastian grumbled.

"Eh." Dorian shrugged. They stepped up next to the Audi. "You good?" he asked.

Bastian's hands were still sweating at the thought of getting back in the seat, but he nodded and pulled the keys out of his pocket.

"You got this," Dorian said gently.

Bastian barely kept himself from swearing at him. They'd only made it here last night because Dorian had kept his big mouth shut while Bastian played some really stupid meditation podcast that their couples counselor had given them and chewed through an entire pack of cinnamon gum. If he was going to start up with the motivational pep talks, Bastian was out.

Apparently, Dorian picked up on his irritation, though, because he flashed an apologetic smile and mouthed *sorry*.

It was fine.

They'd stop at a gas station on the way out of town. Bastian would buy another pack of gum.

Dorian would keep quiet.

They'd queue up another podcast.

And Bastian would drive them both back to Portland.

Loudly snapping another bubble, Bastian slid into the driver's seat and turned the key in the ignition. The car rumbled to life as Dorian buckled.

Then they drove out of the cemetery parking lot, through the gates with the steel letters, down the road lined by sharp wrought iron, and past Zan's lock, which sparkled brilliantly in the blazing sun.

EPILOGUE

Styx

The midi music of the Nintendo filled the office as Zan twirled around on a stool, holding the console so close to his face he was starting to see stars.

GRUMBLE GRUMBLE the screen read.

"Right back atcha," Zan mumbled.

The door creaked open.

Zan swore, swiveling back around. He dropped the Switch onto the desk and quickly threw open the laptop. "Name and location of death," he asked, eyes fixed on the computer screen waiting for the stupid program to load.

"Excuse me?"

He looked up. A girl stood there, about his age. Her hands were shoved into the pockets of her worn jeans, she had on a beaten-up T-shirt with a band slogan across the front. She glared daggers at him, then blew an enormous red bubble and let it snap.

Zan cocked his head. The smell of cinnamon wafted through the room. His stomach twisted. "Name and location of death?"

She mumbled an answer, and he quickly filled it in before letting her pick a key.

They wandered through an enormous concert hall, where a dancer in sparkling white leaped across the stage.

The girl next to him smiled, eyes sliding closed.

The barrier appeared quickly for this one, and Zan reached into his pocket, pressing two coins into the palm of her hand before guiding her over, leaving her mired in the thick water of the river as the Ferryman tore her soul from her throat.

He stepped back into his office, rubbing his neck. The thick smell of cinnamon still permeated the air as he sat down at his desk, staring at the computer screen. The program sat there, bright white light burning his eyes. Zan frowned, then closed the laptop and pulled open the desk drawer, rifling through papers until his fingers found the key ring.

He walked over to the cement wall, flipping until he settled on a large, burnished brass key. The cement flickered in and out of focus before reforming into an orange-painted door. An OPEN sign hung haphazardly in the window, and as he stepped inside, the earthen, papery smell of Fox Books wafted up around him.

Zan smiled.

– End –

Acknowledgements

I have so many thanks to give to those who waded through the River Styx with me.

To Lauren Bittrich, Connor Eck, and the team at Lucinda Lit who worked so hard to give this book every chance it could have.

To my incredible editor, Tamara Grasty, whose enthusiasm made this entire process so joyous. I couldn't have asked for a better champion and having you on this book was a dream.

To the amazing Page Street team: Cassandra Jones, Lauren Knowles, Shannon Dolley, Laura Benton, Rosie Stewart, Emma Hardy, Jane Horovitz, and Lauren Cepero.

To Jenni Howell. I don't know what I did to deserve your constant support, enthusiasm, endless CP efforts, and love, but I am so thankful for it every day. I could write a dissertation filled with all the ways you've helped this book soar, but I'll stop here with: GOOD JOB, ZAN.

To Beatrice, who so frequently dropped everything to help me through edits. Who understood Bastian's grief and Zan's longing like no one else and was always willing to either celebrate with me or berate me over the placement of two obols. I fixed it, okay? Just for you!

To Dani, who spent every day for years listening to me complain, scream, sob, laugh. Who did so much copyediting on so many pages that never even made it into the book. (Sorry. I'm the worst.) 'Til the end of the line, or the sprint channel, whichever comes first!

To the most amazing writing group a person could ever ask for: Stacie, K, Waverly, Jamie, Ellie, Arwyn, Rachel, VV, Anja, Brie, Alice, Crystal, Cristina, Emily, Emmi, Erin, Gina, Monique, Percy, Sara, Kaitee, Miller, the entire #MSMF crew. You all inspire me every single day with your words, your support, and your unflinching perseverance.

To Lin, who beta read one of my very first fanfics and convinced me that, yes, I could do this. Who has always been relentlessly driven and has so many times pulled me out of my own head. Team SBBS!

To my many fandoms over the years. I never thought I stood a chance at writing anything original until your encouragement changed my mind.

To Mr. Patterson, my 7th grade English teacher, who called me a writer. I turned in so many pages of terrible fantasy stories, and you never told me to stop. You'll probably never know how much your kind words mattered. To Karina McGill, easily the best professor I had in my creative writing program. You inspired me so much and opened my eyes to an entire world of poetry. I'll never forget your class. To another unnamed professor in the same program who told me to stop writing: Spite is a powerful motivator, and I'm thrilled to report that I did not quit.

To my friends and family, who have always supported me no matter what. Thank you for your willingness to listen when I hyperfixate on books. To Lydia, Evie, and Cass, who don't know what any of this means and think I've made a million dollars, and we're all now rich and famous.

Lastly, to Travis, who will never read this book. No matter how many first kisses I write, yours will always be the best.

About the Author

Michelle Kulwicki (she/they) grew up in the Pacific Northwest overturning every rock and stick in an unending quest to find portals to worlds far more exciting than her own. After moving to the mountainless Midwest, she earned her bachelor's and master's degrees in music performance, and spent years in the symphony and musical theater pit circuit. She's now a mom by day, musician by night, and writer in all the spaces in between—a life that is somewhat lacking in portals, but is still full of magic.